That Distant Land

WENDELL BERRY

That Distant Land

The Collected Stories

COUNTERPOINT
BERKELEY

This book is a work of fiction. Nothing is in it that has not been imagined.

The author and publisher gratefully acknowledge the editors who have previously published these stories: From *The Wild Birds* (North Point, 1985): "Thicker Than Liquor" and "The Wild Birds" originally published in *Mother Jones* magazine.

From *Fidelity* (Pantheon, 1992): "Pray Without Ceasing" originally published in *The Southern Review*, "A Jonquil for Mary Penn" originally published in *The Atlantic Monthly*, "Making It Home" originally published as "Homecoming" in *The Sewanee Review*, "Fidelity" originally published in *Orion*, "Are You All Right?" originally published in *Wendell Berry*, Vol. IV in the Confluence American Author Series, edited by Paul Merchant.

From *Watch With Me* (Pantheon, 1994): "Nearly to the Fair," "Turn Back the Bed," "A Consent," "A Half-Pint of Old Darling," and "The Solemn Boy" originally published in *The Draft Horse Journal*. "A Consent" was also published as a chapbook by Larkspur Press. "The Lost Bet" was published as a chapbook entitled *How Ptolemy Proudfoot Lost a Bet* by Dim Gray Bar Press.

From *Two More Stories of the Port William Membership* (Gnomon Press, 1997): "A Friend of Mine" and "The Inheritors" originally published in *The Kenyon Review* and *The Draft Horse Journal*.

"The Discovery of Kentucky" was originally published in *The Discovery of Kentucky* (Gnomon Press, 1991).

"The Hurt Man" was originally published in the *Hudson Review*.

The author wishes to thank his friends at Shoemaker & Hoard.

Library of Congress Cataloging-in-Publication Data
Berry, Wendell, 1934–
That distant land : the collected stories of Wendell Berry
p. cm.
Hardcover: ISBN-10 1-59376-027-2 ISBN-13: 978-1-59376-027-4
Paperback: ISBN-10 1-59376-054-X ISBN-13: 978-1-59376-054-0
1. Port William (Ky. : Imaginary place)—Fiction.
2. Kentucky—Social life and customs—Fiction.
3. Pastoral fiction, American. 4. Country life—Fiction. I. Title
PS3552.E75 A6 2004
813'.54—dc22   2003025213

Jacket and text design by David Bullen Design
Map and genealogy designed by Molly O'Halloran
Genealogy prepared by David McCowen

COUNTERPOINT
2560 Ninth St. Suite 318
Berkeley, CA 94710
www.counterpointpress.com

Printed in the United States of America

15 14 13 12 11

Contents

Italics indicate chronological placement of the Port William novels,
which are not included in this collection.

That Distant Land

The Collected Stories

"Oh that I should ever forget We stood by the wagon saying goodbye or trying to & I seen it come over her how far they was a going & she must look at us to remember us forever & it come over her pap and me and the others We stood & looked & knowed it was all the time we had & from now on we must remember We must look now forever Then Will rech down to her from the seat & she clim up by the hub of the wheel & set beside him & he spoke to the team She had been Betsy Rowanberry two days who was bornd Betsy Coulter 21 May 1824 Will turnd the mules & they stepd into the road passd under the oak & soon was out of sight down the hill The last I seen was her hand still raisd still waving after wagon & all was out of sight Oh it was the last I seen of her that little hand Afterwards I would say to myself I could have gone with them as far as the foot of the hill & seen her that much longer I could have gone on as far as the river mouth & footed it back by dark But however far I finaly would have come to wher I would have to stand and see them go on that hand a waving God bless her I never knowd what become of her I will never see her in this world again"

From REMEMBERING

The Hurt Man (1888)

When he was five Mat Feltner, like every other five-year-old who had lived in Port William until then, was still wearing dresses. In his own thoughts he was not yet sure whether he would turn out to be a girl or a boy, though instinct by then had prompted him to take his place near the tail end of the procession of Port William boys. His nearest predecessors in that so far immortal straggle had already taught him the small art of smoking cigars, along with the corollary small art of chewing coffee beans to take the smoke smell off his breath. And so in a rudimentary way he was an outlaw, though he did not know it, for none of his grownups had yet thought to forbid him to smoke.

His outgrown dresses he saw worn daily by a pretty neighbor named Margaret Finley, who to him might as well have been another boy too little to be of interest, or maybe even a girl, though it hardly mattered — and though, because of a different instinct, she would begin to matter to him a great deal in a dozen years, and after that she would matter to him all his life.

The town of Port William consisted of two rows of casually maintained dwellings and other buildings scattered along a thoroughfare that nobody had ever dignified by calling it a street; in wet times it hardly deserved to be called a road. Between the town's two ends the road was unevenly rocked, but otherwise had not much distinguished itself from the buffalo trace it once had been. At one end of the town was the school, at the other the graveyard. In the center there were several stores, two saloons, a church, a bank, a hotel, and a blacksmith shop. The town was the product of its own becoming, which, if not accidental exactly, had also been unplanned. It had no formal government or formal history. It was without pretense or ambition, for it was the sort of place that pretentious or ambitious people were inclined to leave. It had never declared an aspiration to become anything it was not. It did not thrive so much as it merely lived, doing the things it needed to do to stay alive. This tracked and rubbed little settlement had been built in a place of great natural abundance and beauty, which it had never valued highly enough or used well enough, had damaged, and yet had not destroyed. The town's several buildings, shaped less by art than by need and use, had suffered tellingly and even becomingly a hundred years of wear.

Though Port William sat on a ridge of the upland, still it was a river town; its economy and its thoughts turned toward the river. Distance impinged on it from the river, whose waters flowed from the eastward mountains ultimately, as the town always was more or less aware, to the sea, to the world. Its horizon, narrow enough though it reached across the valley to the ridgeland fields and farmsteads on the other side, was pierced by the river, which for the next forty years would still be its main thoroughfare. Commercial people, medicine showmen, evangelists, and other river travelers came up the hill from Dawes Landing to stay at the hotel in Port William, which in its way cherished these transients, learned all it could about them, and talked of what it learned.

Mat would remember the town's then-oldest man, Uncle Bishop Bower, who would confront any stranger, rap on the ground with his long staff, and demand, "Sir! What might your name be?"

And Herman Goslin, no genius, made his scant living by meeting the steamboats and transporting the disembarking passengers, if any, up to the hotel in a gimpy buckboard. One evening as he approached the hotel with a small trunk on his shoulder, followed by a large woman with a parasol, one of the boys playing marbles in the road said, "Here comes Herman Goslin with a fat lady's trunk."

"You boys can kiss that fat lady's ass," said Herman Goslin. "Ain't that tellin 'em, fat lady?"

The town was not built nearer the river perhaps because there was no room for it at the foot of the hill, or perhaps because, as the town loved to reply to the inevitable question from travelers resting on the hotel porch, nobody knew where the river was going to run when they built Port William.

And Port William did look as though it had been itself forever. To Mat at the age of five, as he later would suppose, remembering himself, it must have seemed eternal, like the sky.

However eternal it might have been, the town was also as temporal, lively, and mortal as it possibly could be. It stirred and hummed from early to late with its own life and with the life it drew into itself from the countryside. It was a center, and especially on Saturdays and election days its stores and saloons and the road itself would be crowded with people standing, sitting, talking, whittling, trading, and milling about. This crowd was entirely familiar to itself; it remembered all its history of allegiances, offenses, and resentments, going back from the previous Saturday to the Civil War and long before that. Like every place, it had its angers, and its angers as always, as everywhere, found justifications. And in Port William, a dozen miles by river from the court house and the rule of law, anger had a license that it might not have had in another place. Sometimes violence would break out in one of the saloons or in the road. Then proof of mortality would be given in blood.

And the mortality lived and suffered daily in the town was attested with hopes of immortality by the headstones up in the graveyard, which was even then more populous than the town. Mat knew — at the age of five he had already forgotten when he had found out — that he had a brother and two sisters up there, with carved lambs resting on the tops of their small monuments, their brief lives dated beneath. In all the time he had known her, his mother had worn black.

But to him, when he was five, those deaths were stories told. Nothing in Port William seemed to him to be in passage from any beginning to any end. The living had always been alive, the dead always dead. The world, as he knew it then, simply existed, familiar even in its changes: the town, the farms, the slopes and ridges, the woods, the river, and the sky over it all. He had not yet gone farther from Port William than to Dawes Landing on the river and to his Uncle Jack Beecham's place out on the

Bird's Branch Road, the place his mother spoke of as "out home." He had seen the steamboats on the river and had looked out from the higher ridgetops, and so he understood that the world went on into the distance, but he did not know how much more of it there might be.

Mat had come late into the lives of Nancy and Ben Feltner, after the deaths of their other children, and he had come unexpectedly, "a blessing." They prized him accordingly. For the first four or so years of his life he was closely watched, by his parents and also by Cass and Smoke, Cass's husband, who had been slaves. But now he was five, and it was a household always busy with the work of the place, and often full of company. There had come to be times, because his grown-ups were occupied and he was curious and active, when he would be out of their sight. He would stray off to where something was happening, to the farm buildings behind the house, to the blacksmith shop, to one of the saloons, to wherever the other boys were. He was beginning his long study of the town and its place in the world, gathering up the stories that in years still far off he would hand on to his grandson Andy Catlett, who in his turn would be trying to master the thought of time: that there were times before his time, and would be times after. At the age of five Mat was beginning to prepare himself to help in educating his grandson, though he did not know it.

His grown-ups, more or less willingly, were letting him go. The town had its dangers. There were always horses in the road, and sometimes droves of cattle or sheep or hogs or mules. There were in fact uncountable ways for a boy to get hurt, or worse. But in spite of her losses, Nancy Beechum Feltner was not a frightened woman, as her son would learn. He would learn also that, though she maintained her sorrows with a certain loyalty, wearing her black, she was a woman of practical good sense and strong cheerfulness. She knew that the world was risky and that she must risk her surviving child to it as she had risked the others, and when the time came she straightforwardly did so.

But she knew also that the town had its ways of looking after its own. Where its worst dangers were, grown-ups were apt to be. When Mat was out of the sight of her or his father or Cass or Smoke, he was most likely in the sight of somebody else who would watch him. He would thus be corrected, consciously ignored, snatched out of danger, cursed, teased, hugged, instructed, spanked, or sent home by any grown-up into whose sight he may have strayed. Within that watchfulness he was free — and almost totally free when, later, he had learned to escape it and thus had earned his freedom. "This was a *free* country when I was a boy," he would sometimes say to Andy, his grandson.

When he was five and for some while afterward, his mother drew the line unalterably only between him and the crowds that filled the town on Saturday afternoons and election days when there would be too much drinking, with consequences that were too probable. She would not leave him alone then. She would not let him go into the town, and she would not trust him to go anywhere else, for fear that he would escape into the town from wherever else she let him go. She kept him in sight.

That was why they were sitting together on the front porch for the sake of the breeze there on a hot Saturday afternoon in the late summer of 1888. Mat was sitting close to his mother on the wicker settee, watching her work. She had brought out her sewing basket and was darning socks, stretching the worn-through heels or toes over her darning egg and weaving them whole again with her needle and thread. At such work her fingers moved with a quickness and assurance that fascinated Mat, and he loved to watch her. She would have been telling him a story. She was full of stories. Aside from the small movements of her hands and the sound of her voice, they were quiet with a quietness that seemed to have increased as it had grown upon them. Cass had gone home after the dinner dishes were done. The afternoon had half gone by.

From where they sat they could see down into the town where the Saturday crowd was, and they could hear it. Doors slammed, now and then a horse nickered, the talking of the people was a sustained murmur from which now and then a few intelligible words escaped: a greeting, some bit of raillery, a reprimand to a horse, an oath. It was a large crowd in a small place, a situation in which a small disagreement could become dangerous in a hurry. Such things had happened often enough. That was why Mat was under watch.

And so when a part of the crowd intensified into a knot, voices were raised, and there was a scuffle, Mat and his mother were not surprised. They were not surprised even when a bloodied man broke out of the crowd and began running fast up the street toward them, followed by other running men whose boot heels pounded on the road.

The hurt man ran toward them where they were sitting on the porch. He was hatless. His hair, face, and shirt were bloody, and his blood dripped on the road. Mat felt no intimation of threat or danger. He simply watched, transfixed. He did not see his mother stand and put down her work. When she caught him by the back of his dress and fairly poked him through the front door—"Here! Get inside!"—he still was only alert, unsurprised.

He expected her to come into the house with him. What finally surprised him was that she did not do so. Leaving him alone in the wide hall, she remained outside the door, holding it open for the hurt man. Mat ran halfway up the stairs then and turned and sat down on a step. He was surprised now but not afraid.

When the hurt man ran in through the door, instead of following him in, Nancy Feltner shut the door and stood in front of it. Mat could see her through the door glass, standing with her hand on the knob as the clutch of booted and hatted pursuers came up the porch steps. They bunched at the top of the steps, utterly stopped by the slender woman dressed in mourning, holding the door shut.

And then one of them, snatching off his hat, said, "It's all right, Mrs. Feltner. We're his friends."

She hesitated a moment, studying them, and then she opened the door to them also and turned and came in ahead of them.

The hurt man had run the length of the hall and through the door at the end of it and out onto the back porch. Nancy, with the bunch of men behind her, followed where he had gone, the men almost with delicacy, as it seemed to Mat, avoiding the line of blood drops along the hall floor. And Mat hurried back down the stairs and came along in his usual place at the tail end, trying to see, among the booted legs and carried hats, what had become of the hurt man.

Mat's memory of that day would always be partly incomplete. He never knew who the hurt man was. He knew some of the others. The hurt man had sat down or dropped onto a slatted green bench on the porch. He might have remained nameless to Mat because of the entire strangeness of the look of him. He had shed the look of a man and assumed somehow the look of all things badly hurt. Now that he had stopped running, he looked used up. He was pallid beneath the streaked bright blood, breathing in gasps, his eyes too widely open. He looked as though he had just come up from almost too deep a dive.

Nancy went straight to him, the men, the friends, clustered behind her, deferring, no longer to her authority as the woman of the house, as when she had stopped them at the front door, but now to her unhesitating, unthinking acceptance of that authority.

Looking at the hurt man, whose blood was dripping onto the bench and the porch floor, she said quietly, perhaps only to herself, "Oh my!" It was as though she knew him without ever having known him before.

She leaned and picked up one of his hands. "Listen!" she said, and the man brought his gaze it seemed from nowhere and looked up at her. "You're at Ben Feltner's house," she said. "Your friends are here. You're going to be all right."

She looked around at the rest of them who were standing back, watching her. "Jessie, you and Tom go see if you can find the doctor, if he's findable." She glanced at the water bucket on the shelf over the wash table by the kitchen door, remembering that it was nearly empty. "Les, go bring a fresh bucket of water." To the remaining two she said, "Get his shirt off. Cut it off. Don't try to drag it over his head. So we can see where he's hurt."

She stepped through the kitchen door, and they could hear her going about inside. Presently she came back with a kettle of water still warm from the noon fire and a bundle of clean rags.

"Look up here," she said to the hurt man, and he looked up.

She began gently to wash his face. Wherever he was bleeding, she washed away the blood: first his face, and then his arms, and then his chest and sides. As she washed, exposing the man's wounds, she said softly only to herself, "Oh!" or "Oh my!" She folded the white rags into pads and instructed the hurt man and his friends to press them onto his cuts to stop the bleeding. She said, "It's the Lord's own mercy we've got so many hands," for the man had many wounds. He had begun to tremble. She kept saying to him, as she would have spoken to a child, "You're going to be all right."

Mat had been surprised when she did not follow him into the house, when she waited on the porch and opened the door to the hurt man and then to his friends. But she had not surprised him after that. He saw her as he had known her: a woman who did what the world put before her to do.

At first he stayed well back, for he did not want to be told to get out of the way. But as his mother made order, he grew bolder and drew gradually closer until he was almost at her side. And then he was again surprised, for then he saw her face.

What he saw in her face would remain with him forever. It was pity, but it was more than that. It was a hurt love that seemed to include entirely the hurt man. It included him and disregarded everything else. It disregarded the aura of whiskey that ordinarily she would have resented; it disregarded the blood puddled on the porch floor and the trail of blood through the hall.

Mat was familiar with her tenderness and had thought nothing of it. But now he recognized it in her face and in her hands as they went out to the hurt man's wounds. To him, then, it was as though she leaned in the black of her mourning over the whole hurt world itself, touching its wounds with her tenderness, in her sorrow.

Loss came into his mind then, and he knew what he was years away from telling, even from thinking: that his mother's grief was real; that her children in their graves once had been alive; that everybody lying under the grass up in the graveyard once had been alive and had walked in daylight in Port William. And this was a part, and belonged to the deliverance, of the town's hard history of love.

The hurt man, Mat thought, was not going to die, but he knew from his mother's face that the man *could* die and someday would. She leaned over him, touching his bleeding wounds that she bathed and stanched and bound, and her touch had in it the promise of healing, some profound encouragement.

It was the knowledge of that encouragement, of what it had cost her, of what it would cost her and would cost him, that then finally came to Mat, and he fled away and wept.

What did he learn from his mother that day? He learned it all his life. There are few words for it, perhaps none. After that, her losses would be his. The losses would come. They would come to him and his mother. They would come to him and Margaret, his wife, who as a child had worn his cast-off dresses. They would come, even as Mat watched, growing old, to his grandson, Andy, who would remember his stories and write them down.

But from that day, whatever happened, there was a knowledge in Mat that was unsurprised and at last comforted, until he was old, until he was gone.

Don't Send a Boy to Do a Man's Work (1891)

Athey Keith never knew his mother. She died before he was a year old, leaving him to be raised partly by his father and partly by a widowed Negro woman, Aunt Molly Mulwain, once a slave.

Carter Keith was a good father. He kept Athey with him as much as his work and, later, Athey's schooling would allow. The Keith place was always astir with work in those days. Everybody on the place would be up and the men and boys at the barns while the stars still shone, and at work by first light. Carter Keith followed the rules that he handed on to his son: He made use of all the daylight he had and would ask no man to do anything that he would not do himself. His tenants and hands knew this and so respected him, and they worked hard.

In the fall and winter, in addition to his farming, Carter Keith had made a sideline of trading in livestock, tobacco, corn, hay, and other things that his neighbors had to sell. What he bought, together with the produce of his own place, he gathered at his landing, loaded onto the steamboats, and sent down the rivers to Louisville or beyond.

From the time he could follow, Athey went to work with his father. From the time he could straddle a pony, he went with his father on his trading trips through the neighborhood. They might ride eight or ten miles, winding about through the creek valleys and over the ridges, gathering up a bunch of calves, it might be, or a few weanling mules, and driving them back home by dark (if they were lucky). And so early in his life Athey rode with his father over the same country that later he himself would court, dance, hunt, and trade over. In his life Athey traveled much, though not extensively. He knew more of the history and geography of the country between Bird's Branch and Willow Run than most people know of the United States.

Athey didn't intend ever to be separated from his father. "That boy stays as close to me as my conscience," his father would say. By the time he was six, Athey considered that he had found his work in this world. And so his father had to make him go to school. Carter Keith (and this also his son took from him) did not speak much, but he spoke pointedly.

He said, "Well, by God, you're going, and your opinion in the matter is of no consequence."

And then, seeing that Athey was sulking, Carter said: "Moreover. If you get a thrashing up there, you'll get the full brother to it down here. You mind what I tell you."

And so when school was in session, Athey did his morning chores, ate his breakfast, and walked the children's path up through the woods to Port William School, starting alone and arriving finally with an assortment of children, mainly Rowanberrys and Coulters. And when he walked back down again, no matter how he delayed, he found his evening chores waiting for him. His father would light the lantern and hand it to him. "If you come home in the dark," Carter Keith said, "you have got to do your chores in the dark."

When he was twelve Athey was big enough to harness a mule, and his father let him have a little crop of his own. By then, when his father would go away he would tell Athey, "You look after things." Athey thought himself a man, but he was wrong. He was riding for a fall.

That year his father had an exceptionally nice bunch of shoats, due to be fat and ready by the time the nights turned cold. The word had got out and a number of people had spoken for them—neighbors, people in Port William, some from farther away.

It happened, as hog-killing time came on and the talk went around, that the hog-buyers got together with Carter Keith and made a deal by which they would do the slaughtering and work up the meat down at the Keith place to avoid having to move the live hogs, and Carter in turn would provide scalding box, gam'ling pole, firewood, and other necessities at a small surcharge per head. They were going to kill a full two dozen hogs, which would be a big job, but with all the help they had and some careful management they expected to do everything in two days.

The appointed time, when it came a few days after Thanksgiving, turned out to be more complicated than any man would have expected, let alone a boy. The complications came in stages.

First, Carter Keith had accumulated a shipment of tobacco that he would have to accompany to Louisville on the next boat. Which happened to come so early on the day of the hog-killing that you couldn't even call it "morning." When they first heard the *Falls City* blow it was not a long time after midnight. They dressed and went down with a lantern to hail the boat.

After the hogsheads of tobacco were on board, Carter Keith, standing on the end of the gangplank, shook hands with Athey, who was standing on the shore. "Look after things," he said. "See that they have what they need. They'll know what they're doing."

The boat backed away and headed downstream, its lights soon disappearing around the bend, leaving Athey alone and in charge. This was the first complication, but he wouldn't understand that it was a complication until he had understood the second complication, which was still several hours off.

He returned to the house and got back into bed in his underwear and shirt, hoping for more sleep, but had hardly shut his eyes when the wagons of the hog-killers began arriving. The wagons brought, altogether, ten men: Lute Branch, Dewey Fields, Webster Page, Thad Coulter, Stillman Hayes, John Crop, Miller Quinch, Big Joe and Little Joe Ellis (who were no kin), and a small, stout-built man Athey remembered only as Tomtit. Some had bought hogs; some had come to help.

His father had emptied the barn to give stall room to the visitors. Athey went out with his lantern and showed them where to put their teams. Somebody had brought an extra scalding box, so there were two. He showed them where to dig the trenches for the scalding boxes, one on each side of the long gam'ling pole. They dug the trenches, laid fire in them, set the scalding boxes over the fires, and filled the boxes with water.

While the men stood by the fires, waiting for the water to heat and for the daylight to get strong enough to shoot by, Athey did his morning chores and then rushed to the house to get his breakfast. He did not even take his cap off. He dragged out his chair and sat down in it without drawing it up. "Give me my breakfast!" he said to Aunt Molly, who was bringing it.

She withdrew his plate. "Now," she said, "ain't you something, Mister Man. You take off that cap, and square yourself to that table, and act a nickel's worth civilized."

Whereas his father only ruled him, Aunt Molly owned him outright, at least when he was in the house where she could get at him. He did as she said. She gave him his breakfast. When he had eaten it, she let him go. By the time he got back to the barn lot, two hogs were shot and stuck, ready to scald. He pitched in, determined to do a man's work that day.

The second complication was in the person of Put Woolfork, who left his mother's little farm above Squires Landing before daylight that morning, driving a mule to an old spring wagon with springs relaxed almost to the axles. Only the summer before, Put had acquired a wife to help his mother help him with his farmwork. And he had got wind of the hog-killing.

"He had it planned out," Athey said. "He was a man who believed in thinking if it would get him something for nothing."

If he attended the hog-killing and worked or appeared to work, Put thought, then surely they would give him a couple of heads and maybe a backbone, maybe even a sparerib or two. Maybe the more finicky among them (if anybody could be finicky in that hard time) would make him a present of kidneys or hearts or livers or milts or sweetbreads. At the very least, he would have a day of company and talk and a tub or two of guts to throw out for his chickens and dogs. He had two washtubs for that purpose in his wagon.

On his way downriver along the interconnecting farmtracks that passed for a road in those days, Put stopped at the Billy Landing to see what news of that quarter he might take in trade to the hog-killing. The Billy Landing didn't amount to much. The store there was a rough, nearly empty building where Jim Pete Markman went to appear busy when he got tired of sitting at the house. He and Put understood each other. Jim Pete's actual calling in this world was not storekeeping but whiskey-making. At that he was one of the best. His product was prime stuff, as smooth as a baby's cheek — you could gargle with it — and it had a kick like a three-year-old mule.

When Put had discharged the news from upriver and taken aboard all that Jim Pete could or would contribute, Jim Pete asked him what brought him down that way on so brisk a morning.

"Oh, they're having a monstrous big hog-killing down at the Keith place," Put said. "Fat hogs by the dozen, and I don't know who all."

"Well, where was I?" Jim Pete said. "Nobody told me about it." And for a minute he sat and thought.

"Well," he said, "I'll tell you what. Kill one for me and I'll furnish the whiskey."

"Why, sure. That'll be just fine," said Put, who had no entitlement to agree to any such thing.

Above all things Put loved the taste of somebody else's whiskey. "Why not?" he said.

"No sooner said than done," Jim Pete said.

He brought out a small keg containing maybe three gallons and stood it at Put's feet in the wagon. And Put set forth for the hog-killing, a rich man with his offering.

When he got to Carter Keith's barn lot, he set the keg on a big chopping block that had been upended in a handy place. "Boys," he said, "Jim Pete wants you to kill one for him, and he's furnishing the whiskey."

And there that keg sat in the midst of the people, like the golden calf.

Mr. Dewey Fields, who was the senior man of them, eyed it as if that was exactly what it was. "We ain't having none of that here," he said.

And not another one of them said a word.

"That," Athey later would say, "was when I ought to have picked up the axe that was leaning right there and split that keg wide open. I was big enough to do it and I had the right. But that was when I played the boy and not the man. After that, I stayed a boy more or less to the end of it."

Put Woolfork did help some, and Athey of course helped. The visitors had brought lunches and they ate in shifts, hardly stopping work. Athey went to the house for his dinner. He submitted himself to the eyes of Aunt Molly like a good boy, hoping to get by, but she accused him as soon as he had drawn up to the table.

"What you got out there on top of that block?"

Embarrassed and trying not to sound like it, Athey said, "That's a keg of red-eye that Jim Pete Markman has sent down here for a hog."

"Red-eye!" she said. "Listen at you!"

Athey felt that whatever was going to go wrong at the barn had already been foreseen and judged at the house. He felt himself to be in the hands of fate. He didn't waste any time getting outside again.

By three o'clock, it may have been, they had twenty-five hogs scraped and gutted and hanging from the gam'ling pole. (Athey himself, sure in his confusion that his father would not want to be indebted to Jim Pete Markman, had insisted that they kill the twenty-fifth to pay for the whiskey.)

There was a letup then, and they felt their weariness. At rest, they felt the coldness of the wind. They had much work still ahead. For hours they had been walking by the exalted keg, leaving an empty space around it, a radius of maybe eight feet, as if from suspicion or respect. Now they looked at it.

Big Joe Ellis wiped his mouth on the shoulder of his ragged jacket. "Boys," he said, "I don't know about you all, but a little warming right now would suit me mighty well."

They were silent after that, all of them looking at the keg, until finally Mr. Fields said, "Well, maybe 'twould."

They sent Athey to the house to bring the water bucket and dipper. When he got back they had drawn the bung. He watched the liquor pour from the keg in little gushes, saying, "Good-good-good-good-good." He felt he had a duty of some kind, but he did not know what it was. Also he would have liked to drink from the dipper as it went around and then around again. He did not for fear of Aunt Molly and his father.

"Oh my!" said Lute Branch. "But don't that grease the axle of the old world?"

"Boys, let's get back to it now," said Mr. Fields. "We got a long ways to go and a short time to get there in."

They began blocking out the meat, laying the carcasses down on a table improvised of boards and trestles, removing the quarters, carving out the backbones and spareribs, carrying the pieces into the stripping room to be trimmed the next day, when they would also grind and sack the sausage and render the lard.

But as they worked now, they drank. There is an irresistible ease in dipping whiskey out of a water bucket with a dipper. It takes no time or trouble at all. And gradually the considerable skill that every one of them had been using all day became fumbling and unsure.

"Well," they had begun to say in consolation or in gleeful complacency, "what you don't get on one piece you'll get on another'n."

"Well, if it can't be ham, it'll just have to be sausage."

They wielded their axes and knives with something like abandon, though strangely there was never a finger cut. Athey saw Little Joe Ellis draw forth a sparerib with hide and a few bristles on the outside, and presently he saw him pick up a middling with a hole in it that you could look through like a window.

Put Woolfork always walked with his knees bent, as if expecting to have to sit down in a hurry. He had his bottom closer to the ground now than usual. He was walking toward the stripping room, carrying a large ham skin-side-down. He hooked his right toe precisely behind his left ankle and fell, tumbling the ham meat-side-down onto the ground. "Well," he said, "I'll eat it, I reckon, if nobody else will."

Big Joe Ellis held up a gobbet of fat that he had either mistakenly or accidentally sliced from a middling and then dropped on the ground. He said, in excellent good humor, "Now, that there piece there now, would you call that there piece sausage or skin fat? Well, God bless it, I'm a-calling it sausage. The dirt on it looks just like pepper."

Dewey Fields was warming himself by one of the scalding boxes, standing in the ashes. One of his overshoes had caught fire.

"Mr. Fields," Stillman Hayes said, "it looks to me like your overshoes is on fire."

Mr. Fields said, patiently, "These ain't my overshoes, honey. I borrowed these overshoes offen Isham Quail."

They were nowhere near finishing that day's work by chore time.

"I do believe," said Lute Branch, "that the women are going to have to do the milking."

"And after that cook up a little mess of victuals, I hope, I hope," said Miller Quinch.

"A virtuous woman," Dewey Fields said, "is a crown to her husband. Her price is far above rubies."

Pretty soon it was dark.

The third complication of that day came in the several persons of the Regulators. These were a kind of Ku Klux Klan, an imitation Ku Klux Klan maybe, for they wore sheets and hoods but their business (so far as Athey knew) was not Negroes, of which there were not many in the Port William neighborhood even in those days. The great interest of the Regulators was in sins against domestic tranquility. They were very hard on drinkers, sellers, and makers of whiskey (which they called "the demon rum"), with the perfectly logical result that every maker and seller of whiskey within a radius of several miles became a Regulator, and the actions of the Regulators were nearly all against new or outside competitors. They had a fairly free hand, for the law was in Hargrave, the roads scarcely existed for a good part of the year, and river transport was expensive and slow. And of course they caused trouble.

"If the Devil don't exist," Athey used to say, looking back, "how do you explain that some people are a lot worse than they're smart enough to be?"

Though they disguised themselves, and thought or pretended themselves disguised, the Regulators' "secrecy" was a useless glamour. They were no more secret or anonymous than the town dogs of Port William, for they rode upon horses and mules that were known to every boy above the age of five. Peg Shifter went so far as to nail a shoe to the end of his wooden leg before riding out with this local whiskey monopoly (which is really what it was)—but that too was only comedy, for as he rode his sheet worked up, confirming the truth already revealed by his mule.

When the Regulators came filing up the long lane past the house and into the barn lot, carrying torches and lanterns, the hog-killing crew did not try to run or hide. They just quit, each one right in the midst of whatever motion he was making, and stood and looked.

Big Joe Ellis said, "Did you ever see the like? Well, I never seen the like!"

The Regulators encircled them. Every man who did not carry a light held a shotgun or a rifle. Athey knew them all. They were the Hench twins, Felix and Festus, old man Tucker Thobe, Peg Shifter, Noble Crane, Jim Doyle, Gid Lamar, Guiney McGrother, U. S. Jones, and Jim Pete Markman.

"Well, gentlemen," old man Thobe chirped through his hood, "we done found you all in breach of the peace and the public good. I reckon you all know, now, that we can't let this sort of doings go on unmolested. No woman nor child would be safe. We're impounding this liquor, and we're going to put you away in that stripping room while we decide on further measures."

"I need to be getting on home now," said Put Woolfork, who was standing and swaying with his legs apart. "I ain't killing no hogs. I ain't even here. I got my cow to milk."

"Even if you knew how to milk, your women would have already done done it for you," Felix Hench called out from inside his hood.

The hooded men all laughed. So did some of the others.

He knew them all, but Athey never quite got rid of the shiver it gave him to hear those hooded men speaking. Though they spoke in their own voices, they were not speaking for themselves.

They drove the hog-killing crew into the stripping room and latched and propped the door. There were windows above the bench all along the north side. Did the Regulators think of the windows? If they did, they assumed that no man there would break a window belonging to Carter Keith. Maybe, since it was too dark to see the windows, the hog-killers were too drunk to remember them. Athey made no move to go in, and the Regulators did not make him go.

They emptied every stall in the barn, turning the guest mules and horses out into the pasture with those belonging to Carter Keith, making work for somebody besides themselves, and stabled their own.

They brought wood from the woodpile and made a fire.

"What're you all doing?" Athey said.

"What we don't have to tell you," said Festus Hench, looking through eyeholes over the dipper, which already was passing around. He was holding the bottom of his hood above his mouth so he could drink.

They sent Athey to the house for salt and a skillet.

"And just a leetle dab of meal," Peg Shifter called after him. "About a gallon."

"Two skillets," Guiney McGrother shouted to him, "and two gallon of meal."

Aunt Molly helped him get the things they had asked for. She was furious, though maybe not now at him. He was furious himself.

"They say the bottom rail shall be the rider," Aunt Molly said. "But it's the foam and the filth that biles to the top."

He brought them the skillets and the salt and meal. They began to slice meat from the joints and middlings that had not yet been carried to the stripping room. They took the tenderest cuts — hamstrings, tenderloins, slices of ham and shoulder — and greased the skillets with fat and started frying the meat. They made corn pones and dropped them into the grease.

Although Athey was hungry, he stood away from the fire. But when the good smell of the frying meat came to him he had to holler out: "Why don't you all cut some mouth holes in them things if you aim to eat like mortal humans?"

"Because we ain't got one of them little old mouths that runs like a calf's ass," Felix Hench said.

And Guiney McGrother waved his pistol at Athey and said, "*Get* to the house!"

He made as if to go but went instead and let himself quietly into the corncrib, where he could watch them through the slats.

He could see that somebody in the stripping room was sober enough to have found a match and started a fire in the stove. Otherwise there was no sound from there. They were sleeping.

The Regulators had laid their weapons down and removed their hoods. They feasted on the free pork and drank what to all of them but Jim Pete Markman was free whiskey. Jim Pete was drinking hard in order to reduce his loss. When they finished eating, they dutifully covered their heads again with their hoods to make themselves official. They talked and laughed, sitting and then leaning and then lying around the fire. It was too big a fire, for the firewood also was free to them. Finally they too quieted down and went to sleep. Athey watched and watched, cold and determined — determined to do what, he did not know. He

was no longer a boy who thought himself a man. He was a boy trying
unsurely to make up for his failure to be a man when a man was needed.
It was the first time he ever was awake all night long.

Now that he was a boy no longer thinking of himself as a man, the
spirit of his father seemed to be telling him what a man ought to do.
When the fire had died down almost to coals, he slipped out of the crib
and went over to where the Regulators were sleeping. He knew how to
squirrel hunt, and with what seemed to him in his fear the patience of
the moving stars, he took their guns two at a time and buried them in the
wheat in the granary. After that, he warmed himself at the coals of the
fire, ready to run if anybody moved. It was way into the night by then.
Before long it would be morning. And soon the gray of it rose among
the eastward stars.

In a while he heard a little tapping from the inside of the stripping
room. He went over and leaned to the wall. "What?" he said.

"Athey?" It was Webster Page.

He said, "Yessir."

"Are they asleep?"

"Yessir."

"Where's their guns?"

"I put them away."

"Where?"

"In a place."

"What about Guiney's pistol?" This was Lute Branch.

"I put it away too."

Somebody back in the room groaned and muttered something, and
Lute Branch said, "Damn your head! Stir yourself!"

"Athey," Webster Page said, "are you listening?"

"Yessir."

"Unfasten this door. Now, wait! Listen! As soon as you do that, let
loose all their mules and horses. Run 'em out! Hear?"

"Yessir."

And that was what he did. He unlatched the door and took the props
away, and then ran to the barn. He opened every stall and drove the
beasts out into the dimness.

Somebody among the Regulators cried "Whoa!" and then he heard a great gibberish of cries and curses as the forces of temperance and family order awoke. Before he was out of the barn again he heard the hooves swerve past the waking sleepers, cross the lot, go through the gate and on out the lane past the house.

When he came out of the barn, he saw the little man called Tomtit square himself in the posture of John L. Sullivan in front of a tall gangly Regulator who was probably Guiney McGrother. In their hoods and apart from their horses and voices, it was harder now to tell which Regulator was which. Tomtit danced and sparred impressively in front of the big Regulator and then made the mistake of trying to get close enough to hit him. Long before Tomtit got the Regulator within his reach, he came within reach of the Regulator, who hit him in the face with great force but also indifferently, as he might have swatted a fly, and Tomtit went down as if he had no bones.

And then Guiney, if that was who it was, wound up like a pitcher and swung at Webster Page, and missed, and Webster Page knocked him down.

And then one of them, maybe U. S. Jones, came running at Mr. Fields and tried to jump over a log two steps before he got to it, and then stumbled over the log—and Mr. Fields, of all people, knocked him down.

Given the numbers involved, it really wasn't much of a fight. The hog-killing crew were on average a good deal younger than the Regulators, they were more offended, and they weren't wearing hoods. A hood is far from an ideal garment to wear in a fistfight. Several of the Regulators had trouble aligning their eyes with their eyeholes.

And so the fight didn't take long. On the other hand, it didn't end in a rout as it ought to have done. Nobody felt good enough. The defeated did not feel like running and the victors did not feel like pursuing. Finally the fight just subsided in place like a fire burning out.

The victors were all standing and the others sitting or lying down. Athey heard the *Blue Wing* blow out on the river. Her engine seemed hardly to hesitate as she went by the landing. And then almost too soon Carter Keith had stepped into the barn lot in his black suit and hat, having stayed in Louisville only long enough to receive payment on his shipment of tobacco and catch the next boat home.

Now that he was standing there, they saw the shambles they had made of the place. Carter Keith stopped and stood looking, and he was white around the mouth.

Athey went to face his father. "I ought to busted that keg as soon as it was set down," he said. "It's all my fault."

"I don't believe so," his father said, and he put his arm around Athey.

He said to the Regulators, "You goddamned sackheads get out of here and go home."

He told Athey, "Run yonder and tell Aunt Molly to make some coffee. Tell her to make it strong."

Mr. Fields and Webster Page and the others had begun to stir, trying to get themselves back to work. Athey's father walked among them as if he were wading.

"If there's anything I can't stand," he said, "it's a damned nasty hog-killing."

In the new day Athey ran to the house to tell Aunt Molly to make coffee. She would in a short while fix breakfast for them all, but she grunted as she lifted herself out of her chair at the window where she too had kept awake all night. "Rest me, Jesus!" she said. The Regulators were now filing past the house, carrying their saddles.

The sight of the Regulators had, to Athey, the force of revelation. He saw them now wholly apart from power, seniority, even meanness. They were only men. Peg Shifter, in person, had never been friendly to Athey; as a Regulator, he had seemed terrible. Now he hopped along like a one-legged crow, not keeping up with the others. It occurred to Athey then that it might be possible to feel sorry for Peg Shifter, and in later years he did.

A Consent (1908)

For my friends at Monterey, Kentucky

Ptolemy Proudfoot was nothing if not a farmer. His work was farming, his study and passion were farming, his pleasures and his social life occurred in the intervals between farm jobs and in the jobs themselves. He was not an ambitious farmer—he did not propose to own a large acreage or to become rich—but merely a good and a gifted one. By the time he was twenty-five, he had managed, in spite of the hard times of the 1890s, to make a down payment on the little farm that he husbanded and improved all his life. It was a farm of ninety-eight acres, and Tol never longed even for the two more that would have made it a hundred.

Of pleasures and social life, he had a plenty. The Proudfoots were a large, exuberant clan of large people, though by my time Tol was the last one of them in the Port William neighborhood, and Tol was childless. The Proudfoots were not, if they could help it, solitary workers. They swapped work among themselves and with their neighbors, and their workdays involved a mighty dinner at noontime, much talk and laughter, and much incidental sport.

As an after-dinner amusement and aid to digestion, the Proudfoot big boys and young men would often outline a square or a circle on the ground, and get into it and wrestle. Everybody wrestled with everybody, for the object was to see who would be the last one in the ring. The manpower involved might better have been rated as horsepower, and great feats of strength were accomplished. Now and again great physical damage was accomplished, as when, for example, one Proudfoot would endeavor to throw another Proudfoot out of the ring through the trunk of a large tree. Sometimes, after failing to make headway through a tree trunk or barn door, a Proudfoot would lie very still on the ground for several minutes before he could get up. Sometimes, one Proudfoot or another would be unable to go back to work in the afternoon. These contests would be accompanied by much grunting, and by more laughter, as the Proudfoots were hard to anger. For a Proudfoot boy to become big enough and brave enough finally to set foot in that ring was a rite of passage. For a Proudfoot to stand alone in that ring—as Tol did finally, and then often did—was to know a kind of triumph and a kind of glory. Tol was big even for a Proudfoot, and the others could seldom take him off his feet. He tumbled them out, ass over elbows, one by one, in a manner more workmanly than violent, laughing all the time.

Tol was overabundant in both size and strength. And perhaps because animate creatures tended to get out of his way, he paid not much attention to himself. He damaged his clothes just by being in them, as though surprising them by an assortment of stresses and strains for which they had not been adequately prepared. The people around Port William respected Tol as a farmer; they loved to tell and retell and hear and hear again the tales of his great strength; they were amused by the looks of him, by his good humor, and by his outsized fumblings and foibles. But never, for a long time, would any of them have suspected that his great bulk might embody tender feelings.

But Tol did embody tender feelings, and very powerful tender feelings they were. For Tol, through many years, had maintained somewhere about the center of himself a most noble and humble and never-mentioned admiration for Miss Minnie Quinch. Miss Minnie was as small and quick as Tol was big and lumbering. Like him, she was a Port Williamite. She had taught for many years at Goforth School, grades one through eight, which served the neighborhood of Katy's Branch and Cotman Ridge in which Tol's farm lay. When she was hardly more than a girl, Miss Minnie had gone away to a teacher's college and prepared herself to teach by learning many cunning methods that she never afterward used. For Miss Minnie loved children and she loved books, and she taught merely by introducing the one to the other. When she had trouble with one of the rougher big boys, she went straight to that boy's father and required that measures be taken. And measures usually were taken, so surprisingly direct and demanding was that lady's gaze.

For as many years as Miss Minnie had taught at Goforth School, Tol had admired her from a distance, and without ever looking directly at her when she might have been about to look directly at him. He thought she was the finest, prettiest, nicest little woman he had ever seen. He praised her to himself by saying, "She's just a pocket-size pretty little thing." But he was sure that she would never want to be around a big, rough, unschooled fellow like himself.

Miss Minnie did, from time to time, look directly at Tol, but not ever when he might have been about to look directly at her. More than once she thought rather wistfully that so large and strong a man as Tol ought to be some woman's knight and protector. She was, in fact, somewhat concerned about him, for he was thirty-six, well past the age when men usually got married. That she herself was thirty-four and unmarried was something she also thought from time to time, but always in a different thought. She kept her concern about Tol limited very strictly to concern, for she was conscious of being a small person unable even to hope to arrest the gaze of so splendid a man.

For years, because of mutual avoidance of each other's direct gaze, their paths did not cross. Although they met and passed, they did not do so in a way that required more than a polite nod, which they both accomplished with a seriousness amounting almost to solemnity. And then one morning in Port William, Tol came out of Beater Chatham's store directly face-to-face with Miss Minnie who was coming in, and who smiled at him before she could think and said, "Well, good morning, Mr. Proudfoot!"

Tol's mouth opened, but nothing came out of it. Nothing at all. This was unusual, for Tol, when he felt like it, was a talkative man. He kept walking because he was already walking, but for several yards he got along without any assistance from his faculties. Sight and sense did not return to him until he had walked with some force into the tailgate of his wagon.

All the rest of that day he went about his work in a somewhat vision-
ary state, saying to himself, and to the surprise of his horses and his dog,
"Good morning, mam!" and "How do you do, Miss Minnie?" Once he
even brought himself to say, bowing slightly and removing his hat, "And
a good morning to you, little lady."

And soon, as if they had at last come into each other's orbit, they met
face-to-face again. It was a fine fall afternoon, and Tol happened to be
driving down past Goforth School, slowing his team, of course, so as not
to disturb the concentration of the scholars inside. Miss Minnie was
standing by the pump in front of the schoolhouse, her figure making a
neat blue silhouette against the dingy weatherboarding.

Again she smiled at him. She said, "How do you do, Mr. Proudfoot?"

And Tol startled at the sound of her voice as if he had not seen her
there at all. He could not remember one of the pleasantries he had
invented to say to her. He looked intently into the sky ahead of him and
said quickly as if he had received a threat, "Why, howdy!"

The conversation thus established was a poor thing, Tol knew, so far
as his own participation in it went, but it was something to go on. It gave
him hope. And now I want to tell you how this courtship, conducted for
so long in secret in Tol's mind alone, became public. This is the story of
Miss Minnie's first consent, the beginning of their story together, which
is one of the dear possessions of the history of Port William.

That fall, Miss Minnie and her students had worked hard in prepara-
tion for the annual Harvest Festival at the school. The Harvest Festival
was Miss Minnie's occasion; she had thought it up herself. It might have
been a Halloween party, except that Halloween in that vicinity got
enough out of hand as it was without some public function to bring all
the boys together in one place. And so she had thought of the Harvest
Festival, which always took place two weeks before Halloween. It was a
popular social event, consisting of much visiting, a display of the students' work, recitations by the students, an auction of pies and cakes to
raise money for books and supplies, and abundant refreshments provided by the mothers of the students.

Ptolemy Proudfoot had never been to the Harvest Festival. He had no
children, he told himself, and so did not belong there. But in fact he had
always longed to go, had always been afraid to intrude himself without

excuse into Miss Minnie's world, and had always, as a result, spent an unhappy night at home. But this year, now that he and Miss Minnie were in a manner of becoming friends, he determined that he would go.

Tol had got along as bachelors must. He had even become a fair cook. From the outside, his house was one of the prettiest and best kept in the neighborhood. It was a small house with steep, gingerbreaded gables, and it stood under two white oaks in the bend of the road, just where the road branched off to go down into the Katy's Branch valley where Goforth and its school were. Tol kept the house painted and the yard neat, and he liked to turn in off the road and say to himself, "Well, now, I wonder who lives in such a nice place!" But what he had thought up to do to the inside of the house was not a great deal above what he had thought up to do to the inside of his barn. Like the barn, the house was clean and orderly, but when he went into it, it did not seem to be expecting him, as it did after Miss Minnie came there to live.

On the day of the festival, Tol cut and shocked corn all day, but he thought all day of the festival, too, and he quit early. He did his chores, fixed his supper and ate it, and then, just as he had planned in great detail to do, he began to get ready. He brought his Sunday clothes to the kitchen and laid them out on a chair. He hunted up his Sunday shoes and polished them. He set a large washtub on the floor in front of the stove, dipped hot water into it from the water well at the end of the stove, cooled the hot water with water from the water bucket on the shelf by the door, put soap and washrag and towel on the floor beside the tub. And then he undressed and sat in the tub with his feet outside it on the floor, and scrubbed himself thoroughly from top to toe. He dried himself and put on his pants. Gazing into the mirror over the little wash table by the back door, he shaved so carefully that he cut himself in several places. He put on his shirt, and after several tries buttoned the collar. He put on his tie, tying a knot in it that would have broken the neck of a lesser man and that left even him so nearly strangled that he supposed he must look extremely handsome. He wet his hair and combed it so that when it dried it stuck up stiffly in the air as Proudfoot hair was inclined to do. He put on his suspenders, his gleaming shoes, and his Sunday hat. And then he sat in a chair and sweated and rubbed his hands together until it was time to hitch old Ike to the buggy and drive down to the school.

Before he got to the schoolhouse, he could hear voices, an uninterrupted babble like the sound of Katy's Branch in the spring, and then he
could see a glow. When he got to the bottom of the hill and saw, among
the trunks of the big walnuts and water maples and sycamores that
stood there, the schoolhouse windows gleaming and the school yard
strung with paper lanterns, lighting the bare-worn ground and throwing
the shadows of the trees out in all directions like the spokes of a wheel,
he said, "Whoa, Ike." The light around the old schoolhouse and within
it seemed to him a radiance that emanated from the person of Miss
Minnie herself. And Tol's big heart quaked within him. He had to sit
there in the road behind his stopped horse and think a good while before
he could decide not to go on by, pretending to have an errand elsewhere.

Now that he had stopped, it became quiet where he was; he could
hear the crickets singing, and he was aware of Willow Hole on Katy's
Branch, a little beyond the school, carrying on its accustomed business
in the dark. As he sat and thought — thought hard about nothing that he
could fix in a thought — Tol slid his fingers up beneath his hat from time
to time and scratched, and then jerked the hat down firmly onto his head
again, and each time he did this he rotated the front of his hat a little further toward his right ear. Presently the sound of another buggy coming
down the hill behind him recalled him to himself; he clucked to Ike and
drove on, and found a hitching place among the other buggies and the
wagons and the saddled horses at the edge of the school yard.

There was a perimeter of voices out on the very edge of the light,
where the boys had started a game of tag, unwilling to come nearer the
schoolhouse than they had to. Near the building the men were gathered
in groups, smoking or chewing, talking, as they always talked, of crops,
livestock, weather, work, prices, hunting, and fishing, in that year and the
years before.

Tol, usually a sociable man, had nothing to say. He did not dare to say
anything. He went past the men, merely nodding in response to their
greetings, and since he did not want to talk and so could not stop, and was
headed in that direction, he went on into the schoolhouse, and immediately he realized his mistake. For there were only women and girls in
there, and not one man, not a single one. Beyond the boys' voices out on
the edge of the dark and the men's voices in the school yard was this

bright, warm nucleus of women's voices, and of women themselves and of women's eyes turned to see who had burst through the door with so much force.

Those women would always remember the way Tol looked when he came in that night. After all his waiting and anxiety, his clothes were damp and wrinkled, his shirttail was out, there was horse manure on one of his shoes. His hat sat athwart his head as though left there by somebody else. When, recognizing the multiflorous female presence he was in, he snatched his hat off, his hair stuck up and out and every which way. He came in wide-eyed, purposeful, and alarmed. He looked as if only his suspenders were holding him back—as if, had it not been for that restraint upon his shoulders, he might have charged straight across the room and out through the back wall.

He had made, he thought, a serious mistake, and he was embarrassed. He was embarrassed, too, to show that he knew he had made a mistake. He did not want to stay, and he could not go. Struck dumb, his head as empty of anything sayable as a clapperless bell, he stood in one place and then another, smiling and blushing, an anxious, unhappy look in his eyes.

Finally, a voice began to speak in his mind. It was his own voice. It said, "I would give forty dollars to get out of here. I would give forty-five dollars to get out of here." It consoled him somewhat to rate his misery at so high a price. But he could see nobody to whom he could pay the forty dollars, or the forty-five either. The women had gone back to talking, and the girls to whispering.

But Tol's difficulty and his discomfort had not altogether failed of a compassionate witness. His unexpected presence had not failed to cause a small flutter in the bosom of Miss Minnie and a small change in the color of her face. As soon as she decently could, Miss Minnie excused herself from the circle of women with whom she had been talking. She took the bell from her desk and went to the door and rang it.

Presently the men and boys began to come inside. Tol, though he did not become inconspicuous, began at least to feel inconspicuous, and as his pain decreased, he was able to take intelligent notice of his whereabouts. He saw how prettily the room was done up with streamers and many candles and pictures drawn by the students and bouquets of autumn leaves. And at the head of the room on a large table were the cakes and pies that were to be auctioned off at the end of the evening. In the very center of the table, on a tall stand, was a cake that Tol knew, even before he heard, was the work of Miss Minnie. It was an angel food cake with an icing as white and light and swirly as a summer cloud. It was as white as a bride. The sight of it fairly took his breath—it was the most delicate and wondrous thing that he had ever seen. It looked so beautiful and vulnerable there all alone among the others that he wanted to defend it with his life. It was lucky, he thought, that nobody said anything bad about it—and he just wished somebody would. He took a position in a corner in the front of the room as near the cake as he dared to be, and watched over it defensively, angry at the thought of the possibility that somebody *might* say something bad about it.

"Children, please take your seats!" Miss Minnie said.

The students all dutifully sat down at their desks, leaving the grownups to sit or stand around the walls. There was some confusion and much shuffling of feet as everybody found a place. And then a silence, variously expectant and nervous, fell upon the room. Miss Minnie stepped to the side of her desk. She stood, her posture very correct, regarding her students and her guests in silence a moment, and then she welcomed them one and all to the annual Harvest Festival of Goforth School. She told the grown-ups how pleased she was to see them there so cherishingly gathered around their children. She gave them her heart-felt thanks for their support. She asked Brother Overhold if he would pronounce the invocation.

Brother Overhold called down the blessings of Heaven upon each and every one there assembled, and upon every family there repre-sented; upon Goforth School and Miss Minnie, its beloved teacher; upon the neighborhood of Katy's Branch and Cotman Ridge; upon the town of Port William and all the countryside around it; upon the county, the state, the nation, the world, and the great universe, at the very center of which they were met together that night at Goforth School.

And then Miss Minnie introduced the pupils of the first grade, who were to read a story in unison. The first grade pupils thereupon sat up straight, giving their brains the full support of their erect spinal columns, held their primers upright in front of them, and intoned loudly together:

"Once—there—were—three—*bears*. The—big—bear—was—the

—*poppa*—bear. The—middle—bear—was—the—*momma* bear. The—little—bear—was—the—*baby* bear"—and so on to the discovery of Goldilocks and the conclusion, which produced much applause.

And then, one by one, the older children came forward to stand at the side of the desk, as Miss Minnie had stood, to recite poems or Bible verses or bits of famous oratory.

A small boy, Billy Braymer, recited from Sir Walter Scott:

> *Breathes there the man with soul so dead*
> *Who never to himself hath said:*
> *"This is my own, my native land"?*

—and on for thirteen more lines, and said "Whew!" and sat down to enthusiastic applause. Thelma Settle of the sixth grade, one of the stars of the school, made her way through "Thanatopsis" without fault to the very end. The audience listened to "A Psalm of Life," the First, the Twenty-third, and the Hundredth Psalms, "The Fool's Prayer," "To a Waterfowl," "To Daffodils," "Concord Hymn," "The Choir Invisible," "Wolsey's Farewell to His Greatness," Hamlet's Soliloquy, "The Epitaph" from Gray's "Elegy Written in a Country Church-Yard," and other pieces. Hibernia Hopple of the eighth grade declared with a steadily deepening blush and in furious haste that she loved to the depth and breadth and height her soul could reach. Walter Crow said in a squeaky voice and with bold gestures that he was the master of his fate and the captain of his soul. Buster Niblett implored that he be given liberty or death.

And then Miss Minnie called the name of Burley Coulter, and a large boy stood up in the back of the room and, blushing, made his way to the desk as he would have walked, perhaps, to the gallows. He turned and faced the audience. He shut his eyes tightly, opened them only to find the audience still present, and swallowed. Miss Minnie watched him with her fingers laced at her throat and her eyes moist. He was such a good-looking boy, and—she had no doubt—was smart. Against overpowering evidence she had imagined a triumph for him. She had chosen a poem for him that was masculine, robust, locally applicable, seasonally appropriate, high spirited, and amusing. If he recited it well, she would be so pleased! She had the poem in front of her, just in case.

He stood in silence, as if studying to be as little present as possible, and then announced in an almost inaudible voice, "'When the Frost Is on the Punkin' by James Whitcomb Riley."

He hung his hands at his sides, and then clasped them behind him, and then clasped them in front of him, and then put them into his pockets. He swallowed a dry-mouthed swallow that in the silence was clearly audible, and began:

> *"When the frost is on the punkin and the fodder's in the shock,*
> *And you hear the kyouck and gobble of the struttin' turkey-cock,*
> *And the clackin' of the — of the, uh — the clackin' of the —"*

"Guineys!" Miss Minnie whispered.
"Aw, yeah, guineys," he said:

> *And the clackin' of the guineys, and the cluckin' of the hens,*
> *And the rooster's hallylooer as he tiptoes on the fence*
> *— uh, let's see —"*

"Oh, it's then's . . ."

> *"Oh, it's then's the time's a feller is a-feelin' at his best,*
> *With the risin' sun to greet him from a night of peaceful rest,*
> *When he — uh —"*

"As he leaves . . ."

> *"As he leaves the house, bare-headed, and goes out to feed the stock,*
> *When the frost is on the punkin and the fodder's in the shock."*

He looked at his feet, he scratched his head, his lips moved soundlessly.
"They's something . . ."
"Aw, yeah.

> *"They's something kindo' harty-like about the atmusfere*
> *When the heat of summer's over — uh — kindo' lonesome-like,*
> *but still — uh —*

"Well, let's see. Uh —

"Then your apples — Then your apples all —"

Miss Minnie was reading desperately, trying to piece the poem together as he dismembered it, but he had left her behind and now he was stalled. She looked up to see an expression on his face that she knew too well. The blush was gone; he was grinning; the light of inspiration was in his eyes.

"Well, drot it, folks," he said, "I forgot her. But I'll tell you one I heard."

Miss Minnie rose, smiling, and said in a tone of utter gratification, "*Thank* you, Burley! Now you may be seated."

She then called upon Kate Helen Branch, who came to the front and sang "In the Gloaming" in a voice that was not strong but was clear and true.

That brought the recitations to an appropriate conclusion. There was prolonged applause, after which Miss Minnie again arose. "Mr. Willis Bagby," she said, "will now conduct our auction of pies and cakes."

Mr. Bagby took his place behind the table of pies and cakes.

"Folks," he said, "this here is for the good of the school, and to help out this little teacher here that's doing such a good job a-teaching our children. For what would tomorrow be without the young people of today? And what would our young people be without a fine teacher to teach them to figger and read and write, and to make them do all the fine things we seen them do here on this fine occasion this evening? So now, folks, open up your hearts and let out your pocketbooks. What am I bid for this fine cherry pie?" And he tilted the pie toward the crowd so that all could see the lovely crisscrossing of the top crust.

Tol had stood and watched and listened in a state of anxiety that prevented him from benefiting at all from the program. He had never seen in his life, he thought, such a woman as Miss Minnie — she was so smart and pretty, and so knowing in how to stand and speak. And when she stopped that Burley Coulter and set him down, Tol felt his heart swerve like a flying swift. She was as quick on her feet, he thought, as a good hind-catcher. And yet the more he looked upon her, the higher above him she shone, and the farther he felt beneath her notice.

Now there was old Willis Bagby auctioning off the pies and cakes, which were bringing more or less than fifty cents, depending on what they looked like and who had made them. And Tol was sweating and quaking like a man afraid. For what if her cake brought less than fifty cents? What if—and he felt his heart swerve again—nobody bid on it? He would bid on it himself—but how could he dare to? People would think he was trying to show off. Maybe *she* would think he was trying to show off.

Tol backed into his corner as far as he could, trying to be small, wishing he had not come. But now Willis Bagby put his hands under the beautiful white cake and lifted it gleaming on its stand.

"*Now* look a-here, folks," he said. "For last, we got this fine cake made by this mighty nice lady, our schoolteacher. What am I bid for it?"

"One dollar," said Gilead Hopple, who with his wife, Ag, was standing not far in front of Tol Proudfoot. Gil Hopple was the local magistrate, who now proposed for himself the political gallantry of offering the highest bid for the teacher's cake. After his bid, he uttered a small cough.

"Dollar bid! I've got a dollar bid," said Willis Bagby. "Now, anywhere a half?"

Nobody said anything. Nobody said anything for a time that got longer and longer, while Gil Hopple stood there with his ears sticking out and his white bald head sticking up through its official fringe of red hair.

And Tol Proudfoot was astonished to hear himself say right out and in a voice far too loud, "*Two dollars!*"

Gil Hopple coughed his small cough again and said, his voice slightly higher in pitch than before, "Two and a quarter."

It seemed to Tol that Gil Hopple had defiled that priceless cake with his quarter bid. Gil Hopple happened to be Tol's neighbor, and they had always got along and been friends. But at that moment Tol hated Gil Hopple with a clear, joyful hatred. He said, "*Three* dollars!"

Gil Hopple did not wish to turn all the way around, but he looked first to the right and then to the left. His ears stuck out farther, and the top of his head had turned pink. It had been a dry year. He looked as if the room smelled of an insufficient respect for hard cash. "Three and a quarter," he said in a tone of great weariness.

Willis Bagby was looking uncomfortable himself now. Things obviously were getting out of hand, but it was not up to him to stop it.

Tol said, "Four!"

At that point a revelation came to Miss Minnie. It seemed to her beyond a doubt that Tol Proudfoot, that large, strong man whom she had thought ought to be some woman's knight and protector, was bidding to be *her* knight and protector. It made her dizzy. She managed to keep her composure: she did not blush much, the tears hardly showed in her eyes, by great effort she did not breathe much too fast. But her heart was staggering within her like a drunk person, and she was saying over and over to herself, "Oh, you magnificent man!"

"Four and a quarter," said Gil Hopple.

"*Five!*" said Tol Proudfoot.

"Five and a quarter," said Gil Hopple.

"*Ten!*" shouted Tol Proudfoot.

And at that moment another voice — Ag Hopple's — was raised above the murmuring of the crowd: "Good *lord*, Gil! I'll *make* you a cake!"

Willis Bagby, gratefully seeing his duty, said, "Sold! To Tol Proudfoot yonder in the corner."

Tol could no more move than if he had been turned by his audacity into a statue. He stood in his corner with sweat running down his face, unable to lift his hand to wipe it off, frightened to think how he had showed off right there in front of everybody for her to see.

And then he saw that Miss Minnie was coming to where he was, and his knees shook. She was coming through the crowd, looking straight at him, and smiling. She reached out with her little hand and put it into one of his great ones, which rose of its own accord to receive it. "Mr. Proudfoot," she said, "that was more than kind."

Tol was standing there full in public view, in the midst of a story that Port William would never forget, and as far as he now knew not a soul was present but Miss Minnie and himself.

"Yes, mam — uh, mam — uh, miss — uh, little lady," he said. "Excuse me, mam, but I believe it was worth every cent of it, if you don't mind. And I ain't trying to act smart or anything, and if I do, excuse me, but might I see you home?"

"Oh, Mr. Proudfoot!" Miss Minnie said. "Certainly you may!"

Pray Without Ceasing (1912)

Mat Feltner was my grandfather on my mother's side. Saying it thus, I force myself to reckon again with the strangeness of that verb *was*. The man of whom I once was pleased to say, "He is my grandfather," has become the dead man who was my grandfather. He was, and is no more. And this is a part of the great mystery we call time.

But the past is present also. And this, I think, is a part of the greater mystery we call eternity. Though Mat Feltner has been dead for twenty-five years, and I am now older than he was when I was born and have grandchildren of my own, I know his hands, their way of holding a hammer or a hoe or a set of checklines, as well as I know my own. I know his way of talking, his way of cocking his head when he began a story, the smoking pipe stem held an inch from his lips. I have in my mind, not just as a memory but as a consolation, his welcome to me when I returned home from the university and, later, from jobs in distant cities. When I sat down beside him, his hand would clap lightly onto my leg above the knee; my absence might have lasted many months, but he would say as though we had been together the day before, "Hello, Andy." The shape of his hand is printed on the flesh of my thigh as vividly as a birthmark. This man who was my grandfather is present in me, as I felt always his father to be present in him. His father was Ben. My own live knowledge of the Feltners in Port William begins with Ben, whom I know from my grandparents' stories. That is the known history. The names go back to Ben's father and grandfather.

But even the unknown past is present in us, its silence as persistent as a ringing in the ears. When I stand in the road that passes through Port William, I am standing on the strata of my history that go down through the known past into the unknown: the blacktop rests on state gravel, which rests on county gravel, which rests on the creek rock and cinders laid down by the town when it was still mostly beyond the reach of the county; and under the creek rock and cinders is the dirt track of the town's beginning, the buffalo trace that was the way we came. You work your way into the interior of the present, until finally you come to that beginning in which all things, the world and the light itself, at a Word welled up into being out of their absence. And nothing is here that we are beyond the reach of merely because we do not know about it. It is always the first morning of Creation and always the last day, always the now that is in time and the Now that is not, that has filled time with reminders of Itself.

When my grandfather was dying, I was not thinking about the past. My grandfather was still a man I knew, but as he subsided day by day he was ceasing to be the man I had known. I was experiencing consciously for the first time that transformation in which the living, by dying, pass into the living, and I was full of grief and love and wonder.

And so when I came out of the house one morning after breakfast and found Braymer Hardy sitting in his pickup truck in front of my barn, I wasn't expecting any news. Braymer was an old friend of my father's; he was curious to see what Flora and I would do with the long-abandoned Harford Place that we had bought and were fixing up, and sometimes he visited. His way was not to go to the door and knock. He just drove in and stopped his old truck at the barn and sat looking around until somebody showed up.

"Well, you ain't much of a Catlett," he said, in perfect good humor. "Marce Catlett would have been out and gone two hours ago."

"I do my chores *before* breakfast," I said, embarrassed by the lack of evidence. My grandfather Catlett would, in fact, have been out and gone two hours ago.

"But," Braymer said in an explanatory tone, as if talking to himself, "I reckon your daddy is a late sleeper, being as he's an office man. But that Wheeler was always a shotgun once he *got* out," he went on, clearly implying, and still in excellent humor, that the family line had reached its nadir in me. "But maybe you're a right smart occupied of a night, I don't know." He raked a large cud of tobacco out of his cheek with his forefinger and spat.

He looked around with the air of a man completing an inspection, which is exactly what he was doing. "Well, it looks like you're making a little headway. You got it looking some better. Here," he said, pawing among a litter of paper, tools, and other odds and ends on top of the dashboard and then on the seat beside him, "I brought you something." He eventually forceped forth an old newspaper page folded into a tight rectangle the size of a wallet and handed it through the truck window. "You ought to have it. It ain't no good to me. The madam, you know, is hell for an antique. She bought an old desk at a sale, and that was in one of the drawers."

I unfolded the paper and read the headline: BEN FELTNER, FRIEND TO ALL, SHOT DEAD IN PORT WILLIAM.

"Ben Feltner was your great-granddaddy."

"Yes. I know."

"I remember him. They never made 'em no finer. The last man on earth you'd a thought would get shot."

"So I've heard."

"Thad Coulter was a good kind of feller, too, far as that goes. I don't reckon he was the kind you'd a thought would shoot somebody, either."

He pushed his hat back and scratched his forehead. "One of them things," he said. "They happen."

He scratched his head some more and propped his wrist on top of the steering wheel, letting the hand dangle. "Tell you," he said, "there ain't a way in this world to know what a human creature is going to do next. I loaned a feller five hundred dollars once. He was a good feller, too, wasn't a thing wrong with him far as I knew, I liked him. And dogged if he didn't kill himself fore it was a week."

"Killed himself?" I said.

"*Killed* himself," Braymer said. He meditated a moment, looking off at his memory of the fellow and wiggling two of the fingers that hung over the steering wheel. "Don't you know," he said, "not wishing him no bad luck, but I wished he'd a done it a week or two sooner."

I laughed.

"Well," he said, "I know you want to be at work. I'll get out of your way."

I said, "Don't be in a hurry," but he was starting the truck and didn't hear me. I called, "Thanks!" as he backed around. He raised his hand, not looking at me, and drove away, steering with both hands, with large deliberate motions, as if the truck were the size of a towboat.

There was an upturned feed bucket just inside the barn door. I sat down on it and unfolded the paper again. It was the front page of the Hargrave *Weekly Express,* flimsy and yellow, nearly illegible in some of the creases. It told how, on a Saturday morning in the July of 1912, Ben Feltner, who so far as was known had had no enemies, had been killed by a single shot to the head from a .22 caliber revolver. His assailant, Thad Coulter, had said, upon turning himself in to the sheriff at Hargrave soon after the incident, "I've killed the best friend I ever had." It was not a long article. It told about the interment of Ben Feltner and named his survivors. It told nothing that I did not know, and I knew little more than it told. I knew that Thad Coulter had killed himself in jail, shortly after the murder. And I knew that he was my grandfather Catlett's first cousin.

I had learned that much, not from anyone's attempt, ever, to tell me the story, but from bits and pieces dropped out of conversations among my elders, in and out of the family. Once, for instance, I heard my mother say to my father that she had always been troubled by the thought of Thad Coulter's lonely anguish as he prepared to kill himself in the Hargrave jail. I had learned what I knew, the bare outline of the event, without asking questions, both fearing the pain that I knew surrounded the story and honoring the silence that surrounded the pain.

But sitting in the barn that morning, looking at the old page opened on my knees, I saw how incomplete the story was as the article told it and as I knew it. And seeing it so, I felt incomplete myself. I suddenly wanted to go and see my grandfather. I did not intend to question him. I had never heard him speak so much as a word about his father's death, and I could not have imagined breaking his silence. I only wanted to be in his presence, as if in his presence I could somehow enter into the presence of an agony that I knew had shaped us all.

With the paper folded again in my shirt pocket, I drove to Port William and turned in under the old maples beside the house. When I let myself in, the house was quiet, and I went as quietly as I could to my grandfather's room, thinking he might be asleep. But he was awake, his fingers laced together on top of the bedclothes. He had seen me drive in and was watching the door when I entered the room.

"Morning," I said.

He said, "Morning, son," and lifted one of his hands.

"How're you feeling?"

"Still feeling."

I sat down in the rocker by the bed and told him, in Braymer's words, the story of the too-late suicide.

My grandfather laughed. "I expect that grieved Braymer."

"Is Braymer pretty tight?" I asked, knowing he was.

"I wouldn't say 'tight,' but he'd know the history of every dollar he ever made. Braymer's done a lot of hard work."

My grandmother had heard us talking, and now she called me. "Oh, Andy!"

"I'll be back," I said, and went to see what she wanted.

She was sitting in the small bedroom by the kitchen where she had always done her sewing and where she slept now that my grandfather was ill. She was sitting by the window in the small cane-bottomed rocking chair that was her favorite. Her hands were lying on her lap and she was not rocking. I knew that her arthritis was hurting her; otherwise, at that time of day, she would have been busy at something. She had medicine for the arthritis, but it made her feel unlike herself; up to a certain point of endurability, she preferred the pain. She sat still and let the pain go its way and occupied her mind with thoughts. Or that is what she said she did. I believed, and I was as sure as if she had told me, that when she sat alone that way, hurting or not, she was praying. Though I never heard her pray aloud in my life, it seems to me now that I can reproduce in my mind the very voice of her prayers.

She had called me in to find out things, which was her way. I sat down on the stool in front of her and submitted to examination. She wanted to know what Flora was doing, and what the children were doing, and when I had seen my mother, and what she had been doing. She asked exacting questions that called for much detail in the answers, watching me intently to see that I withheld nothing. She did not tolerate secrets, even the most considerate ones. She had learned that we sometimes omitted or rearranged facts to keep her from worrying, but her objection to that was both principled and passionate. If we were worried, she wanted to worry with us; it was her place, she said.

After a while, she quit asking questions but continued to look at me. And then she said, "You're thinking about something you're not saying. What is it? Tell Granny."

She had said that to me many times in the thirty years I had known her. By then, I thought it was funny. But if I was no longer intimidated, I was still compelled. In thirty years I had never been able to deceive her when she was looking straight at me. I could have lied, but she would have known it and then would have supposed that somebody was sick. I laughed and handed her the paper out of my pocket.

"Braymer Hardy brought that to me this morning."

She unfolded it, read a little of the article but not all, and folded it back up. Her hands lay quiet in her lap again, and she looked out the window, though obviously not seeing what was out there that morning. Another morning had come to her, and she was seeing it again through the interval of fifty-three years.

"It's a wonder," she said, "that Mat didn't kill Thad Coulter that morning."

I said, "Granddad?"

And then she told me the story. She told it quietly, looking through the window into that July morning in 1912. Her hands lay in her lap and never moved. The only effect her telling had on her was a glistening that appeared from time to time in her eyes. She told the story well, giving many details. She had a good memory, and she had lived many years with her mother-in-law, who also had a good one. I have the impression that they, but not my grandfather, had pondered together over the event many times. She spoke as if she were seeing it all happen, even the parts of it that she had in fact not seen.

"If it hadn't been for Jack Beechum, Mat *would* have killed him," my grandmother said.

That was the point. Or it was one of the points—the one, perhaps, that she most wanted me to see. But it was not the beginning of the

story. Adam and Eve and then Cain and Abel began it, as my grandmother depended on me to know. Even in Thad Coulter's part of the
story, the beginning was some years earlier than the July of 1912.

Abner Coulter, Thad's only son, had hired himself out to a grocer in
Hargrave. After a few years, when he had (in his own estimation) learned
the trade, he undertook to go into business for himself in competition
with his former employer. He rented a building right on the courthouse
square. He was enabled to do this by a sizable sum of money borrowed
from the Hargrave bank on a note secured by a mortgage on his father's
farm.

And here Thad's character enters into the story. For Thad not only
secured his son's note with the farm that was all he had in the world and
that he had only recently finished paying for, but he further committed
himself by bragging in Port William of his son's new status as a merchant in the county seat.

"Thad Coulter was not a bad man," my grandmother said. "I believed
then, and I believe now, that he was not a bad man. But we are all as little
children. Some know it and some don't."

She looked at me to see if I was one who knew it, and I nodded, but I
was thirty then and did not know it yet.

"He was as a little child," she said, "and he was in serious trouble."

He had in effect given his life and its entire effort as hostage to the possibility that Abner, his only son, could be made a merchant in a better
place than Port William.

Before two years were out, Abner repaid his father's confidence by
converting many small private fritterings and derelictions into an un-
disguisable public failure and thereupon by riding off to somewhere
unknown on the back of a bay gelding borrowed ostensibly for an overnight trip to Port William. And so Thad's fate was passed from the reckless care of his son to the small mercy of the law. Without more help
than he could confidently expect, he was going to lose his farm. Even
with help, he was going to have to pay for it again, and he was close to
sixty years old.

As he rode home from his interview with the Hargrave banker, in
which the writing on the wall had been made plain to him, he was goug-
ing his heel urgently into his mule's flank. Since he had got up out of the

chair in the banker's office, he had been full of a desire as compelling as thirst to get home, to get low to the ground, as if to prevent himself from falling off the world. For the country that he had known all his life and had depended on, at least in dry weather, to be solid and steady underfoot had suddenly risen under him like a wave.

Needing help as he did, he could not at first bring himself to ask for it. Instead, he spent most of two days propped against a post in his barn, drinking heavily and talking aloud to himself about betrayal, ruin, the cold-heartedness of the Hargrave bankers, and the poor doings of damned fools, meaning both Abner and himself. And he recalled, with shocks of bitterness that only the whiskey could assuage, his confident words in Port William about Abner and his prospects.

"I worked for it, and I come to own it," he said over and over again. "Now them will own it that never worked for it. And him that stood on it to mount up into the world done run to perdition without a patch, damn him, to cover his ass or a rag to hide his face."

When his wife and daughter begged him to come into the house, he said that a man without the sense to keep a house did not deserve to be in one. He said he would shelter with the dogs and hogs, where he belonged.

The logical source of help was Ben Feltner. Ben had helped Thad to buy his farm—had signed his note and stood behind him. Ben was his friend, and friendship mattered to Ben; it may have mattered to him above all. But Thad did not go to Ben until after his second night in the barn. He walked to Ben's house in Port William early in the morning, drunk and unsteady, his mind tattered and raw from repeated plunges through the thorns and thistles of his ruin.

Ben was astonished by the look of him. Thad had always been a man who used himself hard, and he had grown gaunt and stooped, his mouth slowly caving in as he lost his teeth. But that morning he was also soiled, sagging, unshaved and uncombed, his eyes bloodshot and glary. But Ben said, "Come in, Thad. Come in and sit down." And he took him by the arm, led him in to a chair, and sat down facing him.

"They got me, Ben," Thad said, the flesh twitching around his eyes. "They done got me to where I can't get loose." His eyes glazed by tears that never fell, he made as much sense of his calamity as he was able to make: "A poor man don't stand no show." And then, his mind lurching on, unable to stop, he fell to cursing, first Abner, and then the Hargrave bank, and then the ways of the world that afforded no show to a poor man.

Ben listened to it all, sitting with his elbow on the chair arm and his forefinger pointed against his cheek. Thad's language and his ranting in that place would not have been excusable had he been sober. But insofar as Thad was drunk, Ben was patient. He listened attentively, his eyes on Thad's face, except that from time to time he looked down at his beard as if to give Thad an opportunity to see that he should stop.

Finally Ben stopped him. "Thad, I'll tell you what. I don't believe I can talk with you anymore this morning. Go home, now, and get sober and come back. And then we'll see."

Thad did not have to take Ben's words as an insult. But in his circumstances and condition, it was perhaps inevitable that he would. That Ben was his friend made the offense worse — far worse. In refusing to talk to him as he was, Ben, it seemed to Thad, had exiled him from friendship and so withdrawn the last vestige of a possibility that he might find anywhere a redemption for himself, much less for his forfeited land. For Thad was not able then to distinguish between himself as he was and himself as he might be sober. He saw himself already as a proven fool, fit only for the company of dogs and hogs. If he could have accepted this judgment of himself, then his story would at least have been different and would perhaps have been better. But while he felt the force and truth of his own judgment, he raged against it. He had fled to Ben, hoping that somehow, by some means that he could not imagine, Ben could release him from the solitary cage of his self-condemnation. And now Ben had shut the door.

Thad's whole face began to twitch and his hands to move aimlessly, as if his body were being manipulated from the inside by some intention that he could not control. Patches of white appeared under his whiskers. He said, "I cuss you to your damned face, Ben Feltner, for I have come to you with my hat in my hand and you have spit in it. You have throwed in your lot with them sons of bitches against me."

At that Ben reached his limit. Yet even then he did not become angry. He was a large, unfearful man, and his self-defense had something of merriment in it. He stood up. "Now, Thad, my friend," he said, "you must go." And he helped him to the door. He did not do so violently or with an excess of force. But though he was seventy-two years old, Ben was still in hearty strength, and he helped Thad to the door in such a way that Thad had no choice but to go.

But Thad did not go home. He stayed, hovering about the front of the house, for an hour or more.

"It seemed like hours and hours that he stayed out there," my grandmother said. She and my great-grandmother, Nancy, and old Aunt Cass, the cook, had overheard the conversation between Ben and Thad, or had overheard at least Thad's part of it, and afterward they watched him from the windows, for his fury had left an influence. The house was filled with a quiet that seemed to remember with sorrow the quiet that had been in it before Thad had come.

The morning was bright and still, and it was getting hot, but Thad seemed unable to distinguish between sun and shade. There had got to be something fluttery or mothlike about him now, so erratic and unsteady and unceasing were his movements. He was talking to himself, nodding or shaking his head, his hands making sudden strange motions without apparent reference to whatever he might have been saying. Now and again he started resolutely toward the house and then swerved away.

All the while the women watched. To my grandmother, remembering, it seemed that they were surrounded by signs that had not yet revealed their significance. Aunt Cass told her afterward, "I dreamed of the dark, Miss Margaret, all full of the sound of crying, and I knowed it was something bad." And it seemed to my grandmother, as she remembered, that she too had felt the house and town and the bright day itself all enclosed in that dreamed darkness full of the sounds of crying.

Finally, looking out to where the road from upriver came over the rise into town, they saw a team and wagon coming. Presently they recognized Thad Coulter's team, a pair of mare mules, one black and the other once gray and now faded to white. They were driven by Thad's daughter, wearing a sunbonnet, a sun-bleached blue cotton dress, and an apron.

"It's Martha Elizabeth," Nancy said.

And Aunt Cass said, "Poor child."

"Well," Nancy said, relieved, "she'll take him home."

When Martha Elizabeth came to where Thad was, she stopped the mules and got down. So far as they could see from the house, she did not plead with him. She did not say anything at all. She took hold of him, turned him toward the wagon, and led him to it. She held onto him as he climbed unsteadily up into the wagon and sat down on the spring seat, and then, gathering her skirts in one hand, she climbed up and sat beside him. And all the while she was gentle with him. Afterward and always, my grandmother remembered how gentle Martha Elizabeth had been with him.

Martha Elizabeth turned the team around, and the Feltner women watched the wagon with its troubled burden go slowly away.

Ben, who had meant to go to the field where his hands were at work, did not leave the house as long as Thad was waiting about outside. He saw no point in antagonizing Thad when he did not have to, and so he sat down with a newspaper.

When he knew that Thad was gone and had had time to be out of sight, Ben got up and put on his hat and went out. He was worried about the state both of Thad's economy and of his mind. He thought he might find some of the other Coulters in town. He didn't know that he would, but it was Saturday, and he probably would.

The Feltner house stood, as it still does, in the overlap of the northeast corner of the town and the southwest corner of Ben's farm, which spread away from the house and farmstead over the ridges and hollows and down the side of the valley to the river. There was a farmstead at each of the town's four corners. There was, as there still is, only the one road, which climbed out of the river valley, crossed a mile of ridge, passed through the town, and, after staying on the ridge another half mile or so, went back down into the valley again. For most of its extent, at that time, it was little more than a wagon track. Most of the goods that reached the Port William merchants still came to Dawes Landing by steamboat and then up the hill by team and wagon. The town itself consisted of perhaps two dozen houses, a church, a blacksmith shop, a bank, a barber shop, a doctor's office, a hotel, two saloons, and four stores that sold a variety of merchandise from groceries to dry goods to hardware to harness. The road that passed through town was there only as a casual and hardly foreseen result of the comings and goings of the inhabitants. An extemporaneous town government had from time to time caused a few loads of creek rock to be hauled and knapped and spread over it, and the townspeople had flung their ashes into it, but that was all.

Though the houses and shops had been connected for some time by telephone lines carried overhead on peeled and whitewashed locust poles, there was as yet not an automobile in the town. There were times in any year still when Port William could not have been reached by an automobile that was not accompanied by a team of mules to pull it across the creeks and out of the mud holes.

Except for the telephone lines, the town, as it looked to Ben Feltner on that July morning seventy-eight years ago, might have been unchanged for many more years than it had existed. It looked older than its history. And yet in Port William, as everywhere else, it was already the second decade of the twentieth century. And in some of the people of the town and the community surrounding it, one of the characteristic diseases of the twentieth century was making its way: the suspicion that they would be greatly improved if they were someplace else. This disease had entered into Thad Coulter and into Abner. In Thad it was fast coming to crisis. If Port William could not save him, then surely there was another place that could. But Thad could not just leave, as Abner had; Port William had been too much his life for that. And he was held also by his friendship for Ben Feltner, and for himself as a man whom Ben Feltner had befriended—a friendship that Ben Feltner seemed now to have repudiated and made hateful. Port William was a stumbling block to Thad, and he must rid himself of it somehow.

Ben, innocent of the disease that afflicted his friend yet mortally implicated in it and not knowing it, made his way down into the town, looking about in order to gauge its mood, for Port William had its moods, and they needed watching. More energy was generated in the community than the work of the community could consume, and the surplus energy often went into fighting. There had been cuttings and shootings enough. But usually the fighting was more primitive, and the combatants simply threw whatever projectiles came to hand: corncobs, snowballs, green walnuts, or rocks. In the previous winter, a young Coulter by the name of Burley had claimed that he had had an eye blackened by a frozen horse turd thrown, so far as he could determine, by a Power of the Air. But the place that morning was quiet. Most of the crops had been laid by and many of the farmers were already in town, feeling at ease and inclined to rest now that their annual battle with the weeds had ended. They were sitting on benches and kegs or squatting on their heels under the shade trees in front of the stores, or standing in pairs or small groups among the hitched horses along the sides of the road. Ben passed among them, greeting them and pausing to talk, enjoying himself, and all the while on the lookout for one or another of the Coulters.

Martha Elizabeth was Thad's youngest, the last at home. She had, he thought, the levelest head of any of his children and was the best. Assuming the authority that his partiality granted her, she had at fifteen taken charge of the household, supplanting her mother, who was sickly, and her three older sisters, who had married and gone. At seventeen, she was responsible beyond her years. She was a tall, raw-boned girl, with large hands and feet, a red complexion, and hair so red that, in the sun, it appeared to be on fire.

"Everybody loved Martha Elizabeth," my grandmother said. "She was as good as gold."

To Thad it was a relief to obey her, to climb into the wagon under the pressure of her hand on his arm and to sit beside her as she drove the team homeward through the rising heat of the morning. Her concern for him gave him shelter. Holding to the back of the seat, he kept himself upright and, for the moment, rested in being with her.

But when they turned off the ridge onto the narrower road that led down into the little valley called Cattle Pen and came in sight of their place, she could no longer shelter him. It had long been, to Thad's eye, a pretty farm—a hundred or so acres of slope and ridge on the west side of the valley, the lower, gentler slopes divided from the ridge land by a ledgy bluff that was wooded, the log house and other buildings occupying a shelf above the creek bottom. Through all his years of paying for it, he had aspired toward it as toward a Promised Land. To have it, he had worked hard and long and deprived himself, and Rachel, his wife, had deprived herself. He had worked alone more often than not. Abner, as he grew able, had helped, as the girls had, also. But Abner had been reserved for something better. Abner was smart—too smart, as Thad and Rachel agreed, without ever much talking about it, to spend his life farming a hillside. Something would have to be done to start him on his way to something better, a Promised Land yet more distant.

Although he had thought the farm not good enough for Abner, Thad was divided in his mind; for himself he loved it. It was what he had transformed his life into. And now, even in the morning light, it lay under the shadow of his failure, and he could not bear to look at it. It was his life, and he was no longer in it. Somebody else, some other thing that did not even know it, stood ready to take possession of it. He was ashamed in its presence. To look directly at it would be like looking Martha Elizabeth full in the eyes, which he could not do either. And his shame raged in him.

When she stopped in the lot in front of the barn and helped him down, he started unhitching the team. But she took hold of his arm and drew him away gently toward the house.

"Come on, now," she said. "You've got to have you something to eat and some rest."

But he jerked away from her. "Go see to your mammy!"

"No," she said. "Come on." And she attempted again to move him toward the house.

He pushed her away, and she fell. He could have cut off his hand for so misusing her, and yet his rage at himself included her. He reached into the wagon box and took out a short hickory stock with a braid of rawhide knotted to it. He shook it at her.

"Get up," he said. "Get yonder to that house 'fore I wear you out."

He had never spoken to her in such a way, had never imagined himself doing so. He hated what he had done, and he could not undo it.

The heat of the day had established itself now. There was not a breeze anywhere, not a breath. A still haze filled the valley and redoubled the light. Within that blinding glare he occupied a darkness that was loud with accusing cries.

Martha Elizabeth stood at the kitchen door a moment, looking back at him, and then she went inside. Thad turned back to the team then, unhitched them, did up the lines, and led the mules to their stalls in the barn. He moved as if dreaming through these familiar motions that had now estranged themselves from him. The closer he had come to home, the more the force of his failure had gathered there to exclude him.

And it was Ben Feltner who had barred the door and left him without a friend. Ben Feltner, who owed nothing, had turned his back on his friend, who now owed everything.

He said aloud, "Yes, I'll come back sober, God damn you to Hell!"

He lifted the jug out of the white mule's manger, pulled the cob from its mouth, and drank. When he lowered it, it was empty. It had lasted him three days, and now it was empty. He cocked his wrist and broke the jug against an upright.

"Well, that does for you, old holler-head."

He stood, letting the whiskey seek its level in him, and felt himself slowly come into purpose; now he had his anger full and clear. Now he was summoned by an almost visible joy.

He went to the house, drank from the water bucket on the back porch, and stepped through the kitchen door. Rachel and Martha Elizabeth were standing together by the cookstove, facing him.

"Thad, honey, I done fixed dinner," Rachel said. "Set down and eat."

He opened the stairway door, stepped up, and took down his pistol from the little shelf over the door frame.

"No, now," Martha Elizabeth said. "Put that away. You ain't got a use in this world for that."

"Don't contrary me," Thad said. "Don't you say another damned word."

He put the pistol in his hip pocket with the barrel sticking up and turned to the door.

"Wait, Thad," Rachel said. "Eat a little before you go." But she was already so far behind him that he hardly heard her.

He walked to the barn, steadying himself by every upright thing he came to, so that he proceeded by a series of handholds on doorjamb and porch post and gatepost and tree. He could no longer see the place but walked in a shifting aisle of blinding light through a cloud of darkness. Behind him now was almost nothing. And ahead of him was the singular joy to which his heart now beat in answer.

He went into the white mule's stall, unbuckled hame strap and belly-band, and shoved the harness off her back, letting it fall. He unbuckled the collar and let it fall. Again his rage swelled within him, seeming to tighten the skin of his throat, as though his body might fail to contain it, for he had never before in his life allowed a mule's harness to touch the ground if he could help it. But he was not in his life now, and his rage pleased him.

He hooked his finger in the bit ring and led the mule to the drinking trough by the well in front of the barn. The trough was half an oak barrel, nearly full of water. The mule wanted to drink, but he jerked her head up and drew her forward until she stood beside the trough. The shorn stubble of her mane under his hand, he stepped up onto the rim. Springing, he cast himself across the mule's back, straddled her, and sat upright as darkness swung around him. He jerked hard at the left rein.

"Get up, Beck," he said.

The mule was as principled as a martyr. She would have died before she would have trotted a step, and yet he urged her forward with his heel. Even as the hind feet of the mule lifted from their tracks, the thought of Martha Elizabeth formed itself within the world's ruin. She seemed to rise up out of its shambles, like a ghost or an influence. She would follow him. He needed to hurry.

On the fringe of the Saturday bustle in front of the business houses, Ben met Early Rowanberry and his little boy, Arthur. Early was carrying a big sack, and Art a small one. They had started out not long after breakfast; from the log house on the ridgetop where the Rowanberrys had settled before Kentucky was a state, they had gone down the hill, forded the creek known as Sand Ripple, and then walked up the Shade Branch hollow through the Feltner Place and on to town. Early had done his buying and a little talking, had bought a penny's worth of candy for Art, and now they were starting the long walk back. Ben knew that they had made the trip on foot to spare their mules, though the sacks would weigh sorely on their shoulders before they made it home.

"Well, Early," Ben said, "you've got a good hand with you today, I see."

"He's tol'ble good company, Ben, and he packs a little load," Early said.

Ben liked all the Rowanberrys, who had been good neighbors to him all his life, and Early was a better-than-average Rowanberry — a quiet man with a steady gaze and a sort of local fame for his endurance at hard work.

Ben then offered his hand to Art, who shyly held out his own. Ben said, "My boy, are you going to grow up to be a wheelhorse like your pap?" and Art answered without hesitation, "Yes, sir."

"Ah, that's right," Ben said. And he placed his hand on the boy's unladen shoulder.

The two Rowanberrys then resumed their homeward journey, and Ben walked on down the edge of the dusty road into town.

Ben was in no hurry. He had his mission in mind and was somewhat anxious about it, but he gave it its due place in the order of things. Thad's difficulty was not simple; whatever it was possible to do for him could not be done in a hurry. Ben passed slowly through the talk of the place and time, partaking of it. He liked the way the neighborhood gathered into itself on such days. Now and then, in the midst of the more casual conversation, a little trade talk would rouse up over a milk cow or a pocketknife or a saddle or a horse or mule. Or there would be a joke or a story or a bit of news, uprisings of the town's interest in itself that would pass through it and die away like scurries of wind. It was close to noon. It was hot even in the shade now, and the smells of horse sweat and horse manure had grown strong. On the benches and kegs along the storefronts, pocketknives were busy. Profound meditations were coming to bear upon long scrolls of cedar or poplar curling backward over thumbs and wrists and piling over shoetops.

Somebody said, "Well, I can see the heat waves a-rising."

Somebody else said, "Ain't nobody but a lazy man can see them heat waves."

And then Ben saw Thad's cousin, Dave Coulter, and Dave's son, Burley, coming out of one of the stores, Dave with a sack of flour on his shoulder and Burley with a sack of meal on his. Except for his boyish face and grin, Burley was a grown man. He was seventeen, a square-handed, muscular fellow already known for the funny things he said, though his elders knew of them only by hearsay. He and his father turned down the street toward their wagon, and Ben followed them.

When they had hunched the sacks off their shoulders into the wagon, Ben said, "Dave?"

Dave turned to him and stuck out his hand. "Why, howdy, Ben."

"How are you, Dave?"

"'Bout all right, I reckon."

"And how are you, Burley?"

Dave turned to his boy to see that he would answer properly; Burley, grinning, said, "Doing about all right, thank you, sir," and Dave turned back to Ben.

"Had to lay in a little belly timber," he said, "'gainst we run plumb out. And the boy here, he wanted to come see the sights."

"Well, my boy," Ben said, "have you learned anything worthwhile?"

Burley grinned again, gave a quick nod, and said, "Yessir."

"Oh, hit's an educational place," Dave said. "We hung into one of them educational conversations yonder in the store. That's why we ain't hardly going to make it home by dinnertime."

"Well, I won't hold you up for long," Ben said. And he told Dave as much as he had understood of Thad's trouble. They were leaning against the wagon box, facing away from the road. Burley, who had gone to untie the mules, was still standing at their heads.

"Well," Dave said, "hit's been norated around that Abner weren't doing just the way he ought to. Tell you the truth, I been juberous about that loan proposition ever since Thad put his name to it. Put his whole foothold in that damned boy's pocket is what he done. And now you say it's all gone up the spout."

"He's in a serious fix, no question about it."

"Well, is there anything a feller can do for him?"

"Well, there's one thing for certain. He was drunk when he came to see me. He was cussing and raring. If you, or some of you, could get him sober, it would help. And then we could see if we can help him out of his scrape."

"Talking rough, was he?"

"Rough enough."

"I'm sorry, Ben. Thad don't often drink, but when he does he drinks like the Lord appointed him to get rid of it all."

Somebody cried, "Look out!"

They turned to see Thad and the white mule almost abreast of them. Thad was holding the pistol.

"They said he just looked awful," my grandmother said. "He looked like death warmed over."

Ben said, without raising his voice, in the same reasonable tone in which he had been speaking to Dave, "Hold on, Thad."

And Thad fired.

Dave saw a small round red spot appear in the center of Ben's forehead. A perplexed look came to his face, as if he had been intending to say something more and had forgot what it was. For a moment, he remained standing just as he had been, one hand on the rim of the wagon box. And then he fell. As he went down, his shoulder struck the hub of the wagon wheel so that he fell onto his side, his hat rolling underneath the wagon.

Thad put the pistol back into his pocket. The mule had stood as still after he had halted her as if she were not there at all but at home under a tree in the pasture. When Thad kicked her, she went on again.

Ben Feltner never had believed in working on Sunday, and he did not believe in not working on workdays. Those two principles had shaped all his weeks. He liked to make his hay cuttings and begin other large, urgent jobs as early in the week as possible in order to have them finished before Sunday. On Saturdays, he and Mat and the hands worked in the crops if necessary; otherwise, that day was given to the small jobs of maintenance that the farm constantly required and to preparations for Sunday, when they would do nothing except milk and feed. When the work was caught up and the farm in order, Ben liked to have everybody quit early on Saturday afternoon. He liked the quiet that descended over the place then, with the day of rest ahead.

On that Saturday morning he had sent Old Smoke, Aunt Cass's husband, and their son, Samp, and Samp's boy, Joe, to mend a fence back on the river bluff. Mat he sent to the blacksmith shop to have the shoes reset on Governor, his buggy horse. They would not need Governor to go to church; they walked to church. But when they had no company on Sunday afternoon and the day was fair, Ben and Nancy liked to drive around the neighborhood, looking at the crops and stopping at various households to visit. They liked especially to visit Nancy's brother, Jack Beechum, and his wife, Ruth, who lived on the Beechum place, the place that Nancy always spoke of as "out home."

And so Mat that morning, after his chores were done, had slipped a halter on Governor and led him down through town to the blacksmith's. He had to wait—there were several horses and mules already in line—and so he tied Governor to the rail in front of the shop and went in among the others who were waiting and talking, figuring that he would be late for dinner.

It was a good place. The shop stood well back from the street, leaving in front of it a tree-shaded, cinder-covered yard, which made room for the hitch rail and for the wagons, sleds, and other implements waiting to be repaired. The shop itself was a single large, dirt-floored room, meticulously clean—every surface swept and every tool in place. Work-benches went around three walls. Near the large open doorway were the forge and anvil.

The blacksmith—a low, broad, grizzled man by the name of Elder Johnson—was the best within many miles, a fact well known to himself, which sometimes made him difficult. He also remembered precisely every horse or mule he had ever nailed a shoe on, and so he was one of the keepers of the town's memory.

Elder was shoeing a colt that was nervous and was giving him trouble. He was working fast so as to cause the colt as little discomfort as he could. He picked up the left hind hoof, caught it between his aproned knees, and laid the shoe on it. The shoe was too wide at the heel, and he let the colt's foot go back to the floor. A small sharp-faced man smoking a cob pipe was waiting, holding out a broken singletree for Elder's inspection as he passed on his way back to the forge.

Elder looked as if the broken tree were not the sort of thing that could concern him.

"Could I get this done by this evening?" the man asked. His name was Skeets Willard, and his work was always in some state of emergency. "I can't turn a wheel," he said, "till I get that fixed."

Elder let fall the merest glance at the two pieces of the singletree, and then looked point-blank at the man himself as if surprised not only by his presence but by his existence. "What the hell do you think I am? A hammer with a brain? Do you see all them horses and mules tied up out there? If you want that fixed, I'll fix it when I can. If you don't, take it home."

Skeets Willard elected to lay the pieces down in a conspicuous place by the forge. And Elder, whose outburst had not interrupted the flow of talk among the bystanders, caught the shoe in his tongs and shoved it in among the coals of the forge. He cranked the bellows and made small flames spike up out of the coals. As he turned the handle, he stared in a kind of trance at the light of the open doorway, and the light shone in his eyes, and his face and his arms were shining with sweat. Presently he drew the shoe, glowing, out of the coals and, laying it on the horn of the anvil, turned in the heel. He then plunged the shoe into the slack tub from which it raised a brief shriek of steam.

Somebody turned out of the conversation and said, "Say, Elder, do you remember that little red mule come in here with a bunch of year-lings Marce Catlett bought up around Lexington? Ned, I think they called him."

"Newt," Elder said in so even a voice that Skeets Willard might never have been there. "You bet I remember him."

He took the cooled shoe from the slack tub and, picking up the colt's foot and straddling it again, quickly nailed one nail in each side, raking the points over with the claws of his hammer. He let the colt stand on his foot again to see how the shoe set. "You bet I remember him," he said. "That mule could kick the lard out of a biscuit."

And then they heard the single voice raised in warning out in the road, followed immediately by the shot and by a rising murmur of excited, indistinguishable voices as the whole Saturday crowd turned its attention to the one thing.

Mat hurried out with the others and saw the crowd wedged in be-tween the storefronts and Dave Coulter's wagon. He only began to real-ize that the occasion concerned him when the crowd began to make way for him as he approached.

"Let him through! Let him through!" the crowd said.

The crowd opened to let him through, turning its faces to him, falling silent as it saw who he was. And then he saw what was left of the man who had been his father lying against the wagon wheel. Those nearest him heard him say, "Oh!" and it did not sound like him at all. He stepped forward and knelt and took his father's wrist in his hand to feel for the pulse that he did not expect, having seen the wound and the fixed unsighted eyes. The crowd now was as quiet around him as the still tree-tops along the road. For what seemed a long time Mat knelt there with his father's dead wrist in his hand, while his mind arrived and arrived and yet arrived at that place and time and that body lying still on the soiled and bloodied stones. When he looked up again, he did not look like the man they had known at all.

"Who did this?" he said.

And the crowd answered, "Thad Coulter, he done it."

"Where'd he go?"

"He taken down the road yonder towards Hargrave. He was on that old white mule, old May."

When Mat stood up again from his father's side, he was a man new-created by rage. All that he had been and thought and done gave way to his one desire to kill the man who had killed his father. He ached, mind and body, with the elation of that one thought. He was not armed, but he never thought of that. He would go for the horse he had left tied at the blacksmith's. He would ride Thad Coulter down. He would come up beside him and club him off the mule. He would beat him down out of the air. And in that thought, which lived more in his right arm than in his head, both he and his enemy were as clear of history as if newborn.

By the time Mat was free of the crowd, he was running.

Jack Beechum had sold a team of mules the day before, and so he had a check to carry to the bank. He also had a list of things that Ruth wanted from town, and now that he had money ahead he wanted to settle his account at Chatham's store. His plan was to do his errands in town and get back home by dinner; that afternoon, he wanted to mow a field of hay, hoping it would cure by Monday. He rode to town on a good black gelding, called Socks for his four white pasterns.

He tied the horse some distance from the center of town in a place of better shade and fewer flies. He went to the bank first and then went about gathering the things that Ruth needed, ending up at Chatham's.

He was sitting by Beater Chatham's desk in the back, watching Beater total up his account, when they heard the shot out in the street.

"Sounds like they're getting Saturday started out there," Jack said.

"I reckon," Beater said, checking his figures.

"They're going to keep on until they shoot somebody who don't deserve it."

Beater looked at him then over the tops of his glasses. "Well, I reckon they'll have to look hard to find him." He filled out a check for the amount of the bill and handed the check to Jack for him to sign.

And then somebody who had just stepped out of the store stepped back in again and said, "Jack, you'd better come. They've shot Ben Feltner."

Jack never signed the check that day or for several days. He ran to the door. When he was outside, he saw first the crowd and then Mat running toward him out of it. Without breaking his own stride, he caught Mat and held him.

They were both moving at some speed, and the crowd heard the shock of the impact as the two men came together. Jack could hardly have known what he was doing. He had had no time to think. He may have been moved by an impulse simply to stop things until he *could* think. At any rate, as soon as Jack had taken hold of Mat, he understood that he *had* to hold him. And he knew that he had never taken hold of any such thing before. He had caught Mat in a sideways hug that clamped his arms to his sides. Jack's sole task was to keep Mat from freeing his arms. But Mat was little more than half Jack's age; he was in the prime of his strength. And now he twisted and strained with the concentration of fury, uttering cries that could have been either grunts or sobs, forcing Jack both to hold him and to hold him up. They strove there a long time, heaving and staggering, and the dust rose up around them. Jack felt that his arms would pull apart at the joints. He ached afterward. Something went out of him that day, and he was not the same again.

And what went out of Jack came into Mat. Or so it seemed, for in that desperate embrace he became a stronger man than he had been. A strength came into him that held his grief and his anger as Jack had held him. And Jack knew of the coming of this strength, not because it enabled Mat to break free but because it enabled Jack to turn him loose. He stepped away, allowing himself to be recognized, and Mat stood still. To Jack, it was as though he had caught one man and let another go.

But he put his eye on Mat, not willing yet to trust him entirely to himself, and waited.

They both were winded, wet with sweat, and for a moment they only breathed, watched by the crowd, Jack watching Mat, Mat looking at nothing.

As they stood so, the girl, Martha Elizabeth, walked by in the road. She did not look at them or at the wagon or at the body crumpled on the ground. She walked past it all, looking ahead, as if she already saw what she was walking toward.

Coming aware that Jack was waiting on him, Mat looked up; he met Jack's gaze. He said, "Pa's dead. Thad Coulter has shot him."

They waited, looking at each other still, while the earth shook under them.

Mat said, "I'll go tell Ma. You bring Pa, but give me a little time."

Dinner was ready, and the men were late.

"It wasn't usual for them to be late," my grandmother said, "but we didn't think yet that anything was wrong. Your mother was just a little girl then, and she was telling us a story about a girl and a dog and a horse."

Aunt Cass stood by the stove, keeping an eye on the griddle. Nancy was sweeping the floor under the firebox of the stove; she was a woman who was always doing. Margaret, having set the table, had turned one of the chairs out into the floor and sat down. All three were listening to Bess, who presently stopped her story, rolled her eyes, and said, "I hear my innards a-growling. I reckon I must be hungry."

They laughed.

"I spect so, I spect so," Aunt Cass said. "Well, you'll eat fore long."

When she heard Mat at the kitchen door, Aunt Cass said, "Miss Nancy, you want to take the hoecake up?" And then seeing the change in Mat's face, which was new to it but old to the world, she hushed and stood still. Nancy, seeing the expression on Cass's face, turned to look at Mat.

Bess said, "Goody! Now we can eat!"

Mat looked at his mother and then down at Bess and smiled. "You can eat directly," he said.

And then he said, "Margaret, take Bess and go upstairs. I think she's got a book up there she wants you to read to her."

"I knew what it was then," my grandmother said. "Oh, I felt it go all over me before I knew it in my mind. I just wanted to crawl away. But I had your mother to think about. You always have somebody to think about, and it's a blessing."

She said, "Come on, Bess, let's go read a story. We'll eat in a little bit."

As soon as he heard their footsteps going up the stairs, Mat looked at his mother again. As the silence gathered against him, he said, "Ma, I'm sorry. Pa's dead."

She was already wearing black. She had borne four children and raised one. Two of her children she had buried in the same week of a diphtheria epidemic, of which she had nearly died herself. After the third child had died, she never wore colors again. It was not that she chose to be ostentatiously bereaved. She could not have chosen to be ostentatious about anything. She was, in fact, a woman possessed of a strong native cheerfulness. And yet she had accepted a certain darkness that she had lived in too intimately to deny.

She stood, looking at Mat, while she steadied herself and steadied the room around her, in the quiet that, having suddenly begun there, would not end for a long time. And then she said to Mat, "Sit down."

She said, "Cass, sit down."

They turned chairs away from the table and sat down, and then she did.

"Now," she said, "I want to know what happened."

In the quiet Mat told as much, as little, as he knew.

As if to exert herself against the silence that too quickly filled the room, Nancy stood again. She laid her hand on the shoulder of Mat's wet shirt and patted it once.

"Cass," she said, "we mustn't cry," though there were tears on her own face.

"Mat," she said, "go get Smoke and Samp and Joe. Tell them, and tell them to come here."

To Aunt Cass again, she said, "We must fix the bed. They'll need a place to lay him."

And then they heard the burdened footsteps at the door.

In his cresting anger in the minutes before he stopped the mule in the road in Port William and fired the one shot that he ever fired in anger in his life, Thad Coulter knew a fierce, fulfilling joy. He saw the shot home to the mark, saw Ben Feltner stand a moment and go down, and then he kicked the mule hard in the side and rode on. He went on because all behind him that he might once have turned back to was gone from his mind, and perhaps even in his joy he knew that from that time there was to be no going back.

Even before the town was out of sight behind him, his anger and his joy began to leave him. It was as if his life's blood were running out of him, and he tried to stanch the flow by muttering aloud the curses of his rage. But they had no force, and his depletion continued.

His first thought beyond his anger was of the mule. She was thirsty, he knew, and he had denied her a drink.

"When we get to the creek," he said.

The mule followed the windings of the road down off the upland. Below the cleared ridges, they passed through woods. On the gentler open slopes below, they came into the blank sunlight again, and he could see the river winding between its wooded banks toward its meeting with the Ohio at Hargrave.

At the foot of the hill, the road dipped under trees again and forded a creek. Thad rode the mule into the pool above the ford, loosened the rein, and let her drink. It was a quiet, deeply shaded place, the water unrippled until the mule stepped into it. For the first time in three days Thad could hear the quiet, and a bottomless sorrow opened in him, causing him suddenly to clutch his belly and groan aloud.

When the mule had finished drinking, he rode her out of the pool, dismounted, and, unbuckling one end of the rein from the bit, led her into a clump of bushes and tall weeds and tied her there. For now the thought of pursuit had come to him, and he knew he would have to go the rest of the way on foot. The mule could not be hurried, and she would be difficult to hide.

He went back to the pool and knelt at the edge of it and drank, and then he washed his hands and in his cupped hands lifted the clear water to his face.

Presently, he became still, listening. He had heard, he thought, nothing but the cicadas in the surrounding trees. And then he heard, coming fast, the sound of loud talking and the rapid hooftread of horses. He stepped into a patch of weeds and watched several riders go by on the road. They were boys and young men from the town who, having waited through the aftermath of the shooting, had now been carried by their excitement into pursuit of him. "Boys," he thought. He felt in no danger from them — he did not think of the pistol — and yet he feared them. He imagined himself hurrying on foot along the road, while the young riders picked and pecked at him.

The quiet returned, and he could feel, as if in the hair roots and pores of his skin, that Martha Elizabeth was coming near. He went back to the road again.

The walking and the water drying on his face cleared his mind, and now he knew himself as he had been and as he was and knew that he was changed beyond unchanging into something he did not love. Now that his anger had drained away, his body seemed to him not only to be a burden almost too heavy to carry but to be on the verge of caving in. He walked with one hand pressed to his belly where the collapse seemed already to have begun.

The best way between Port William and Hargrave was still the river. The road found its way as if by guess, bent this way and that by the whims of topography and the convenience of landowners. At intervals, it was interrupted by farm gates.

After a while, hearing several more horses coming behind him, he stepped out of the road and lay down in a small canebrake. When they had passed, he returned to the road and went on. Always he was watchful of the houses he passed, but he stayed in the road. If he was to protect the one choice of which he was still master, he had to hurry.

And now, as he had not been able to do when he left it, he could see his farm. It shone in his mind as if inwardly lighted in the darkness that now surrounded both him and it. He could see it with the morning sun dew-bright on the woods and the sloping pastures, on the little croplands on the ridge and in the bottoms along the creek. He could see its cool shadows stretching out in the evening and the milk cows coming down the path to the barn. It was irrevocably behind him now, as if a great sword had fallen between him and it.

He was slow and small on the long road. The sun was slow overhead. The air was heavy and unmoving. He watched the steady stepping of his feet, the road going backward beneath them. He had to get out of the road only twice again: once for a family in a spring wagon coming up from Hargrave and once for another horse and rider coming down from Port William. Except for those, nothing moved in the still heat but himself. Except for the cicadas, the only sounds he heard were his own steady footfalls on the dry dust.

He seemed to see always not only the changing road beneath his feet but also that other world in which he had lived, now lighted in the dark behind him, and it came to him that on that day two lives had ended for a possibility that never had existed: for Abner Coulter's mounting up to a better place. And he felt the emptiness open wider in him and again heard himself groan. He wondered, so great was the pain of that emptiness, that he did not weep, but it exceeded weeping as it exceeded words. Beyond the scope of one man's grief, it cried out in the air around him, as if in that day's hot light the trees and the fields and the dust of the road all grieved. An inward pressure that had given his body its shape seemed to have been withdrawn, and he walked, holding himself, resisting step by step the urge to bend around the emptiness opening in his middle and let himself fall.

Where the valley began to widen toward the river's mouth, the road passed a large bottom planted in corn. Thad looked back, expecting that he would see Martha Elizabeth, and he did see her. She was maybe three-quarters of a mile behind him, small in the distance, and the heat rising off the field shimmered and shook between them, but he knew her. He walked faster, and he did not look back again. It seemed to him that she knew everything he knew, and loved him anyhow. She loved him, minute by minute, not only as he had been but as he had become. It was a wonderful and a fearful thing to him that he had caused such a love for himself to come into the world and then had failed it. He could not have bowed low enough before it and remained above ground. He could not bear to think of it. But he knew that she walked behind him — balanced across the distance, in the same hot light, the same darkness, the same crying air — ever at the same speed that he walked.

Finally he came to the cluster of houses at Ellville, at the end of the bridge, and went across into Hargrave. From the bridge to the court-house, he went ever deeper into the Saturday crowd, but he did not alter his gait or look at anybody. If anybody looked at him, he did not know it. At the cross streets, he could see on the river a towboat pushing a line of barges slowly upstream, black smoke gushing from its stacks. The walks were full of people, and the streets were full of buggies and wagons. He crossed the courthouse yard where people sat on benches or stood talk-ing in little groups under the shade trees. It seemed to him that he walked in a world from which he had departed.

When he went through the front door of the courthouse into the sudden cool darkness of the hallway, he could not see. Lights swam in his eyes in the dark, and he had to prop himself against the wall. The place smelled of old paper and tobacco and of human beings, washed and unwashed. When he could see again, he walked to a door under a sign that said "Sheriff" and went in. It was a tall room lighted by two tall windows. There was a row of chairs for people to wait in, and several spittoons, placed at the presumed convenience of spitters, that had been as much missed as hit. No one was there but a large man in a broad-brimmed straw hat and a suit somewhat too small, who was standing behind a high desk, writing something. At first he did not look up. When he finally did look up, he stared at Thad for some time, as if not suffi-ciently convinced of what he saw.

"In a minute," he said, and looked down again and finished what he was writing. There was a badge pinned lopsidedly to the pocket of his shirt, and he held an unlit cigar like another pen in his left hand. He said as he wrote, "You look like most of you has been wore off."

"Yes," Thad said. "I have killed a man."

The sheriff laid the pen on the blotter and looked up. "Who?"

Thad said, "Ben Feltner, the best friend I ever had." His eyes suddenly brimmed with tears, but they did not fall. He made no sound and he did not move.

"You're a Coulter, ain't you? From up about Port William?"

"Thad," Thad said.

The sheriff would have preferred that Thad had remained a fugitive. He did not want a self-confessed murderer on his hands — especially not one fresh from a Saturday killing in Port William. He knew Ben Feltner, knew he was liked, and feared there would be a commotion. Port William, as far as he was concerned, was nothing but trouble, almost beyond the law's reach and certainly beyond its convenience — a source, as far as he was concerned, of never foreseeable bad news. He did not know what would come next, but he thought that something would, and he did not approve of it.

"I wish to hell," he said, "that everybody up there who is going to kill each other would just by God go ahead and do it." He looked at Thad for some time in silence, as if giving him an opportunity to disappear.

"Well," he said, finally, "I reckon you just as well give me that pistol."

He gestured toward Thad's sagging hip pocket, and Thad took out the pistol and gave it to him.

"Come on," the sheriff said.

Thad followed him out a rear door into the small paved yard of the jail, where the sheriff rang for the jailer.

The sheriff had hardly got back into the office and taken up his work again when a new motion in the doorway alerted him. He looked up and saw a big red-faced girl standing just outside the door as if uncertain whether or not it was lawful to enter. She wore a sunbonnet, a faded blue dress that reached to her ankles, and an apron. Though she was obviously timid and unused to public places, she returned his look with perfect candor.

"Come in," he said.

She crossed the threshold and again stopped.

"What can I do for you, miss?"

"I'm a-looking for Mr. Thad Coulter from up to Port William, please, sir."

"You his daughter?"

"Yes, sir."

"Well, he's here. I got him locked up. He claims he killed a fellow."

"He did," the girl said. "Is it allowed to see him?"

"Not now," the sheriff said. "You come back in the morning, miss. You can see him then."

She stood looking at him another moment, as if to make sure that he had said what he meant, and then she said, "Well, I thank you," and went out.

An hour or so later, when he shut the office and started home to supper, she was sitting on the end of one of the benches under the shade trees, looking down at her hands in her lap.

"You see," my grandmother said, "there are two deaths in this — Mr. Feltner's and Thad Coulter's. We know Mr. Feltner's because we had to know it. It was ours. That we know Thad's is because of Martha Elizabeth. The Martha Elizabeth you know."

I knew her, but it came strange to me now to think of her — to be asked to see her — as a girl. She was what I considered an old woman when I first remember her; she was perhaps eight or ten years younger than my grandmother, the red long gone from her hair. She was a woman always near to smiling, sometimes to laughter. Her face, it seemed, had been made to smile. It was a face that assented wholly to the being of whatever and whomever she looked at. She had gone with her father to the world's edge and had come back with this smile on her face. Miss Martha Elizabeth, we younger ones called her. Everybody loved her.

When the sheriff came back from supper, she was still there on the bench, the Saturday night shoppers and talkers, standers and passers leaving a kind of island around her, as if unwilling to acknowledge the absolute submission they sensed in her. The sheriff knew as soon as he laid eyes on her this time that she was not going to go away. Perhaps he understood that she had no place to go that she could get to before it would be time to come back.

"Come on with me," he said, and he did not sound like a sheriff now but only a man.

She got up and followed him through the hallway of the courthouse, past the locked doors of the offices, out again, and across the little iron-fenced courtyard in front of the jail. The sheriff unlocked a heavy sheet-iron door, opened it, and closed it behind them, and they were in a large room of stone, steel, and concrete, containing several cages, barred from floor to ceiling, the whole interior lighted by one kerosene lamp hanging in the corridor.

Among the bars gleaming dimly and the shadows of bars thrown back against concrete and stone, she saw her father sitting on the edge of a bunk that was only an iron shelf let down on chains from the wall, with a thin mattress laid on it. He had paid no attention when they entered. He sat still, staring at the wall, one hand pressed against his belly, the other holding to one of the chains that supported the bunk.

The sheriff opened the cell door and stood aside to let her in. "I'll come back after while," he said.

The door closed and was locked behind her, and she stood still until Thad felt her presence and looked up. When he recognized her, he covered his face with both hands.

"He put his hands over his face like a man ashamed," my grandmother said. "But he was like a man, too, who had seen what he couldn't bear."

She sat without speaking a moment, looking at me, for she had much to ask of me.

"Maybe Thad saw his guilt full and clear then. But what he saw that he couldn't bear was something else."

And again she paused, looking at me. We sat facing each other on either side of the window; my grandfather lay in one of his lengthening sleeps nearby. The old house in that moment seemed filled with a quiet that extended not only out into the whole broad morning but endlessly both ways in time.

"People sometimes talk of God's love as if it's a pleasant thing. But it is terrible, in a way. Think of all it includes. It included Thad Coulter, drunk and mean and foolish, before he killed Mr. Feltner, and it included him afterwards."

She reached out then and touched the back of my right hand with her fingers; my hand still bears that touch, invisible and yet indelible as a tattoo.

"That's what Thad saw. He saw his guilt. He had killed his friend. He had done what he couldn't undo; he had destroyed what he couldn't make. But in the same moment he saw his guilt included in love that stood as near him as Martha Elizabeth and at that moment wore her flesh. It was surely weak and wrong of him to kill himself—to sit in judgment that way over himself. But surely God's love includes people who can't bear it."

The sheriff took Martha Elizabeth home with him that night; his wife fed her and turned back the bed for her in the spare room. The next day she sat with her father in his cell.

"All that day," my grandmother said, "he would hardly take his hands from his face. Martha Elizabeth fed him what little he would eat and raised the cup to his lips for what little he would drink. And he ate and drank only because she asked him to, almost not at all. I don't know what they said. Maybe nothing."

At bedtime again that night Martha Elizabeth went home with the sheriff. When they returned to the courthouse on Monday morning, Thad Coulter was dead by his own hand.

"It's a hard story to have to know," my grandmother said. "The mercy of it was Martha Elizabeth."

She still had more to tell, but she paused again, and again she looked at me and touched my hand.

"If God loves the ones we can't," she said, "then finally maybe we can. All these years I've thought of him sitting in those shadows, with Martha Elizabeth standing beside him, and his work-sore old hands over his face."

Once the body of Ben Feltner was laid on his bed, the men who had helped Jack to carry him home went quietly out through the kitchen and the back door, as they had come in, muttering or nodding their commiseration in response to Nancy's "Thank you." And Jack stayed. He stayed to be within sight or call of his sister when she needed him, and he stayed to keep his eye on Mat. Their struggle in front of Chatham's store, Jack knew, had changed them both. Because he did not yet know how or how much or if it was complete, it was not yet a change that he was willing, or that he dared, to turn his back on.

Someone was sent to take word to Rebecca Finley, Margaret's mother, and to ask her to come for Bess.

When Rebecca came, Margaret brought Bess down the stairs into the quiet that the women now did their best to disguise. But Bess, who did not know what was wrong and who tactfully allowed the pretense that nothing was, knew nevertheless that the habits of the house were now broken, and she had heard the quiet that she would never forget.

"Grandma Finley is here to take you home with her," Margaret said, giving her voice the lilt of cheerfulness. "You've been talking about going to stay with her, haven't you?"

And Bess said, dutifully supplying the smile she felt her mother wanted, "Yes, mam."

"We're going to bake some cookies just as soon as we get home," Rebecca said. "Do you want to bake a gingerbread boy?"

"Yes, mam," Bess said.

She removed her hand from her mother's hand and placed it in her grandmother's. They went out the door.

The quiet returned. From then on, though there was much that had to be done and the house stayed full of kin and neighbors coming and going or staying to help, and though by midafternoon women were already bringing food, the house preserved a quiet against all sound. No voice was raised. No door was slammed. Everybody moved as if in consideration, not of each other, but of the quiet itself—as if the quiet denoted some fragile peacefulness in Ben's new sleep that must not be intruded upon.

Jack Beechum was party to that quiet. He made no sound. He said nothing, for his own silence had become wonderful to him and he could not bear to break it. Though Nancy, after the death of their mother, had given Jack much of his upbringing and had been perhaps more his mother than his sister, Ben had never presumed to be a father to him. From the time Jack was eight years old, Ben had been simply his friend—had encouraged, instructed, corrected, helped, and stood by him; had placed a kindly, humorous, forbearing expectation upon him that he could not shed or shirk and had at last lived up to. They had been companions. And yet, through the rest of that day, Jack had his mind more on Mat than on Ben.

Jack watched Mat as he would have watched a newborn colt weak on its legs that he had helped to stand, that might continue to stand or might not. All afternoon Jack did not sit down because Mat did not. Sometimes there were things to do, and they were busy. Space for the coffin had to be made in the living room. Furniture had to be moved. When the time came, the laden coffin had to be moved into place. But, busy or not, Mat was almost constantly moving, as if seeking his place in a world newly made that day, a world still shaking and doubtful underfoot. And Jack both moved with him and stayed apart from him, watching. When they spoke again, they would speak on different terms. In its quiet, the house seemed to be straining to accommodate Ben's absence, made undeniable by the presence of his body lying still under his folded hands.

Jack would come later to his own reckoning with that loss, the horror and the pity of it, and the grief, the awe and gratitude and love and sorrow and regret, when Ben, newly dead and renewing sorrow for others dead before, would wholly occupy his mind in the night, and could give no comfort, and would not leave. But now Jack stayed by Mat and helped as he could.

In the latter part of the afternoon came Della Budge, Miss Della, bearing an iced cake on a stand like a lighted lamp. As she left the kitchen and started for the front door, she laid her eyes on Jack, who was standing in the door between the living room and the hall. She was a large woman, far gone in years. It was a labor for her to walk. She advanced each foot ahead of the other with care, panting, her hand on her hip, rocking from side to side. She wore many clothes, for her blood was thin and she was easily chilled, and she carried a fan, for sometimes she got too warm. Her little dustcap struggled to stay on top of her head. A tiny pair of spectacles perched awry on her nose. She had a face like a shriveled apple, and the creases at the corners of her mouth were stained with snuff. Once, she had been Jack's teacher. For years they had waged a contest in which she had endeavored to teach him the begats from Abraham to Jesus and he had refused to learn them. He was one of her failures, but she maintained a proprietary interest in him nonetheless. She was the only one left alive who called him "Jackie."

As she came up to him he said, "Hello, Miss Della."

"Well, Jackie," she said, lifting and canting her nose to bring her spectacles to bear upon him, "poor Ben has met his time."

"Yes, mam," Jack said. "One of them things."

"When your time comes you must go, by the hand of man or the stroke of God."

"Yes, mam," Jack said. He was standing with his hands behind him, leaning back against the doorjamb.

"It'll come by surprise," she said. "It's a time appointed, but we'll not be notified."

Jack said he knew it. He did know it.

"So we must always be ready," she said. "Pray without ceasing."

"Yes, mam."

"Well, God bless Ben Feltner. He was a good man. God rest his soul."

Jack stepped ahead of her to help her out the door and down the porch steps.

"Why, thank you, Jackie," she said as she set foot at last on the walk.

He stood and watched her going away, walking, it seemed to him, a tottering edge between eternity and time.

Toward evening Margaret laid the table, and the family and several of the neighbor women gathered in the kitchen. Only two or three men had come, and they were sitting in the living room by the coffin. The table was spread with the abundance of food that had been brought in. They were just preparing to sit down when the murmur of voices they had been hearing from the road down in front of the stores seemed to converge and to move in their direction. Those in the kitchen stood and listened a moment, and then Mat started for the front of the house. The others followed him through the hall and out onto the porch.

The sun was down, the light cool and directionless, so that the colors of the foliage and of the houses and storefronts of the town seemed to glow. Chattering swifts circled and swerved above the chimneys. Nothing else moved except the crowd that made its way at an almost formal pace into the yard. The people standing on the porch were as still as everything else, except for Jack Beechum who quietly made his way forward until he stood behind and a little to the left of Mat, who was standing at the top of the steps.

The crowd moved up near the porch and stopped. There was a moment of hesitation while it murmured and jostled inside itself.

"Be quiet, boys," somebody said. "Let Doc do the talking."

They became still, and then Doctor Starns, who stood in the front rank, took a step forward.

"Mat," he said, "we're here as your daddy's friends. We've got word that Thad Coulter's locked up in the jail at Hargrave. We want you to know that we won't stand for the thing he did."

Several voices said, "No!" and "Nosir!"

"We don't think we can stand for it, or that we ought to, or that we ought to wait on somebody else's opinion about it."

Somebody said, "That's right!"

"We think it's our business, and we propose to make it so."

"That's right!" said several voices.

"It's only up to you to say the word, and we'll put justice beyond question."

And in the now-silent crowd someone held up a coil of rope, a noose already tied.

The doctor gave a slight bow of his head to Mat and then to Nancy who now stood behind Mat and to his right. And again the crowd murmured and slightly stirred within itself.

For what seemed to Jack a long time, Mat did not speak or move. The crowd grew quiet again, and again they could hear the swifts chattering in the air. Jack's right hand ached to reach out to Mat. It seemed to him again that he felt the earth shaking under his feet, as Mat felt it. But though it shook and though they felt it, Mat now stood resolved and calm upon it. Looking at the back of his head, Jack could still see the boy in him, but the head was up. The voice, when it came, was steady:

"No, gentlemen. I appreciate it. We all do. But I ask you not to do that."

And Jack, who had not sat down since morning, stepped back and sat down.

Nancy, under whose feet the earth was not shaking, if it ever had, stepped up beside her son and took his arm.

She said to the crowd, "I know you are my husband's friends. I thank you. I, too, must ask you not to do as you propose. Mat has asked you; I have asked you; if Ben could, he would ask you. Let us make what peace is left for us to make."

Mat said, "Come and be with us. We have food, and you all are welcome."

He had said, in all, six brief sentences. He was not a forward man. This, I think, was the only public speech of his life.

"I can see him yet," my grandmother said, her eyes, full of sudden moisture, again turned to the window. "I wish you could have seen him."

And now, after so many years, perhaps I have. I have sought that moment out, or it has sought me, and I see him standing without prop in the deepening twilight, asking his father's friends to renounce the vengeance that a few hours before he himself had been furious to exact.

This is the man who will be my grandfather—the man who will be the man who was my grandfather. The tenses slur and slide under the pressure of collapsed time. For that moment on the porch is not a now that was but a now that is and will be, inhabiting all the history of Port William that followed and will follow. I know that in the days after his father's death—and after Thad Coulter, concurring in the verdict of his would-be jurors in Port William, hanged himself in the Hargrave jail and so released Martha Elizabeth from her watch—my grandfather renewed and carried on his friendship with the Coulters: with Thad's widow and daughters, with Dave Coulter and his family, and with another first cousin of Thad's, Marce Catlett, my grandfather on my father's side. And when my father asked leave of the Feltners to marry their daughter Bess, my mother, he was made welcome.

Mat Feltner dealt with Ben's murder by not talking about it and thus keeping it in the past. In his last years, I liked to get him to tell me about the violent old times of the town, the hard drinking and the fighting. And he would oblige me up to a point, enjoying the outrageous stories himself, I think. But always there would come a time in the midst of the telling when he would become silent, shake his head, lift one hand and let it fall; and I would know—I know better now than I did then—that he had remembered his father's death.

No Feltner or Coulter of the name is left now in Port William. But the Feltner line continues, joined to the Coulter line, in me, and I am here. I am blood kin to both sides of that moment when Ben Feltner turned to face Thad Coulter in the road and Thad pulled the trigger. The two families, sundered in the ruin of a friendship, were united again first in new friendship and then in marriage. My grandfather made a peace here that has joined many who would otherwise have been divided. I am the child of his forgiveness.

After Mat spoke the second time, inviting them in, the crowd loosened and came apart. Some straggled back down into the town; others, as Mat had asked, came into the house, where their wives already were.

But Jack did not stay with them. As soon as he knew he was free, his thoughts went to other things. His horse had stood a long time, saddled, without water or feed. The evening chores were not yet done. Ruth would be wondering what had happened. In the morning they would come back together, to be of use if they could. And there would be, for Jack as for the others, the long wearing of grief. But now he could stay no longer.

As soon as the porch was cleared, he retrieved his hat from the hall tree and walked quietly out across the yard under the maples and the descending night. So as not to be waylaid by talk, he walked rapidly in the middle of the road to where he had tied his horse. Lamps had now been lighted in the stores and the houses. As he approached, his horse nickered to him.

"I know it," Jack said.

As soon as the horse felt his rider's weight in the stirrup, he started. Soon the lights and noises of the town were behind them, and there were only a few stars, a low red streak in the west, and the horse's eager footfalls on the road.

Watch with Me (1916)

One of the vital organs of Ptolemy Proudfoot's farm was a small square building called simply "the shop." Here Tol worked, according to necessity, as a blacksmith, farrier, carpenter, and mender of harness and shoes. The shop contained a forge with a cranking bellows and an anvil resting on an oak block. A workbench, with a stout vise attached, ran along one wall under three small windows. Tools and spare parts and usable scraps lay on the bench or stood propped in corners or hung from nails. On good days when they could be left open, large double doors at the front end admitted a fine flow of light.

On days when the weather prevented work outdoors, Tol would go to the shop and putter, or he would go there and sit and think. But he puttered and thought to advantage, for he earned more than he spent and sold more than he bought. He would be in the shop in the fall and winter more than in the spring and summer. In the spring and summer it was a good place to set a hen, and a couple of boxes for that purpose were fastened to the wall at the end of the workbench nearest the front doors.

Tol and his wife, Miss Minnie, and their neighbors killed hogs as soon as the nights became dependably cold in the fall. They wintered on backbone and spareribs and sausage and souse, with a shoulder or ham now and then. By spring they would begin to be a little tired of pork; fried chicken began to be easy to imagine. That was when Miss Minnie would begin to save eggs and watch for her hens to start setting. She liked to put

several hens on eggs, in the henhouse and in the shop, just as soon as the
weather began to warm up.

On the morning when this story begins, the chickens of that year
were nearly all hatched. There was only one red hen still hovering sixteen eggs in one of the boxes in the shop. It was a fine morning early in
August, dewy and bright; the Katy's Branch valley was still covered with
a shining cloud of fog. It was 1916 and a new kind of world was in the
making on the battlefields of France, but you could not have told it,
standing on Cotman Ridge with that dazzling cloud lying over Goforth
in the valley, and the woods and the ridgetops looking as clear and clean
as Resurrection Morning. Birds were singing. And Tol could hear roosters crowing, it seemed to him, all the way to Port William.

He had just stepped out after breakfast. It was later than usual, because
the day had begun crosswise. When he had called his milk cows, they had
not come. He had walked in the weak dawn-light down into the woods
along the branch, where he found a water gap torn out by a recent
freshet. From there he tracked the three cows down the wooded slopes
halfway to Goforth before he found them and started them home. He
drove them through the rent in the fence, wired it back with his hands
well enough to hold until he could return with proper tools and more
wire, and went on up the hill to chain them in their places in the barn.

And then when he was milking the third cow—a light-colored Jersey
by the name of Blanche of whom he was particularly fond—she sol-
emnly raised her right hind foot, plastered with manure, and set it down
again in the half-filled bucket of milk.

Though he was a large, physically exuberant man who had been a
wrestler famous all the way to Hargrave in his younger days, Tol was not
a man of violence. But once he got Blanche's foot out of the bucket, he
had to sit there on his stool a good while before he could rid himself of
the thought of joyful revenge. On the one hand, he sympathized with the
cow. He thought he knew how she felt. It would be exasperating, after
finding a hole in the fence and escaping into the wide world, to be driven
home again, chained to a stanchion, and required to yield one's milk into
a bucket. On the other hand, Tol's sense of justice was outraged. He had
raised the cow lovingly from a calf; he had sheltered and fed and doc-
tored her; he had loved and petted and pampered her—and now just

look how she had treated him! He leaned his head back into her flank and began to milk again.

"Blanche," he said, "I ought to knock you in the head." He milked on in silence, his anger ebbing away. "But I don't reckon I will."

He stripped her dry, poured the bucket of ruined milk into the hog trough, turned the cows back into the pasture, and went to the house for breakfast, carrying one empty milk bucket and one full one.

"Did you have trouble with the cows?" Miss Minnie asked. She set Tol's breakfast before him and started straining the milk.

Tol told her.

"Why, the old hussy!" Miss Minnie said. "I'll bet you wanted to knock her in the head. Did you?"

"Not this time," Tol said. And that made him laugh, for he thought he was at the end of the story, but he was not at the end of it yet.

The day had begun so contrarily that when Tol went by the shop to see about the setting hen on his way to the barn, he was not much surprised to hear her squawking in extreme dismay before he opened the door. When he opened the door he saw what the fuss was about. A big snake had climbed the locust tree next to the shop, crawled out along a limb and under the eave of the building, and was now descending along a crossbrace toward the hen's nest. The snake was the kind known as a cowsucker, and it was big enough to swallow every egg in the nest. Tol was not particularly afraid of snakes, though he preferred not to walk up on one by surprise, nor did he hate them. He rather liked to have them around to catch mice, and now and then he would capture one to put in his corncrib. All the same, he did not welcome them into his hens' nests.

"You got to change your mind, boy," he said to the snake, who was now looking at him with its head erect, flickering its tongue. "You going to have to take your business elsewhere."

Tol thought at first that he would just catch the snake by the end of the tail and buy its goodwill by letting it catch mice a while in the corncrib. But a cowsucker is a grouchy kind of snake, much inclined to stand on its rights, and when Tol reached out for its tail, the snake contracted into loops and threatened to bite Tol's hand. There is no danger of being poisoned by a cowsucker's bite, but when one threatens to bite you, you are very much inclined to draw back in a hurry whatever you have stuck out, and you are inclined to take the gesture as an insult.

Tol was a man slow to anger, but when the snake made as if to strike his hand, his mental state reverted to the moment, by no means long enough ago, when the cow had put her foot in the bucket.

"Well," he said to the snake, "if you don't need killing, then Hell ain't hot."

Tol was thoroughly mad by then, and also anxious for the hen and her nest of eggs. On her account, he wanted to get rid of the snake with the least possible commotion and in the biggest possible hurry.

So he ran back to the house and put a shell into the chamber of the old ten-gauge shotgun that he had inherited from his father. It was a hard-shooting, single-barreled weapon that Tol's father had called Old Fetcher, "for it was a sure way to send for fresh meat."

When he got back to the shop, Tol flung the door open for light, stood back so as to minimize disturbance to the hen, leveled the long, rusty barrel point-blank at the snake's head, and fired — only to see the snake, with maddening dignity and aplomb, slowly depart by way of the hole that Old Fetcher had blasted through the wall.

Tol fully appreciated how funny that was, but he had no trouble in postponing his laughter. The hen, for one thing, was off the nest now and raising Cain, as if Tol and not the snake were the chief threat to her peace of mind.

"Get back on that nest and shut up," Tol said.

He picked up a stick and ran around to the side of the building, but the snake, after the manner of its kind, was nowhere to be seen. And so Tol patched the hole he had made in the wall, and chinked up the place under the eave where he thought the snake had come in. He shooed the offended hen back into the shop and shut the door.

"Be quiet, now," he said. "You're going to live."

He went back to the house, got another shell for the gun, reloaded it, and propped it against the shop door.

Tol went to the garden then, unhooked his hoe from the fence, sharpened it, and began cleaning out a row of late cabbages.

Steady work quiets the mind. Tol began to feel that he had got the day off to a straight start at last. He had nearly finished the cabbage row when he saw Sam Hanks's truck come in and stop in front of the barn.

Sam got out and came strolling into the garden. He wanted to borrow Tol's posthole-digging tools so he could set a clothesline post for his mother.

Sam was Miss Minnie's favorite nephew, the only son of her only sister and Warren Hanks, a hardworking but somehow luckless tenant farmer. Sam had not followed in his father's footsteps. "He loves a damned wheel," his father had said, and Sam earned a modest living for himself and his now-widowed mother by hauling livestock and other things in his truck. He owned plenty of mechanic's tools, but when he needed something to dig with, he came to Tol.

For that matter, Sam was apt to show up at Tol's and Miss Minnie's pretty often, even when he didn't want to borrow something. He returned his aunt's affection, and he liked Tol. Moreover, he enjoyed Tol. When Sam came walking into the garden that morning, Tol looked completely in character. He stood amid the rows of his garden, which he kept with an almost perfect attention to detail. And in the midst of that neatness and order, Tol could have been a scarecrow, albeit an unusually big one. He wore an utterly shapeless old straw hat. And he had now been long enough beyond the reach and influence of Miss Minnie that part of his shirttail was out, one of his cuffs was unbuttoned, and his left shoe was untied. Tol's clothes always looked as if they were making a strenuous and perhaps hopeless effort just to stay somewhere in his vicinity.

"Well," Sam Hanks said to him, "looks like I been elected to put up a clothesline. Don't reckon I could borrow your diggers and all."

"Why, sure," Tol said. "They're yonder in the shop. Watch, now, when you go in and don't get snakebit."

Tol then told Sam what had happened. But he just said he had let the snake get away from him; he didn't tell about shooting the hole in the wall. He wanted to save that for when he could laugh about it. He was a man who had been mistreated by a cow and a snake all in the same morning, and he felt sore and aggrieved.

But while he was still commenting to Sam on the cowsucker's extreme ill humor, he saw his neighbor, Thacker Hample, coming over the ridge, and then another trouble returned to his mind.

Thacker Hample belonged to a large family locally noted for the fact that from one generation to another not a one of them had worked quite right. Their commonest flaw was poor vision. When he could find them or somebody found them for him, Thacker wore glasses with lenses as thick as shoe soles. Walter Cotman said that if Nightlife's nose had been a quarter of an inch longer, he would have been illiterate — but that was Walter Cotman. They called Thacker Nightlife on the theory that he could not tell daylight from dark, and therefore was liable to conduct his nightlife in the daytime. The name had a certain sexual glamour that appealed to Thacker Hample himself. When he had occasion to call himself by name, he usually called himself Nightlife — though he didn't ordinarily say much of anything to anybody.

But Nightlife was incomplete, too, in some other way. There were times when spells came on him, when he would be sad and angry and confused and maybe dangerous, and nobody could help him. And sometimes he would have to be sent away to the asylum where, Uncle Othy Dagget said, they would file him down and reset his teeth.

When he was quiet, he was quieter than anybody, and Nightlife had been quiet for a long time. But then the week came for the annual revival at Goforth Church, and unbeknownst to anybody but himself, Nightlife decided that on the third night he himself would be the preacher, and he spent most of the preceding night getting ready. He made up a sermon and a prayer or two, and picked out some appropriate hymns. And on the night before Tol's trouble with the cow and the snake, Nightlife presented himself to the regular preacher and the visiting preacher and told them that he was going to preach the evening's sermon. In his sermon, as Tol and the others would understand later, Nightlife wanted to tell what it was like to be himself. It had to come out because at that time anyhow, it was all he had in him.

It would have been better if the two preachers had just said all right. But they, who well knew that they knew neither the day nor the hour of the coming of the Son of Man, were in fact not prepared for anything unscheduled. They told Nightlife that the evening's service would have to proceed as planned. And that was when Nightlife's time of quietness came to an end and, as the eyewitnesses all agreed, he throwed a reg'lar fit.

He flung his Bible down at the feet of the horrified young preachers. He threw his arms wide apart, laughed a loud contemptuous laugh, and asked them whose church they thought it was. They thought it was their church, he said, but he reckoned they just might be a little bit mistaken: it was Jesus's church. And when Jesus came back, He would fork the likes of them into Hell as quick as look at them, and he, Nightlife, would at that time enjoy hearing them sing a different tune. He laughed again and bestowed upon them several epithets not normally used in church.

And so that evening's service did not, after all, proceed as planned. By a sort of general and unspoken deference, Tol Proudfoot, who was certainly the biggest of them and was probably the kindest, was elected to deal with Nightlife Hample. While the others stood around and listened and then, tiring, began to drift away, Tol talked to Nightlife, whose anger had begun to subside into confusions of sorrow, regret, and self-pity. No clever persuasion was involved. With his big hand resting on Nightlife's shoulder or his knee, Tol told him that everybody liked him and didn't hold anything against him and thought he was a good fellow and wanted him to go home now and get a good night's sleep. Tol told him all that over and over again, and finally Nightlife allowed his old mother to lead him home.

But nobody, least of all Tol, thought it would end there. Tol figured that having dealt with Nightlife once, he would have to deal with him again. And so when he saw Nightlife flinging himself over the ridgetop and down toward the barn, he wasn't surprised, though he certainly was sorry.

"Trouble comes in bunches," he said to Sam.

From where Nightlife came over the ridge, he could look right into Tol's garden, and he had on his glasses. That he saw Tol and Sam was obvious enough to them; he even seemed to have the idea of coming directly to where they were. But then when he crossed the road and entered Tol's driveway, Nightlife appeared to lose his intention; perhaps he had wanted to talk with Tol alone, and Sam's presence put him off. He wandered past the house into the barn lot. Now he was pretending, perhaps, that he did not know they were there and that he was just looking around to see if Tol was at home.

"You looking for me?" Tol called. "Here I am."

Nightlife then started toward the garden gate, went past the shop, saw Tol's old shotgun leaning there, and picked it up. He opened the breech to see if it was loaded. When he closed the breech again they could hear the snap of the lock all the way up there in the garden. Nightlife balanced the gun in his hands for a moment as if he were thinking of buying it. And then he laid it over his shoulder and turned away.

"Uh-oh," Tol said. He started toward the gate with Sam Hanks stepping between the same pair of rows behind him.

"Don't take my gun, Nightlife!" Tol called, trying to sound not too much concerned, and yet unable to keep the tone of pleading entirely out of his voice. "I'm liable to need it!"

Tol had started to hurry. He hung his hoe on the fence by the gate and went on toward the shop.

Nightlife was hesitating. He turned back toward the door of the shop, as though he might actually put the gun back where he got it.

But then he turned away again. He said, not to Tol and Sam, rather to himself, but in too loud a voice, as if he did not quite expect himself to be able to hear, "Why, a damned fellow just as well shoot hisself, I reckon."

"Wait, Nightlife!" Tol said. And then he added an endearment, as he usually did, to soften what might have seemed a reprimand: "Hold on, sweetheart."

But Nightlife was already starting down through the pasture toward the woods with the gun on his shoulder.

"I expect I'll just ease along with him a ways," Tol said to Sam. "You go tell Miss Minnie, and then drive over and tell Walter Cotman and Tom and Braymer. Or send word to them if they're out at work. And then you come with us."

Tol was watching Nightlife while he talked to Sam. "Mind that old gun, now. If he's crazy enough to shoot hisself, he might be crazy enough to shoot you."

"Or you," Sam said.

"Or me," Tol said. He stepped off down the slope, following the dark path Nightlife had made in the dewy grass.

When he heard the screen door slam as Sam stepped into the kitchen, a kind of wonder came over Tol, for almost in the twinkling of an eye he had crossed the boundary between two worlds. In spite of the several small troubles of that morning, he had been in a world that was more or less the world he thought it was, and where at least some things happened more or less as he intended. But now he was walking down through the wet grass of his cow pasture toward the edge of his woods, a place as familiar to him as the palm of his own hand, in a world and a day in which he intended only to follow Nightlife and foresaw nothing.

He hurried a little, not to catch up with Nightlife, but to keep him in sight, which would be harder to do once they were in the woods. And it was into the woods that Nightlife was going. He was not going in a hurry, but he was not loitering either. He walked like a man with a desti-nation — though where, in that direction, he could be going was a mys-tery to Tol.

And then Nightlife took the gun from his shoulder, placed it in the crook of his right arm, and went in among the young cedars that bor-dered the woods' edge at that place. He disappeared as completely as if he had suddenly dived into water, but with less commotion. Not a bush trembled after he disappeared, and Tol feared that he would lose him. He went in himself at the same place, and for a while, among the cedars and other young low-branching trees, he could not see six feet ahead. And then, not far from the edge, the woods became taller and more open, and Tol could see Nightlife again.

He was no longer going so directly down the slope, but was slanting to his right as though he intended to go toward the river along that side of the Katy's Branch valley, and soon, when he was well into the woods, he again altered his course so that he was not going downhill at all, but was going along the level contour of the slope. He was not walking fast, nor did he appear to be looking at anything. He seemed totally preoccu-pied, as though all his attention were demanded by whatever was in his mind.

Tol had thought of calling out to Nightlife, but had rejected the thought. The presence of Old Fetcher made it hard to know what to say.

Tol had known Nightlife as long as Nightlife had been in this world to be known, but when one of his spells was on him, Nightlife was a stranger to everybody. There was no telling, then, what he might or might not do. Tol didn't want to cause him to shoot himself in order to win an argument about whether or not he was going to shoot himself. Nor was Tol on his own account at all eager to face the business end of Old Fetcher.

He decided just to follow along, keeping Nightlife in sight as best he could. He would not try to catch up; he would try not to fall too far behind; he would say nothing. And Tol's decision then established what he and the others would do the rest of that day and into the next. They would let whatever it was run its course, if it would. They would stop Nightlife from using the gun, if they had to and if they were able. At every considerable change of direction, Tol broke a branch end and left it dangling as a mark for Sam. Otherwise, the passage of two men over the dead leaves of the woods' floor ought to be legible enough.

Nightlife and his widowed mother lived on a farm of maybe fifty acres that lay back in one of the several hollows that drained into Katy's Branch. The farm was mostly hillside. It contained no ridgeland at all, and no bottomland except for a narrow shelf along the branch where the Hamples had their garden and where they had built a small log barn with a corncrib beside it. The house, built of logs like the barn, stood on the slope above the scrap of bottom, with privy and henhouse and smokehouse behind it. So far as the neighborhood remembered, nobody but Hamples had ever lived there. The farm was a remnant of land that had been overlooked or left out of the surveys of the larger boundaries that once surrounded it, or it had been sold off one of the larger boundaries at some time during the frenzy of settlement and speculation that accompanied the white people's first taking of the land.

There had been a time — way back when the trees of the original forest were yet growing on it — when the place was fertile. But the first-comers, having no other land to farm, cut the trees from the slopes, patch by patch, growing little crops of tobacco and corn until fertility declined by the combined action of plow and rain, and then abandoning the land again to bushes and then trees, only to repeat the whole process in forty or fifty years. In the early days, perhaps, the Hamples lived up to the standard of most of their neighbors. They had the produce of what was still a productive little farm. They had what they could kill or pick or dig up in the stands of virgin forest that still stood all around.

But as the forests were cut down and the wild bounty of the country diminished and the soil of the slopes fled away beneath the axes and jumper plows of generation after generation of Hamples, the family's life became ever more marginal. They kept a milk cow or two, a team of mules, meat hogs, and poultry. They raised a patch of corn and a little shirttail crop of tobacco. They kept the garden. They hunted and fished and trapped, dug roots and stripped bark, gathered the wild potherbs and fruit. From the corn that they and their animals did not eat, they distilled a palatable and potent whiskey, of which they sold as much as they did not drink. And yet their life declined until they were reduced to dependence on daywork for their neighbors, who did not need much help. And yet the Hamples persevered, and even provided a sort of hearty and bitter amusement to themselves. Delbert, Nightlife's father, as an old man became famous for his boast, often repeated in the store at Goforth or in the bank at Port William: "I started out with damn near nothing, and I have multiplied it by hard work until I am going to end up with damn near what I started out with."

But the Hamples were known, too, for their handiness. The neighborhood liked to boast of them that they could "make anything or fix anything." They seemed to be born, virtually every one of them, with an uncanny mastery of tools and materials. When weak vision got bred into the line — which it did fairly early — it apparently made little difference, for Hample hands were so adept that they seemed to possess a second sight in their very fingertips. As industrial farm machinery entered the country and became more complicated, the Hamples in a way came into their own. None of them ever had the enterprise to open a proper shop, but their neighbors were forever bringing them something to fix.

Large families of Hamples had been raised in their snug hollow with its two slopes facing one another across the rocky notch of the branch, for the Hample men, whatever the condition of their fields, were fertile, and they married fertile women. As soon as they got big enough to leave or to marry, the Hample generations scattered like seeds from an opened pod. Always, until now, somebody would be left to start the cycle again. But after his father died, Nightlife stayed at home with his mother; he did not marry, and nobody thought he ever would. Even as a Hample, Nightlife was an oddity, and nobody could quite account for him. He had inherited the mechanical gifts of the Hamples; people said that he could do anything with his hands. And yet he seemed also to have been endowed with an ineptitude that was all his own. For instance, when he was about ten years old he contrived a jew's harp out of an old clock spring and a piece of walnut; it was a marvel of cunning artistry, as everybody affirmed, but when he attempted to play it, it very nearly cut off his tongue. He was a Hample, plain enough, but it was as though when he was a baby his mechanically minded siblings had taken him apart and lost some of the pieces, which they then replaced with just whatever they found lying around. Nightlife lacked almost entirely the rough sense of humor that had accompanied other Hamples into and out of this world. And in addition to the capability of becoming drunk, which all Hample men before him had had in varying degrees, Nightlife had the capability of becoming crazy. His mind, which contained the lighted countryside of Katy's Branch and Cotman Ridge, had a leak in it somewhere, some little hole through which now and again would pour the whole darkness of the darkest night — so that instead of walking in the country he knew and among his kinfolks and neighbors, he would be afoot in a limitless and undivided universe, completely dark, inhabited only by himself. From there he would want to call out for rescue, and that was when nobody could tell what he was going to do next, and perhaps he could not tell either.

Or that was what it looked like to Tol, who had thought much about it. And that was what Nightlife himself looked like that morning when Tol followed him down into the woods — he looked like somebody who didn't know where in all the world he was, who didn't know anybody else was there to see him, much less follow along after him.

Tol followed him nevertheless, and yet he did so with a sense of foregone conclusion. He had too much courtesy, if he had not had too much sense, to believe for sure that Nightlife would die by his own hand that day, or even soon, if ever. But he believed that he would die somehow sometime, and that when he did die, the name and the prospects of the Hamples would depart forever from what until then would be known as the Hample Place.

In assuming that the history and the future of the Hamples in their native hollow would end with Nightlife, Tol was right. Fifty years later, on a Sunday ramble with Elton Penn and the Rowanberry brothers and Burley Coulter, I walked up the branch through what once had been the Hample Place. It was early April. The spring work had started. When Elton and I drove down to the Rowanberry Place after dinner that day, the Rowanberrys said they were stiff and sore and needed to walk. So we climbed up through the woods onto the Coulter Ridge where we ran into Burley, who had nothing better to do, he said, than to go with us. There were five of us then, not hurrying or going anyplace in particular; we were just walking along and looking at the season and the weather, talking of whatever the places we came to reminded us of.

We walked down the hollow the Coulters call Stepstone, past the old barn that stands there, and on down to the Katy's Branch road. We followed the road up Katy's Branch a little beyond Goforth, and then we crossed the branch and went up into the woods along the hollow that divided the Hample Place. By then the Hample Place, the Tol Proudfoot Place, the Cotman Place, and others had all been dissolved into one large property that belonged to a Louisville doctor, who had bought it for a weekend retreat and then lost interest in it. Now, except for the best of the ridges, which were rented and farmed badly, the land was neither farmed nor lived on. Every building on it was ruining or already ruined, and the good hillside pastures were covered with young trees — which Burley Coulter said was all right with him.

"It's a damned shame, anyhow," said Elton, who did not want to forgive the neglect.

"Well, a fellow looking for something better, he don't want to stay in a place like this," Art Rowanberry said.

"Was that doctor looking for something better when he bought it?" Mart said.

"I reckon he thought he already had something better."

"Well," Mart said, laughing a little to refuse the argument with his brother, "anyhow, I reckon the more trees, the more coons."

They were all hunters. All the country around us was thickly criss-crossed with the nighttime passages of their hunts. They had worked over it, too, and as boys had played over it. They knew it by day and by night, and knew something about every scrap of it. As we came up by Goforth Church, the long-abandoned store building, and the site of the vanished schoolhouse, and then passed the Goforth Hill road that went up alongside the Proudfoot Place, they began to tell stories about Tol Proudfoot, quoting the things he had said that nobody who had known him ever forgot. And then when we started up along the Hample branch, they told about the time Nightlife threw his fit, and about Tol and the others following him through the woods.

"What kind of farmers were the Hamples?" I asked.

And Art Rowanberry said, "Oh, they growed a very good *winter* crop."

The Hample Place, when we got to it, no longer looked like anybody's place. The woods, which had started to return after Delbert Hample's death, had now completely overgrown it. The young trees had grown big enough to have begun to shade out the undergrowth. The barn and other outbuildings were gone without a trace. The house had slowly weathered away beneath its tin roof, which with its gables intact had sunk down onto the collapsed walls. Only the rock chimney stood, its corners still as straight as on the day they were laid. We peered under one of the fallen gables and looked straight into a buzzard's nest containing one fuzzy white chick and one unhatched egg.

We had come as far as we wanted to go, and we rested there a while before we started back. It was a pleasant place, sheltered, opening to the west, so that the sun would have warmed it on winter afternoons. The north slope above the house would have been good land once, and now with the woods thriving on it again, you could imagine how it once might have evoked a vision of home in whatever landless, wandering Hample had first come — though his and his descendants' attempt to farm there could only have proved it no place to farm. Their way of farming, in fact, had destroyed maybe forever the possibility of farming there. And so you felt that the trees had returned as a kind of justice. They had only drawn back and paused a moment while a futile human experiment had been tried and suffered in that place, and had failed at last as it was bound to do.

As we were leaving, we wandered past the fallen house and across the old garden spot to the branch. And then we saw that the chimney was not the only thing left standing, for there in the middle of the streambed stood a cylinder of laid rock that once had lined the Hamples' well, and now it stood free like another chimney, turned wrong side out, where the stream had cut the earth from around it.

And so the Hamples had come and gone and left their ruin. And now the trees had returned. The trees on the little shelf where the garden had been were tall young tulip poplars that lifted their opening buds into the still light and air of that evening with such an unassuming calm that you could almost believe they had been there always.

Art Rowanberry, I remember, stood looking at them a long time. And then, turning to go, he said, "Well, old Nightlife didn't have to leave this world for want of wood, I don't reckon."

And so Tol was right. The Hamples did die out on the Hample Place. But they did not die out of the community. There are still plenty of Hamples, on Cotman Ridge and elsewhere, to this day.

Tol had just begun to wonder when Sam was going to show up when Sam showed up. Tol raised his hand to him, and Sam nodded. In silence then they picked their way along together, Sam walking behind Tol. Between themselves and Nightlife, they kept a sort of room of visibility, the size of which varied according to the density of the foliage. They meant to stay separate from Nightlife by the full breadth of that room. When the foliage thickened, they drew closer to Nightlife to keep him in sight. Where the trees were old and there was not much undergrowth, they slowed down and let him get farther ahead.

After a while Nightlife came to a pile of rocks that had been carried from some long-abandoned corn or tobacco patch, and he sat down, laying the gun across his lap. He appeared now to be carrying the gun as if it were some mere hand tool, not recognizing what it was, just as he appeared to grant no recognition to himself or to where he was. When he stopped and sat down, Tol and Sam stood still. When he got up and started on again, they followed.

After a while Braymer Hardy was there behind Sam. And not long after that, when Tol again looked back, Walter Cotman and Tom Hardy were there. Tol stopped them then, and beckoned them close. He was older than the oldest of them by twenty years; he could have been father to them all, and they came obediently into whispering distance.

"Boys," he said, "ain't no use in us walking lined up so that old gun could hit us all with one shot. Kind of fan out. We'll keep him in sight better that way."

They fanned out as he said. And now the room of sight that had been defined only by a diameter was given a circumference as well. As they moved along, they continued to draw closer together or move farther apart, according to visibility. In that moving room that at once divided and held them together the only clarity was their intent not to let Nightlife be further divided from them.

They moved along with him wherever he moved. He went, still, pretty much level along the face of the slope, into the draws and out around the points, through old woods and through thicket, across pastures and tobacco patches, but mostly in the woods. Sometimes he would stop or sit down, and then they would wait, and when he went ahead they would go with him. That Nightlife was not himself, that he had become merely the vehicle of something he suffered that they had not suffered, they could tell by the way he moved and carried himself, the way he looked always straight ahead and always at the ground. He moved like a man in the concentration of urgent bodily pain, though they knew his pain was not of the body. Maybe he was not going to kill himself, they thought. Maybe he just needed something he did not have, had never had, did not know how to ask for, and maybe did not know the name of. But they knew also that Old Fetcher was an influential weapon. It was not a squirrel rifle — not a gun with which you could confidently undertake to shoot yourself just a little. If you picked up Old Fetcher, declaring that you might as well shoot yourself, then they knew as surely as if they held it in their own hands, you couldn't put that gun down again without deciding not to shoot yourself.

It was a long time since morning now, and the day was getting hot. In the woods it was still and close. All five of them had sweated through their shirts. And still they moved along with Nightlife, and still they formed their rough and ever-shifting semicircle at the limit of sight. They were squirrel hunters and they knew how to move unobtrusively and quietly in the woods. In the spell of Nightlife's silence and their own, strangeness came over them, as if they had died and come back in another time. Everything familiar had become strange. What they saw around them now seemed no longer to be what they knew and had always known, but seemed only to remind them of a time when they had known those things. They were following a man whom it had never occurred to them to follow before, who now had become central to their lives, and who perhaps was trying to find his way out of this world.

By noon they had come all the way down the Katy's Branch valley and turned into the valley of the river, still keeping along the mostly wooded face of the bluff, high up. Now they were conscious of the bigger space and larger light; down through openings among the treetops they could see the river itself bending across the valley floor between its two parallel rows of trees, leaving the wide bottomlands first on one side and then the other. They could see the cornfields and houses and farm buildings in the bottoms on down into the blue distance halfway to Hargrave. Off somewhere on the far side of the river they heard a dinner bell.

And now they were aware also of the world going on, unaware of them and their extraordinary worry and purpose. It seemed unaccountable to them that they should know so well where they were when nobody else in all the world had any idea.

Presently they came to a deep crease in the face of the slope, worn there over the millennia by a steep wet-weather stream known as Squire's Branch. And here instead of turning into the hollow in order to keep on the level as he had been doing, Nightlife slanted down into the dry bed of the branch and then turned straight down toward the river, stair-stepping down the tumbled rocks of the streambed. The others followed in their half-circle, with Tol in the center and the others fanned out on either side.

They stayed in the wooded hollow, but as the slopes gentled they could see open pasture off through the trees first on the left and then also on the right. And then they could see a little tobacco patch on the left. From time to time, the foliage opening, they could see the little store at Squire's Landing and the house on the slope above it where Uncle Othy and Aunt Cordie Dagget lived and farmed a little and fished a little and kept the store and the landing and kept an eye on the comings and goings of the neighborhood.

When Uncle Othy and Aunt Cordie's house came full into sight, Nightlife climbed out of the streambed onto the open slope. And then he walked down across Uncle Othy's cow pasture, through the yard gate, across the yard, up onto the back porch, and through the kitchen door without so much as a knock.

Tol stopped at the edge of the woods and the others came up beside him.

"What now?" Walter Cotman said.

Tol uttered a sound that was partly a laugh and partly a grunt. What he should have done was all too clear to him now, and to the rest of them, too. He should have sent Sam Hanks and Tom Hardy, who were on that side of the branch, to Uncle Othy's ahead of Nightlife. But it had not occurred to him that Nightlife, who earlier had avoided him and Sam and who had spent the whole morning skulking along in the woods by himself, would think of going right into somebody's house. Tol had his lower lip between his teeth.

"Well, what are we going to do?" Braymer Hardy said.

"Boy, there ain't nothing *to* do. We can't go barging into Aunt Cordie's kitchen ourselves. He's the only one that's got a gun. And if we had guns they wouldn't do us any good, unless we wanted to shoot somebody or get shot, which I reckon we don't."

"So I reckon we're going to wait," Walter Cotman said. And he sat down.

The others seemed to consider sitting down also for they would not have minded a rest, but nobody but Walter did so. Nor could they stay where they were. Watching the house always, they eased gradually down into the yard. They did not go closer to the house than the yard gate for fear of inciting Nightlife to some damage they feared without naming. The worst they could imagine now had as good a license to happen as the best, and there was nothing at the moment that they could do. They did not go to the shade for the same reason that they did not sit down: it would not have been right. All the morning, it seemed to them, they had been walking the rim of the world, a narrow, shadowy, steeply sloping margin between life and death, and this imposed a strict propriety on them all. But from where they stood even with the kitchen windows open, they could not tell what was happening inside.

They weren't going to know what was happening inside until after the story was over and Uncle Othy told Sam Hanks and Sam told Tol and Tol told the others at church on Sunday morning.

Uncle Othy and Aunt Cordie were eating dinner. It was fried catfish. The others knew that much; they could smell it out in the yard. It smelled better than they wanted it to, for they were hungry.

"Do you want some cornbread, Othy?" Aunt Cordie said.

And then the screen door opened and here came Nightlife right into the kitchen with that old gun cradled in the crook of his left arm and looking like he was trying hard to remember something that he only barely remembered forgetting. They had not heard him until he put hand to the door and the spring sang.

He got clear into the middle of the kitchen before he seemed to realize that he was among people.

When he saw Uncle Othy and Aunt Cordie sitting at the table, looking at him, their laden forks suspended between their plates and their mouths, he said, "Let us earnestly compose our hearts for prayer."

"Son," Uncle Othy said later to Sam Hanks, "I did earnestly compose my heart for prayer. I was afraid if I looked up I'd find my head in my plate."

When Uncle Othy and Aunt Cordie bowed their heads, Nightlife prayed. What he said Uncle Othy was unable to report to Sam, for he said his mind had been occupied with a few words in his own behalf.

It was, anyhow, a long prayer that Nightlife prayed; Uncle Othy ran out of anything to say in his own behalf before it was over, and under the circumstances he was unable to think of anything to say in anybody else's behalf. He and Aunt Cordie sat there with their heads down while that good fish got cold on the platter and Nightlife prayed, but not for them or at them; he prayed as if he were off somewhere by himself, and out loud but not too loud, Uncle Othy said, as if he suspected Old Marster was present but too deaf to overhear a thought or a whisper.

Aunt Cordie kept her head bowed to the end, for she would honor even a crazy man's prayer. But when Nightlife said, "Amen," she looked straight at him. "Thacker Hample, now what is all this foolishness? Sit down, child, and let me fix you a plate."

But Nightlife just stared at her and at Uncle Othy, too, as if they, who had known him all his life, were strangers. His face was covered by a sort of blur of incomprehension, as if he not only did not recognize them but had no idea where he was.

"Son," Uncle Othy said, "put down that dad-damned old gun, now, and get yourself something to eat."

"I can't eat of that river," Nightlife said, "for it's of the passing of the flesh. I don't know where it has come from nor where it's a-going."

"Son, that river has come from up and it's a-going down. Take a chair, and let the woman fix you a bite of fish."

Aunt Cordie, who had got up, said, "Yes!" and reached out toward Nightlife as if to take hold of his arm.

Nightlife shrank away from her hand like a wild horse, and went back out the kitchen door.

"I went to the kitchen door and watched him go," Uncle Othy told Sam, "and then I seen you all was following along after him. So I sat down again and told the woman to pass the cornbread, for I had to eat and I didn't have all day."

When they had come out of the shadowy woods, the whole hillside, buildings and trees and all, quaked in the still sunlight. Under the strong light, the maples in Uncle Othy's yard seemed bent in profound meditation on their shadows now drawn in at their feet. Standing together just inside the yard gate, Tol and the other three quaked, too, and sweated in the fierce, bright fall of the noon heat. Not a leaf stirred anywhere. They heard what they would later know was Nightlife's prayer—not the words, but just the rising and falling sound of it. And then, more briefly, they heard the voices of Aunt Cordie and Uncle Othy.

And then the screen door was flung open and Nightlife came out, letting the door clap to behind him. When he stepped off the porch, he looked straight at the little band of men standing inside the yard gate with no more sign of recognition than if they had been posts or trees or

not there at all. He followed the path around the house and down past
the little store that would be closed until Uncle Othy finished his dinner.
He turned upriver along the road; beyond the wooden bridge over
Squire's Branch, he crossed the narrow bottom to the river and turned
upstream again at the top of the bank.

They were following him again, easing along behind him as before,
keeping him in sight. If he knew he was thus accompanied, he gave no
sign, and he did not look back. They walked nonetheless in fear that he
would look back, would see and recognize them, and that the sight of
them would cause him to do they did not know what. They were too
busy, picking their way along and keeping him and each other in sight, to
have time to think much about anything else, but they never ceased to be
conscious of the gun, and of the immense difference it made. It was the
wand that transformed them all. Without it, they would have been men
merely walking on the world. Having it there before them in the hands
of a man who might do with it they did not know what, they were men
walking between this present world and the larger one that lies beyond it
and contains it.

When they had passed the store they had seen Put Woolfork sitting in
the shade under the porch roof, waiting for Uncle Othy to come down
and open up for the afternoon. Put, as they knew, had a misery that
wouldn't let him work much in hot weather, and so he would walk down
to the landing in the afternoon to fill himself up with Uncle Othy's gossip and free advice. They had not passed near enough to him to speak,
though Tol had raised his hand. Put did not raise his hand in reply, for he
was too absorbed in watching them. They knew that they would be the
first subject of conversation in the store that afternoon. They expected
that as soon as Put was fully informed of the dinnertime events in the
Daggets' kitchen, he would be along.

They were right. Now that Nightlife was walking along the river, he
began to stop more often. The river seemed to have attracted his notice
as nothing had since he had spied Old Fetcher leaning against Tol's shop
door. As he went along now, he would pause to stand and look at the
shady water beneath the overleaning trees. Or if he came to a stump or a
drift log, he would sit down and look. And so it was no trouble for Put,
once he had been informed, to catch up with them. Tol was soon aware

that somebody was coming along behind them, and before he looked he knew who it was. Glancing back, he would see Put watching them from a weed patch or from behind a tree, his face sticking out, curious — in truth, fascinated — and yet afraid. He had come to observe and report.

Put was a man of about Tol's age, somewhere past his mid-forties, though his face showed not a wrinkle. He was round of eye and face and form, as tight-skinned and smooth as an apple. "Put" was a foreshortening of Pussel Gut, a name that had been conferred upon him on his first day in school. Put lived on a tiny farm where the Cotman Ridge road came down into the river bottom. He kept three or four cows, which his wife milked, and with the help of his wife and his neighbors, he grew a little crop. The misery that kept him from working much in hot weather also did not allow him to work much in cold weather or in wet weather, or ever to do any work for very long if it was very hard. Put walked with his knees bent and his posterior slightly lowered as if at any moment he might be called upon to squat, so that even walking on level ground, he gave the impression that he was going down a steep hill. It was not a good idea to ask him how he was, for he would tell you. Tol nevertheless always asked him how he was. Tol was as good a friend as Put had.

Still, it made him uneasy to have Put tagging along. Though he did not like to know it, and would never have said so, he knew that Put, beyond being useless, could be a burden. He knew also that unlike most of the neighborhood, who either tolerated Put or ignored him, Walter Cotman despised him. It had not been but a few days since Tol had heard Walter say in Put's presence — as if Put were not there or as if it did not matter if he was — that he was "as no-account as a shit-for-a-living damned old housecat." Walter was a good farmer and a good dependable young man, and yet Tol knew that Walter had an edge to him as hard, sharp, and forthright as a good saw. Walter was a fastidious, demanding man, who did good work himself, who had no patience with bad work, and who said exactly and without hesitation whatever he thought. Walter's tongue, as Tol often said to Miss Minnie, was connected directly to his mind.

Tol knew furthermore that when Walter laid one of those opinions of his in front of all the world, the Hardy brothers would laugh at it. The Hardys were stout, good-natured, smiling fellows, enough alike almost to be twins, except that Tom pitched and Braymer caught, and Braymer never owned anything he wouldn't trade and Tom never owned anything he would. They were half Proudfoot, the sons of Tol's sister, and Tol took much pleasure and pride in them. But they were young yet, too willing to laugh at somebody's failings. So far as he could, Tol would go along with Put just as he would go along with Nightlife; he would do what he had to do, or what he could do. If, after it was over, it made a good story, then he would tell it; if it was funny, he would laugh. But now was no time for laughter.

Nightlife had stopped again. He had come to one of the rare places where the bank slanted down gently almost to the water's edge. He sat down on the exposed roots of a big water maple that leaned out over the water; the gun lay across his lap and his hands rested on the gun. All the trees were big there, the riverbank was clear of brush, and Tol and the others had fallen a long way back. From his distance behind them, Put could no longer see Nightlife at all. Presently Tol saw Put break cover and start forward. Put was curious; he wanted to be where he could look at Nightlife. But Tol knew that he also had got lonesome and was longing for company and approval. Wanting no more commotion than necessary, Tol eased quietly back to forestall him.

"How're you, Put?" Tol said.

"Aw, Tol, I ain't no good," Put said. "I've had my misery a right smart lately. You know how this weather does me. How you, Tol?" he asked sympathetically, as if Tol suffered from the same misery.

"Fine," Tol said.

"Well, Uncle Othy was telling me about Nightlife and all. What do you reckon is going to happen? You reckon he's going to shoot hisself?"

They were talking under the white limbs of a large sycamore, well out of sight of Nightlife, but Put was peering ahead, trying to see him; he had hardly looked at Tol. "Where's he at?"

"He's yonder," Tol said.

Now, having seen Tol move back, the others were coming, too.

Walter Cotman came up beside Tol just as Put said, "Well, I just thought you might need some help."

And Tol imagined Walter saying to Put—or to one of the others, for he would say it in front of Put but not to him, "If somebody's going to get shot, he'd like to be on hand to see it, long as it ain't much trouble." Tol could hear it as plainly as if Walter had said it, though so far Walter had said nothing.

"Honey," Tol said to Walter, "I expect one of us ought to keep an eye on Nightlife. We don't want him to go off without us."

Walter nodded and went back.

"Why, sure," Tol said to Put. "A fellow never knows when he'll need help."

After Nightlife got up from the roots of the maple and started on, it was a long time before he stopped again. He stayed near the river, avoiding the farmsteads, using farm roads or cow paths when he came to them and they were going in his direction; where there was no beaten way, he kept to his course anyhow. Briar patches he went around; other obstacles he climbed or went through apparently without granting them notice of their existence. He went through patches of nettles up to his waist. He went through brakes of horseweed that were over his head. He was not hurrying, but neither did he alter his pace or stop. And Tol followed just as steadily behind him, with the young men spread out on either side of him as before and Put Woolfork coming along behind. The crops having been laid by, the six of them walked in a deserted country even there among the fields, and as they walked, the hot bright after-noon stood tall and still above them. Around them, in the heat, the low fields shimmered and swayed.

Tol was hungry. He had not forgotten the smell of fried fish wafting out from Aunt Cordie Dagget's kitchen. He was sorry he had not thought to leave Walter or Sam to wait for Uncle Othy to open the store and bring along maybe some cheese and some crackers, or maybe a few cans of sardines. He did not wish to indulge such thoughts, but they came to him uninvited, for he was a big man and he was used to three big meals a day.

But he was troubled also because he knew—he had known ever since that moment at the Daggets' when he had watched Nightlife walk unchecked and preceded by no warning through Aunt Cordie's kitchen door—that the day was beyond their control. The only man who had control was Nightlife, who did not know he had it. Their proven help-lessness at the Daggets' forced Tol to acknowledge that he could not foretell any of the bad outcomes that might lie ahead—or any outcome at all, for that matter. Maybe, he thought, you could keep a crazy man with a gun from shooting you or somebody else, if you could guess cor-rectly what he was going to do and watch closely enough and keep far enough away. But how in the world you could keep him from shooting himself if he wanted to, unless you had a gun yourself and shot him first, Tol could not imagine.

And so along with heat and hunger and the beginning of weariness, Tol's mind began to be afflicted by a sense of the futility, even the fool-ishness, of what he and the others were doing. For a while his thoughts lurched here and there as if unable to accept that there was not some-thing better to do, or a better way to do what they were doing, some reasonability or sense that could be invited in. But he gave that up, as he gave up with the same motion of his mind the hope of food or rest or comfort.

It was not going to make sense, not yet, and maybe not for a long time, if ever. And for a while, maybe a longish while, there would not be food or rest or comfort either. When they got to the end of the story, he reckoned, they would at least eat. He said to himself, "I reckon it would be better not to have got involved." But he knew even so that, helpless or not, hopeless or not, he would go along with Nightlife until whatever happened that would allow him to cease to go along had happened. And he knew that Walter and Sam and the Hardys would keep going as long as he did, just as he knew that Put would not. He thought, "I reckon I am involved."

They had had a quick drink where a spring fed into Squire's Branch just above Uncle Othy's tobacco patch, and none since. Nightlife had not stopped to drink at all. Now they saw Nightlife veer away from the river toward an isolated barn where they knew there was a cistern. The cis-tern was in a small lot now in the shade at one of the barn's eastward corners. Keeping their distance, they watched Nightlife enter the lot, unhook a tin can from the barn wall, and pump himself a drink. He leaned the gun against the barn when he took down the can, and now he sat down on the cistern top with his back to the gun and with the full can of water in his hand.

"Lordy Lord," Tol thought, "if only one of these boys was close enough to snatch that old gun and run with it!"

But they were not close enough. They were standing in the sun at the edge of a cornfield, scattered out as before. Except for Put who had kept his distance from them as they from Nightlife, they were well within sight of one another, watching Nightlife who was sitting and resting in the shade with that can of cool water in his hand. With the cistern in sight, they suffered from their thirst. Nightlife took his time. The shade held him, and he sat there, sipping water from the can, while the barn swallows dipped and circled around him and overhead. And still he kept the same straight-ahead fixation on whatever was on his mind; he did not turn his head this way or that; he did not appear to be looking at anything.

After a while — an almost insufferable while for those who watched, thirsty, at the weedy edge of the cornfield, furnishing dinner to the sweatbees and the deerflies — he got up, hung the can back on its nail, picked up the gun, and went on in the same direction as before.

When Nightlife went out of sight into a wooded hollow, well beyond gun range of the barn, Tol's little company headed for the cistern — the Hardy brothers first, running, Sam Hanks not far behind them, and then Walter Cotman, who disdained to concede by any haste that he was as thirsty as the others, and then Tol. When Tol got almost to the little cistern lot, Put Woolfork emerged from the cornfield.

Now that they were close enough to one another, the Hardy brothers were almost as eager to talk as to drink.

"Whew!" Tom was saying as Tol came up. "When I seen him go in at Uncle Othy's, I didn't know what."

He had pumped for Sam, and now he pumped again while Braymer held the can under the spout.

"I sure didn't want to hear that old gun go off," Braymer said. He grinned, shook his head, and wiped his mouth. "Uncle Tol," he said, "I don't reckon you was worried."

Tol laid his hat on the cistern top and wiped his face on his sleeve. "No," he said, "I wasn't worried. A man has a fit one night in church, and the next day picks up a loaded gun and goes off into the woods by hisself, and then walks in on an old couple at dinnertime without a knock or a 'come in,' that ain't no kind of a worry."

"What I want to know," Braymer said, having drunk and handed the can to his brother, "is how long can he keep up this traveling. Don't you reckon he'll get hungry before long? He ain't had no dinner."

"We ain't either," Sam said, "that I noticed."

"I reckon a man going to shoot hisself don't need to worry much about dinner," Tom said.

"How do you know he's going to shoot hisself?"

"Well, he said he was, didn't he?"

"He said he might as well. Maybe he ain't going to."

"Maybe he ain't."

Walter filled the can and offered it to Tol.

"Drink," Tol said.

Walter drank, refilled the can, and handed it to Tol.

"Well," Walter said, gazing off where Nightlife had disappeared, "if the damned fool is going to shoot hisself, why don't he go on and do it, and let the rest of us get back to work?"

That was Walter exactly, Tol thought. He would not leave a thought unsaid. And he could not ignore a difference.

But Walter did not leave, as Tol—and Walter himself—knew he would not. He said no more. He simply snorted, seeing that Put had now come up and seated himself on the cistern top.

Having emptied the can once fast and once more slowly, Tol handed it to Tom Hardy who was still at the pump, and stepped off toward the woods' edge, begrudging himself the three or four minutes he had stopped to drink.

Tol had not gone many steps from the barn before Sam Hanks put his hat back on and started after him. If there was danger in Nightlife, then Tol walked at risk now as he approached the woods; though Tol could not see Nightlife, Nightlife, if he wished, could see Tol. Once again it was possible for Sam to imagine the single abrupt syllable that was Old

Fetcher's entire vocabulary. Sometimes during that day it had been pos-sible to forget the old gun's plain and sudden eloquence; sometimes it had not been. Sam remembered it now with an exact presentiment of the difference it could make. He was glad to see that Tol circled out well wide of the place where Nightlife had entered the woods.

In his battered and frazzled old straw hat that no longer by its shape distinguished front from back, and his increasingly disheveled clothes now soaked with sweat, Tol reminded Sam of a tree. He was like a tree walking. Over the difficult terrain of that day he had taken the footing as it came, uphill or down, sidling or flat, brushy or open, as concentrated in his way as Nightlife in his.

The others also were coming now, hurrying to catch up, Walter Cot-man and the Hardys positioning themselves in relation to Tol as before, Put Woolfork falling back into his accustomed place at the rear.

Their little delay at the cistern had cost them; now, for the first time since the beginning, they did not have Nightlife in sight and did not know in which direction he had gone. Once they were in the woods, they cir-cled about in order to cross his track.

In a little while Walter Cotman said quietly, "Here he went."

And now they arranged themselves according to the known reference of Nightlife's track, which curved around a slue and then on out of the woods into another grass field where, at last, they had him in sight again.

From the barn where they drank, Nightlife had not gone back to the river, but slanted across the bottom generally in the direction of the mouth of Willow Run. He went on as before, straying around impas-sable obstacles, avoiding places where there might be people. For Tol and the others, following him had ceased to seem unusual. In the heat and the difficulty of their constant effort to keep just within sight of their strange neighbor, who had become at once their fear, their quarry, and their leader, they had ceased even to wonder what end they were moving toward. This wild pursuit that at first had seemed an interruption of their work had become their work. Now they could hardly imagine what they would be doing if they were home.

At the edge of a tobacco patch, they came upon two rows of toma-toes. Going by, they each picked two or three ripe ones. Tom Hardy picked a half-rotten one and aimed a perfect throw at the back of his brother's head. If the tomato had been anything harder, it would have knocked Braymer down. Braymer returned the fire with two tomatoes, one of which, aimed at Tom's head, caused him to duck, the second knocking off his hat. This exchange occurred in perfect good humor and in absolute silence.

Tol, who had a large tomato in each hand, whispered, "Boys! Boys! Boys!" and kept walking.

Tom made as if to throw a tomato at Tol's back, grinned at his brother, and followed Tol, eating the tomato.

Nightlife reached the river again just a little downstream from the mouth of Willow Run. He kicked aside a few little pieces of driftwood and made himself a place to sit down and then he sat down, leaning his back against a large sycamore. There were several big trees there, water maples and sycamores and cottonwoods, making the shade deep.

A good breeze, the first they had felt all day, was coming up the river. They would have been comfortable, waiting there, except that they were thirsty again, and even if they had wanted to drink out of the river in dog days, they could not have gone down the bank now without putting themselves too much into view.

And so they just stopped when Nightlife stopped, and stood still, only taking their hats off to let the breeze cool their heads. After they had been there, unmoving, a little while, the stillness of the place sealed itself over them. Even the little wind ripples on the water seemed to grow attentive and still.

And that was when they heard Put Woolfork squall.

It was really not much of a squall, just the single abrupt syllable, "Wa!"—a statement that Put would not be allowed to forget for the rest of his life. It might have been merely the startled, despairing outcry of some unfortunate animal.

But Tol knew what it was, and he thought, "Boys!"

If Nightlife had heard, he gave no sign. He did not move. Tol looked then to see which of his young companions was missing, and found that no one was. They were all looking at him.

He started back toward the place the squall had come from. Seeing that all four of the others had started back with him, he stopped; he motioned to Sam to stay and keep an eye on Nightlife, and then went on, Walter and the Hardys moving quietly along with him.

Presently they saw, standing at the foot of a tall cottonwood, Burley Coulter with three days' whiskers, holding an unlit lantern, grinning at Put Woolfork, who was fussing at him in a whisper.

"It ain't a damn bit funny," Put was saying. "You just done it because it was me. I'd like to see you try it on Walter Cotman."

Burley simply continued to grin. And then when he saw Tol and Walter and the Hardys coming up, he shifted his grin to them.

For a few seconds nobody said anything, and then Tol said, "I knowed it was a boy. I just didn't know which boy it was."

Burley was twenty-one that year, old enough to take the word *boy* either as a judgment or as a pleasantry. Tol offered it as both, and Burley received it with his grin unaltered.

"Howdy, Burley," Walter Cotman said. "Has Put treed a squirrel?"

Burley told what there was to tell. He had been in a patch of elderberries at the edge of the riverbank trees, just ready to step into the shade to cool off and maybe take a swim in the river, when he saw Nightlife coming along with the gun; Burley recognized it as Tol's Old Fetcher. From Nightlife's possession of the gun and from the look of him, Burley knew that something was out of fix. He kept still. Presently he saw Tol and Sam and Walter and the Hardy brothers, who obviously were following Nightlife. And then, coming way behind, he saw Put. When Tol and the others stopped, Put, who could not see Nightlife, stepped behind the big cottonwood and began to peep around it. He was so given over to his curiosity that Burley could not resist the temptation to creep up behind him and poke him in the back with a stick. Thereupon, expecting to die, Put had uttered the aforementioned famous exclamation.

The circumstances did not permit laughter, but even Tol smiled.

And Put said, "Slip up on a fellow that way! It's about what you'd expect."

"If you expected it, what did you holler for?" Burley said.

Burley was a wild young man. As the others knew, Put was an eager carrier of tales about Burley; they knew that Burley knew it, and knew that Put knew that Burley knew it.

"Well, what are *you* doing here?" Walter asked Burley.

"I've got a young dog disappeared over in here somewhere. Running a fox, I reckon."

"How come you're hunting this time of year?"

"I ain't hunting. *He's* hunting. I'm hunting *him*. You all got anything to eat? I had a few biscuits but they're long gone."

"No. We ain't got a crumb. How long you been gone?"

Burley grinned, not much wanting to say, but finally saying, "Since night before last. What you boys doing?"

They told him.

Put, whose sense of grievance had been growing, said, "It's done already chore time. I got to go home."

"Don't go, Put," Tol said. He knew that was what Put wanted him to say, but he said it anyhow. "It ain't no use in going."

"Well," Put said sadly, "I ain't got no business here."

Having thus expressed his dissatisfaction with them all, Put headed home.

And so, while following Nightlife to keep from losing him somewhere ahead of them, they had lost Put Woolfork behind them. And Tol was sorry, for he had not meant to lose anybody. He knew Put exactly for what he was. And yet in some way that Tol could not have explained, now that Put had gone off offended, they needed him. Or anyhow Tol did.

"He ain't going home yet," Walter said. "Not till his women have had time to get the milking done."

"Well," Tol said, "he don't mean no harm."

"Nor no good neither."

"Well, but no harm."

Tol was not sure there was no harm in Put—he was at least a gossip and probably a troublemaker—but he did not want to say so, and he did not want Walter to say so. It was a time of day when you could be sorrowful if you were not at home. Tol felt himself pressed out again onto that verge that Nightlife was walking. The conviction welled up in him that Put was better with them than he was alone—even allowing for the trouble that attended him, or that he brought, when he was with them.

"How about you boys?" he asked. "You all have got chores, too."

"Well, how about you?" Braymer Hardy said.

"I ain't got much. Miss Minnie can do what I've got."

"Well, our wives can do ours," Braymer said.

"How about Josie?" Tol said to Tom Hardy, who was the one most recently married. "Can she milk?"

"Why, I reckon!" Braymer said. "She's a better hand than Tom."

"Walter," Tom said, "can you do like Put and leave your chores for your wife?"

"Why, sure," Walter said.

Tol — who had not ceased to watch Sam Hanks, who had not ceased to watch Nightlife — now saw Sam motion to them to come on.

"Come on, boys," Tol said.

"Burley," Walter Cotman said, "you just as well come along."

"I reckon I just as well," Burley said.

And so he came along.

From the mouth of Willow Run, where the river curved in close to the hill again, Nightlife led them back up along the wooded bluffs. Now they left the river valley and walked upstream along the westward slope of the valley of Willow Run. Once he was well up into the woods, Nightlife followed the level contour of the slope out around the points and in and out of the hollows, as he had done before, and they followed him.

In one hollow a tiny stream of water flowed, and Nightlife followed it straight up the slope to where a spring issued from a cleft in the rock. They watched him kneel and drink, and waited while he sat down to rest.

Waiting, they looked at one another and grinned. They were again suffering from thirst, and again Nightlife took his time.

When finally he rose and went on and disappeared in the foliage, Tol motioned to Burley to go and drink. There was room for only one to drink at a time, and Tol did not want as much commotion and delay as there had been at the barn.

They watched as Burley knelt and drank and went on, and then one by one Tol waved the others forward: Walter, and then the two Hardys, and then Sam.

When Sam had finished, Tol drank and followed after the others, leaving the woods quiet again around the spring.

They would be in the woods now for a long time, for the west slope of the valley was poor land, most of which had been cut over at one time or another but not plowed. They were passing through some stands of large trees, mostly hickory and oak, and it was pretty walking, though too steep to be comfortable. Going along behind the others, Tol thought that if he were not hungry and did not have Nightlife to worry about, he would be having a pretty good time. And then he thought that he was having a pretty good time anyhow.

The evening shade had come to that side of the valley by the time Tol caught up with the others. It was cooling off a little. They would have been grateful for some supper—they were all thinking of things they would like to eat—but they were enjoying the cool. A little breeze had begun drifting down the slope, drying the sweat from their faces.

The light now lost its strength and heat as if detached from its source. Stray glows and luminescences floated among the trees. Sometimes they would hear a wood thrush sing, a flute suddenly trilled and then fading, somewhere beyond or behind. And before all the daylight was gone, there was a moon.

While Tol still had enough light to see them all, he gathered them to him. "We can't all stay close enough to see him after dark," he said. "So let Burley follow Nightlife, and we'll follow Burley. With that moon, we ought to be able to stay together pretty good."

And that was what they did.

After it got dark, Nightlife wandered a little more than he had earlier; he went a little slower and stopped more often. But he went on and on, Burley followed him, and they followed Burley. They kept always alert, for if Burley lost sight of Nightlife or they lost sight of Burley, anything could happen. Or so they felt. They felt that they could not afford to risk confusion. They certainly did not want to become disoriented and blunder into Nightlife and Old Fetcher in the dark. Enough moonlight filtered down through the foliage to give vigilance an edge over confusion, but barely enough. The light filled the woods with shadows, and at times the very effort of sight seemed to call forth phantoms and apparitions, motions where nothing moved. They lost all sense of where they were except in relation to one another. They forgot their tiredness and their hunger. They would have been thirsty again if they had remembered thirst, but they had forgotten it. They seemed to have become enlarged out of their bodies into sight itself and the effort of sight, and they walked owl-eyed among the confusions of things and the shadows of things.

They knew only what they saw, and they saw only shadows within a shadow. Nightlife led them through a maze that did not exist before he led them through it. They went in silence, for the dew had softened the dry leaves underfoot, and still they walked with care. Now and again, when they passed above a house, dogs would bark. Now and again, way off, they would hear an owl. Once, coming suddenly to the edge of an open field, they seemed to plunge headlong out of the dark into the moon-flooded sky.

The moon shone way into the night. And then, unexpectedly, for they had not seen the sky in a while, clouds covered the moon, and it was suddenly so dark that they could not see to the ends of their own arms; when they held their hands up before their faces and wiggled their fingers, they could not see them. It was, Walter Cotman told Elton Penn, who told me, "as black as a coker's ass, and all at once."

They stopped and waited, for that was all they could do. They knew that somewhere in the dark ahead of them Burley was trying out the problem of following Nightlife by sound, of getting close enough to him to know where he was without touching him. And so they waited.

They waited a long time, and saw nothing at all. They heard anonymous, inexplicable stirrings here and there. They heard a dog bark, way off—not at them this time. They heard a small owl trill sweetly and another answer from farther away. And that was all.

They were beginning to think of sitting down when they saw a dim yellow light suddenly bloom out of a hollow not far behind them. They turned and eased back toward it. When they got close enough, they recognized Burley. He had lit his lantern. They gathered around him.

"He never stopped," Burley said. "He kept right on going."

"Course he went on!" Walter said. "A man that can't see in the daytime, what does it matter to him if he can't see in the dark?"

"I stayed with him for a while," Burley said. "I was close enough to him that I could hear him walking, I thought. And then I got to where I couldn't tell what I was hearing. I was starting to hear things, and I couldn't tell if they was actually things or not. I got scared I'd walk smack into him, so I held back. And then I lost him. He either stopped or went on, I didn't know which. And so I eased away."

"Well, we don't want that light, do we?" Tol said.

"He's too far to see it where he is," Burley said, "I think, unless he followed me back." He grinned at Walter Cotman.

The lantern, turned low, sat on the ground at their feet. It showed them their faces, and cast their shadows out around them like spokes.

They fell silent now, for the knowledge of their failure had suddenly come over them. The potency of Tol's old shotgun entered their thoughts again. They knew that at any time, from somewhere out in the dark, they might hear its one short and final exclamation. And only then would they know where to go.

"Well," Tol Proudfoot said, after a time that seemed longer than it was, "I reckon we've lost him."

"I reckon if he's lost, he ain't by hisself," Tom Hardy said. "Do you know where we are?"

"I know within three or four miles, I reckon," Tol said.

"Do you know, Burley?"

"Right here," Burley said.

They were speaking almost in whispers.

"What're we going to do, then?" Walter Cotman said. "Stand here till sunup, with that lantern lighting us up for him to shoot at?"

"That lantern ain't going to burn till sunup," Burley said, "unless one of you all brought some coal oil."

"We could build us a little fire, I reckon," Braymer said.

Tol knew then that they were going to build a fire. He already objected to the lantern—or the caution in him objected to it. But after the darkness, it was a comfort and a pleasure. That they would build a fire he knew because he knew he could not bring himself to stop them from building it.

He was nonetheless relieved to hear Walter Cotman say, "We're too close to him here to build any fire."

"Well," Burley said, "we could drop down this hollow till we're out of the woods. He'll stay in the woods, won't he? That's his pattern."

They made their way slowly down the rocky bed of the stream. They came to a water gap in a rock fence, and crossed into what they knew to be a pasture, for now they saw cattle tracks and smelled cattle, and the foliage had been browsed nearly to the height of a man. There were trees still along the hollow, but here there would be grass fields out on the slopes on either side.

Burley led them up out of the streambed onto a little bench. By the light of the lantern or by feel they gathered up kindling and bigger wood for a fire. They helped the kindling with a tiny splatter of oil from the lantern, and soon they had a small fire going. Burley raised the globe and blew out the lantern flame. The fire cheered them; it forced back the dark and the damp of the night a little, and they were glad to sit down beside it. They were tired, and the fire made them a resting place.

And yet sitting there in the room of light it made was a fearfully simple, almost a brutal, act of faith. It made them visible to all the distances around them, and made those distances invisible to them. All they could hope was that if Nightlife saw the light of their fire, he would come into it and not shoot into it. They did not *think* he would see it, but the chance that he might shaped that odd little hope in them, and it kept them silent for a while, glowing, all of them, in the firelight.

Finally Walter Cotman said quietly, "It'll rain tomorrow."

"I'd say so," Tol said.

"Well, we need a rain."

"Yes, we do. If it don't come too hard."

"It could come hard. It's been mighty hot."

"We need one of them good old dizz-dozzlers," Braymer Hardy said. "This time of year, it would be money in the bank."

"A good rain now surely would ruin them little cabbages of mine," Tol said.

"Why?"

"It would make big ones out of 'em."

What they had said had not made so welcome an effect on the silence around them as their fire had made on the darkness. They let the silence come back. The fire eased them, and they thought of their tobacco. Walter and Burley made cigarettes; Sam and Tol filled and lit cob pipes; the others took chews.

After a while Walter said in the same quiet voice as before, "Tom, you reckon Josie'll still be at your house when you get home?"

"It ain't every newly married man that you find wandering about the woods of a night," Tol said.

"Pore thing," Braymer said, "it's just a blessing she don't care nothing about him, or this sort of doings would break her heart."

Except for Tom's, every face around the fire remained solemn. Tom grinned.

Tol said, "You take a young fellow like that, now, ugly and mean and nothing to offer but beans and hard work, and he fools a nice, smart, pretty girl into marrying him — you'd think he wouldn't leave home, day nor night."

"It's a shame," Walter said. "The women are all talking about it."

"I growed my crop close to the house, the first year I got married," Braymer said, "didn't you, Uncle Tol?"

"Yessir, I did," Tol said.

"Tom," Walter said, "when you get up of a morning and you see these little specks floating on top of your coffee and you try to blow them off and they don't blow off, that's because they ain't there."

And then, way off, on their side of the valley but in a place they had not yet come to, a hound's voice opened the darkness like a flare.

They hushed to listen.

The hound puzzled for several minutes over the scent he had announced, as if he were cold-trailing, perhaps, or going in the wrong direction. And then his cries rose full and confident.

"Is that your dog, Burley?" Sam Hanks asked.

"It's him," Burley said.

"Well, that ain't no fox he's running now."

"No. He's running a coon now."

Tol said, "He's a sweet-mouthed dog, ain't he?"

They listened. Presently the cries became more urgent. The coon had treed.

"That was quick," Sam said.

"Probably a sow with young ones," Burley said.

The hound's voice now seemed to fill the world with longing. The voice seemed to speak for the world. It spoke for Nightlife. It spoke for them all.

It seemed to them also to be an outlandish breach of propriety — so close and, in the face of their difficulty, so insistent on the normal order of things. The hound was Burley's, and the others kept quiet for fear that Burley was going to say, in spite of Nightlife's despair somewhere nearby in the dark, "Well, I reckon we ought to go see if a coon is what it is." Burley himself kept quiet for fear that one of the others might say it in courtesy to him. And so for a long time nobody but the hound said anything.

Without warning, a hectoring, humorous voice came out of the nearby dark: "Well, by God, if you fellows is hunting, why don't you go to your dog?"

The voice lifted them to varying heights above their resting places before they recognized it and let themselves back down again. Lester Proudfoot stepped into the firelight, holding his lantern up as if he had found what he was looking for.

"We ain't hunting," Burley said. "We're just setting here improving."

"I don't reckon you brought anything to eat," Tom Hardy said. "Or drink."

"Naw, nor nothing to sleep with neither. What in the hell are *you* doing, running around in the woods of a night? Something got wrong with young women since my day? Tol, how you making it?"

Lester bore all the distinguishing marks of a Proudfoot. He was Tol's first cousin, and he looked like Tol, though he was not as big. He possessed to the full the Proudfoot gregariousness, always ready to do anything that could be done in company. Lester would talk to anybody anywhere, under any circumstances, at any time, at any length. A hunter himself, he had been awakened by the hound and then, looking out his kitchen window, had seen the fire up on the hillside.

Tol told him why they were there.

"And Nightlife's up yonder in the woods somewhere with a gun?" Lester said.

"I reckon. Sit down, Les."

Lester sat down. He extinguished his lantern. "And you boys is waiting here either for him to see this fire and come to it, or take a shot at one of you all?"

"Or shoot hisself," Walter Cotman said. "Or wander on from hell to breakfast, the way he's been doing."

"He's done already wandered around equal to Moses," Tom Hardy said.

"He's wandered around equal to old Daniel Boone hisself," Braymer said.

"Well, I hope he discovers Kentucky pretty soon and settles down," Walter said.

"What the matter with him is he's a Hample," Lester said. "Ain't that his chief difficulty? He don't fit the hole that was bored for him."

"Les," Tol said, "tell about that time Nightlife's granddaddy swore off drinking."

"Uncle Norey," Lester said. "Uncle Norey got to where he would always get drunk and down before the crop was made, and leave the hardest part for Aunt Nancy and the children. Aunt Nancy told him he'd have to stop that, and he did, he swore off. And then when they finally got the crop made and ready for the market, Uncle Norey said, 'Here I've put in a whole crop year from Genesis to Revelation, and nare a drop of liquor has defiled my lips. Hand me that jug!'"

After Lester's noisy entrance among them, their conversation had been quiet. Now they laughed as quietly as they had spoken. And then, except for the hound still clamoring at the tree, the quiet restored itself.

For some time, where they were, it was silent altogether.

And then Tom Hardy said, "A man would think of killing hisself, he ain't at hisself, surely."

"He's at hisself, all right," Tol said. "He ain't nowhere *but* at hisself. Look at old Nightlife just rambling on, not looking right nor left, going like he knows where, and he don't know."

"The way he is now," Walter said, "he just as well stayed home or stayed asleep. Or never been born. He don't know where he is."

"Don't matter where he is," Tol said. "He's just wandering around inside hisself, looking for the way out. In there where he is, it's dark sure enough."

"Well, here we are. Or there we were. Right there with him."

"And what did we do? Or what could we? For he ain't just wandering around inside hisself; he's wandering around out of reach — by about the range of that old gun."

"You got to live whether you want to or not," Tom Hardy said.

Tol said, "Boy, I think you've got to want to." He said nothing for a long time then, and then he said, "You've got to *like* to live in this world. You can't just mortal it out from one day to the next for three score years and ten."

They were quiet again for a while, and then Lester stood up and relit his lantern. He said, "I reckon being as that keen-eyed fellow's up there with Tol's gun, I won't bother about your dog now, Burley. I'll slip up there after daylight and bring him down to the house. You get him when you can."

"I'd be much obliged," Burley said.

Lester stepped out of the firelight then. For a few seconds they heard his footsteps descending the slope, and then it was quiet. They could hear the hound, and that was all.

When Lester had gone, they began to feel their weariness. One by one they lay down beside the fire and slept.

"Couldn't you stay awake? Couldn't you stay awake?"

Gray daylight had come. The fire had burned down to white ash. Now, though the hound was exactly where he had been before, his voice sounded farther away and smaller. But what had wakened them was Nightlife standing over them, one foot in the ashes. He was holding the gun, but not threatening them with it. It dangled from his hand as unregarded as if it had been the bail of an empty bucket.

"Couldn't you stay awake?"

The lenses of his glasses apparently as opaque as bark, he was looking right at them and not seeing them. They were frightened, astonished, tickled at their own and one another's fright and astonishment, and most of all ashamed.

"Sit down, Nightlife," Tol said. "Sit down, old bud. We'll go home pretty soon and get some breakfast."

"You think there ain't no breakfast here?" Nightlife said. "Where the hell you think breakfast is at? I've got breakfast right here."

His voice had grown louder, and now he raised the gun and gestured with it in a way that caused them to make various motions backward. "Couldn't you stay awake?" he said.

"Well, we thought if you shot yourself it would wake us up," said Walter Cotman.

Nightlife went on then. He stepped out of the circle of men around the dead fire, and started back up into the woods. They lay there with their heads raised and watched him go.

"Shoo!" Tom Hardy said quietly. It seemed to them all that they now began to breathe again.

Tol grunted, getting himself to his feet. "If he hadn't found us," he said, "I don't reckon we ever would have found him."

The others got up slowly and followed—"three meals in arrears by then," Sam Hanks would say years later, "and we were feeling it, I can tell you."

In a little while it seemed to them that they had never stopped. They went on as before. Even their hunger and thirst were familiar. They came to another spring and drank, and then they were only hungry.

They were going upstream through the woods on the westward side of Willow Run valley, which was the eastward side of Cotman Ridge, the westward side of which they had gone down the morning before. They were approaching Tol Proudfoot's place from the direction opposite to that of their departure.

When Nightlife stopped again, Tol dropped back a little and beckoned Sam to him.

"Looks like we'll be pretty close to home again before long," he said.

"Maybe he'll circle right back to there," Sam said. "You reckon?"

"Maybe so. If he don't, maybe we can at least get a bite to eat as we go by. If you don't mind, would you just cut straight across to my house and ask Miss Minnie would she kindly see if she can't scrape us up a little something to eat?"

"Why, sure," Sam said. "Looks like that Nightlife would get hungry sooner or later hisself. Don't you reckon a good meal mightn't get him unfittified?"

"It might," Tol said. "There's a world of sanity in a little meat and gravy. It sho would help me."

The women, of course, had anticipated this hunger. When Sam stepped into Miss Minnie's kitchen, Thelma Cotman and the two Josie Hardys, Josie Braymer and Josie Tom, were frying chicken and baking biscuits and making gravy and slicing tomatoes and boiling beans and potatoes. Even old Mrs. Hample, Nightlife's mother, was there. Miss Minnie had sent for her, and she had walked up not long after daylight, worried and needing company. She was making a kind of dutiful effort to help the other women, but was so distracted and full of hesitations that she was only getting in their way, wringing her hands beneath her apron and trying to disguise her repeated glances out the windows and the door. "I just don't know what's got into that boy's head," she kept saying. "I just wisht I knowed."

The smell in the kitchen was almost too much for Sam Hanks. "I thought I was going to faint," he said. "I had to sit down and hold on to the table."

But he delivered his message: One way or another, sooner or later, they would be there to eat. They would need a lot. They were hungry.

"I should think so," Miss Minnie said. "Poor Thacker Hample!"

"Poor Thacker Hample!" Sam said. "Good God!"

To appease him and to comfort him on his walk back into the woods, she gave him two chicken legs and three biscuits, which in pure kindness Sam ate in a hurry, so as not to torment Tol and the others by the sight.

It was not a true circle that Nightlife had traveled in. He had been governed too much both by the lay of the land and by his craziness for his course to have assumed any sort of regular shape. Nevertheless, it was clear by midmorning that he was headed back toward their starting place. He came up out of the woods and began picking his way across the pastures and hayfields and around the tobacco and corn patches of the ridgetop, and he was tending generally in the direction of Tol Proudfoot's place.

For some time they had been hearing thunder in the distance, and every leaf in the woods had held still. When they came out of the woods onto the high and open ground, they could see under the general overcast a dark cloud sharply outlined above the horizon in the southwest. And the thunder was louder. They could hear it rumbling and stuttering. It had about it the quality of preoccupation, as if the Power inhabiting the cloud was too intent upon his preparations to concern himself yet with what he was going to do.

Keeping Nightlife in sight was no longer a problem now that they were on the open ridge. He went his way as before, looking neither left nor right, as if he were the only human being left on earth. Tol and the others maintained their distance from him, safely out of gun range, close enough to see him. When they got to the top of the ridge and could look down and see Tol's house and outbuildings, Tol beckoned to Sam and Burley and Walter.

"Boys, work your way around on the right, now. Stay between him and the house. *Don't* let him go to the house. Sam, you go tell the women to lock the doors."

So now Tol and the Hardys followed Nightlife as before, but Walter and Burley and Sam walked almost even with him, well out to his right. And now the sky lowered and darkened until it seemed to enclose them all.

The road across from Tol's place was bordered by a rock fence. Because they were approaching at an angle to the road, the three who were walking to Nightlife's right got to the fence before he did, and crossed it and stepped down the bank into the road. Nightlife then approached the fence and started to cross.

And that was the last that Tol and the Hardys saw of him before the storm hit. It fell upon them all of a sudden—lightning and thunder and wind and hard rain all at once. Tom and Braymer started running and also disappeared from sight. The rain fell hard, so nearly a solid spout that, Burley said, "a fish could have swum up it." When the big drops struck and splashed, the wind seized the spray and sped it along in sheets.

Tol went down the slope to the rock fence, clambered over it, fell, and slid down the bank into the road. He glimpsed the opening of the driveway, and went in under the greater darkness of the yard trees. By then he, too, was running.

The shop was the first outbuilding reachable from the road. And now Tol could see that the door of the shop was open, and he knew the others had gone inside. He was not fast on his feet, but he passed one other man who, he realized only after he had gone by, was walking, and carrying a gun.

"No, boys!" he called into the shop as he ran. "Wait! Come out!"

He stumbled into the dark interior of the shop only a step or two ahead of Nightlife, who stopped just inside the door.

When Nightlife stepped through the door behind Tol, and took his stand, cradling the gun in his hands as if expecting a covey of quail to flush at any second, that put an end to the little breathless laughter that had started among the others because of their wild run through the storm and their escape into shelter at last.

They hushed and stood still in their sopping clothes. Sam Hanks then quietly sat down on a nail keg in front of the forge. Now that they looked at Nightlife face-to-face, after all he had caused them to do and to think, they were struck by how ordinary he looked. He looked like his same old self — except that, looking straight at them, he appeared not to see them, or to be looking through them at whatever was behind them.

"Brethren," he said, "let us stand and sing." And he began, alone at first, to sing "The Unclouded Day."

Staggeringly, the others began to join in. And here it was discovered that Sam Hanks, who was the only one sitting down, had not stood up. He had instead managed to find a dry match and had lit his pipe.

"Sam," Tom Hardy said to him in a whisper, "ain't you going to sing?"

"*Naw*sir!" Sam said out loud. "I ain't a-going to sing just because the likes of him tells me to."

"Well, he's liable to shoot you."

"Well, he'll just have to do it, then, because I ain't going to sing." And Sam expelled several small complacent puffs of smoke, looking out past Nightlife into the rain.

But the others sang, and sang pretty well, too, Burley's and Tol's strong voices carrying the others:

O the land of cloudless day,
O the land of an unclouded day;
O they tell me of a home where no storm clouds rise,
O they tell me of an unclouded day.

They lifted the fine old song up against the rattle of hard rain on the roof and up over the roof and out into the gray, rainy light — as if in them the neighborhood sang, even under threat, its love for itself and its grief for itself, greater than the terms of this world allow. By the time they got to the second verse, the onsetting force of the storm having abated, Miss Minnie and Thelma and the two Josies and old Mrs. Hample could hear them all the way to the kitchen, and I can hear them now:

O they tell me of a home where my friends have gone,
O they tell me of a land far away,
Where the tree of life in eternal bloom
Sheds its fragrance thro' the unclouded day.

When they finished the hymn, Nightlife began his sermon — the one, as they supposed, that he had prepared for the revival service of the night before last. His text was Matthew 18:12, which he knew by heart:

How think ye? if a man have an hundred sheep, and one of them be gone astray, doth he not leave the ninety and nine, and goeth into the mountains, and seeketh that which is gone astray?

Though Christ, in speaking this parable, asked his hearers to think of the shepherd, Nightlife understood it entirely from the viewpoint of the lost sheep, who could imagine fully the condition of being lost and even the hope of rescue, but could not imagine rescue itself.

"Oh, it's a dark place, my brethren," Nightlife said. "It's a dark place where the lost sheep tries to find his way, and can't. The slopes is steep and the footing hard. The ground is rough and stumbly and dark, and overgrowed with bushes and briars, a hilly and a hollery place. And the shepherd comes a-looking and a-calling to his lost sheep, and the sheep knows the shepherd's voice and he wants to go to it, but he can't find the path, and he can't make it."

The others knew that Nightlife knew what he was talking about. They knew he was telling what it was to be him. And they were moved.

Long afterward, Elton Penn asked Walter Cotman, "Did what he said make sense? I mean, did you feel for him?"

"Me?" Walter said. "*Course* I felt for him! The son of a bitch could preach!"

They were moved. Even Sam Hanks was moved. But they also began to be amused — begging sympathy's pardon — because Miss Minnie's old setting hen had returned from wherever she had been to breakfast, only to find Nightlife standing and preaching right in front of her nest. The hen began to walk back and forth at Nightlife's feet, crying out with rapidly increasing hysteria, "My children! My children! What will become of my children?" Now and again, she squatted and opened her wings as if to fly up to her nest, and then changed her mind.

At last she crouched almost directly in front of Nightlife, and with a leap, a desperate, panic-stricken, determined outcry, and a great flapping of wings, she launched herself upward.

But she had miscalculated Nightlife's height; he continued to rise up in front of her long past the point at which she had expected him to stop. She got up a little above breast height, and then either lost her nerve or decided to stop and reconsider. She hung there, flapping and squawking, right in Nightlife's face, and Nightlife struck her an open-handed blow that Walter Cotman said would have given second thoughts to a mule.

After Nightlife hit the hen, Walter told Elton, she hung suspended in the air for many seconds, whirling like a pinwheel and shedding feathers around her in spirals.

That was all it took. By the time the hen hit the ground, still squawking, a change had come over Nightlife. He looked around like a man just awakened, and it was plain to the others that he saw that they were there with him and that he knew them. It looked to them as though the very lenses of his glasses were clarified by intelligence. He leaned the shotgun against the bench, and stood free of it.

Tol then stepped up beside Nightlife and picked up the gun. He said, "Nightlife, honey, I want you to see my gun. My daddy had it before me. It's an old one."

He opened the breech, removed the shell, and put the shell into his pocket. He snapped the breech shut again and handed the gun to Nightlife, who took it and looked it over.

"It looks like a right good old gun, Tol," Nightlife said, and he handed it back.

They heard the dinner bell then, for Miss Minnie, feeling that she should do something, and not knowing what else to do, had sent Josie Tom out to ring it.

"Boys," Tol said, "I believe Old Marster and the good women have kept us in mind. Let's go eat!"

"Oh, that was a meal that was a joy to set on the table!" Miss Minnie said.

She and her nephew, Sam Hanks, had been telling Granny and me the story of Nightlife's spell and his long ramble through the woods. It had taken most of the afternoon. Miss Minnie's account of all they had to eat and of all they ate had been a small epic in itself.

It was a story I never forgot, and as time went on I would pick up bits of it from Braymer Hardy, from Walter Cotman by way of Elton Penn, and from others. But Miss Minnie, I think, understood it better than anybody. She had taught at least four of those young men at the Goforth school: Nightlife, Burley Coulter, and the two Hardys. And she and Tol had been neighbors to them all. She knew pretty exactly by what precarious interplay of effort and grace the neighborhood had lived.

"Poor old Thacker Hample," she said. "They kept him alive that time, anyhow. They and the Good Lord."

"And that old hen," Sam Hanks said.

"Yes, that old hen," Miss Minnie said.

She mused a while, rocking in her chair. Finally she said, "And don't you know that old hen survived it all. She hatched fourteen chicks and raised them, every one!"

A Half-Pint of
Old Darling (1920)

Ptolemy Proudfoot and Miss Minnie did not often take a lively interest in politics. They were Democrats, like virtually everybody else in the vicinity of Cotman Ridge and Goforth. They had been born Democrats, had never been anything but Democrats, and had never thought of being anything but Democrats. To them, being Democrats was much the same sort of thing as being vertebrates; it was not a matter of lively interest. Their daily lives were full of matters that were in the most literal sense lively: gardens and crops and livestock, kitchen and smokehouse and cellar, shed and barn and pen, plantings and births and harvests, washing and ironing and cooking and canning and cleaning, feeding and milking, patching and mending. That their life was surrounded by great public issues they knew and considered, and yet found a little strange.

The year 1920, however, was one of unusually lively political interest, especially for Miss Minnie. In January of that year, the constitutional amendment forbidding "the manufacture, sale, or transportation of intoxicating liquors" went into effect. And in August the women's suffrage amendment was ratified. Miss Minnie did not approve of drinking intoxicating liquors, which she believed often led to habitual drunkenness. And she certainly did believe that women ought to have the vote.

Tol, for his part, enjoyed a bottle of beer occasionally, and occasionally he had been known to enjoy a good drink of somebody else's whiskey —

whether homemade or bottled in bond he did not particularly care, so long as it was good. He liked whiskey of a quality to cure a sore throat, not cause one. This was not something that Miss Minnie knew or that Tol had ever considered telling her. It was not something she had ever had any occasion—or, so far as he knew, any need—to know. Liquor also was something that he could easily go without. If the country chose not to drink, then he could comfortably endure the deprivation as long as the country could.

And so very little was said between them on the subject of the Prohibition amendment. Miss Minnie belonged to the Women's Christian Temperance Union, and supported the amendment, and that was all right with Tol, and that was that.

On the question of the suffrage amendment, Tol's conclusion was that if he had the vote, and if (as he believed) Miss Minnie was smarter than he was, then Miss Minnie should have the vote. Miss Minnie (who did not think she was smarter than Tol, and did not wish to be) said that though Tol had not accurately weighed all the evidence, his reasoning was perfect.

"The vote," said Tol, "means that us onlookers and bystanders get to have a little bit of say-so."

"And I want my little bit," Miss Minnie said.

"So it's out with the whiskey and in with the women," Tol said.

Miss Minnie let him have a smile then, for she loved his wit, but she said that by and large she thought that was the way it would have to be, for women hated liquor because of all they'd had to suffer from drunken men. She had seen some of her own students grow up to be worthless drunkards.

Tol said that she was right there, and he knew it. By and large, he was content to believe as she believed. She had been a schoolteacher and knew books, and he looked up to her.

To say that Tol looked up to Miss Minnie is to use a figure of speech, for Tol was an unusually big man and Miss Minnie an unusually small woman. And so at the moment when he was in spirit looking up to her, he was in the flesh beaming down upon her from beneath a swatch of hair that projected above his brows like a porch roof.

It was still dark on a morning in the middle of November. Tol had done his chores while Miss Minnie fixed breakfast; they had eaten and, having completed their conversation, had stood up from the table. Tol's hair, which he had wetted and combed when he washed his face, had reverted to its habit of sticking out this way and that. This condition had been aggravated by Tol's habit of scratching under his cap from time to time without taking it off. To an impartial observer Tol might have looked a little funny, as though he had put a pile of jackstraws on his head.

Miss Minnie, however, was not an impartial observer. To her he looked comfortable. To her he was shelter and warmth. When he smiled down at her that way, it was to her as though the sun itself had looked kindly at her through the foliage of a tall tree.

It was a Saturday morning. That day they were going to make one of their twice- or thrice-yearly trips to Hargrave, the county seat, ten miles down the river from Port William.

Tol said he had a few odds and ends to do at the barn before he harnessed Redbird. And Miss Minnie said that would be fine, for she had to finish up in the house and ought to be ready by the time he would be.

Tol said, well, he thought they needn't be in a big hurry, for it was a little nippy out, and maybe they should give it a chance to warm up. And Miss Minnie said, yes, that was fine.

And so in the slowly strengthening gray November daylight Tol set things to rights around the barn, the way he liked to do on Saturday, and brought Redbird out of his stall and curried and brushed and harnessed him, and left him tied in the driveway of the barn. Tol pulled the buggy out of its shed then and went back to the house. He shaved at the washstand by the kitchen door and put on the fresh clothes that Miss Minnie had laid out for him.

Miss Minnie had the gift of neatness. Her house was neat, and she was neat herself. Even in her everyday dresses she always looked as if she were expecting company. This in addition to her fineness of mind and character made her, Tol thought, a person of quality. Tol loved the word *quality* much as he loved the words of horse anatomy such as *pastern*, *stifle*, and *hock*. He liked it when a buyer said to him of his crop or a load of lambs or steers, "Well, Mr. Proudfoot, I see you've come with quality again this year." And when he thought about what a fine woman Miss Minnie was, with her neat ways and her book learning and her correct grammar, he enjoyed saying to himself, "She's got quality."

Tol was like Miss Minnie in his love of neatness, and his farm was neatly kept. His barn was as neat in its way as Miss Minnie's house. But Tol was not a neat person. He was both too big, I assume, and too forget-ful of himself to look neat in his clothes. The only time Tol's clothes looked good was before he put them on. In putting them on, he forgot about them and began, without the slightest malice toward them, to subject them to various forms of abuse. When he had got them on that morning, Miss Minnie came in and went over them, straightening his shirtfront, buttoning his cuffs, tucking in his pocket handkerchief and the end of his belt. She pecked over his clothes with concentrated haste, like a banty hen pecking over a barn floor, as if Tol were not occupying them at all, Tol meanwhile ignoring her as he transferred his pocket stuff from his discarded pants and put on his cap and coat.

"Now you look all nice," she said.

And Tol said, "You look mighty nice, too, little lady." That was his endearment, and she gave him a pat.

The sun had come up behind clouds, and from the looks of the sky it would be cloudy all day.

"Is it going to rain?" Miss Minnie said.

"I doubt it," Tol said. "May snow along about evening, from the looks of things and the feel of that wind."

They went together to where the buggy stood. Tol brought Redbird from the barn and put him between the shafts, handed Miss Minnie up into the buggy, and got in himself, the buggy tilting somewhat to his side as his weight bore on the springs, so that it was natural for Miss Minnie to sit close to him. Sitting close to him was not something she ever minded, but on that morning it was particularly gratifying, for the wind, as Tol said, was "a little blue around the edges." They snugged the lap robe around them and drove out onto the road.

For a while they did not talk. Redbird was a young horse in those days, Tol having hitched him for the first time only that spring, and he was feeling good. The sharp air made him edgy. He was startled by the steam clouds of his breath, and he enjoyed the notion that he was in danger of being run over by the buggy rolling behind him.

"Cutting up like a new pair of scissors, ain't he?" Tol said. "Whoa, my little Redbird! Whoa, my boy! Settle down, now!" Tol sang to the colt in a low, soothing voice. "You'll be thinking different thoughts by dark."

Redbird and his notions amused Tol. He gave him his head a little, letting him trot at some speed.

"He requires a steady hand, doesn't he?" Miss Minnie said, impressed as always by Tol's horsemanship.

"He's a little notional," Tol said. "He'll get over it."

Redbird abandoned his notions about halfway up the first long hill, and settled down to a steady jog. Tol could relax then, and he and Miss Minnie resumed their never-ending conversation about the things they saw along the road and the things those sights reminded them of, and this morning, too, they talked more from time to time about politics.

What brought the subject up now, as at breakfast, was that in this year of unusual political interest Latham Gallagher was running for the office of state representative. "The Gallagher boy," as Miss Minnie called him, had been sheriff and court clerk, and now he aspired to the seat of government in Frankfort. He was the son of an old friend of Miss Minnie's, and for that reason Miss Minnie thought him fine and handsome and an excellent orator. A month or so ago she and Tol had gone to hear him speak on the porch of the old hotel in Port William.

Tol thought that the Gallagher boy had already made far too much of some of his opportunities, and he did not like oratory made up of too many sentences beginning "My fellow Kentuckians," but he kept his opinions to himself. The boy, after all, was a Democrat, which meant that there was at least one worse thing he could have been.

Now and again as they drove along, Tol and Miss Minnie would see one of the Gallagher boy's posters attached to a tree or a telephone pole. "Gallagher for Representative," the posters said, "A Fair Shake for the Little Man."

"A Fair Shake for the Little Woman," said Tol Proudfoot, nudging Miss Minnie beneath the lap robe, and she nudged him back.

They went through Port William and on down the river road to Ellville and over the bridge into Hargrave, talking the whole way. It had been a busy fall; Tol had been out of the house from daylight to dark, and Miss Minnie had been equally preoccupied with her own work, preparing for winter. So it was pleasant to ride along behind the now-dutiful Redbird, in no particular hurry, and just visit, telling each other all they'd thought of and meant to say as soon as they found a chance.

When they got to Hargrave, they left Redbird at the livery stable where he could rest well and have some hay to eat and a ration of grain while they went about their errands. At first they did a little shopping together, and carried their purchases back and stored them in the buggy. And then they went to the Broadfield Hotel to eat dinner. This was a place Tol particularly favored because they did not bring the meals out on individual plates to little separate tables, but instead the patrons sat together at long tables, and the food was set before them on heaped platters and in large bowls, and pans of hot biscuits and cornbread were passing around almost continuously, and pitchers of sweet milk and buttermilk and pots of coffee were always in reach, and when a person's plate began to look clean, there would be waiters coming around with various kinds of pie, and all of it was good. It was a place where a man like Tol could eat all he wanted without calling too much attention to himself—cooking for him, Miss Minnie had been heard to say, was like cooking for a hotel—and where also he could have his fill of conversation. Tol loved to eat and he loved to talk. The hotel dining room appealed to him because while he ate there he could expect to be in the company of some people he knew and of some he did not know, and in the course of a meal he would extract from all of them a great deal of information about themselves, their families, and their businesses or farms—also their opinions about the national and local economies, the market prospects for tobacco, cattle, sheep, and hogs, and any other opinions they might care to express. The meal characteristically would take an hour and a half or two hours, for Tol stretched to the limit the leisure and the pleasure of it. It was one of the main reasons for their trip to Hargrave, as Miss Minnie knew, though Tol never said so. He ate and talked and laughed and complimented the cooks and urged more food on his fellow guests just as if he were at home.

When the meal was over and they had lingered, talking, at the table for long enough, Tol and Miss Minnie strolled out onto the hotel porch, from which they could see the broad Ohio River flowing past and the mouth of their own smaller river opening into it. The ferry that connected Hargrave with the nearby towns in Indiana pulled away from the dock while they watched.

And then Miss Minnie, who wanted to buy Tol's Christmas present, a little awkwardly presented the falsehood that she had "a few little errands" and would meet him at the livery stable in an hour and a half. Her business would not require that long, but she knew that Tol, wherever he went, would get to talking and would be that long at least. Tol, who wished to do some private shopping of his own, agreed, and they parted.

Tol first returned to a dry goods store that he and Miss Minnie had visited together that morning. He had heard her say to a clerk of a certain bolt of cloth, intending perhaps that he should overhear, "Now *that's* pretty." He bought her enough of the cloth to make a dress. And then, because it took so little cloth to make a dress for Miss Minnie, he went to another store and bought her a pretty comb that caught his eye, and also—what he had never done before—he bought a bottle of perfume, which lasted for years and years because, as Miss Minnie said, it smelled so wonderful that she used it seldom and only the teensiest bit at a time. He stuck these things into various pockets to be smuggled home, talked with the clerk until another customer came in, and went back out to the street.

The thought struck him then that he might not get back to Hargrave before his ewes started to lamb, and he was out of whiskey. Tol always liked to keep a little whiskey on hand during lambing. Some sheepmen would say that if you had a weak lamb and a bottle of whiskey, it paid better to knock the lamb in the head and drink the whiskey yourself. But Tol believed that "a drop or two," on a bitter night, would sometimes encourage a little heart to continue beating—as, despite his religion and Miss Minnie, he believed it had sometimes encouraged bigger ones to do.

And so, without giving the matter much thought, he went to the drugstore where he was used to buying the occasional half-pint that he needed. And then, as he entered the door, he thought, "Prohibition!" And then he thought, "Well, no harm in trying."

So he went up to the druggist, whom he knew, who was leaning against a wall of shelves behind the counter in the back.

"I don't reckon you could let me have half a pint of whiskey," Tol said to him in a low voice.

"Medicinal?" the druggist asked.

"Medicinal," Tol said, nodding.

The druggist handed him a half-pint bottle, and Tol stuck it into his pocket and paid. It was a local brand known as Old Darling—a leftover, Tol supposed.

The druggist, also a conversationalist, said, "Somebody a little under the weather?"

"No," Tol said. "Lambs. I like to have a little on hand when I'm lambing."

There followed an exchange of some length in which Tol and the druggist told each other a number of things that both of them already knew.

When he was back at the livery stable, hitching Redbird to the buggy, Tol remembered the bottle and tossed it onto the floor of the buggy box under the seat, thinking not much about it one way or another.

Redbird, well rested and fed and now going in his favorite direction, required a good bit of attention at first. They were across the bridge and well out into the country again before he settled down. When he settled down, Tol settled down, too, and so did Miss Minnie. The interests and pleasures of the town were all behind them, the trip had fulfilled its purposes, and now they had ahead of them only the long drive home and their evening chores, which would seem a little strange after their day in town. Tol drove with his eye on Redbird and the road ahead, humming to himself in a grunty, tuneless way that meant, Miss Minnie knew, that he had gone way off among his thoughts and no longer knew she was there. "Mr. Proudfoot," she had actually said to him once, "when you are thinking you might as well be asleep."

That made him laugh, for he enjoyed a good joke on himself. But it was true. Sometimes, in his thoughts, he departed from where he was.

Tol and Miss Minnie had been married for twelve years. In that time they had found how secret their lives had been before. They had made many small discoveries that were sometimes exciting, sometimes not. One of the best had been Tol's discovery that Miss Minnie could whistle.

Though he had known a whistling woman or two in his time, he had always known also the proverb holding that

> *These will come to no good end:*
> *A whistling woman and a crowing hen,*

and he assumed that Miss Minnie, who had quality, would be the last woman on earth to whistle. Imagine his surprise, then, not long after they were married, when he was going by the house one morning and overheard Miss Minnie rattling the breakfast dishes and whistling "Old Joe Clark" as prettily and effortlessly as a songbird.

That night after supper, when they were sitting together by the fire, he said to her, "Go ahead. Whistle. I know you can do it. I heard you."

So she whistled for him—"Soldier's Joy" this time. It was a secret revelation. It made them so gleeful she could hardly control her pucker.

And now I am going to tell about the more famous revelation by which Miss Minnie learned Tol's method of reviving a weak lamb.

Tol had been humming and thinking only a little while when Miss Minnie needed to blow her nose. Her handkerchief was in her purse, which she had set behind her heels under the seat of the buggy. She fished under the lap robe with her hand to bring it up and so encountered the cold hard shape of Tol's half-pint bottle of Old Darling. It was a shape that, as an avid student of the problem of drunkenness, she knew very well. Thereupon a suspicion flew into her mind—as sudden and dark as a bat this suspicion was, and as hard to ignore in such close quarters.

She felt the bottle again to make sure, and then stealthily drew it up to the light on the side opposite Tol, and looked at it. At the sight of it, she could have wept and cried out with anger and with bitter, bitter disappointment. The label carried the seductive name of Old Darling, and it declared shamelessly that the bottle contained whiskey, ninety proof. That the amber liquid inside the bottle was actually rather beautiful to the eye did not surprise her, for she knew that the devil made sin attractive.

She almost flung the bottle into the roadside weeds right there and then, but two thoughts prevented her. First, she imagined that if the bottle did not hit a rock and break, then some innocent boy or young man might come along and find it and be tempted to drink the whiskey, and that would not do. Second — and perhaps this thought was not even second, for her mind was working fast — she remembered that whiskey was an expensive product. When she thought, "It would be a shame to waste it," she meant of course the money that Tol had spent for the whiskey, not the whiskey itself.

But she did think, "It would be a shame to waste it," and the thought put her in a quandary. For if she did not want to throw the whiskey away, neither did she want to put it back under the seat to be carried home and drunk by her wayward husband, from the mystery of whose being this bottle had emerged.

And now Miss Minnie's mind revolved in a curious metamorphosis from the great virtue of thriftiness to the much smaller virtue of romantic self-sacrifice. Her anger and disappointment at Tol as she now had discovered him to be only increased her love for him as she had thought him to be — and as he might, in fact, become, if only she could save him from his addiction to the evil drug that she at that moment held in her hand. For such a man as he *might* be, she felt, she would do anything. She had read much of loyalties given and sacrifices made by the wives of drinking men. In her love for Tol, she had at times already wished to be capable of some legendary fidelity or sacrifice to make her worthy of her happiness in him. And by how much now was this wish magnified by her thought of Tol fallen and redeemed! "Oh," she thought, "I will do it! I will say to the world I did it without hesitation." She shifted as she might have shifted if she had wanted to look at something interesting off to the right-hand side of the road.

She broke the paper seal and twisted out the cork. She put her nose carefully over the opening and sniffed the vile fumes. *"Awful!"* she thought. And the thought of its awfulness made her sacrifice more pleasing to her. She tilted the bottle and drew forth bravely half a mouthful and swallowed it.

It was fire itself in her throat. If she had looked quickly enough, she thought, she would have seen a short orange flame protruding from her nose. Though she sternly suppressed the impulse to cough, there was no refusing the tears that filled her eyes.

But then as the fiery swallow descended into her stomach, a most pleasing warmth, a warmth at once calming and invigorating, began to radiate from it. For a few minutes she bestowed upon this warmth the meditation that it seemed to require, and then she tried another swallow, a more wholehearted one. The effect this time was less harsh, because less surprising, and the radiance even warmer and more reassuring than before. She felt strangely ennobled by the third, as if the rewards of her sacrifice were already accruing to her. The radiance within her had begun to gleam also in a sort of nimbus around her. If the devil made sin attractive, then she would have to admit that he had done a splendid job with Old Darling.

She sat half turned away from Tol, and leaning back so that she sat also a little behind him. He was still departed in his thoughts, no more aware of what she was doing than were the occupants of the occasional buggies and wagons that they met.

Miss Minnie sipped from time to time as they drove along, finding her sacrifice not nearly so difficult as she had expected. In fact, she was amazed at how quickly she was getting rid of the repulsive contents of the bottle. It occurred to her that perhaps she should drink more slowly, for soon there would be none left.

Suddenly she experienced a motion that recalled her to her school days when she had swung in swings and ridden on seesaws. But the likeness was only approximate, for Redbird, the buggy, the road, and indeed the whole landscape had just executed a motion not quite like any she had ever known.

"Whoo!" said Miss Minnie.

Tol had been humming along, figuring and refiguring how much he might get for his crop in view of the various speculations and surmises he had heard in town. When Miss Minnie said "Whoo!" it was news to him. "What?" he said.

"Do that again," she said. "Oh! Whoo!"

He said, "What?"

"Old Darling," she said. "Whoo!"

"Mam?" Tol Proudfoot said.

And then he saw the bottle in her hand. For a moment he thought he was going to laugh, and then he thought he wasn't. "Oh, Lordy!" he said. "Oh, Lordy Lord! Oh, Lord!"

Now as they went around a curve in the road they met another couple in a buggy. Miss Minnie leaned forward and called out to them momentously the name of Gallagher. "A vote for Gallagher," she cried, "is a vote for the little man!"

"Come up, Redbird," said Tol Proudfoot.

But as luck would have it, speeding up only brought them more quickly face-to-face with the next buggy coming down the road.

"Gallagher!" cried Miss Minnie. "A fair shake for the little man is a fair shake for the little woman!"

"Miss Minnie," Tol said, "I believe you've had about all you need of that."

He held out his hand for the bottle, and was surprised to see, when she handed it to him, how little was left.

"Take it, then!" she said. "Drunkard!"

"Drunkard?" he said, and then put out his hand again to steady her, for she was attempting to stand up, the better to point her finger at him. "No, mam. I'm not no drunkard. You know better."

"Then *what*," Miss Minnie said, pointing to the incontrovertible evidence, "were you doing with *that*?"

"Lambs," Tol said.

"You get little lambs drunk," Miss Minnie declared. "Oh, my dear man, you are the limit."

"For when they're born on the cold nights," Tol said. "Sometimes it'll help the weak ones live."

"Ha!" said Miss Minnie.

Tol said no more. Miss Minnie spoke only to urge Gallagher upon the people they met — though, fortunately, they met only a few.

By the time they went through Port William, she had ceased to call out, but she was saying in a rather loud voice and to nobody in particular that though she was not sure, she was sure the Gallagher boy had never taken a drink in *his* life — and though she was not sure, she was sure that *he* at least understood that now that women had the vote, there would be no more liquor drinking in the land of the free and the home of the brave. Her voice quivered patriotically.

When they drove in beside the house at last, and Redbird gladly stopped in front of the buggy shed, Tol stepped down and turned to help Miss Minnie, who stood, somewhat grandly spurning his offer, and fell directly into his arms.

Tol carried her to the house, helped her to remove her hat and coat and to lie down on the sofa in the living room. He covered her with the afghan, built up the fire, and returned to the barn to do his chores.

The house was dark when he came back in. Miss Minnie was lying quietly on the sofa with her forearm resting across her brow. Tol tiptoed in and sat down.

After a little while, Miss Minnie said, "Was it really just for the lambs?"

Tol said, "Yessum."

And then Miss Minnie's crying jag began. Regrets flew at her from all sides, and she wept and wept. Of all her sorrows the worst was for her suspicion of Tol. But she mourned also, for his sake and her own, the public display that she had made of herself. "I surely am the degradedest woman who ever lived," she said. "I have shamed myself, and most of all you."

Tol sat beside her for a long time in the dark, patting her with his big hand and saying, "Naw, now. Naw, now. You didn't do no such of a thing."

It was, as Miss Minnie would later say, a lovely time.

When at last she grew quiet and sleepy, Tol helped her to bed and waited beside her until her breath came in little snores. And then he went down to the kitchen and cooked himself a good big supper, for it had been a hard day.

This was, oddly, a tale that Miss Minnie enjoyed telling. "It was my only binge," she would say, giggling a little. And she liked especially to quote herself: "I surely am the degradedest woman who ever lived."

She said, "Mr. Proudfoot was horrified. But after it was over, he just had to rear back and laugh. Oh, he was a man of splendid qualities!"

The Lost Bet (1929)

After Ptolemy Proudfoot and Miss Minnie bought their Model A and partly quit using their buggy, they got around in the neighborhood more than they used to. But only a little more. Tol was never the master of the Model A that he was of a horse; if the car increased by a little bit the frequency of their going about, it increased their range almost not at all — except once, which is another story. For Tol and Miss Minnie, the Model A was an experiment — the only one they ever made — and it did not completely replace their horse and buggy, which Tol kept and continued to use for shorter trips until his death. He *liked* horses better than he liked the Model A, and he drove them better, too.

Before and after the advent of the Model A, Tol and Miss Minnie lived their lives almost entirely within a radius of about six miles. They cleaned up after dinner every Saturday and drove to Port William to take their cream and eggs, and to buy the few things they needed that they did not grow or make for themselves. All their business never took more than an hour, but they made an afternoon of it, visiting and talking with everybody else who had come in for the same purposes, and always getting back home in plenty of time to milk and feed.

On Sunday morning they went down the hill to the Goforth church, usually going back again for the evening services. And once a month Miss Minnie attended the all-day meeting of the Missionary Society. And that was most of their going, except when they went to a wedding or a funeral or to a neighbor's house to visit or help with the work.

And except for an occasional trip, which Tol sometimes made alone, to Hargrave or to the stockyards in Louisville. He sold his tobacco at Hargrave, where there was also a small stockyard. But Tol was a pretty shrewd businessman, and when he had enough stock to justify the haulage — as when he shipped his lambs in June, and his finished steers in November — he liked to try the market at the Bourbon Stockyards in Louisville. The prices were noticeably better there than at Hargrave, but that was not all the reason. The rest of it was that Tol enjoyed making the trip with Sam Hanks, the trucker who hauled the stock. And Sam Hanks found it necessary to admit that he enjoyed making the trip with Tol. Sam Hanks was Miss Minnie's favorite nephew, a lean, seldom-speaking man, who might go all day and not speak ten words, just doing his work and watching and being amused. He was a little amused at whatever happened — at least in his younger days. His major amusements were baseball and Tol. Over the years he collected a lot of stories about Tol, and he liked to tell them.

Tol would be up long before daylight on the appointed day, getting the steers or the lambs penned and ready to load. And then he would feed and milk and eat breakfast and clean up, so as to be ready when, maybe still before daylight, Sam's truck would rattle up the driveway past the house into the barn lot, and back up to the loading chute.

Tol was a fellow who was neat as a pin in all his work, but who was to about the same degree careless of his own appearance. His little farm was almost as clean and orderly as Miss Minnie's kitchen, which was immaculate. When he drove his team to the field they were as well groomed and harnessed as if he were driving them to town. And he used a plow or a mowing machine as precisely as some people use a comb. But he wore his clothes, as Sam Hanks said, the way a hog wears mud.

When he left the house to load his stock, he would be as clean and neat as Miss Minnie's repeated instructions and inspections could make him. He would be washed and shaved and combed, dressed in his best everyday clothes, which would be spotless, as stiff with starch as if made of tin. By the time the stock were loaded, all the creases would be criss-crossed with wrinkles; there would be mud and manure on his shoes and britches and maybe on his shirt; he would have a loose cuff or suspender; after much head scratching, his cap or hat would be on crooked and some stray swatch of hair would be hanging in his eyes or sticking out over one ear.

After they got to the stockyards and got unloaded, Tol followed a procedure that in its general outlines never varied. And Sam always went along in a state of alert expectancy, because in its details it was never twice the same. Say it was in the fall. They would go back through the yards to where Tol's steers were penned, and lean against the gate to wait for the buyers to come around. But it wasn't just the buyers, Sam knew, that Tol was waiting for. Tol always had good steers — good in their individual quality, uniform as a lot, and well finished, showing a lot of bloom — and he liked to hear them praised. And so he stood there, leaning proprietarily against the gate, watching the drovers and the commission men and the farmers go by. And when one of them stopped to look into the pen at Tol's cattle, Tol would look at him in such a way that the fellow nearly always asked, "Those your steers?"

And Tol would say, "*Yessir!*" as if it ought to have been obvious.

And then the fellow would say something like "Mighty nice" or "Well, they're the right kind."

And Tol would say, "*Yessir!*" in a way that showed he knew the fellow had made pretty much of an understatement — which sometimes caused the fellow to try to say something even better and more intelligent about the cattle, and sometimes did not.

If it did not, Tol would turn the conversation to the subject of the fellow himself — what his name was, where he was from, whom he had married, how his family was, how much rain he'd had, how his crops had turned off, and so on. Tol loved that kind of visiting, and he talked to everybody he met whether the body in question wanted to be talked to or not. Sam followed these conversations with as much interest as he followed baseball. The thing was that Tol mostly liked everybody, and because he liked them he was genuinely interested in everything about them, and he pumped information out of them, Sam figured, that would be news to their wives. Tol never forgot them or anything he learned about them, and he was always glad to see them when he met them again. He had got acquainted with a lot of people in this way. But Sam knew that on these trips, because they were his adventures, Tol much preferred strangers to acquaintances.

When the cattle were sold and the talking was finished, they went to the office for their checks. Except for the few times when Tol thought his stock had been graded too low, Sam never heard him complain about the size of his check. He appeared to accept it simply as the necessary completion of a business in which he had ceased to have any live interest the moment the cattle ceased to belong to him.

And then Tol would invite Sam to be his guest at a certain saloon where, if it was fall, they would eat fried oysters, which Tol loved. The meal lasted an hour or two. They stood at the bar and ate, and Tol talked to whatever stranger happened to be standing next to him. Now, for Sam, the quality of the interest changed, for here Tol was less likely to be talking to a farmer and more likely to be talking to some city fellow who would not appreciate a stranger's interest in his personal affairs. Sam had seen Tol get into some pretty tough spots. He was never sure that Tol ever realized that he was in a tough spot when he was in one; and Tol always got out of whatever tough spot he was in, and he never got out of it either by fighting or by shutting up. It was better than baseball, when Sam could maintain his detachment; when he couldn't, it was worse.

After the oysters, Tol would always have something or other he wanted to buy that he couldn't buy closer to home. And even if it wasn't but one thing, shopping for it would take exactly all the rest of the time they had.

The time I am going to tell you about, Tol was looking for navy beans. He and Miss Minnie always grew a big garden and put up most of the stuff they needed, but something they never tried to grow was navy beans. And so one of Tol's regular fall chores was to buy a two-bushel bag of them, which was usually enough to see them through the winter — some to keep and some to give away, according to the first rule of the Proudfoot household.

This year, Tol had found no navy beans in Port William and none in Hargrave. And so he made them the business of his and Sam's annual cattle-selling trip to Louisville. Sam followed him through the Haymarket, a couple of steps behind, picking his teeth, watching Tol with the patient interest with which a man already satisfied awaits further satisfaction.

Navy beans were scarce in Louisville, too, it turned out, for Tol visited all the likely places he knew without luck, and then they worked their way out into strange territory.

They finally went into a store that was not the sort of feed-and-seed establishment usually patronized by farmers, but a grocery store obviously set up to cater to the city trade — and, by the look of it, prosperous. There was a long wall of shelves full of canned goods, and a long counter in front of that, and in front of that a long row of wire baskets of fresh produce: potatoes, turnips, parsnips, eggs, cabbages, apples, and pears. In the back there were three fellows in suits — drummers, Sam thought — standing by a big iron stove, for it was cold that day. And behind the counter, talking to them, was a dapper fellow with a round face and round eyeglasses, his hair parted in the middle, garters on his sleeves, and a cigar in his mouth.

When Tol walked in with Sam behind him, the drummers and the clerk quit talking and looked. And they kept on looking. By that time, Sam said, Tol had been beyond the reach and influence of Miss Minnie long enough to look unusual. He looked as tall and wide as the door. He wore a sheepskin coat, unbuttoned, that flared out at the back and sides, giving the impression of great forward momentum. Half his shirttail was out. The bill of his next-best winter cap hovered between his right eye and his right ear. His britches legs were stuffed into the top of a pair of gum boots plastered with manure. He had bought a big sack of hard candy as a gift for Miss Minnie, and the twisted neck of the sack now stuck out as though he carried a setting goose in his pocket.

The three drummers and the proprietor looked at Tol. They watched him come back through the store, and then the drummers looked at each other and grinned. The proprietor watched Tol until he stopped and faced him across the counter.

"What can I do for you, Otis?" the proprietor asked. He never cracked a smile, but he gave the drummers just the slightest little wink, and the drummers chuckled.

None of them saw the look that crossed Tol's face, drawing one eye just a fraction of an inch narrower than the other, and if they had seen it they probably wouldn't have known what to make of it. But Sam, who was hanging back near the door, did see it, and did know what to make of it, and he made himself comfortable against the doorjamb and folded his arms.

Tol's eyes were set under bristly brows, and were much wrinkled at the corners. Mostly there was great candor in them; you could look through them right into his mind. But sometimes you could not see into his mind. At such times, thinking was going on in there that Tol didn't want anybody to find out about. When Tol thought, Sam Hanks said, he looked like he wasn't thinking at all; he looked like he was listening to a low rumble in his guts. And that was the way he looked for maybe about three seconds after the proprietor called him "Otis." And then, as if suddenly remembering where he was, he looked back at the proprietor.

"Two bushel of navy beans, if you go 'em, please, sir," said Ptolemy Proudfoot. If they had known their man, the proprietor and the drummers might have heard a very precise comment in the way Tol said "sir," but they missed that, too.

"I don't customarily sell them by the bushel, Timothy," the proprietor said, "but I believe I can let you have them."

"I'd be mightily obliged," said Tol.

The proprietor walked to a door in the back and called, "A bag of navy beans for Mr. Wheatly here."

Every time he called Tol by a new name, he glanced at the drummers, who seemed to be appreciating his wit a great deal, for they were grinning and nudging each other and whispering. And Sam appreciated it, too, in his way, for he knew, as they did not, that they were watching a contest.

A colored fellow came through the door in the back with the bag of beans on a hand truck and stood the bag up beside Tol.

The proprietor beat a little drumbeat on the edge of the counter with his hands. "Will that be all for you today, Mr. Bulltrack?"

"Well, I believe so," Tol said. "How much, if you please, sir?"

The proprietor told him, and Tol began grabbling in his pocket. He held his suspenders with one hand and grabbled with the other, and finally drew out clenched in his fist an assortment of wadded bills, some coins, half a cut plug, a pocketknife, and the last three inches of a pencil. He made order of all this on one large stretched-out palm, and laid the price of the beans a bill or a coin at a time on the counter in front of the proprietor, the exact amount. And then he poked around in his hand and came up with a quarter.

He smiled over at the proprietor. "Ever see one of them disappear? I can make that disappear."

"Why, you're a magician, too, are you, Mr. Briarly?" the proprietor said, winking at the drummers. "Let me see."

Tol made a violent jerk with his right hand that sent the coin bouncing to the floor between two baskets of produce. He got down, grunting, onto his hands and knees and laboriously retrieved it. The drummers were laughing out loud now, and the proprietor's face had begun to wear the smile of the successful host.

"He'd done lost me," Sam would say later when he would tell the story. "Looked like he was *trying* to make a fool of himself. I thought, 'Now what?'"

"Well, you made it disappear, all right," the proprietor said.

"Wait a minute," Tol said, coming up with the quarter. "Watch it this time."

He made the same jerk, and sent the quarter spinning under the stove, and crawled after it. The drummers were holding onto themselves.

"Well, that ain't all the tricks I can do," Tol said. "I'll bet you this quarter I can jump into that basket of eggs and not break a one."

"Well, Spud, old boy, I'll just bet you can't," said the proprietor. And then he caught that look in Tol's eye that Sam had been watching all along, and his own eyes got wide. "Wup," he said.

He was too late. His lips had just shut on that little "wup" when Tol leapt into the air as light as a fox and came down with both feet in the basket of eggs. There was a loud crunch that totaled up the breaking of many small shells, and a viscous puddle began to spread slowly around the basket.

Tol's light leap and heavy descent were funny, Sam told me, but nobody laughed.

"Didn't you laugh?" I asked him.

"Hell, naw!" he said. "I was trying to act like I was there by myself. It was as quiet as a church with nobody in it. It was as quiet as a graveyard at midnight."

Tol stood in the basket of broken eggs with what Sam described as "a sweet, innocent smile," holding his quarter out to the proprietor. "Well, you got me. Dogged if you ain't a hard man to get ahead of."

The proprietor stood looking at Tol's quarter with his mouth open. "And then," Sam told me, "I swan if that fellow didn't reach out, still not quite able to get his mouth to shut, and take that quarter and put it in his pocket."

Tol stepped out of the basket, shouldered his sack of beans, and walked to the door, which Sam was holding open.

I heard Sam Hanks tell the story in town one July afternoon, and the next time I stopped by to see Miss Minnie, it occurred to me to ask her if she had ever heard it.

She had, of course. And she told it much as Sam had told it, but a good deal shorter. She was sitting in her rocker in the kitchen of the little house where she and Tol had passed the time their lives had been joined together. Now, their lives put asunder, Miss Minnie told the story with the mixture of approval and amusement with which she usually remembered Tol. When she finished the telling, she laughed. And then she sat in silence, reflecting, I knew, on the opposing claims of charity and justice in the story, and on the conflict of extravagance and gentleness in Tol's character. The late sun threw a patch of warm light on the wall behind her. The clock ticked.

"Mr. Proudfoot was that way," she said, and smiled. "But he was half sorry just as soon as he did it."

Thicker than Liquor (1930)

When the telephone rang, Wheeler Catlett was thinking about his future. Not that he knew much about it. The future was going to surprise him, as it had surprised all his mothers and fathers before him, but he had hopes. He had come back from his eastern law school four years ago, set himself up as a lawyer in two upstairs rooms overlooking the courthouse square in Hargrave, and increased his yearly income from nearly nothing to almost a living, with prospects for improvement. And now he was a married man with a future that needed thinking about.

Between his own hard times and those of the nation, Wheeler had grown familiar with the scarcity of money—indeed, as the son of a struggling small farmer, he had never known an abundance of it—and the present year of drouth and depression certainly offered no promise of financial astonishment. But he had worked hard, been careful, paid attention, lost no time, wasted nothing, and in spite of the hard times, he now and again had a few small bills to rub together. And that was partly what he was thinking about: the heartwarming friction of one piece of legal tender against another. These were not thoughts that could be considered mercenary; he had no yearning for mere money in a pile. He was thirty years old, he had been married just under a month, and money, for him, was as symbolic as it should be. His need for it tended as much toward substantiality as did his love for his bride. He was thinking about a home of his own, a place of his own. He liked his thoughts—which were, in fact, visions of Bess as happy as she deserved to be — and that was why he let the phone ring three times before he answered.

"I'm trying to get hold of Mr. Wheeler Catlett."

"This is Wheeler Catlett speaking."

"Mr. Catlett, this is the desk at the Stag Hotel in Louisville. We have a message for you from Mr. Leonidas Wheeler, who is staying here."

"Well, what's the message?"

"He says to tell you that he's sick, and he has no way to get home."

"Is he drunk?"

"I'm afraid so, sir. And, ah, his situation with respect to his bill appears to be somewhat embarrassing."

"I'll bet it is." Wheeler looked at his watch. "All right. I'll be there as soon as I can."

He hung up, and then rang and asked for his home number.

"Hello," Bess said.

"Would this be the beautiful young widder Catlett?"

"Herself. What did he die of?"

"Love, of course."

"For me?"

"For you."

"Well, wasn't that sweet!"

"Bess, my star client, Uncle Peach, requires my services at Louisville."

"Oh goodness! Is Uncle Peach having one of his attacks?"

"He's about down to the lower side of one, it sounds like. I don't know when I'll be home."

"I'll expect you when I see you?"

"I'm afraid so, Bess. I'm sorry."

"I'll miss you. Give my love to Uncle Peach."

"I don't think I will," Wheeler said.

When he had hung up, he sat still for a minute to think, and then he counted the few doomed bills that he had in his wallet.

Wheeler's earliest associations with Uncle Peach were among his privileges. In those days, when he was sober, and Wheeler only knew him sober in those days, Uncle Peach was a good-looking, good-humored man who could be charmingly attentive to a small boy. He was the first man Wheeler wanted to be like when he grew up.

"What do you want to be when you grow up?" his father asked him. It was after supper, and Wheeler was sitting in his father's lap by the kitchen stove.

"I want to be like Uncle Peach."

His father laughed. "Well, I'll be damned! You do, do you?"

And his mother said quietly, "Marce."

And then one night — it must not have been long after that, Wheeler must not have been more than five — he was waked up by a commotion in the house, and when he went to see what it was, he met his mother coming out of the spare bedroom, carrying a lamp.

"Go back to bed. Uncle Peach is sick."

"What's he got?"

"He's having one of his spells. Go back to bed, now, like I told you."

But he did not go back to bed. He went into the spare room where his mother had left Uncle Peach.

Uncle Peach had all his clothes off down to his underwear. "Hello, Wheeler boy," he said. "Uncle Peach is sick. Uncle Peach been going at a fast pace through the thorns and thistles that the ground has brought forth." And then he said, "*Oh*, me!"

Uncle Peach was standing in the middle of the floor, aiming at the bed, his feet wandering here and there and the rest of him staying mainly still.

"It's coming around!" he said. And he watched the bed and said again, "It's coming around!"

He made a mighty leap then toward the bed, but it was coming around too fast and he missed. He landed in the corner by the washstand, and lay there the way he fell, with his arms and legs strewn around him. Wheeler's mother came running back into the room. "Oh, Peach!" she said, in a way Wheeler had never heard her talk before. "What is ever to become of you?"

And Uncle Peach said, "Sing 'Yellow Rose o' Texas' to me, madam."

Uncle Peach was Dorie Catlett's trial. He was her baby brother. Their mother died when Peach was born, when Dorie, the oldest child, was thirteen. Their father never remarried. The story was that Andrew Wheeler had to take Peach to the field with him to plow when Peach was still a baby in arms. Andrew would take off his coat at the field edge, and spread it on the ground with his purse and all his money in one of its pockets and Peach asleep on top of it. Andrew's brother, James, would say later that if a thief had stolen Peach and all the money and left the coat, Andrew would have had the best of the trade. That was a story that Wheeler had often heard his mother tell. And she always quoted Uncle James and laughed, and then said, "Hmh!" not in refusal, Wheeler thought, but simply in dismissal; it was a judgment that she understood but did not find possible. She had had much of the raising of Peach, and he was her failure, or so she felt.

He never married, for the reason, according to him, that he could never accomplish a short courtship; no woman who came to know him well enough to make up her mind about him would make it up in his favor. And so his dependence on Dorie continued. He was always departing from her in a spirit of high resolve, going off, a new man, to seek his fortune, and always returning to her failed, drunk, sick, and broke, to be nursed to sobriety and health again, and reinfused with the notion that he was master of a better fate than available evidence encouraged even her to expect. He was her trial because she let him be, because she loved him and would not give him up.

He was Marce's trial for the opposite reason. Marce did not love him. He was constrained to be kind to him without benefit of love. He tolerated him, was patient with him, even helped him so far as he was able, for Dorie's sake, and for the sake of principle, but he found no excuse for him, and he gave up on him on fairly short acquaintance.

As a child, Wheeler was soon aware of his father's judgment and his mother's grief, and after the time when he wanted to be like Uncle Peach there was a time when he held him in gleeful contempt. Once, when Uncle Peach had come in drunk, and eaten, and fallen asleep in his chair, his head tilted back and his mouth open, Wheeler and Andrew his older brother took the pepper shaker and half filled Uncle Peach's mouth with pepper, and Uncle Peach woke up after a while and said, "I feel like I'm going to sneeze!"

That was the last time Uncle Peach came to the house drunk. There must have been words between him and Marce about it, because after that Uncle Peach came sober and he came sick, but he did not come drunk.

When he worked, which was far from all the time, Uncle Peach was a carpenter, and for a while he was known as a good one. His failing in his younger years was merely infidelity. He was absolutely dependable as long as his pockets were empty. Money made him thirsty; once he got thirsty, he left; and then there was no getting him back until he had passed through flight, gallantry, drunkenness, devastation, and convalescence.

He was never a fast worker, but in his ponderous way, by much deliberation and some trial and error, he was capable of working well. People who were not in a hurry liked to hire him, for he cheapened his work in accordance with his own estimate of his faults, he was easy to get along with — was good company, in fact — and in the long run, if they had time for the long run, he satisfied his employers.

Later, as hopelessness and carelessness and perplexity grew upon him, his work became rougher. He declined gradually in public esteem until nobody would hire him to build a house, and declined further until nobody would hire him to build a barn. He became finally an odd-jobs man, a mender of leaky roofs, an overhauler of small outbuildings. He lost such habits of neatness and order as he had ever had, and worked in the midst of steadily increasing confusion. Whatever he was done with, for the day or the moment, he dropped wherever he was, until he built under his feet a sort of midden of lumber, scraps, and tools, in which whatever he needed at any given moment was lost.

In his puzzlement, he fell into the habit of talking to himself. He would go lurching and stumbling, sweating and puffing among the shambles of his work, picking up scraps and tools in one place, flinging them out of the way only to increase the disorder someplace else, muttering all the while to himself in steady commentary on his problem: "Now *where* did I put that damned saw? Did I lay it under here? No, sir. Did I lay it over *there*? No, sir." Sometimes what he was looking for was in plain sight. Sometimes it was in his hand.

Once, when he was about fifteen, Wheeler watched Uncle Peach try to untangle a hundred feet of inch rope. Instead of imposing order on the tangle, he became more and more involved in it, until finally, trying to take up a length that was looped around his foot, he fell into the midst of it. What most impressed Wheeler at the time was that Uncle Peach

was not embarrassed. He seemed too implicated in his clumsiness even
to be aware of it. It was Wheeler who was embarrassed. Uncle Peach lay
on his back, toiling like Laocoön among the interloopings of the rope,
and Wheeler was astonished. It took him a year to see that it was funny.

And still, when Uncle Peach was down and sick and needed help,
Dorie would help him. She would put him in bed in the spare room at
home. Or he would send for her, and Marce would drive her in the
buggy the ten miles to Uncle Peach's little farm over by Floyd's Station.
The farm had been partly Marce's idea. He had encouraged and then
helped Uncle Peach to buy it. It was the sort of place, Marce thought,
that could put a sound footing under a tradesman's economy. And he
probably thought too, or so Wheeler guessed, that the ten miles would
put Uncle Peach out of the way. But if that was what he thought, he was
mistaken; the distance was too short for impossibility and too long for
convenience.

Seeing how his mother troubled herself with Uncle Peach and
mourned over him, Wheeler said, bullying her in her own defense as a
seventeen-year-old boy is apt to do, "To hell with him! Why don't you let
him get on by himself the best way he can? What's he done for you?"

Dorie answered his first question, ignoring the second: "Because
blood is thicker than water."

And Wheeler said, mocking her, "Blood is thicker than liquor."

"Yes," she said. "Thicker than liquor too."

The day was warm and clear, the sky an immaculate brilliance. The
brighter leaves had all fallen, leaving only the oaks still darkly red or
brown. After the long summer of drouth, there had been rain through
the fall, and now the pastures were green. Wheeler had planned to end
the day outdoors with his dog and gun. It was a day for which there were
many better uses than the present one, and Wheeler was full of the bitterness of waste and loss. "Why don't I just leave the old son of a bitch
down there?" he asked himself, driving too fast down the gravel road, a
long white cloud of dust blooming behind him. And though he knew
very well why, the question seemed to remain unanswered.

He wanted to be done with ordeals. The summer had been an ordeal.
One hot, rainless day had followed another while pastures withered,

crops parched, and ponds and springs went dry. Marce Catlett kept his stock alive by hauling water in barrels from the one spring that stayed constant. He hauled load after load, day after day, dipping the water out of the walled basin of the spring with a bucket. When he could leave the office early enough, Wheeler would drive up to help him, to ease the work a little and to keep him company.

One afternoon, when they had watered the cattle and were watching them drink, Marce looked at his son and smiled. "Awful, ain't it?"

"Yes," Wheeler said, and he did think so. Another merciless day was ending, the sun glared on the burnt world, the cattle were poor, the grass all but gone, and the sight depressed him.

"Well, I've seen dry years before this, and I'll tell you something. It's so miserable you think you'll never get over it. You're ready for the world to end. But it'll pass. There'll come a time when you won't think about it."

Marce raised his hat, ran his hand over his white hair, and put his hat back on, looking sideways, still smiling, at Wheeler.

They were sitting side by side on the edge of the wagon bed. The emptied barrels gleamed where water had spilled down their sides. All around them the late sunlight slanted brazenly over the greenless, dusty fields, and over the fly-covered backs of the lean steers. And Marce Catlett sat looking at his son with a light in his eye that came from another direction entirely, waiting to see if he saw.

It was a moment that would live with Wheeler for the rest of his life, for he saw his father then as he had at last grown old enough to see him, not only as he declared himself, but as he was. And in that seeing Wheeler became aware of a pattern, that his father both embodied and was embodied in, that also contained the drouth and made light of it, that contained other hardships also and made light of them. For his father's good work was on that place in a way that granted and collaborated in its own endurance, that had carried them thus far, and would carry them on. Looking at his father, Wheeler knew, and would not forget, that though they were surrounded by the marks and leavings of a bad year, they were surrounded also by the marks and leavings of good work, which for that year and any other proposed an end and a new beginning.

He slowed down as he entered the town of Langlay. In the center of town he turned off the main road, drove to the railroad station, and parked his car. He did not have long to wait to catch the interurban, and soon he was seated in a nearly empty car, looking out the windows at the farms and little towns as the rail joints clicked under the wheels.

It seemed to him that for the last hour he had been passing through the stages of an abandonment of his own will, working his way toward a leap past which his own wishes would be idle dreams. At each stage, it seemed to him, turning back had become less possible. Now, sliding down toward the city along the same tracks that Uncle Peach had followed days ago, it was easy for Wheeler to imagine himself telling the desk clerk, "I don't know anybody named Leonidas Wheeler." But he knew better than that. He knew that he had not passed the place of turning back that day, or that year. He may, he thought, have been born on the downhill side of it.

When Wheeler headed home from law school, he did not have Uncle Peach much in mind, one way or another. But when he arrived, there was Uncle Peach, older, grayer, worse for wear, traveling at a slower pace now among the thorns and thistles that the ground brought forth, but still on the same route. And Dorie was still seeing him through.

"Blood is thicker than liquor," Wheeler said to her, no longer mocking, but gently stating the fact as he knew she saw it.

"Yes," she said, and smiled. "It is."

And as he knew by then, she had more than that in mind. Uncle Peach was, she thought, "one of the least of these my brethren"—a qualification for her care that the blood connection only compounded. If one of the least of Christ's brethren happened to be her brother, then the obligation was as clear as the penalty. She had long ago given up hope for Uncle Peach. She cared for him without hope, because she had passed the place of turning back or looking back. Quietly, almost submissively, she propped herself against him, because in her fate and faith she was opposed to his ruin.

Marce, who was the most craftsmanly of farmers, the artist of his particular domain of earth and flesh, stood outside this push and pull of opposition. He was Uncle Peach's opposite, all right, but Marce could stand opposite without opposing. Dorie opposed Uncle Peach because she loved him. Wheeler had opposed him, so far, because he was affronted by him. Marce merely maintained his difference. He was a man of simple preferences and complex abilities — a better carpenter, for instance, in answer to his own occasional need to be one, than Uncle Peach had ever been. He simply knew what he desired, and worked toward it with whatever means he had, without fuss. Not having inherited Uncle Peach, he patiently tolerated as much of him as he thought tolerable. The rest he ignored.

Wheeler, who loved his father and liked his ways, assumed that he thought and felt as his father did. But Wheeler loved his mother too, and so he inherited Uncle Peach. When he returned home, Uncle Peach devolved upon him.

When the train stopped, Wheeler stepped off so quickly that he did not stop. He went through the station to the street, and set off on foot for the hotel, too impatient to wait for a streetcar. He went through the Haymarket, stepping past boxes and bags and bins and baskets of produce, crates of eggs, chickens in cages along the edge of the sidewalk. And then, the street opening in front of him again, free of encumbrances, he went on toward the stockyards and its satellite businesses and shops catering to the needs and the weaknesses of country people.

He came to the hotel, a turreted corner building of dingy elegance, with its name in white block letters on windows and door, went in, and stopped and let the door shut behind him. He stopped because at that point he had come to a place he would never have come to on his own. He had been there before, for the same reason, and the lobby was familiar to him: the white tiled floor mopped with dirty water, the black wainscoting, the hard chairs pushed back to the walls, the spittoons gaping up at the pressed-metal ceiling — a room meager and stark from the expectation of hard use. In the chairs a few men merely sat, as they had been sitting, so far as Wheeler could tell, when he was there last.

Behind the desk, the clerk stood leaning against a wall of pigeonholes, reading a newspaper. When Wheeler crossed the lobby and stopped at the desk, it seemed to him that he came to the end of the slant he had been on; now he spoke the words that sent him, like a diver, into the air: "Mr. Leonidas Wheeler?"

"Oh," the clerk said, looking up and folding his paper, "you must be Mr. Catlett." He fingered his ledger.

"What's his bill?"

The clerk named the sum, and Wheeler paid.

"Thank you very much, sir."

And then the clerk spoke to a Negro porter who was mopping the floor in the hallway off the lobby: "Take him up. Mr. Wheeler's room."

"This way, sir," the porter said, and led the way to the elevator in long, pushing strides. He held the door for Wheeler, and then shut it, and they started up.

"You Mr. Wheeler's kinfolks?" the porter asked over the bumping and groaning of the elevator.

"I'm his nephew."

The porter gave a somewhat embarrassed laugh, as unwilling to intrude as to leave Wheeler unwarned. "Mr. Wheeler done got hisself plumb down."

Before the elevator even reached the floor where Uncle Peach's room was, Wheeler could hear him roaring. "Oh ho ho ho!" he was saying. "Oh, Lord! Oh, me! Oh ho ho ho ho!"

Wheeler glanced at the porter, who smiled obligingly and said, "He been doing that quite some time."

When they unlocked the door and went in, Uncle Peach never even heard them. It was a tiny room, its one window looking out at a blank wall across an alley, and it was as much a shambles as one man could have made it without the use of tools. The room's one table and chair were turned over on the floor. Uncle Peach's pants, shirt, shoes, socks, necktie, coat, and hat were scattered all over it. Bedclothes and pillows had been flung off the bed in several directions. Beside the sagging bed was a wastebasket that Uncle Peach had attempted to vomit into, but missed. Uncle Peach was lying on the bed under a blanket with his feet sticking out, his face a mess, his eyes shut tight, still hollering.

"Be still, Uncle Peach!" Wheeler said sharply.

Uncle Peach instantly quieted down.

"Huh?" he said. "Who is it?"

"It's Wheeler. What in the world have you done to yourself?"

"You know damned good and well what I've done to myself."

"I got your message," Wheeler said. "Are you ready to go home?"

Uncle Peach groaned. He lay still a moment. And then he opened his eyes and looked at Wheeler. He cleared his throat. "I'm ready, Wheeler boy, but I've got to have a drink before I can move." As his way was at such times, he spoke of himself so matter-of-factly that Wheeler knew he was telling the truth.

Wheeler turned to the porter, who was still standing in the open door. "Can you give him a bath and a shave?"

"Yes, sir. For a consideration."

Wheeler grinned at the delicacy of that. "What do you consider a consideration?"

"One dollar."

Wheeler handed him a dollar. "As cold as possible," he said.

In the street again, Wheeler stopped to think. He knew beyond doubt, having seen the evidence, that whiskey was within reach, but he did not know where to find it. He had not asked Uncle Peach for directions because he knew that Uncle Peach's directions, even when he was sober, were not followable. He was almost ready to turn back and lay his problem before the desk clerk, when he saw a man coming toward him in a swaying, hobbling gait that he recognized unmistakably. It was Laban Jones, Wheeler's friend from childhood, a Port William farmer's son, crippled from birth, who was working in an office at the stockyards. Wheeler caught his arm. "Laban," he said. The face that turned to look at him was as sweet and honest as the day itself.

"Why, hello, Wheeler. How in the world are you?"

"All right," Wheeler said. "*Nearly* all right. I need a half-pint of whiskey, and I don't know where to find it."

"*You* do, Wheeler?" Laban laughed. As always his hat was set far back on his head as if that was just the place he kept it in case he might want to put it on.

Wheeler laughed too. "I *may* need it before this is over. But at present Uncle Peach is the one in need."

Laban widened his eyes and nodded. "I see. You've got to patch him up and get him home."

"That's right."

"Well, come with me."

Laban turned and started back the way he had come, hobbling along at a pace Wheeler had to hurry to keep up with. Laban's eagerness to be of use was familiar to Wheeler, but it was strange to him to have Laban as a guide. Always before, it had been the other way around. Wheeler had been the one who knew, Laban the innocent who learned late. Once he had actually sawed off a tree limb that a squirrel was on, forgetting that he himself was standing on the same limb. Now he was guiding Wheeler through the invisible world that lay beneath the visible one. Wheeler walked along beside him obediently and asked no questions.

They went several blocks, and then Laban abruptly entered a hardware store. Wheeler walking behind him now, they went through the store, through a large stockroom at the back, winding their way among stacks of boxes, crates, and kegs. And then Laban opened another door and they emerged in the bottom of what appeared to be a deep shaft, brick walled, with a tiny patch of sky at the top. It was a dark, damp place, smelling of mold, as hidden from the rest of the world as the bottom of a well. The place astonished Wheeler, and he was grateful not to be there alone.

Laban pointed to a ragged hole in one of the brick walls. "Hand a dollar bill through that hole."

"Through *that* hole?" Wheeler said.

Laban was grinning, greatly amused. "That's right."

Wheeler did as he was told, although, as much as he trusted Laban, he did not do so gladly. But he felt the bill gently withdrawn from his fingers, and felt the cold glass of a small bottle pressed firmly upon the palm of his hand.

He slipped the bottle into his pocket, and followed Laban back out through the meanders they had come in by and into the daylit street.

"Well, that ought to fix him up," Laban said. "He'll be a new man now."

"He's been a new man many a time before this," Wheeler said. "Thanks."

"My pleasure," Laban said, and hobbled away before Wheeler could ask the question he had in mind.

Uncle Peach, scrubbed, shaved, and reassembled in his blue suit and tie, his hat, reshaped, on his knee, was sitting in the chair in the middle of the room, which the porter was now setting to rights. The suit was the only one Uncle Peach had; he used it only to get drunk in. It was a garment a man could feel comfortable either wearing or walking on, as need might be. And Uncle Peach looked as old and exhausted as his suit, pale and wasted, his neck too small for his collar. And yet his head, despite its snow-white hair, was somehow still a boy's head, the ears sticking innocently too far out, the hair, which had been wetted and combed down, already drying and rising stiffly like the hackles on a dog's neck. Wheeler could see a crooked vein pulsing at his temple.

"Here," he said. "See if that'll help."

Uncle Peach held the bottle of colorless whiskey up, trembling, against the window light, and looked through it, and then he pulled the cork and drank. "Ah!" he said, and made a face.

Wheeler took the bottle back.

"*Ter'ble* stuff! *Aw*ful stuff!" Uncle Peach said, fighting for breath.

"But you like it," Wheeler said and laughed. He had begun to feel a little relieved; he was involved in the problem now, getting something done.

"I like a little, from time to time," Uncle Peach said, and then, feeling a sudden access of moral seriousness, he said to Wheeler and the porter and anyone who might be passing by in the hall, "But don't never drink, my boys. Stay clean away from it."

And then the three of them stayed quiet for what must have been several minutes in that little room that, even straightened up, oppressed Wheeler by its measliness, Wheeler and the porter watching Uncle Peach who was staring at the window. Slowly he seemed to grow steadier within himself. He took a deep, tremulous breath and smacked his mouth as though tasting the air. And then he reached for the bottle. "Bird can't fly with one wing, Wheeler boy."

Wheeler, who had flight in mind, let him have another drink. But when he took the bottle back that time he handed it to the porter. "That's all," he said to Uncle Peach.

"That's all," Uncle Peach said, in a tone of finality in which Wheeler recognized the familiar intention of reform. For a while now Uncle Peach would be a prohibitionist, a new man. "I'm going to wipe the slate clean!"

But far from flying, when they put his hat on and helped him up,

Uncle Peach collapsed back onto the chair and would have continued to the floor, had they not held him. He shook his head. "Whoo!"

"You're going to have to work at this," Wheeler told him. "Pay attention."

Uncle Peach paid attention, and when they got him up again, he stood. They walked him out to the elevator, they descended with him to the lobby, and then the porter walked ahead and held open the street door.

If he could keep Uncle Peach on his feet, Wheeler was determined to walk to the station. Uncle Peach needed the effort and the fresh air, Wheeler thought, and he was right, for as they went along Uncle Peach recovered some of his capabilities. He was not standing up on his own, but he was walking on his own. And Wheeler began to be a little hopeful. Maybe, he thought, he could get Uncle Peach back in charge of himself by nightfall. Wheeler wanted to go home. He imagined himself finally free of this story he was in, telling it to Bess. Encumbered as he was, he imagined how neatly and nimbly *she* would walk beside him.

As he and Uncle Peach made their way slowly along, they necessarily attracted the attention of the passersby — a handsome, erect, nicely dressed young man walking arm in arm with an aging drunk. Wheeler bore it well enough, for he had expected to have to, and he knew there was no escape. But the pressure of so many curious, amused, or disapproving stares produced in Uncle Peach a desire to rise above his condition. If he was a man who obviously *did* disgrace and degrade himself with drink, he wished at least to appear to be a man who *knew* that he should not.

"My boy," he said loudly, "there's a moral lesson in this for you, if you'll only learn it. Here's a awful example right before your eyes."

"Hush," Wheeler said. "Just please hush."

But Uncle Peach's heart was full. His voice was trembling. "You got a good mother and daddy. Finest a man ever had. You don't have to be like old Uncle Peach. Let this be a lesson to you, Wheeler boy. I know what a life like mine goes to show."

"For God's *sake*, be quiet," Wheeler said. And then, though he knew better, he said, "Lesson to *me*! If it's no lesson to you, why should it be a lesson to me?"

"It *is* a lesson to me. I've learnt it a thousand times."

Wheeler usually put up with Uncle Peach by finding him funny, which was easy enough, for Uncle Peach's life and conversation were rich in absurdities, and Wheeler's involvements with him invariably made good stories. But underlying the possibility of laughter was the possibility of anger, and he was close to that now. He did not need a moral lesson from Uncle Peach. He did not need Uncle Peach, so far as he was aware, for anything—not him or the likes of him. So far as he was aware, nobody did.

"There's no moral lesson in a man's inability to learn a moral lesson," he said, and wondered if that was true. But Uncle Peach's thoughts had strayed to other matters; if he heard, he did not answer.

The train was crowded, people were standing in the aisle, and the car was hot. Wheeler tried to open a window, but cold weather had come officially, if not in fact, and the windows had been locked shut.

When the train gained speed outside the city and the car began to sway, Uncle Peach became sick again. He swallowed and smacked his mouth, and drops of sweat ran down his face. Wheeler looked for a way out, perhaps to the vestibule at the end of the car, but with the aisle full of people escape appeared to be impossible, and anyhow it was too late, for suddenly Uncle Peach leaned forward and, with awful retches and groans, vomited between his spread knees. Wheeler caught hold of him and held him. All around them people were giving them looks and drawing their feet away. Wheeler gave Uncle Peach his handkerchief, helped him out of his coat, and fanned him with his hat, encouraging and helping him the best he could. But the spasms came repeatedly, with unabated violence, and with each one Uncle Peach's gasps and groans and roars of supplication became louder. "Ohhhh, Lord!" he said. "Ohhhh, me! Ohhhh, Lord, help me!" Wheeler's pleadings with him to be quiet might as well have been addressed to a panic-stricken horse. As soon as he would be almost recovered and quiet, suddenly he would lean forward again. "Uuuuuup! *Oh,* my God!" And when the spasm passed he would roll his head against the seatback. "Ohhhh, me!"

It was an awful intimacy carried on in public. To Wheeler, it was endurable only because it was inescapable. He knew that Uncle Peach was suffering, and yet his suffering seemed merely the cause, the relatively minor cause, of the calamitous uproar that he was filling the car with. And yet, in the very midst of it, Wheeler knew that it was rare. It would make a good story, as soon as he could get out of it. But it was not funny now.

Once they had landed, mercifully, on the station platform at Langlay, Wheeler steadied Uncle Peach a moment to let him secure his balance, and then he said, "Let's go."

"All right," Uncle Peach said.

His hand caught firmly under Uncle Peach's arm, Wheeler turned then to walk to his car, only to feel Uncle Peach turn in the opposite direction, a difference of intention that came close to bringing them both down.

"*What are you doing?*" Wheeler said, angry sure enough now.

"Got to get the old mare and buggy."

Wheeler turned him loose, half hoping he would fall, for Uncle Peach, who had used up the afternoon, had now laid claim to the night as well. Wheeler was not going to get home by breakfast, let alone supper. His leap had not ended yet. "Well, damn it to hell!" he said. "Let's go get the damned old mare."

"*Got* to get her," Uncle Peach said. "Got to have her."

And so they went to the livery stable and had Uncle Peach's old sorrel mare, Godiva, harnessed and hitched to the buggy. Wheeler paid the bill there too, and they started for Uncle Peach's place, Wheeler driving and Uncle Peach leaning back in the seat, holding on.

It was a long six miles. Uncle Peach's stomach objected as strenuously to the motion of the buggy as it had to that of the train. He had long ago emptied himself, but the spasms came anyhow, prolonged clenches that left him fighting for balance and breath. And each time, Wheeler had to stop the mare and hold Uncle Peach to keep him from falling out of the buggy.

Finally, after this had happened perhaps half a dozen times, Wheeler, who had remained angry, said, "I hope you puke your damned guts out."

And Uncle Peach, who lay, quaking and white, against the seatback, said, "Oh, Lord, honey, you can't mean that."

As if his anger had finally stripped all else away, suddenly Wheeler saw Uncle Peach as perhaps Dorie had always seen him—a poor, hurt, weak mortal, twice hurt because he *knew* himself to be hurt and weak and mortal. And then Wheeler knew what he did need from Uncle Peach. He needed him to be comforted. That was all. He put his arm around Uncle Peach, then, and patted him as if he were a child. "No," he said. "I don't mean it."

When they got to the house it was almost nightfall. Wheeler left the mare standing at the back door while he helped Uncle Peach into the house. It was a bachelor's house, rudimentary, spare, unadorned, and, on top of that, a mess, for as he always did, Uncle Peach had lost interest in housekeeping as he gained interest in travel. Wheeler led him to a chair, and then he straightened the bedclothes on the bed and took off Uncle Peach's shoes and helped him to lie down.

In the failing light he drove the mare to the barn, unhitched her, watered her at the cistern trough, unharnessed and fed her. She applied herself to her supper as though all were well.

Uncle Peach's little farm had always endeared itself to Wheeler, and he could remember when Uncle Peach had kept it moderately well. Now, like Uncle Peach himself, it was running down. The fences barely served to contain and the brushy pastures to feed the one old mare. The garden was ragged with tall frost-killed weeds. The tobacco crop was hanging cured in the barn, poorer than the year.

Lying on the bed in the lamplight, Uncle Peach looked like a corpse, and lay as still as one. Wheeler stood and watched him a moment to make sure he was breathing. And then he lighted a lamp in the kitchen and moved around for some time, straightening the place up. He drew a fresh bucket of water from the well, drank, and built a fire in the cooking stove. But when he searched the kitchen for food he found nothing except—under a cloth spread over the table—a jar of jam, half a can of pork and beans covered with gray mold like a mouse's pelt, and most of a box of stale crackers.

"Well, *damn* it!" he said, for he was hungry himself, and he knew he needed to get something in the way of food into Uncle Peach. He lighted the lantern that he found beside the woodbox, and went out. Searching the henhouse, the hayloft, and every trough and manger in the barn, he found five eggs.

As he walked back to the house, carrying the eggs in his hat, peering beyond the lantern light into the dark, and the rising wind, it seemed to him strange beyond belief that he was where he was, doing what he was doing. It seemed to him that he was still in his leap, still falling, still attached to Uncle Peach, who was still falling. Sooner or later they would hit bottom together and could start climbing out. He did not know when. He did not know how he was going to get back to his car. All the world to him now was the darkness and the wind, himself and Uncle Peach — two needy men and five eggs. Between the stars and the ground the only lights he could see were the lantern he carried and the windows of Uncle Peach's house. The only sound was the long breath of the wind in the top of the old locust by the back door. He no longer thought of telling his story to Bess. He only missed her. He missed his life.

He was glad to get back inside, where the stove had made it warm. He scrambled the eggs, and warmed some of the crackers in the oven to make them crisp again. He got Uncle Peach up and fed him, and ate what was left himself. He found clean sheets and remade the bed, and helped Uncle Peach to undress and get under the covers. He quickly washed the dishes they had used, thinking to have a little time, finally, to sit down in and be still.

But Uncle Peach began to dream bad dreams, struggling and crying out in his sleep: "*Oh!* Lord God, I see him a-coming! On his old smoky horse!" And Wheeler lay down beside him to quiet him. For a while he did sleep quietly, and then his dreams returned again. Wheeler was awake for hours, soothing and consoling Uncle Peach when he fretted and muttered and cried out, struggling with him when he fought.

And so they waged the night, Uncle Peach striving with the Devil, Wheeler striving with Uncle Peach. It seemed to Wheeler that the two of them were lost together there in the dark house in the dark sky. He could not have told the time within three hours.

Once, after they had passed through yet another nightmare, Uncle Peach, who had momentarily waked, said slowly into the darkness,

"Wheeler boy, this is a hell of a way for a young man just married to have to pass the night."

"I thought of that," Wheeler said. "But it's all right." And he patted Uncle Peach, who went back to sleep and for a while was quiet.

Later, Wheeler himself went to sleep, his hand remaining on Uncle Peach's shoulder where it had come to rest.

And that is where daylight found him, far from home.

Nearly to the Fair (1932)

In the neighborhood of Cotman Ridge and Goforth, and even as far away as Port William, Ptolemy Proudfoot had earned a small fame as a horseman. He never had need on his ninety-eight acres for more than three horses at once, and had rarely owned a brood mare; still, it was understood around and about that Tol was a good judge of horses and that he "had a way" with them. He was a good hand to break a colt, and he had been known to take an older horse that was spoiled or mean and settle him down to a life of useful citizenship. People knew that in his dealings with horses Tol could accomplish pretty much what he wanted or needed to, and without so much as raising his voice. "He was half horse himself," Sam Hanks liked to say.

He always kept as a work team a well-matched pair, usually of geldings, grays if he could find them. And he kept a somewhat lighter third horse that he drove to his buggy, and used with his team on the cutting harrow or breaking plow. The buggy horse, like the workhorses, would be a good one, and when Tol and Miss Minnie set out for town or for church, they traveled in some style. They looked, perhaps, as any moderately prosperous farm couple of that time and place would have looked, except for one thing. Tol, who was large in all dimensions, weighed in the neighborhood of three hundred pounds and Miss Minnie never more than about ninety, and so, when they traveled together in the buggy, the buggy leaned to Tol's side and Miss Minnie, as a consequence, always sat very close to Tol. Fortunately, Miss Minnie felt romantic about Tol — he was her bulwark, she said; it was not merely gravity that drew her to his side. But perhaps it was not ordinary in their time and place for a couple on the far side of middle age to sit as closely together as Tol and Miss Minnie did.

On his part, Tol's affection for Miss Minnie was always somewhat breathlessly mingled with awe. Miss Minnie had been a schoolteacher, and Tol looked up to her for her book learning and her correct grammar. For him, a certain romance adhered to their marriage because of his conviction that she was above him, that she deserved not only all he could do for her, but more.

And that, probably, is why he bought the little Model A coupe in 1929, just before the Depression. Tol, I think, would have been satisfied to stick to his horse and buggy for the rest of his days. Traveling in cooperation with a good horse interested him more than any other form of travel could have done. When they drove together he was in the habit of saying to Miss Minnie from time to time, gesturing toward Ike or Fiddler or Redbird or Sunfish or Hickory, "He's a good one, ain't he?" or "Stepping out now, ain't he?"—just as he liked often to say to her, when they had been away and had come back into sight of their neat gingerbreaded house and its outbuildings that stood just where the Goforth Hill road dropped down off Cotman Ridge toward Goforth in the valley, "Now I wonder who lives in that pretty place."

But Tol was no stranger to the fact that automobiles had come to be the thing. It got so that almost every time they went onto the road they met one — if it was good weather, that is, and the road was passable for automobiles. When they went down to Goforth to church, there several automobiles would be, not lined up at the hitch rail, but scattered hither and yon, not needing to be tied to anything when you were not using them. Even old Uncle Arn Ekrum had bought one; when it threatened to rust, he had covered it with a coat of whitewash so that now it looked like a ghost. And it came to Tol that Miss Minnie, abreast of things as he knew her to be, undoubtedly longed secretly in her heart to ride in an automobile of their own.

Tol could not bear the thought that Miss Minnie might long secretly in her heart for anything that he could provide. And so the next time they went to Hargrave — a trip they didn't make but two or three times a year — Tol, speaking of a "surprise" he said he had for her, and revealing his own excitement by a smile that made his face shine like a ripe tomato, drove her to the place where a man sold automobiles and, stopping in front of a glossy Model A coupe, merely held out his hand, palm open, like Columbus presenting the New World to the Queen of Spain. And Miss Minnie — who despite Tol's suspicions had never dreamed of owning an automobile, who in fact loved Tol's way with a horse and loved to sit beside him while he drove, and who, now that she was suddenly face-to-face with a car of their own, thought it the homeliest black bug she had ever seen — assuming that it was something that Tol had longed for secretly in his heart, said, "Why, Mr. Proudfoot, it is perfectly beautiful!"

The next day the salesman delivered the car and taught Tol how to drive it: how to start it by twisting its crank, how to guide it by twisting its steering wheel, how to make it go forward and backward. Tol did not know what to expect it to do next. But he got good enough finally to drive it three times slowly around the front pasture and then out the gate and down the road to Goforth, and then back up the hill and into the yard again, with the salesman beside him, smiling and saying, "You're getting the hang of it, sir. Just go easy."

And so Tol and Miss Minnie went easy into the modern world, never really getting the hang of it. She sat close to him in the Model A as she had in the buggy, because of the same conditions of gravity and attraction. And in the automobile, as in the buggy when the horse trotted, she always held her hat on with one hand, even when the windows were shut. All the neighbors, except when they had to meet him in the road, enjoyed watching the way Tol drove, as later they would enjoy remembering it. When Tol traveled by horse and buggy, his horse stayed in the road more or less on its own, leaving Tol free to look around. Though the Model A required much more supervision than a horse, Tol still spent a good deal of time looking around. It would have seemed to him a discourtesy to travel through the country without looking at it. His course therefore involved a series of strayings to one side or another, alternating with sudden corrections. The corrections were usually inspired by the warnings of Miss Minnie, who always spoke in the nick of time (who, on those journeys, *lived* in the nick of time), and who nevertheless retained to the end of her days an almost devout admiration of Tol's ability to run an automobile.

Because they never entirely trusted their new machine, which Tol always referred to as "the Trick," and because they had an almost superstitious fear of getting it wet or muddy, they kept their horse and buggy for use in emergencies and when the weather was bad and when Tol needed to go somewhere by himself, for he would not go anywhere in the Trick without Miss Minnie. And so the Model A stood in the wagon shed as innocent of rain or mud as a pet canary, and gleaming as on the day it was new, for Miss Minnie went over the outside of it almost every day with her dust mop.

Having an automobile might have caused them to think many thoughts that they had never thought before, but in fact it only caused one such thought. For the most part, they continued in their familiar, modest, frugal ways. They went to Port William to shop and visit a while on Saturday afternoon. They went down to Goforth to church on Sunday. They went to a neighbor's sometimes and sat till bedtime, or some of the neighbors would come to sit with them. And pretty often they would have company and Miss Minnie would load the table with one of her bountiful meals, and these were Tol's favorite occasions, for he loved food and talk and laughter. In the fall Tol would go to Hargrave to market his tobacco crop. He would go to the stockyards at Louisville in June to sell his lambs, and again in November to sell his steers. Occasionally Miss Minnie and the other women of the Missionary Society would hold a bake sale. But mostly she and Tol stayed home and stayed busy in the leisurely way of people who know exactly what they have to do and how to do it and have got used to doing it, and who don't have to do too much.

The one thought that the automobile caused them to think was the thought of the State Fair, which took place in Louisville at the end of every summer. They had heard of the Fair, and they had dreamed of it. They had heard of the perfect ears of corn laid side by side in rows, and of the perfect garden vegetables, the fruits and the canned goods, the needlework, the flowers; of the cages of beautiful chickens and ducks and geese, of guinea fowl and pigeons, of turkeys bronze and white; of ranks of fine cattle, and pens of excellent sheep and hogs; of the mule show and the horse show. Tol and Miss Minnie knew what good things were, and they had but to close their eyes to see them at the Fair as they must have been: all the produce of the cultivated earth, perfect in all its shapes and colors, cherished and gleaming. But they had never seen it with their own eyes. They had never gone.

But now that they possessed an automobile, they could think of going, for the world had changed. Now they could think of going fifty miles to the Fair and fifty miles home again on the same day, and only because they *wanted* to. It fairly took their breath. They talked about it for three years.

"If we wanted to go," Tol said prophetically to Miss Minnie, "the Trick could take us there."

"Yes, it's the modern world now," Miss Minnie replied. "People do such things."

But the truth was that in his heart Tol knew he belonged to an older world, and he was afraid. For him, to walk the aisles of the great exhibit halls among fruits and vegetables grown splendidly ripe, and to see the good animals fed and groomed to a royal excellence, would have been to set foot in Eden itself. But now, as never before, the thought of these things set off a tremor of anxiety in his mind. Getting there would be the problem.

And then one day something happened that enabled Tol Proudfoot to think of getting there. It was the middle of the summer, and Tol had walked through the field to Corbin Crane's to see if he could borrow back the corn planter that Corbin had borrowed from him in the spring. He thought that if he came walking, Corbin might offer to bring the planter home with his own team rather than wait, as he usually did, for Tol to come with his team to get it. Tol had thought it best to ask for the return of the planter several months ahead of time because if he knew Corbin, the planter would need fixing before it could be used. Corbin was hard on tools, as he was on everything else, which was perhaps why he saw fit to get along without any of his own.

He did, however, own a car. And when Tol came over the ridge, he saw the car running at what appeared to be terrific speed around the corner of the barn. It made a big loop in the pasture, disappeared again around the same corner of the barn, and reappeared in the lane, heading out toward the road gate. It disappeared again, and then in a few minutes it came back into sight, going backward nearly as fast as it had gone forward.

Tol, who had continued walking, stopped then and stood by the lane where it came up between the house and the barn. When the car flew backward past him, he hollered, "Whoa!" and the car stopped. Behind the wheel Tol saw his friend Elton Penn, Corbin Crane's stepson. Elton was twelve years old that summer, and as he raised his hand in greeting to Tol he had a grin on his face that could have been distributed among three or four boys and still showed them all to be in a good humor.

"Want a ride?" Elton said.

"No, thanks. Not today," Tol said. "Where's Corbin?"

"Over to Braymer Hardy's, putting up hay," Elton said.

"Your mammy, too?"

Elton nodded.

"I thought so."

"They sent me home to milk."

"Well, why ain't you milking?"

Tol knew what Elton was doing. He was not just enjoying himself; he was taking revenge on Corbin Crane, who did not like him and was mean to him. It was because of Corbin's meanness to Elton that Tol and Elton had got to be friends.

One day Tol had stopped to talk to Corbin when Corbin and Elton were hoeing tobacco. While the two men talked, Elton, who was only about nine at the time, got to fiddling with the water jug, and he dropped it. It didn't break, but some water spilled, and Corbin turned around and cracked Elton across the wrist with his hoe handle. It was a hard reckless lick, and Elton started to cry.

Tol heard no more of what Corbin was telling him. He reached down with his big old hand and picked up Elton's hand and led him away.

"If you don't mind," he said, not looking back at Corbin Crane, "I'm going to borrow this boy for a while."

They walked along together, Tol not saying anything, and Elton blubbering and sniffling. After a while Elton said, "Someday I'm going to kill that son of a bitch."

"Aw, son," Tol said, "you don't want to do that."

"I taken a shine to the boy," Tol told Miss Minnie later that day, meaning that from then on he was going to be Elton's friend.

And they were friends from then on. Tol would pay Elton a dime or a quarter to help him out with some job. Or Miss Minnie would make cookies and lemonade, and they would call Elton on the party line to come over and play croquet. And often at night Tol would call Elton up and play Miss Minnie's Victrola for him over the telephone. A many a night Elton stood by the wall with the receiver to his ear, listening to "Mother Machree" or "There's a Cradle in Carolina" or, his and Tol's favorite, a song called "Nothing but Something Cool."

Once Tol offered Elton a dime to split a pile of stove wood. The wood split hard and the job took Elton a long time. Tol paid him his dime, and then showed him how to play the game of heads-or-tails.

"Now," Tol said, "look. If we bet a dime and you win, you'll have two dimes instead of one."

"All right," Elton said.

So they flipped.

"Call it," Tol Proudfoot said.

"Tails—wup—I mean heads!" Elton said.

And Tol showed his coin and took Elton's dime. Elton sat down on the pile of split wood and was not able to say anything, and Tol stood and looked down at him. After the suffering had gone on as long as Tol could stand it, he handed Elton back his dime.

"Son," he said, "don't never gamble."

And sometimes they just sat together while Tol told things.

One night, Tol said, when there was a full moon, he woke up, it must have been about three o'clock, and he could see Miss Minnie lying beside him on her back with her mouth open. Tol took the end of his forefinger and dabbled it into Miss Minnie's mouth and wiggled it around. And then he composed himself and breathed deeply. He heard Miss Minnie smacking her mouth. And then she sat straight up in bed.

"Mr. Proudfoot! Mr. Proudfoot, wake up! I have swallowed a mouse!"

"Miss Minnie," said Tol, his laughter shaking the bed so that, of course, she caught him, "there ain't much I know of to do for somebody that's swallowed a mouse."

Elton was a fine addition to Tol's and Miss Minnie's life. He liked them, they made him welcome, and it got so he would be over at their place whenever he could escape from home. He was a help. He didn't mind work, and he was bright. He saw things. He was interested in things. It often turned out that something Tol or Miss Minnie needed to have done and did not much want to do was something Elton was glad to do. He not only wanted to earn one of Tol's dimes or quarters and eat quite a lot of Miss Minnie's good cooking—he wanted to do the work. He seemed a godsend to Tol and Miss Minnie, who had no child of their own. They loved every little opportunity to pay attention to him. When he ate with them, they stuffed him like a sausage. Miss Minnie served him biscuits two at a time; when he bit into the second one, she popped two more hot ones onto his plate; while he buttered them, Tol would refill his glass. Miss Minnie baked pies and cookies for him, and brought him little snacks where he was at work.

When Tol saw how apt Elton was at driving a car, all his worry about getting to the Fair melted right out of his mind and flowed away. He saw that Elton, being young himself, belonged to the young world of machines. Whereas Tol could drive an automobile only fearfully, and certainly with no skill, this Elton was already master of it, even at so young an age, and had no fear.

"Miss Minnie," Tol said, "the boy can drive. He can take us to the Fair."

And Miss Minnie said, "Oh, why didn't we think of that before?"

She thought and then added, "But, Mr. Proudfoot, won't it be too expensive?" They were then in the very pit of the Depression and, though she and Tol owed nothing and had savings, she felt that it was appropriate to worry.

"Well," Tol said, "we ain't going probably but this once. If we average in all the times we haven't gone and all the times we ain't going to go, it'll come out pretty cheap."

"It *would* be nice to go once," she said.

"You ought to see him go," Tol said, laughing. "That boy's worth a share in the railroad."

They secured Elton's agreement, broaching the subject with some care lest, after all, he might not want to undertake so daunting a project.

"Why, sure!" Elton said, grinning on behalf of himself and several others. "I imagine I can drive her."

They set the date. They told Elton to get permission from his folks.

And Elton did. Understanding the situation a good deal better than they did, Elton got permission from his folks to help Tol clean a fence-row on that day, which, as it happened, was a Saturday. He said he was supposed to stay overnight and go to church with Tol and Miss Minnie the next day, so he would need to take his Sunday clothes.

As a last precaution, Miss Minnie got her nephew Sam Hanks, who drove a cattle truck, to draw her a map showing how to get to the Fair. Sam sat between Tol and Miss Minnie at the kitchen table.

"Now here's the stockyards, Tol. You know how to get there."

"Aw, I know how to get *there,* all right!" Tol said.

"Well, starting from there, here's what you do." And Sam drew the streets onto a paper, telling them the various buildings and other land-marks by which they would recognize the turns, and they watched and listened and nodded their heads. He folded the map when he had fin-ished and handed it to Miss Minnie, who laid it by her place at the table so she would remember to put it in her purse.

Sam had his doubts about Tol's driving. If they had had a bigger auto-mobile, he might have offered to drive them himself, but he didn't favor being squeezed into that little coupe with Tol and Miss Minnie, and so he let it slide, only hinting a little warning to Tol.

"You'll be all right, now, won't you, Tol?"

"Sure."

"You sure?"

"Sure I'm sure."

If he had known their driver was to be a twelve-year-old boy, he surely would have interfered, but they didn't tell him, because he didn't ask. As for them, they just took for granted that if Elton could drive in a pasture, he could drive anywhere — and as it turned out, they were right.

Elton had to raise his chin to see over the dashboard, but under his guid-ance the Trick, as Tol Proudfoot pointed out to Miss Minnie, performed like a circus horse. They pulled out onto the road just as the sun was coming up. For the first dozen miles or so, they were on roads that were dry enough, but were chug-holey and narrow, and they had to go slow and be careful. And then they got onto the blacktop and just went whirling along, going faster by a good deal than Tol and Miss Minnie had ever gone in their lives. Elton drove with a big grin on his face, concentrating on his work, and Tol and Miss Minnie watched the country fly past and commented on what they saw. And every so often Tol would point out to Miss Minnie how splendidly Elton was driving.

Tol was having a wonderful time. For there they went, speeding through the world in the early morning, the Trick running as dependably as a good horse, but much faster; Tol had left his cares behind. And even though she had been a schoolteacher and felt a certain obligation to remain serious in the presence of the young, Miss Minnie, too, felt the intoxication of their speed and became merry and carefree.

"I just wish you would look at that young man, how he can drive!" Tol said. "Why, he can handle this Trick like he's a piece of it."

"I'm just the nut on the steering wheel," Elton said.

And Miss Minnie said, "Well, Mr. Nut, drive right on!"

That was when the left hind tire went "pish-pish-pish-pish," and Elton had to pull off on the side of the road.

Tol, who could do anything that needed doing with a horse and any of the tools he had been raised with, was utterly perplexed when confronted with a flat tire. Largely because of Tol's eager help, it took Elton the better part of forty-five minutes to get the car jacked up and the impaired wheel off and the spare on and the car jacked back down again.

"Well, I don't expect we'll have any more flat tires today, do you?" Tol said when they were going again.

"There is no way to know what to expect," Miss Minnie said pleasantly but with a noticeable diminution of merriment. "We had better have that one fixed."

And so at the next filling station they came to, they turned in. Only one man was working there, and he was busy, and they had to wait. There was a car ahead of them, also with a flat tire, and cars kept coming to the gas pump. It was getting hot now, and Tol and Elton got out to watch the mechanic while he worked, and Miss Minnie sat in the Trick with her white-gloved hands crossed on top of her purse in her lap, the picture of patience.

When the mechanic started work on their tire, which gave them license to draw closer, Tol started passing the time of day with the mechanic. Commercial transactions embarrassed Tol. When he had to receive payment from somebody, the feeling would always come over him that it was too much; when he had to give payment, the same feeling would suggest that it was too little. The passage of money seemed to him to discount all else that might pass between people. And so he always strove to see to it that when the money finally had to pass, it would pass as if in secret under cover of much sociable conversation. And besides, he was interested in people and curious about them.

He found out the man's name, which was Bob Shifter. He found out where he lived, and where he had lived before. He found out that Bob Shifter was no kin to old man Claude Shifter who used to live close to Ellville down by Hargrave, or if he was he didn't know it. He found out how long Bob Shifter had been married and how many children he had. He found out the mechanic's wife's maiden name and his mother's maiden name. He found out all that and a lot more, and he didn't have to ask more than three or four direct questions, for Bob Shifter was more than glad to tell the story of his life, and not in much of a hurry, once the talk started, to fix the tire.

The day was no longer young by the time they paid Mr. Shifter and got a good drink out of their water jug and started on again. But soon they were coming into the outskirts of the city. Now Tol began to experience their adventure as a reality, for the outskirts stretched out a long way before the city itself began. They would go through some of the city before they got to the stockyards, and there was a vast amount of it beyond.

He cleared his throat and said, "When you get me beyond the stockyards, by thunder, you've lost me!"

Nobody said anything.

After a while, to make sure they understood exactly what his qualifications were, he said again, "When you get me past the stockyards, I don't know left from right, nor up from down. I don't for a fact."

But by then they were approaching the stockyards, and Miss Minnie was digging in her purse for Sam Hanks's map.

"Now!" she said, drawing it out and unfolding it.

And then it was her turn to be assaulted by the reality of that day, for the map, past the stockyards, which had been boldly labeled "STOCK

YARDS," did not have a single name on it. Beyond the stockyards, where they now were, and going past in a hurry, the map was just a squiggle of straight lines and right-angle turns. And Miss Minnie understood, in a sort of lightning flash, the urban experience of her well-traveled nephew: When he drove his truck in the city, he went by landmarks, even such landmarks as he had recited while he drew his map, causing her and Tol to see visions of where they were going; past the stockyards, he didn't know the name of anything.

"Well, there is an example of misplaced faith," said Miss Minnie in a voice that was precise and restrained and carried unmistakably the tone of familial exasperation.

They stopped for a red light and then went on again.

"What's the matter?" Tol said. Miss Minnie had never taken that tone with him, but he knew how he would have felt if she ever had, and so he felt sorry for Sam Hanks.

"There are no street names," Miss Minnie said. "The map is perfectly useless."

"Aw, naw, now, it's not," Tol said.

"I fear it is," said Miss Minnie.

"Well, it shows you where to turn," Tol said, putting his big forefinger down onto the paper. "Here. Look a-here. Right here. Turn!" he said to Elton, pointing the way.

And Elton turned left out of the middle of the great street they were on into a smaller one.

"Listen to all the horns," Tol said.

"If we don't know the names of the streets," Miss Minnie said, "how can we know where to turn?"

"Well, we just turn where the line turns," said Tol. "Keep a watch out now. Sam told us what to look for. Maybe he said the names of the streets. Maybe we'll remember some of them. Look at the signs."

So they began watching for the street signs. Miss Minnie was wearing a black straw hat with a stiff brim. "She was turning her head this way and that, looking for signs," as Elton would tell it later, "and that hat like to sawed off Tol's left arm and my head."

"Now," Tol said, "didn't he say to turn past that big building yonder?"

"Yes, perhaps he did," Miss Minnie said.

Elton turned, and they went along another street, and before long they turned again. They went on that way for a considerable time. Finally they could no longer be sure which of the anonymous angles on their map they had come to.

"Well," Miss Minnie said, "we're lost."

"Well, we know something for sure, anyhow," Tol said, and Miss Minnie allowed him to laugh at that all by himself.

"Why don't we ask somebody?" Elton said. "Looks like some of these people ought to know." Elton had never ceased to grin. He was having a good time. As long as he was driving, he didn't care whether they were lost or not.

Miss Minnie, too, had thought of asking somebody, but she had her pride. If there was anything worse than being a person who did not know where she was, it was *appearing* to be a person who did not know where she was. Perhaps she understood also that by giving Tol an opening for conversation with the public at large, they might delay their arrival at the Fair indefinitely. And now that her confidence had failed, she saw pretty clearly that they would have to ask not one person but many. She saw that the place was complicated beyond her imagining or her ability to imagine. She saw that even if they had good directions, they would get them wrong. There was no telling the mistakes they would make.

"It would be reasonable," she said, having calmly resolved to think it through again, "since the Fair is so large an event, that there ought to be signs along the way, saying, 'To the Fair.' And so perhaps if we just look around a little we will see one of those signs."

Buoyed up by the cheerfulness of logical thought, Tol agreed.

"And it seems to me," she said, pointing with her gloved forefinger, "that a promising direction would be *that* way."

And so they wandered about for a while, looking for a sign, and found none.

"Well," Tol said finally, "why don't we just look for a big street where a lot of people are going in the same direction. They'll probably be going to the Fair, for there's a many of them that goes. And we can just follow along. Don't you see?"

But it had got to where thinking did not much help either their spirits or their condition. And though they came to some more big streets, it appeared that about the same numbers of people were going in both directions.

"We must go back to the stockyards and begin again," Miss Minnie said.

And that was the worst thought of all, for only then did they understand how lost they were. That they did not know where they were suddenly proved to them that they did not know where the stockyards were. They did not know where home was.

Failure and despair came upon them. They could no longer say that they were on their way to the Fair. They had come to a place of railroad spurs, tall chimneys, and low buildings — a sooty, ugly, purposeful place that sunlight did not improve. And all the time they were wandering around lost, wasting their precious day, the Fair was happening; it was fleeing as a bird to the mountain. Miss Minnie had a vision of the light fading from the polished skins of apples and pears and plums.

"Oh, goodness!" she said, and Elton thought she was going to cry, but she did not.

And then a sort of wonder happened. Until he was about forty-five — when it was revealed to him that if he was going to get up early he ought to go to bed early — Tol Proudfoot had been a coon hunter, and so he was accustomed to being lost and to finding himself again. Once he understood that Miss Minnie herself was hopelessly bewildered, and that all rational measures had failed, Tol's sense of direction began to operate. "Now, the stockyards," he said, "if that's where we want to go, is right over yonder." And he pointed the direction.

It was a direction diagonal to the streets, and so they had to go in a zigzag, tacking back and forth like a sailboat.

"Slant her over that way a little, son," Tol would say. And then, in a little while, "Now cut her back over this way."

And finally they were going pretty fast, amid much traffic, down the middle of a long, broad street, and they could see, far down at the end of it, the stockyards. Tol was waving his hand, signaling to Elton to go straight ahead.

"Oh, Mr. Proudfoot!" said Miss Minnie. "Where would we be without you?"

And then, over on the left-hand side of the street, Tol spied a man on tall stilts, carrying a sandwich board that said:

> *You'll find it, friend,*
> *At the Outside Inn.*

It was perhaps the chief spectacle of the day so far. For fear the others would not see it, Tol lunged in the direction of the sandwich man and extended his hand to indicate where to look.

"Look a-yonder!" he said.

He had stuck his hand right in front of Elton's face. His hand looked as big, Elton said, as a billboard. And when they had seen the sandwich man and exclaimed and Tol withdrew his hand, the world had changed. The car in front of them was stopping in a hurry for a red light. Elton clapped his foot onto the brake. And what happened after that happened faster than it can be explained.

When the man in front applied his brake, as Elton would tell it, "his ass-end as-cended." When Elton applied his brake, which he did a little too late, the Trick's front end de-scended. And as everything stopped and got level again, the back bumper of the car in front chomped down onto the front bumper of the Trick.

Elton and Tol got right out to see what the damage was.

"It's all right," Elton said. "It didn't make a scratch."

But Tol Proudfoot knew a calamity when he saw one. "Hung like two dogs!" he said. "By thunder, son, they're hung like two dogs!"

The car in front was far longer and far shinier than the Trick. And now its driver had got out and come back to see also. He had a white mustache and a red face and was wearing a suit and was in a hurry.

Elton was grinning as if he could not wait for the world to show forth more of its wonders.

"What do you propose to *do* about this, sir?" the man said, and then, seeing that he addressed a mere boy, turned to Tol Proudfoot and said, "Sir, what do you propose to do about this?"

At that point the light turned green, and the traffic began to pour along on both sides of them, and behind them horns began to blow.

It seemed to Tol that the world, or anyhow his part of it, had come to an end, for he could see no way out. If he had any conviction still in force, it was that when a calamity has happened to somebody, other people ought to come to a respectful and helpful stop. But there he and Elton and Miss Minnie were, trapped and defeated beyond the power of man to conceive, and nothing stopped. The cars and trucks and streetcars and wagons sped past, horns blew, and people shouted. The high, hot sun glared down into the crevice of the street without the mercy of a single tree.

He lifted his voice across their conjoined vehicles to the man with the mustache. "Hung like two dogs!" He spoke as sympathetically as he was able at the required volume, as if hoping to ease their predicament by so apt a description of it. He was sweating with heat and with panic. Behind him, in the Trick, Miss Minnie's eyes were round and watery with unfallen tears, and her lips were shut tight together; her hands in their white gloves lay crossed over her purse in her lap and did not move.

"You must do something about this," the man shouted to Tol. "I don't have all day for this. I'm in a hurry!"

Tol then saw it through, as far at least as indignation. "Drive on!" he shouted back. "I reckon we can drag as fast as you can haul!"

Elton, who had been waving his hand for attention for some time, then said, "Mr. Tol, stand right here," and he pointed to the two stout brackets to which the Trick's bumper was attached.

"What?" Tol said.

"Stand on these!"

Elton showed him again. Propping himself on the back end of the other car, Tol clambered up onto the brackets, and the Trick bowed down under his weight.

"Now take hold of that other bumper and lift up," Elton said.

When Tol lifted—which he did, Miss Minnie said, "as with the strength of ten"—Elton applied himself with all his strength to the left front fender of the Trick, which rolled back and came free. The man in a hurry, without looking again at them, stepped back into his machine and slammed the door.

Elton got back in behind the steering wheel. Tol, whose conviction held further that all calamities should be followed by conversation, stood in disappointment, watching the other car drive away. And then he got in, too.

"Well," Elton said, still grinning, "where does that map say to go now?"

"Home, son." Tol Proudfoot laughed a little, as if to himself, and patted Miss Minnie's crossed hands. "By thunder, it says to go home."

"Yes," Miss Minnie said, "let us go home."

That is the story as I heard it many times from Elton Penn — and from Sam Hanks, too, of course, for he had his version of it, though Elton was its principal eyewitness.

One day, when I happened by to see Miss Minnie, it occurred to me to ask her about that famous trip. She had been long a widow by then, and we neighbors often made a point of happening by. We needed to know that she was all right, but also it was good for us to see her and to have her pleasant greeting.

"Oh, yes!" she said, when I brought the subject up. "We weren't able to get all the way to the Fair. We got *nearly* all the way. I'm sure it was wonderful. But we did succeed in getting all the way home. And wasn't Mr. Proudfoot happy to be here!"

The Solemn Boy (1934)

Ptolemy Proudfoot's ninety-eight-acre farm lay along the Goforth Hill road between the Cotman Ridge road and Katy's Branch. It included some very good ridgeland, some wooded hillside above the creek, and, down between Katy's Branch and the Katy's Branch road, two acres or so of bottomland. This creek-bottom field, small and narrow and awkwardly placed, seemed hardly to belong to the farm at all, and yet it was the one piece of truly excellent land that Tol owned. He called it the Watch Fob. He kept it sowed in red clover and timothy or lespedeza and timothy, and every three or four years he would break it and plant it in corn.

Since the Watch Fob was so out of the way, whatever work Tol had to do there tended to be put off until last. And yet, such was the quality of the crops that came from that land, and such the pleasantness of the place, down among the trees beside the creek, that Tol always looked forward to working there. The little field was quiet and solitary. No house or other building was visible from it, and the road was not much traveled. When Tol worked there, he felt off to himself and satisfied. There were some fine big sycamores along the creek, and while Tol worked, he would now and then hear the cry of a shikepoke or a kingfisher. Life there was different from life up on the ridge.

Nineteen thirty-four was one of the years when Tol planted the Watch Fob in corn. And that was fortunate, for it was a dry year; the ridge fields produced less than usual, and the Watch Fob made up a good part of the difference. Tol cut and shocked that field last, and then he shucked and cribbed the upland corn before he went back again to the creek bottom.

Perhaps Tol agreed with the sage of Proverbs who held that "he that hasteth with his feet sinneth"—I don't know. It is a fact, anyhow, that Tol never hurried. He was not by nature an anxious or a fearful man. But I suspect that he was unhurried also by principle. Tol loved his little farm, and he loved farming. It would have seemed to him a kind of sacrilege to rush through his work without getting the good of it. He never went to the field without the company of a hound or two. At the time I am telling about, he had a large black-and-tan mostly hound named Pokerface. And when Tol went to work, he would often carry his rifle. If, while he was working, Pokerface treed a squirrel or a young groundhog, then the workday would be interrupted by a little hunting, and Miss Minnie would have wild meat on the table the next day. When Tol went down to the Watch Fob to cultivate his corn, he always took his fishing pole. While he worked with plow or hoe, he would have a baited hook in the water. And from time to time he would take a rest, sitting with his back against a tree in the deep shade, watching his cork. In this leisurely way, he did good work, and his work was timely. His crops were clean. His pastures were well grassed and were faithfully clipped every year. His lambs and his steers almost always topped the market. His harvested corn gleamed in the crib, as clean of shuck and silk as if Tol had prepared it for a crowd of knowledgeable spectators, though as like as not he would be the only one who ever saw it.

By the time Tol got around to shucking the corn down on the Watch Fob that fall, it was past Thanksgiving. People had begun to think of Christmas. Tol had put off the job for two or three days, saying to himself, "I'll go tomorrow." But when he woke up on the morning he had resolved to go, he wished that he never had planted the Watch Fob in corn in the first place. Tol was sixty-two years old in 1934. He had not been young for several years, as he liked to say. And that morning when he woke, he could hear the wind ripping past the eaves and corners of the little farmstead, and rattling the bare branches of the trees.

"I'm getting old," he thought as he heaved his big self off the mattress and felt beneath the bedrail for his socks.

"I'm getting old"—he had said that a number of times in the last few years, each time with surprise and with sudden sympathy for his forebears who had got old before him.

But he got up and dressed in the dark, leaving Miss Minnie to lie abed until he built up the fires. Tol was a big man. When he dressed, as Miss Minnie's nephew Sam Hanks said, it was like upholstering a sofa. In sixty-two years Tol had never become good at it. In fact, putting on his clothes was an affair not in the direct line of his interests, and he did not pay it much attention. Later, while he sat with his coffee after breakfast and was thus within her reach, Miss Minnie would see that his shirt collar was turned down and that all his buttons had engaged the appropriate buttonholes.

Tol, anyhow, approximately dressed himself, went down the stairs, built up the fire in the living room, and lit a fire in the cooking range in the kitchen. He sat by the crackling firebox of the range, wearing his cap and coat now, and put on his shoes. And then he sat and thought a little while. Tol had always been a man who could sit and think if he had to. But until lately he had not usually done so the first thing in the morning. Now it seemed that his sixty-two years had brought him to a new place, in which some days it was easier to imagine staying in by the fire than going out to work. He had an ache or two and a twinge or two, and he knew without imagining that the wind was from the north and he knew how cold it was. Tol thought on these things for some time there by the warming stove, and he thought that of all his troubles thinking about them was the worst. After a while he heard Miss Minnie's quick footsteps on the floor upstairs. He picked up the milk buckets then and went to the barn.

A little later, having eaten a good breakfast and hitched his team to the wagon, Tol experienced a transformation that he had experienced many times before. He passed through all his thoughts and dreads about the day, emerging at last into the day itself, and he liked it.

The wind was still whistling down from the north over the hard-frozen ground. But his horses looked wonderful, as horses tend to do on such a morning, with every hair standing on end and their necks arched, wanting to trot with the wagon's weight pressing onto their britchings as they went down the hill, and their breath coming in clouds that streamed away on the wind. Tol's fingers grew numb in his gloves with holding them back.

They quieted down presently, and he drove on to the Watch Fob, sticking first one hand and then the other into his armpits to warm his fingers. And then he untied the first shock, slipped his shucking peg onto his right hand, and began tossing the clean yellow ears into the wagon. It was not yet full daylight. He settled into the work, so that presently he paid less attention to it, and his hands went about their business almost on their own. He looked around, enjoying the look of the little field. Even on so gray a day it was pretty. After he had cut and shocked the corn, he had disked the ground and sowed it in wheat, and now the shocks stood in their straight rows on a sort of lawn that was green, even though it was frozen. And it was pleasant to see the humanly ordered small clearing among the trees. Nearby the creek flowed under thin ice and then broke into the open and into sound as it went over a riffle and back again under ice. But the best thing of all was the quiet. Though he could hear the wind clashing and rattling in the trees around the rim of the valley, there was hardly a breeze down there in the Watch Fob. Surrounded by the wind's commotion, the quietness of the little cornfield gave it a sort of intimacy and a sort of expectancy. As his work warmed him, he unbuttoned his jacket. A while later he took it off.

A little past the middle of the morning, snowflakes began to fall. It was nothing at all like a snowstorm, but just a few flakes drifting down. Up on the ridgetops, Tol knew, the wind would be carrying the flakes almost straight across. "Up there," he thought, "it ain't one of them snows that falls. It's one of them snows that just passes by." But down where he was, the flakes sifted lackadaisically out of the sky as if they had the day off and no place in particular to go, becoming visible as they came down past the treetops and then pretty much disappearing when they lit. It would take hours of such snowing to make even a skift of whiteness on the ground. Pokerface, who in dog years was older than Tol, nevertheless took shelter under the wagon.

"Well, if *you* ain't something!" Tol said to him. "Go tree a squirrel."

Pokerface had a good sense of humor, but he did not appreciate sarcasm. He acknowledged the justice of Tol's criticism by beating his tail two or three times on the ground, but he did not come out.

There had been a time when a Proudfoot almost never worked alone. The Proudfoots were a big family of big people whose farms were scattered about in the Katy's Branch valley and on Cotman Ridge. They liked to work together and to be together. Often, even when a Proudfoot was at work on a job he could not be helped with, another Proudfoot would be sitting nearby to watch and talk. The First World War killed some of them and scattered others. Since then, the old had died and the young had gone, until by now Tol was the only one left. Tol was the last of the Proudfoots, for he and Miss Minnie had no children. And now, though he swapped work with his neighbors when many hands were needed, he often worked alone, amused or saddened sometimes to remember various departed Proudfoots and the old stories, but at other times just present there in the place and the day and the work, more or less as his dog and his horses were. When he was remembering he would sometimes laugh or grunt or mutter at what he remembered, and then the old dog would look at him and the horses would tilt their ears back to ask what he meant. When he wasn't remembering, he talked to the horses and the dog.

"Me and you," he said to Pokerface, "we're a fine pair of half-wore-out old poots. What are we going to do when we get old?"

It amused him to see that Pokerface had no idea either.

For a while after Tol started that morning's work, it seemed to him that he would never cover the bottom of the wagon box. But after he quit paying so much attention he would be surprised, when he did look, at how the corn was accumulating. He laid the stalks down as he snapped off the ears, and then when he had finished all the stalks, he stood them back up in a shock and tied them. The shucked ears were piling up nearly to the top of the wagon box by the time Tol judged it was getting on toward eleven o'clock. By then his stomach had begun to form the conclusion that his throat had been cut, as Proudfoot stomachs had always tended to do at that time of day. And now he began to converse with himself about how long it would take to get back up the hill and water and feed his horses. He knew that Miss Minnie would begin to listen for him at about eleven-thirty, and he didn't want to get to the kitchen much later than that. He thought that he *could* go in with what corn he had, but then he thought he might shuck just a *little* more. He had conducted thousands of such conversations with himself, and he knew just how to do it. He urged himself on with one "little more" after another until he filled the wagon properly to the brim, and in plenty of time, too.

The day was still cold. As soon as he quit work, he had to put his jacket back on and button it up. The thought of reentering the wind made him hunch his shoulders and draw his neck down into his collar like a terrapin.

He climbed up onto the wagon seat and picked up the lines. "Come here, boys," he said to the team. And they turned and drew the creaking load out of the field.

If Tol had a favorite thing to do, it was driving a loaded wagon home from the field. As he drove out toward the road, he could not help glancing back at the wagon box brimming with corn. It was a kind of wonder to him now that he had handled every ear of the load. Behind him, the little field seemed to resume a deeper quietness as he was leaving it, the flakes of snow still drifting idly down upon it.

When they started up the hill the horses had to get tight in their collars. It was a long pull up to the first bend in the road. When they got there, Tol stopped on the outside of the bend and cramped the wheels to let the horses rest.

"Take a breath or two, boys," he said.

"Come on, old Poke," he said to the dog, who had fallen a little behind, and now came and sat down proprietarily beside the front wheel.

Where they were now they could feel the wind. The snowflakes flew by them purposefully, as if they knew of a better place farther on and had only a short time to get there.

Pretty soon the cold began to get inside Tol's clothes. He was ready to speak to the team again when he heard Pokerface growl. It was a quiet, confidential growl to notify Tol of the approach of something that Pokerface had not made up his mind about.

When Tol looked back the way Pokerface was looking, he saw a man and a small boy walking up the road. Tol saw immediately that he did not know them, and that they were poorly dressed for the weather. The man was wearing an old felt hat that left his ears in the cold and a thin, raggedy work jacket. The boy had on a big old blue toboggan that covered his ears and looked warm, but his coat was the kind that had once belonged to a suit, not much to it, the lapels pinned shut at the throat. The sleeves of the boy's coat and the legs of his pants were too short. The man walked behind the boy, perhaps to shelter him a little from the wind. They both had their hands in their pockets and their shoulders hunched up under their ears.

"Hush, Poker," Tol said.

When the man and boy came up beside the wagon, the boy did not look up. The man glanced quickly up at Tol and looked away.

"Well," Tol said cheerfully, for he was curious about those people and wanted to hear where they came from and where they were going, "can I give you a lift the rest of the way up the hill?"

The man appeared inclined to go on past without looking at Tol again.

"Give the boy a little rest?" Tol said.

The man stopped and looked at the boy. Tol could tell that the man wanted to let the boy ride, but was afraid or embarrassed or proud, it was hard to tell which. Tol sat smiling down upon them, waiting.

"I reckon," the man said.

Tol put down his hand and gave the boy a lift up onto the load of corn. The man climbed up behind him.

"We hate to put the burden on your team," the man said.

Tol said, "Well, it's all right. All they been doing is putting in the time. Get up, boys."

"They're right good ones," the man said.

Tol knew the man said that to be polite, but it was a pleasing compliment anyhow, for the man spoke as if he knew horses. Tol said, "They do very well."

And then he said, "You all come far?" hoping the man would tell something about himself.

But the man didn't. He said, "Tolable."

Tol glanced back and saw that the man had positioned his son between his spread legs and had opened his own coat to shelter him within it. As soon as he had stopped walking, the boy had begun to shiver. And now

Tol saw their shoes. The man had on a pair of street shoes with the heels almost worn off, the boy a pair of brogans, too big for him, that looked as stiff as iron.

"Poor," Tol thought. Such men were scattered around the country everywhere, he knew — drifting about, wearing their hand-me-downs or grab-me-ups, looking for a little work or a little something to eat. Even in so out-of-the-way a place as Cotman Ridge Tol and Miss Minnie had given a meal or a little work to two or three. But till now they had seen no boy. The boy, Tol thought, was a different matter altogether.

Tol wanted to ask more questions, but the man held himself and the boy apart.

"That wind's right brisk this morning, ain't it?" Tol said.

"Tolable so," the man said.

"I'm Tol Proudfoot," Tol said.

The man only nodded, as if the fact were obvious.

After that, Tol could think of nothing more to say. But now he had the boy on his mind. The boy couldn't have been more than nine or ten years old — just a little, skinny, peaked boy, who might not have had much breakfast, by the look of him. And who might, Tol thought, not have much to look forward to in the way of dinner or supper either.

"That's my place up ahead yonder," he said to the man. "I imagine Miss Minnie's got a biscuit or two in the oven. Won't you come in and eat a bite with us?"

"Thank you, but we'll be on our way," the man said.

Tol looked at the boy then; he couldn't help himself. "Be nice to get that boy up beside the stove where he can get warm," he said. "And a bean or two and a hot biscuit in his belly wouldn't hurt him either, I don't expect."

He saw the man swallow and look down at the boy. "We'd be mightily obliged," the man said.

So when they came to his driveway, Tol turned in, and when they came up beside the house he stopped.

"You'll find Miss Minnie in the kitchen," Tol said. "Just go around to the back porch and in that way. She'll be glad to see you. Get that boy up close to the stove, now. Get him warm."

The man and boy got down and started around the back of the house.

Tol spoke to his team and drove on into the barn lot. He positioned the wagon in front of the corncrib, so he could scoop the load off after dinner, and then he unhitched the horses. He watered them, led them to their stalls, and fed them.

"Eat, boys, eat," he said.

And then he started to the house. As he walked along he opened his hand, and the old dog put his head under it.

The man and boy evidently had done as he had told them, for they were not in sight. Tol already knew how Miss Minnie would have greeted them.

"Well, come on in!" she would have said, opening the door and seeing the little boy. "Looks like we're having company for dinner! Come in here, honey, and get warm!"

He knew how the sight of that little shivering boy would have called the heart right out of her. Tol and Miss Minnie had married late, and time had gone by, and no child of their own had come. Now they were stricken in age, and it had long ceased to be with Miss Minnie after the manner of women.

He told the old dog to lie down on the porch, opened the kitchen door, and stepped inside. The room was warm, well lit from the two big windows in the opposite wall, and filled with the smells of things cooking. They had killed hogs only a week or so before, and the kitchen was full of the smell of frying sausage. Tol could hear it sizzling in the skillet. He stood just inside the door, unbuttoning his coat and looking around. The boy was sitting close to the stove, a little sleepy looking now in the warmth, some color coming into his face. The man was standing near the boy, looking out the window — feeling himself a stranger, poor fellow, and trying to pretend he was somewhere else.

Tol took off his outdoor clothes and hung them up. He nodded to Miss Minnie, who gave him a smile. She was rolling out the dough for an extra pan of biscuits. Aside from that, the preparations looked about as usual. Miss Minnie ordinarily cooked enough at dinner so that there would be leftovers to warm up or eat cold for supper. There would be plenty. The presence of the two strangers made Tol newly aware of the abundance, fragrance, and warmth of that kitchen.

"Cold out," Miss Minnie said. "This boy was nearly frozen."

Tol saw that she had had no luck either in learning who their guests were. "Yes," he said. "Pretty cold."

He turned to the little washstand beside the door, dipped water from the bucket into the wash pan, warmed it with water from the teakettle on the stove. He washed his hands, splashed his face, groped for the towel.

As soon as Tol quit looking at his guests, they began to look at him. Only now that they saw him standing up could they have seen how big he was. He was broad and wide and tall. All his movements had about them an air of casualness or indifference as if he were not conscious of his whole strength. He wore his clothes with the same carelessness, evidently not having thought of them since he put them on. And though the little boy had not smiled, at least not where Tol or Miss Minnie could see him, he must at least have wanted to smile at the way Tol's stiff gray hair stuck out hither and yon after Tol combed it, as indifferent to the comb as if the comb had been merely fingers or a stick. But when Tol turned away from the washstand, the man looked back to the window and the boy looked down at his knee.

"It's ready," Miss Minnie said to Tol, as she took a pan of biscuits from the oven and slid another in.

Tol went to the chair at the end of the table farthest from the stove. He gestured to the two chairs on either side of the table. "Make yourself at home, now," he said to the man and the boy. "Sit down, sit down."

He sat down himself and the two guests sat down.

"We're mightily obliged," the man said.

"Don't wait on me," Miss Minnie said. "I'll be there in just a minute."

"My boy, reach for that sausage," Tol said. "Take two and pass 'em.

"Have biscuits," he said to the man. "Naw, that ain't enough. Take two or three. There's plenty of 'em."

There was plenty of everything: a platter of sausage, and more already in the skillet on the stove; biscuits brown and light, and more in the oven; a big bowl of navy beans, and more in the kettle on the stove, a big bowl of applesauce and one of mashed potatoes. There was a pitcher of milk and one of buttermilk.

Tol heaped his plate, and saw to it that his guests heaped theirs. "Eat till it's gone," he said, "and don't ask for nothing you don't see."

Miss Minnie sat down presently, and they all ate. Now and again Tol and Miss Minnie glanced at each other, each wanting to be sure the other saw how their guests applied themselves to the food. For the man and the boy ate hungrily without looking up, as though to avoid acknowledging that others saw how hungry they were. And Tol thought, "No breakfast." In his concern for the little boy, he forgot his curiosity about where the two had come from and where they were going.

Miss Minnie helped the boy to more sausage and more beans, and she buttered two more biscuits and put them on his plate. Tol saw how her hand hovered above the boy's shoulder, wanting to touch him. He was a nice-looking little boy, but he never smiled. Tol passed the boy the potatoes and refilled his glass with milk.

"Why, he eats so much it makes him poor to carry it," Tol said. "That boy can put it away!"

The boy looked up, but he did not smile or say anything. Neither Tol nor Miss Minnie had heard one peep out of him. Tol passed everything to the man, who helped himself and did not look up.

"We surely are obliged," he said.

Tol said, "Why, I wish you would look. Every time that boy's elbow bends, his mouth flies open."

But the boy did not smile. He was a solemn boy, far too solemn for his age.

"Well, we know somebody else whose mouth's connected to his elbow, don't we?" Miss Minnie said to the boy, who did not look up and did not smile. "Honey, don't you want another biscuit?"

The men appeared to be finishing up now. She rose and brought to the table a pitcher of sorghum molasses, and she brought the second pan of biscuits, hot from the oven.

The two men buttered biscuits, and then, when the butter had melted, laid them open on their plates and covered them with molasses. And Miss Minnie did the same for the boy. She longed to see him smile, and so did Tol.

"Now, Miss Minnie," Tol said, "that boy will want to go easy on them biscuits from here on, for we ain't got but three or four hundred of 'em left."

But the boy only ate his biscuits and molasses and did not look at anybody.

And now the meal was ending, and what were they going to do? Tol and Miss Minnie yearned toward that nice, skinny, really pretty little boy, and the old kitchen filled with their yearning, and maybe there was to be no answer. Maybe that man and this little boy would just get up in their silence and say, "Much obliged," and go away, and leave nothing of themselves at all.

"My boy," Tol said—he had his glass half-full of buttermilk in his hand, and was holding it up. "My boy, when you drink buttermilk, always remember to drink from the near side of the glass—like this." Tol tilted his glass and took a sip from the near side. "For drinking from the far side, as you'll find out, don't work anything like so well." And then— and perhaps to his own surprise—he applied the far side of the glass to his lips, turned it up, and poured the rest of the buttermilk right down the front of his shirt. And then he looked at Miss Minnie with an expression of absolute astonishment.

For several seconds nobody made a sound. They all were looking at Tol, and Tol, with his hair asserting itself in all directions and buttermilk on his chin and his shirt and alarm and wonder in his eyes, was looking at Miss Minnie.

And then Miss Minnie said quietly, "Mr. Proudfoot, you *are* the limit."

And then they heard the boy. At first it sounded like he had an obstruction in his throat that he worked at with a sort of strangling. And then he laughed.

He laughed with a free, strong laugh that seemed to open his throat as wide as a stovepipe. It was the laugh of a boy who was completely tickled. It transformed everything. Miss Minnie smiled. And then Tol laughed his big hollering laugh. And then Miss Minnie laughed. And then the boy's father laughed. The man and the boy looked up, they all looked full into one another's eyes, and they laughed.

They laughed until Miss Minnie had to wipe her eyes with the hem of her apron.

"Lord," she said, getting up, "what's next?" She went to get Tol a clean shirt.

"Let's have some more biscuits," Tol said. And they all buttered more biscuits and passed the molasses again.

When Miss Minnie brought the clean shirt and handed it to him, Tol just held it in his hand, for he knew that if he stood up to change shirts the meal would end, and he was not ready for it to end yet. The new warmth and easiness of their laughter, the straight way they all had looked at one another, had made the table a lovely place to be. And he liked the boy even better than he had before.

Tol began to talk then. He talked about his place and when he had bought it. He told what kind of year it had been. He spoke of the Proudfoots and their various connections, and wondered if maybe his guests had heard of any of them.

No, the man said, he had never known a Proudfoot until that day. He went so far as to say he knew he had missed something.

Tol then told about marrying Miss Minnie, and said that things had looked up around there on that happy day, which caused Miss Minnie to blush. Miss Minnie had come from a line of folks by the name of Quinch. Had their guests, by any chance, ever run into any Quinches?

But the man said no, there were no Quinches where he came from.

Which brought Tol to the brink of asking the man point-blank where he came from and where he was going. But then the man retrieved his hat from under his chair, and so put an end to all further questions forever, leaving Tol and Miss Minnie to wonder for the rest of their lives.

The man stood up. "We better be on our way," he said. "We're much obliged," he said to Tol. "It was mighty fine," he said to Miss Minnie.

"But wait!" Miss Minnie said. Suddenly she was all in a flutter. "Wait, wait!" she said. "Don't go until I come back!"

She hurried away. All three of them stood now, saying nothing, for a kind of embarrassment had come over them. Now that the meal had ended, now that they had eaten and talked and laughed together for a moment, they saw how little there was that held them. They heard Miss Minnie's footsteps hurry into the front of the house and up the stairs. And then they heard only the wind and the fire crackling quietly in the stove. And then they heard her footsteps coming back.

When she came into the kitchen again, she was carrying over her left arm an old work jacket of Tol's, and holding open with both hands a winter coat of her own that she had kept for second best. She put it on the boy, who obediently put his arms into the sleeves, as if used to doing as a woman told him.

But when she offered the work jacket to the man, he shook his head. The jacket was much patched, worn and washed until it was nearly white.

"It's old, but it's warm," Miss Minnie said.

"No, mam," the man said. For himself, he had reached some unshakable limit of taking. "I can't take the jacket, mam," he said. "But for the boy, I thank you."

He started toward the door then. Miss Minnie hurriedly buttoned the boy into the coat. Tol made as if to help her by prodding the coat here and there with his fingers, feeling between the weather and the boy's skinny back and shoulders the reassuring intervention of so much cloth.

"It's not a fit exactly, but maybe it'll keep him warm," Miss Minnie said as if only to herself. The coat hung nearly to the top of the boy's shoes. "It's good and long," she said.

Her hands darted about nervously, turning the collar up, rolling up the sleeves so that they did not dangle and yet covered the boy's hands. She tucked the boy into the coat as if she were putting him to bed. She snatched a paper bag from a shelf, dumped the remaining biscuits into it out of the pan, and at the last moment, before letting the boy go, shoved the sack into the right-hand pocket of the coat. "There!" she said.

And then they lifted their hands and allowed the boy to go with his father out the door. They followed. They went with the man and boy around the back of the house to the driveway.

The man stopped and turned to them. He raised his hand. "We're mightily obliged," he said. He turned to Miss Minnie, "We're mightily obliged, mam."

"You might as well leave that boy with us," Tol said. He was joking, and yet he meant it with his whole heart. "We could use a boy like that."

The man smiled. "He's a good boy," he said. "I can't hardly get along without this boy."

The two of them turned then and walked away. They went out to the road, through the wind and the gray afternoon and the flying snow, and out of sight.

Tol and Miss Minnie watched them go, and then they went back into the house. Tol put on the clean shirt and his jacket and cap and gloves. Miss Minnie began to clear the table. For the rest of that day, they did not look at each other.

Tol lived nine more years after that, and Miss Minnie twenty more. She was my grandmother's friend, and one day Granddad left Granny and me at the Proudfoot house to visit while he went someplace else. The war was still going on, and Tol had not been dead a year. I sat and listened as the two women talked of the time and of other times. When they spoke of the Depression, Miss Minnie was reminded of the story of the solemn boy, and she told it again, stopping with Tol's words, "We could use a boy like that."

And I remember how she sat, looking down at her apron and smoothing it with her hands. "Mr. Proudfoot always wished we'd had some children," she said. "He never said so, but I know he did."

A Jonquil
for Mary Penn (1940)

Mary Penn was sick, though she said nothing about it when she heard Elton get up and light the lamp and renew the fires. He dressed and went out with the lantern to milk and to feed and harness his team. It was early March, and she could hear the wind blowing, rattling things. She threw the covers off and sat up on the side of the bed, feeling as she did how easy it would be to let her head lean down onto her knees. But she got up, put on her dress and sweater, and went to the kitchen.

Nor did she mention it when Elton came back in, bringing the milk, with the smell of the barn cold in his clothes.

"How're you this morning?" he asked her, giving her a pat as she strained the milk.

And she said, not looking at him, for she did not want him to know how she felt, "Just fine."

He ate hungrily the eggs, sausage, and biscuits that she set in front of him, twice emptying the glass that he replenished from a large pitcher of milk. She loved to watch him eat — there was something curiously delicate in the way he used his large hands — but this morning she busied herself about the kitchen, not looking at him, for she knew he was watching her. She had not even set a place for herself.

"You're not hungry?" he asked.

"Not very. I'll eat something after while."

He put sugar and cream in his coffee and stirred rapidly with the spoon. Now he lingered a little. He did not indulge himself often, but this was one of his moments of leisure. He gave himself to his pleasures as concentratedly as to his work. He was never partial about anything; he never felt two ways at the same time. It was, she thought, a kind of childishness in him. When he was happy, he was entirely happy, and he could be as entirely sad or angry. His glooms were the darkest she had ever seen. He worked as a hungry dog ate, and yet he could play at croquet or cards with the self-forgetful exuberance of a boy. It was for his concentratedness, she supposed, if such a thing could be supposed about, that she loved him. That and her yen just to look at him, for it was wonderful to her the way he was himself in his slightest look or gesture. She did not understand him in everything he did, and yet she recognized him in everything he did. She had not been prepared—she was hardly prepared yet—for the assent she had given to him.

Though he might loiter a moment over his coffee, the day, she knew, had already possessed him; its momentum was on him. When he rose from bed in the morning, he stepped into the day's work, impelled into it by the tension, never apart from him, between what he wanted to do and what he could do. The little hillside place that they had rented from his mother afforded him no proper scope for his ability and desire. They always needed money, but, day by day, they were getting by. Though the times were hard, they were not going to be in want. But she knew his need to surround her with a margin of pleasure and ease. This was his need, not hers; still, when he was not working at home, he would be working, or looking for work, for pay.

This morning, delaying his own plowing, he was going to help Walter Cotman plow his corn ground. She could feel the knowledge of what he had to do tightening in him like a spring. She thought of him and Walter plowing, starting in the early light, and the two teams leaning into the collars all day, while the men walked in the opening furrows, and the steady wind shivered the dry grass, shook the dead weeds, and rattled the treetops in the woods.

He stood and pushed in his chair. She came to be hugged as she knew he wanted her to.

"It's mean out," he said. "Stay in today. Take some care of yourself."

"You, too," she said. "Have you got on plenty of clothes?"

"When I get 'em all on, I will." He was already wearing an extra shirt and a pair of overalls over his corduroys. Now he put on a sweater, his work jacket, his cap and gloves. He started out the door and then turned back. "Don't worry about the chores. I'll be back in time to do everything."

"All right," she said.

He shut the door. And now the kitchen was a cell of still lamplight under the long wind that passed without inflection over the ridges.

She cleared the table. She washed the few dishes he had dirtied and put them away. The kitchen contained the table and four chairs, and the small dish cabinet that they had bought, and the large iron cookstove that looked more permanent than the house. The stove, along with the bed and a few other sticks of furniture, had been there when they came.

She heard Elton go by with the team, heading out the lane. The daylight would be coming now, though the windowpanes still reflected the lamplight. She took the broom from its corner by the back door and swept and tidied up the room. They had been able to do nothing to improve the house, which had never been a good one and had seen hard use. The wallpaper, and probably the plaster behind, had cracked in places. The finish had worn off the linoleum rugs near the doorways and around the stoves. But she kept the house clean. She had made curtains. The curtains in the kitchen were of the same blue-and-white checkered gingham as the tablecloth. The bed stands were orange crates for which she had made skirts of the same cloth. Though the house was poor and hard to keep, she had made it neat and homey. It was her first house, and usually it made her happy. But not now.

She was sick. At first it was a consolation to her to have the whole day to herself to be sick in. But by the time she got the kitchen straightened up, even that small happiness had left her. She had a fever, she guessed, for every motion she made seemed to carry her uneasily beyond the vertical. She had a floaty feeling that made her unreal to herself. And finally, when she put the broom away, she let herself sag down into one of the chairs at the table. She ached. She was overpoweringly tired.

She had rarely been sick and never since she married. And now she did something else that was unlike her: she allowed herself to feel sorry for herself. She remembered that she and Elton had quarreled the night before — about what, she could not remember; perhaps it was not rememberable; perhaps she did not know. She remembered the heavy, mostly silent force of his anger. It had been only another of those tumultuous darknesses that came over him as suddenly and sometimes as unaccountably as a July storm. She was miserable, she told herself. She was sick and alone. And perhaps the sorrow that she felt for herself was not altogether unjustified.

She and Elton had married a year and a half earlier, when she was seventeen and he eighteen. She had never seen anybody like him. He had a wild way of rejoicing, like a healthy child, singing songs, joking, driving his old car as if he were drunk and the road not wide enough. He could make her weak with laughing at him. And yet he was already a man as few men were. He had been making his own living since he was fourteen, when he had quit school. His father had been dead by then for five years. He had hated his stepfather. When a neighbor had offered him crop ground, room, and wages, he had taken charge of himself and, though he was still a boy, he had become a man. He wanted, he said, to have to say thank you to nobody. Or to nobody but her. He would be glad, he said with a large grin, to say thank you to her. And he could *do* things. It was wonderful what he could accomplish with those enormous hands of his. She could have put her hand into his and walked right off the edge of the world. Which, in a way, is what she did.

She had grown up in a substantial house on a good upland farm. Her family was not wealthy, but it was an old family, proud of itself, always conscious of its position and of its responsibility to be itself. She had known from childhood that she would be sent to college. Almost from childhood she had understood that she was destined to be married to a solid professional man, a doctor perhaps, or (and this her mother particularly favored) perhaps a minister.

And so when she married Elton she did so without telling her family. She already knew their judgment of Elton: "He's nothing." She and Elton simply drove down to Hargrave late one October night, awakened a preacher, and got married, hoping that their marriage would be

accepted as an accomplished fact. They were wrong. It was not accept-
able, and it was never going to be. She no longer belonged in that house,
her parents told her. She no longer belonged to that family. To them it
would be as if she had never lived.

She was seventeen, she had attended a small denominational college
for less than two months, and now her life as it had been had ended. The
day would come when she would know herself to be a woman of faith.
Now she merely loved and trusted. Nobody was living then on Elton's
mother's little farm on Cotman Ridge, where Elton had lived for a while
when he was a child. They rented the place and moved in, having just
enough money to pay for the new dish cabinet and the table and four
chairs. Elton, as it happened, already owned a milk cow in addition to his
team and a few tools.

It was a different world, a new world to her, that she came into then —
a world of poverty and community. They were in a neighborhood of six
households, counting their own, all within half a mile of one another.
Besides themselves there were Braymer and Josie Hardy and their children; Tom Hardy and his wife, also named Josie; Walter and Thelma Cotman and their daughter, Irene; Jonah and Daisy Hample and their children; and Uncle Isham and Aunt Frances Quail, who were Thelma
Cotman's and Daisy Hample's parents. The two Josies, to save confusion, were called Josie Braymer and Josie Tom. Josie Tom was Walter
Cotman's sister. In the world that Mary Penn had given up, a place of far
larger and richer farms, work was sometimes exchanged, but the families were conscious of themselves in a way that set them apart from
one another. Here, in this new world, neighbors were always working
together. "Many hands make light work," Uncle Isham Quail loved to
say, though his own old hands were no longer able to work much.

Some work only the men did together, like haying and harvesting the
corn. Some work only the women did together: sewing or quilting or
wallpapering or house-cleaning; and whenever the men were together
working, the women would be together cooking. Some work the men
and women did together: harvesting tobacco or killing hogs or any other
job that needed many hands. It was an old community. They all had
worked together a long time. They all knew what each one was good at.
When they worked together, not much needed to be explained. When
they went down to the little weather-boarded church at Goforth on Sun-

day morning, they were glad to see one another and had much to say, though they had seen each other almost daily during the week.

This neighborhood opened to Mary and Elton and took them in with a warmth that answered her parents' rejection. The men, without asking or being asked, included Elton in whatever they were doing. They told him when and where they needed him. They came to him when he needed them. He was an apt and able hand, and they were glad to have his help. He learned from them all but liked best to work with Walter Cotman, who was a fine farmer. He and Walter were, up to a point, two of a kind; both were impatient of disorder—"I can't stand a damned mess," said Walter, and he made none—and both loved the employment of their minds in their work. They were unlike in that Walter was satisfied within the boundaries of his little farm, but Elton could not have been. Nonetheless, Elton loved his growing understanding of Walter's character and his ways. Though he was a quiet man and gave neither instruction nor advice, Walter was Elton's teacher, and Elton was consciously his student.

Once, when they had killed hogs and Elton and Mary had stayed at home to finish rendering their lard, the boiling fat had foamed up and begun to run over the sides of the kettle. Mary ran to the house and called Walter on the party line.

"Tell him to throw the fire to it," Walter said. "Tell him to dip out some lard and throw it on the fire."

Elton did so, unbelieving, but the fire flared, grew hotter, the foaming lard subsided in the kettle, and Elton's face relaxed from anxiety and self-accusation into a grin. "Well," he said, quoting Walter in Walter's voice, "it's all in knowing how."

Mary, who had more to learn than Elton, became a daughter to every woman in the community. She came knowing little, barely enough to begin, and they taught her much. Thelma, Daisy, and the two Josies taught her their ways of cooking, cleaning, and sewing; they taught her to can, pickle, and preserve; they taught her to do the women's jobs in the hog killing. They took her on their expeditions to one another's houses to cook harvest meals or to houseclean or to gather corn from the fields and can it. One day they all walked down to Goforth to do some wallpapering for Josie Tom's mother. They papered two rooms, had a good time, and Josie Tom's mother fixed them a dinner of fried chicken, creamed new potatoes and peas, hot biscuits, and cherry cobbler.

In cold weather they sat all afternoon in one another's houses, quilting or sewing or embroidering. Josie Tom was the best at needlework. Everything she made was a wonder. From spring to fall, for a Christmas present for someone, she always embroidered a long cloth that began with the earliest flowers of spring and ended with the last flowers of fall. She drew the flowers on the cloth with a pencil and worked them in with her needle and colored threads. She included the flowers of the woods and fields, the dooryards and gardens. She loved to point to the penciled outlines and name the flowers as if calling them up in their beauty into her imagination. "Look-a-there," she would say. "I even put in a jimson-weed." "And a bull thistle," said Tom Hardy, who had his doubts about weeds and thistles but was proud of her for leaving nothing out.

Josie Tom was a plump, pretty, happy woman, childless but the mother of any child in reach. Mary Penn loved her the best, perhaps, but she loved them all. They were only in their late thirties or early forties, but to Mary they seemed to belong to the ageless, eternal generation of mothers, unimaginably older and more experienced than herself. She called them Miss Josie, Miss Daisy, and Miss Thelma. They warmed and sheltered her. Sometimes she could just have tossed herself at them like a little girl to be hugged.

They were capable, unasking, generous, humorous women, and sometimes, among themselves, they were raucous and free, unlike the other women she had known. On their way home from picking black-berries one afternoon, they had to get through a new barbed wire fence. Josie Tom held two wires apart while the other four gathered their skirts, leaned down, and straddled through. Josie Tom handed their filled buckets over. And then Josie Braymer held the wires apart, and Josie Tom, stooping through, got the back of her dress hung on the top wire.

"I *knew* it!" she said, and she began to laugh.

They all laughed, and nobody laughed more than Josie Tom, who was standing spraddled and stooped, helpless to move without tearing her dress.

"Josie Braymer," she said, "are you going to just stand there, or are you going to unhook me from this shitten fence?"

And there on the ridgetop in the low sunlight they danced the dance of women laughing, bending and straightening, raising and lowering their hands, swaying and stepping with their heads back.

Daylight was full in the windows now. Mary made herself get up and extinguish the lamp on the table. The lamps all needed to be cleaned and trimmed and refilled, and she had planned to do that today. The whole house needed to be dusted and swept. And she had mending to do. She tied a scarf around her head, put on her coat, and went out.

Only day before yesterday it had been spring — warm, sunny, and still. Elton said the wildflowers were starting up in the leafless woods, and she found a yellow crocus in the yard. And then this dry and bitter wind had come, driving down from the north as if it were as long and wide as time, and the sky was as gray as if the sun had never shone. The wind went through her coat, pressed her fluttering skirt tight against her legs, tore at her scarf. It chilled her to the bone. She went first to the privy in a back corner of the yard and then on to the henhouse, where she shelled corn for the hens and gave them fresh water.

On her way back to the house she stood a moment, looking off in the direction in which she knew Elton and Walter Cotman were plowing. By now they would have accepted even this day as it was; by now they might have shed their jackets. Later they would go in and wash and sit down in Thelma's warm kitchen for their dinner, hungry, glad to be at rest for a little while before going back again to work through the long afternoon. Though they were not far away, though she could see them in her mind's eye, their day and hers seemed estranged, divided by great distance and long time. She was cold, and the wind's insistence wearied her; the wind was like a living creature, rearing and pressing against her so that she might have cried out to it in exasperation, "*What* do you want?"

When she got back into the house, she was shivering, her teeth chattering. She unbuttoned her coat without taking it off and sat down close to the stove. They heated only two rooms, the kitchen and the front room where they slept. The stove in the front room might be warmer, she thought, and she could sit in the rocking chair by it; but having already sat down, she did not get up. She had much that she needed to be doing, she told herself. She ought at least to get up and make the bed.

And she wanted to tend to the lamps; it always pleased her to have them clean. But she did not get up. The stove's heat drove the cold out of her clothes, and gradually her shivering stopped.

They had had a hard enough time of it their first winter. They had no fuel, no food laid up. Elton had raised a crop but no garden. He borrowed against the crop to buy a meat hog. He cut and hauled in firewood. He worked for wages to buy groceries, but the times were hard and he could not always find work. Sometimes their meals consisted of biscuits and a gravy made of lard and flour.

And yet they were often happy. Often the world afforded them something to laugh about. Elton stayed alert for anything that was funny and brought the stories home. He told her how the tickle-ass grass got into Uncle Isham's pants, and how Daisy Hample clucked to her nearsighted husband and children like a hen with half-grown chicks, and how Jonah Hample, missing the steps, walked off the edge of Braymer Hardy's front porch, fell into a rosebush, and said, "Now, I didn't go to do that!" Elton could make the funny things happen again in the dark as they lay in bed at night; sometimes they would laugh until their eyes were wet with tears. When they got snowed in that winter, they would drive the old car down the hill until it stalled in the drifts, drag it out with the team, and ram it into the drifts again, laughing until the horses looked at them in wonder.

When the next year came, they began at the beginning, and though the times had not improved, they improved themselves. They bought a few hens and a rooster from Josie Braymer. They bought a second cow. They put in a garden. They bought two shoats to raise for meat. Mary learned to preserve the food they would need for winter. When the cows freshened, she learned to milk. She took a small bucket of cream and a few eggs to Port William every Saturday night and used the money she made to buy groceries and to pay on their debts.

Slowly she learned to imagine where she was. The ridge named for Walter Cotman's family is a long one, curving out toward the river between the two creek valleys of Willow Run and Katie's Branch. As it comes near to the river valley it gets narrower, its sides steeper and more deeply incised by hollows. When Elton and Mary Penn were making their beginning there, the uplands were divided into many farms, few of which contained as much as a hundred acres. The hollows, the steeper hillsides, the bluffs along the sides of the two creek valleys were covered with thicket or woods. From where the hawks saw it, the ridge would have seemed a long, irregular promontory reaching out into a sea of trees. And it bore on its back crisscrossings of other trees along the stone or rail or wire fences, trees in thickets and groves, trees in the house-yards. And on rises of ground or tucked into folds were the gray, paint-less buildings of the farmsteads, connected to one another by lanes and paths. Now she thought of herself as belonging there, not just because of her marriage to Elton but also because of the economy that the two of them had made around themselves and with their neighbors. She had learned to think of herself as living and working at the center of a won-derful provisioning: the kitchen and garden, hog pen and smokehouse, henhouse and cellar of her own household; the little commerce of giv-ing and taking that spoked out along the paths connecting her house-hold to the others; the two creeks in their valleys on either side; and all this at the heart of the weather and the world.

On a bright, still day in the late fall, after all the leaves were down, she had stood on the highest point and had seen the six smokes of the six houses rising straight up into the wide downfalling light. She knew which smoke came from which house. It was like watching the rising up of prayers or some less acknowledged communication between Earth and Heaven. She could not say to herself how it made her feel.

She loved her jars of vegetables and preserves on the cellar shelves, and the potato bin beneath, the cured hams and shoulders and bacons hanging in the smokehouse, the two hens already brooding their clutches of marked eggs, the egg basket and the cream bucket slowly fill-ing, week after week. But today these things seemed precious and far away, as if remembered from another world or another life. Her sickness made things seem arbitrary and awry. Nothing had to be the way it was. As easily as she could see the house as it was, she could imagine it empty, windowless, the tin roof blowing away, the chimneys crumbling, the cellar caved in, weeds in the yard. She could imagine Elton and herself gone, and the rest of them—Hardy, Hample, Cotman, and Quail— gone too.

Elton could spend an hour telling her—and himself—how Walter Cotman went about his work. Elton was a man in love with farming, and she
could see him picking his way into it with his understanding. He wanted
to know the best ways of doing things. He wanted to see how a way of
doing came out of a way of thinking and a way of living. He was interested in the ways people talked and wore their clothes.

The Hamples were another of his studies. Jonah Hample and his
young ones were almost useless as farmers because, as Elton maintained,
they could not see all the way to the ground. They did not own a car
because they could not see well enough to drive—"They need to drive
something with eyes," Elton said—and yet they were all born mechan-
ics. They could fix anything. While Daisy Hample stood on the porch
clucking about the weeds in their crops, Jonah and his boys and sometimes his girls, too, would be busy with some machine that somebody
had brought for them to fix. The Hample children went about the neighborhood in a drove, pushing a fairly usable old bicycle that they loved but
could not ride.

Elton watched Braymer, too. Unlike his brother and Walter Cotman,
Braymer liked to know what was going on in the world. Like the rest of
them, Braymer had no cash to spare, but he liked to think about what he
would do with money if he had it. He liked knowing where something
could be bought for a good price. He liked to hear what somebody had
done to make a little money and then to think about it and tell the others
about it while they worked. "Braymer would be a trader if he had a
chance," Elton told Mary. "He'd like to try a little of this and a little of
that, and see how he did with it. Walter and Tom like what they've got."

"And you don't like what you've got," Mary said.

He grinned big at her, as he always did when she read his mind. "I like
some of it," he said.

At the end of the summer, when she and Elton were beginning their
first tobacco harvest in the neighborhood, Tom Hardy said to Elton,
"Now, Josie Braymer can outcut us all, Elton. If she gets ahead of you,
just don't pay it any mind."

"Tom," Elton said, "I'm going to leave here now and go to the other
end of this row. If Josie Braymer's there when I get there, I'm going
home."

When he got there Josie Braymer was not there, and neither were any of the men. It was not that he did not want to be bested by a woman; he did not want to be bested by anybody. One thing Mary would never have to do was wonder which way he was. She knew he would rather die than be beaten. It was maybe not the best way to be, she thought, but it was the way he was, and she loved him. It was both a trouble and a comfort to her to know that he would always require the most of himself. And he was beautiful, the way he moved in his work. It stirred her.

She could feel ambition constantly pressing in him. He could do more than he had done, and he was always looking for the way. He was like an axman at work in a tangled thicket, cutting and cutting at the brush and the vines and the low limbs, trying to make room for a full swing. For this year he had rented corn ground from Josie Tom's mother down by Goforth, two miles away. When he went down with his team to work, he would have to take his dinner. It would mean more work for them both, but he was desperate for room to exert himself. They were poor as the times, they saw more obstacles than openings, and yet she believed without doubt that Elton was on his way.

It was not his ambition—his constant, tireless, often exhilarated pre-occupation with work—that troubled her. She could stay with him in that. She had learned that she could do, and do well and gladly enough, whatever she would have to do. She had no fear. What troubled her were the dark and mostly silent angers that often settled upon him and estranged him from everything. At those times, she knew, he doubted himself, and he suffered and raged in his doubt. He may have been born with this doubt in him, she sometimes imagined; it was as though his soul were like a little moon that would be dark at times and bright at others. But she knew also that her parents' rejection had cost him dearly. Even as he defied them to matter to him, they held a power over him that he could not shake off. In his inability to forgive them, he consented to this power, and their rejection stood by him and measured him day by day. Her parents' pride was social, belonging, even in its extremity, to their kind and time. But Elton's pride was merely creaturely, albeit that of an extraordinary creature; it was a creature's naked claim on the right to respect itself, a claim that no creature's life, of itself, could invariably sup-port. At times he seemed to her a man in the light in daily struggle with a man in the dark, and sometimes the man in the dark had the upper hand.

Elton never felt that any mistake was affordable; he and Mary were living within margins that were too narrow. He required perfection of himself. When he failed, he was like the sun in a cloud, alone and burning, furious in his doubt, furious at her because she trusted in him though he doubted. How could she dare to love him, who did not love himself? And then, sometimes accountably, sometimes not, the cloud would move away, and he would light up everything around him. His own force and intelligence would be clear within him then; he would be skillful and joyful, passionate in his love of order, funny and tender.

At his best, Elton was a man in love — with her but not just with her. He was in love too with the world, with their place in the world, with that scanty farm, with his own life, with farming. At those times she lived in his love as in a spacious house.

Walter Cotman always spoke of Mary as Elton's "better half." In spite of his sulks and silences, she would not go so far as "better." That she was his half, she had no doubt at all. He needed her. At times she knew with a joyous ache that she completed him, just as she knew with the same joy that she needed him and he completed her. How beautiful a thing it was, she thought, to be a half, to be completed by such another half! When had there ever been such a yearning of halves toward each other, such a longing, even in quarrels, to be whole? And sometimes they would be whole. Their wholeness came upon them as a rush of light, around them and within them, so that she felt they must be shining in the dark.

But now that wholeness was not imaginable; she felt herself a part without counterpart, a mere fragment of something unknown, dark and broken off. The fire had burned low in the stove. Though she still wore her coat, she was chilled again and shaking. For a long time, perhaps, she had been thinking of nothing, and now misery alerted her again to the room. The wind ranted and sucked at the house's corners. She could hear its billows and shocks, as if somebody off in the distance were shaking a great rug. She felt, not a draft, but the whole atmosphere of the room moving coldly against her. She went into the other room, but the fire there also needed building up. She could not bring herself to do it. She was shaking, she ached, she could think only of lying down. Standing near the stove, she undressed, put on her nightgown again, and got into the bed.

She lay chattering and shivering while the bedclothes warmed around her. It seemed to her that a time might come when sickness would be a great blessing, for she truly did not care if she died. She thought of Elton, caught up in the day's wind, who could not even look at her and see that she was sick. If she had not been too miserable, she would have cried. But then her thoughts began to slip away, like dishes sliding along a table pitched as steeply as a roof. She went to sleep.

When she woke, the room was warm. A teakettle on the heating stove was muttering and steaming. Though the wind was still blowing hard, the room was full of sunlight. The lamp on the narrow mantel shelf behind the stove was filled and clean, its chimney gleaming, and so was the one on the stand by the bed. Josie Tom was sitting in the rocker by the window, sunlight flowing in on the unfinished long embroidery she had draped over her lap. She was bowed over her work, filling in with her needle and a length of yellow thread the bright corolla of a jonquil — or "Easter lily," as she would have called it. She was humming the tune of an old hymn, something she often did while she was working, apparently without awareness that she was doing it. Her voice was resonant, low, and quiet, barely audible, as if it were coming out of the air and she, too, were merely listening to it. The yellow flower was nearly complete.

And so Mary knew all the story of her day. Elton, going by Josie Tom's in the half-light, had stopped and called.

She could hear his voice, raised to carry through the wind: "Mrs. Hardy, Mary's sick, and I have to go over to Walter's to plow."

So he had known. He had thought of her. He had told Josie Tom.

Feeling herself looked at, Josie Tom raised her head and smiled. "Well, are you awake? Are you all right?"

"Oh, I'm wonderful," Mary said. And she slept again.

Turn Back the Bed (1941)

To some, it seemed that Ptolemy Proudfoot didn't laugh like a Christian. He laughed too loud and too long, and his merriment seemed a little too self-sufficient — as if, had there been enough funny stories and enough breath to laugh at them with, he might not *need* to go to Heaven.

What tickled him as much as anything were his own stories about his grandfather, Mark Anthony Proudfoot, known as Ant'ny and later, of course, as Old Ant'ny. Old Ant'ny was, you might say, the Tol Proudfoot of his generation, with a few differences, the main one being that whereas Tol was childless, Old Ant'ny sired a nation of Proudfoots. Once his progeny had grown up and acquired in-laws and produced scions of their own, they seemed as numerous as the sand that is upon the seashore.

The great events of Tol's boyhood were the family gatherings that took place three or four times a year at Old Ant'ny's place above Goforth in the Katy's Branch valley. By that time Ant'ny was in his old age. He had always been a big man, and now, with less activity and no loss of appetite, he had grown immense. He sat at these meetings, as massive and permanent-seeming almost as the old log house itself, holding a cane in his hand, seldom stirring from the chair that one of his sons had constructed for him out of poplar two-by-fours. He sat erect and mostly in silence, looking straight ahead, his white beard reaching down to his fourth shirt button. Now and then he would say something in a rolling deep voice that whoever was in the room would stop and listen to. And now and then he would reach out with his cane and hook a passing grandson or great-grandson, whose name and the name of whose parents he would demand to know. But for the most part he sat in silence, his patriarchal influence extending to a radius of about six feet, while round him the fruit of his loins revolved, battering floor and walls, like a storm.

Old Ant'ny was a provider, and he did provide. He saw to it that twelve hogs were slaughtered for his own use every fall — and twenty-four hams and twenty-four shoulders and twenty-four middlings were hung in his smokehouse. And his wife, Maw Proudfoot, kept a flock of turkeys and a flock of geese and a flock of guineas, and her henhouse was as populous as a county seat. And long after he was "too old to farm," Old Ant'ny grew a garden as big as some people's crop. He picked and dug and fetched, and Maw Proudfoot canned and preserved and pickled and cured as if they had an army to feed — which they more or less did, for there were not only the announced family gatherings but always somebody or some few happening by, and always somebody to give something to.

The Proudfoot family gatherings were famous. As feasts, as collections and concentrations of good things, they were unequaled. Especially in summer there was nothing like them, for then there would be old ham and fried chicken and gravy, and two or three kinds of fish, and hot biscuits and three kinds of cornbread, and potatoes and beans and roasting ears and carrots and beets and onions, and corn pudding and corn creamed and fried, and cabbage boiled and scalloped, and tomatoes stewed and sliced, and fresh cucumbers soaked in vinegar, and three or four kinds of pickles, and if it was late enough in the summer there would be watermelons and muskmelons, and there would be pies and cakes and cobblers and dumplings, and milk and coffee by the gallon. And there would be, too, half a dozen or so gallon or half-gallon stone jugs making their way from one adult male to another as surreptitious as moles. For in those days the Proudfoot homeplace, with its broad cornfields in the creek bottom, was famous also for the excellence of its whiskey.

So of course these affairs were numerously attended. When the word went out to family and in-laws it was bound to be overheard, and people came in whose veins Proudfoot blood ran extremely thin, if at all. And there would be babble and uproar all day, for every door stood open, and the old house was not ceiled; the upstairs floorboards were simply nailed to the naked joists, leaving cracks that you could not only hear through but in places see through. Whatever happened anywhere could be heard everywhere.

The storm of feet and voices would continue unabated from not long after sunup until after sundown when the voice of Old Ant'ny would rise abruptly over the multitude: "Well, Maw, turn back the bed. These folks want to be gettin' on home." And then, as if at the bidding of some Heavenly sign, the family sorted itself into its branches. Children and shoes and hats were found, identified, and claimed; horses were hitched; and the tribes of the children of Old Ant'ny Proudfoot set out in their various directions in the twilight.

In himself and in his life, Tol Proudfoot had come a considerable way from the frontier independence and uproariousness of Old Ant'ny's household. He was a gentler, a more modest, perhaps a smarter man than his grandfather. And he had submitted, at least somewhat, to the quieting and ordering influence of Miss Minnie. But there was something in Tol, in his spirit as well as in his memory, that hung back there in the time of those great family feasts, which had been a godsend to every boy, at least, who ever attended one.

By the time I came to know him, Tol was well along in years. He had become an elder of the community, and had recognized his memories, the good ones anyhow, as gifts, to himself and to the rest of us. His stories of Old Ant'ny and the high old family times were much in demand, not just because they were good to listen to in their own right, but because certain people enjoyed hearing—and watching—Tol laugh at them. Once he got tickled enough, you could never tell what would happen. He had broken the backs off half a dozen chairs, rearing back in them to laugh. Once, at an ice cream supper, he fell backward onto a table full of cakes.

My grandparents took me to a picnic one Sunday at the Goforth church where Tol and Miss Minnie went. After the morning service, the women spread the food out on tables under the big old oak trees in the churchyard, and then we gathered around and sang "Blessed Be the

Tie That Binds," and the minister gave thanks for the food, and we ate together, some finding places at the tables, some sitting in the shade of the trees, holding their plates on their laps.

Afterward the men drew off to themselves, carrying their chairs up to the edge of the graveyard. There was a good breeze there on the higher ground, and fine dark shade under the cedars. They took smokes and chews, and the talk started, first about crops and weather and then about other things. I don't remember exactly how, but a little merriment started. Then somebody said, "Tol, tell that un about Old Ant'ny and the chamber pot."

They were sitting more or less in a circle in the shade of two big cedars, and in the silences you could hear the breeze pulling through the branches. Tol was sitting with his back to the graveyard, his chair tilted back, the gravestones spread out behind him. He had outlived nearly everybody he would tell about, some of whom lay within the sound of his voice, and he was sitting not far from the spot where we would lay him to rest before two more years had passed.

Below us the women were sitting together near the tables, where they had finished straightening up. You could hear the sound of their voices but not what they said. I remember the colors of their dresses: white and pink and yellow, ginghams and flower prints; the widows all in dark blue or black, the dresses of the older women reaching to their ankles. And I remember how perfect it all seemed, so still and comfortable. The Second World War had started in Europe, but in my memory it seems that none of us yet knew it.

Tol had picked up a dead cedar branch to whittle. His knife was sharp, and the long, fine, fragrant shavings curled and fell backward over his wrists. He was smiling.

"Boys," he said, "I couldn't tell it all in a day."

He laughed a little and said no more. Nobody else said anything either. After a minute he began to tell the story. I wasn't anything but a boy then. I can't tell it the way he told it, but this is the way he put it in my mind.

It was a fine, bright Sunday in October, the year Tol was five years old. The Proudfoots had gathered at Old Ant'ny's. The family had drawn in its various branches, in-laws, and acquaintances. Old Ant'ny had turned out his own mules and horses to make stall room, and by midmorning the barn was full, and saddled horses and harnessed teams stood tied to fence posts.

All the wives had brought food and other necessaries to add to the bounty already laid in and prepared by Old Ant'ny and Maw Proudfoot, and the big kitchen and back porch were full of women and the older girls, setting out dishes and pitchers and glasses and bowls on tables spread with white cloths.

The Proudfoot men were gathered around the hearth in what was called "the front room," where Old Ant'ny sat and where in the early morning there had been a fire. Later, as their numbers grew and the day warmed, some of them sat along the edge of the front porch and others in the open doorway of the barn.

The girls who were too little to help played or visited quietly enough with each other. They were well acquainted, happy to be together again, and possessed of a certain civility and dignity. There was never much trouble from them.

The trouble came from the boys, or, more exactly, from the boys between the ages of about five and about eleven, who did not come with any plans or expectations, and who therefore took their entertainment as a matter of adventure, making do with whatever came to hand. There were, Tol said, "a dozen, maybe twenty" of them.

Before dinner they were kept fairly well under control. They were getting hungry, for one thing, and that held them close to the house. For another thing, the parents were more alert before dinner than they would be afterward. Afterward, they would be full and comfortable and a little sleepy, and most of the men would be a little sleepier and more comfortable than the women, for by then they would have met with some stealthily wandering jug of Old Ant'ny's whiskey.

That was the way it always worked. During the morning the boys were kept within eyesight of the grown-ups, and pretty well apart from each other. They fretted and jiggled and asked when dinner would be ready, and got corrected and fussed at and threatened. And then after dinner the range of grown-up eyesight shortened, and that was when the boys got together and began to run. This was their time of freedom, and to preserve it they ran. Whenever they were near the house, where they knew they might be seen and called down, they ran. They ran in a pack, the big ones in front, the little ones behind. Tol was the littlest one that year, and the farthest behind, but he kept the rest of them in sight. Most of them were Proudfoots, and they all looked more or less like Proudfoots. And as long as there were so many of them and they were all running, by the time one of them could be recognized and called to, they all would be gone.

They ran up the hill behind the barn and over into a wooded draw where their band raveled out into a game of tag, and then a game of hide-and-go-seek — a great crashing and scuffling in the fallen dry leaves. The biggest boy that year was Tol's cousin Lester, whose hair, plastered down with water early that morning, now stuck up like the tail of a young rooster, and whose eyes were wide open in expectation.

Tag and hide-and-go-seek didn't last long. Lester kept changing the rules until nobody wanted to play. Then Old Ant'ny's hounds treed a groundhog in a little slippery elm, and Lester climbed up to shake him out. Lester took his jacket off so he could climb better. When he threw it down, the dogs, thinking it was the groundhog, piled on it and tore it up. While they were tearing up Lester's jacket, the groundhog jumped out of the tree and ran into a hole. The big boys found a couple of sticks and helped the dogs dig until they came to a rock ledge and had to give up.

All that took a while. They had been missed by then, and Aunt Belle was on the back porch, calling, "Oh, Lester!" So they answered and went back, running, allowing themselves to be seen and forgotten again, and ran on across the cornfield to the creek.

They played follow-the-leader, which lasted a long time, because Lester was the leader. They went along the rocks at the edge of the creek and then waded a riffle and came back across walking a fallen tree trunk. And then Lester said, "Follow my tracks," and started taking giant steps across a sand bar. It was a long straddle, and by the time Tol got there the tracks were a foot deep and full of water. He got stuck with his feet apart and fell over sideways.

"Come here, mud man," Lester said. "Come here, mud boy." And he soused Tol, clothes and all, down into the deep cold water and rinsed him off.

Tol started crying. He said a word he had learned from Uncle O. R. and threw a rock at Lester, and everybody laughed, and then Tol did.

Aunt Belle was on the front porch now, hollering again. She was a big

woman with a strong voice. Lester answered and they all started running back toward the house, leaving Tol behind. He was getting tired,
and so he walked on to the house. When he got there the other boys
were gone again, out of sight. He went up on the back porch, taking care
to avoid notice, and found a plate of biscuits under a cloth on the wash
table and took two and went on toward the front door. The women were
in the kitchen and in the parlor, talking. Old Ant'ny and Uncle O. R. and
Uncle George Washington and Uncle Will and Uncle Fowler and some
others were in the front room. A brown and white jug, stoppered with a
corncob, was sitting by Uncle Fowler's chair like a contented cat. They
weren't going to pay any attention to Tol, and he stepped inside the door
to eat his biscuits. Uncle Fowler leaned forward in his chair to spit in the
fireplace and fell headfirst into the ashes. Old Ant'ny never even looked.
The others may have looked or they may not. They never said anything.
But Uncle O. R. looked. He was standing on the corner of the hearth,
leaning one shoulder against the mantel. He said, "Fowler, you're putting a right smart effort into your spitting, seems like."

Uncle Fowler got himself out of the ashes and into his chair again.
"Whoo, Lordy, Lordy!" he said, and fanned himself with his hand, causing a few ashes to float out of his mustache.

Tol crammed the whole second biscuit into his mouth, and ran back
through the house and out the back door, blowing crumbs ahead of him
as he ran.

Lester was up on the roof. He had climbed up on the cellar, and then
onto the cellar house roof, and then onto the back porch roof, and then
onto the roof of the ell that held the kitchen and dining room, and now
he was walking up the slope of the roof over the living room and the bedroom above it toward the chimney. Maw Proudfoot's yellow tomcat was
weaving in and out between Lester's feet, stroking himself on Lester's
legs. The pack of boys had backed up as Lester climbed, keeping him in
sight.

It was a big rock chimney built against the end of the house. Lester
reached into it, and held up a black palm for the others to see. The yellow
cat climbed up onto the chimney beside Lester. He walked back and forth
along the copestones, rubbing himself against Lester's shoulder, his tail
stuck straight up, with a little crook on the end of it like a walking cane.

It was past sundown now. The light was going out of the sky, and it was turning cool. Except for the pack of boys, everybody was in the house. Nobody had started home. They would get home in the dark and still have the milking to do; maybe the thought of that had quieted them. The old house hovered over them now like a mother hen.

Lester backed away a step, and he and the yellow cat stood looking at each other, balanced across the foot or so of air that divided them. Some fascination grew upon them. The boys watching down in the yard felt it. And then Lester raised his hand and gave a little push.

When Lester pushed the cat, he said, "Wup!"

The cat disappeared, clean out of sight, as if the sky had bitten it off. They heard a fit of scratching inside the chimney, and then it ceased. Lester looked over into the chimney mouth. And then he looked around and down at his cousins. His eyes were as wide open as if he had never batted one of them once in his life.

"He didn't go all the way down," Lester said. "He ain't going to make it back up."

Lester looked down at his cousins, and they looked up at him. Nobody moved or spoke. For maybe as long as a minute, nobody had any idea what would happen next. And then Lester's eye fell on Toby.

Several hounds were sitting alongside the pack of boys, watching too, with the same balked expectancy, and Toby was with them. Toby was Old Ant'ny's feist, white with black ears and a black spot in front of his tail. He was a nervous little dog who had courage instead of brains. He would fight anything, would go unhesitatingly into a hole after a varmint, or anywhere after a cat.

"Send up old Tobe," Lester said.

One of the older boys put Toby in the crook of his arm and carried him up onto the kitchen roof. Lester met him and took the dog. He went back up to the chimney and held Toby so he could look in. He might have intended just to show Toby to the cat so as maybe to scare the cat into going on down. Tol didn't know. But whatever Lester intended to do turned out to be beside the point. When the cat saw Toby, he spit at him. They could hear it all the way down in the yard. Toby gave a little yelp, in horror probably at what he was about to do, and jumped out of Lester's arms onto the lip of the chimney and down onto the cat.

The boys had already started running before Toby jumped. When they passed the chimney, they heard Toby and the cat inside, falling and fighting.

They went on around and through the front door and into the living room just in time to see the ashes in the fireplace rise up in a cloud. And then the cat, with Toby behind him, broke out and ran up Uncle Fowler's leg and up his belly and up over the top of his head and off the back of his chair and through the crowd of boys and out into the hall. Old Ant'ny never looked, never turned his head. He just sat there like some people's idea of God, as if having set this stir in motion, he would let it play itself out on its own, as if he despaired of any other way of stopping it. Uncle Fowler, who had been asleep, woke up, spitting ashes, just as Toby cleared the chair back.

"Pew!" Uncle Fowler said. He sighed and shut his eyes again in great weariness.

The only one with enough presence of mind to move at all was Uncle O. R., who started out, running after Toby, only to get tangled up in the crowd of boys standing in the door.

The cat treed under the chiffonier in the hall, but Toby brought him out of there, and by the time Uncle O. R. got free of the boys, the cat had run into the kitchen and down the middle of the table, with Toby still on his heels, and over Aunt Belle's shoulder and out the window. They left a sooty streak down the middle of the cloth.

Aunt Belle was on her feet now. "Who the *hell* let that cat in? And that *damn* dog? *Where* are you, Lester?"

Uncle O. R. ran on out through the kitchen. The pack of boys, who had been following Uncle O. R., got to the dining room door just in time to run smack into Aunt Belle, who was coming out. She was red in the face and already puffing; she just bounced them all out of the way and ran on up the hall toward the front door. They fell in behind her, running as dutifully as if they were still playing follow-the-leader.

Aunt Belle ran out the front door and across the porch and down the porch steps and out in the yard just as Lester came around the corner of the house with Uncle O.R. gaining on him. Lester's eyes were wider open than ever, his hair was sticking up stiff and straight.

Aunt Belle was still running, too. She was light on her feet for a big woman, and when Lester dodged she turned back quick as a turkey hen.

The pack of boys was in the way, so Lester couldn't run on past the porch steps; without intending to, they headed him, and Aunt Belle and Uncle O.R. drove him up onto the porch and through the front door. The women had all come out of the kitchen into the hall, and Uncle George Washington and Uncle Will were starting out of the living room. Lester took the only open route — up the stairs.

Aunt Belle had cut in ahead of Uncle O. R., and she started up, too. She had her skirts bundled in front of her like a load of laundry, and she was going as fast as Lester.

He got to the top of the stairs and ran into the room over the living room, flinging the door to behind him. But Aunt Belle was right there and caught it before it slammed. When Aunt Belle and Uncle O. R. and the rest of the boys went into the room there was nobody in sight, but they could hear the sound of breathing under the bed. And through the cracks between the floorboards they could hear Uncle Fowler snoring by the fire down in the living room.

Aunt Belle got down on her hands and knees and looked under.

"Uh *huh!*" she said. "Young mister, I been a-laying for you."

She crawled partway under, caught Lester by the foot, and dragged him out spread-eagled, turning over a chamber pot that had been left unemptied under the edge of the bed.

The boys got downstairs again in time to see the golden shower spend its last drops upon the head and shoulders of Old Ant'ny, who sat unmoving as before, looking straight ahead, as though he had foreseen it all years ago and was resigned.

"Lor-dee!" Uncle O. R. said.

It was getting dark now. There was a lamp burning in the room, and you could no longer see out the windows. There was a moment that seemed to be the moment before anything else could happen.

And then Old Ant'ny's hat brim jerked upward just a fraction of an inch. "Maw, turn back the bed. These folks want to be gettin' on home."

Little snorts of laughter had been leaking out of Tol for some time, and now he let himself laugh. It was a good laugh, broad and free and loud, including all of us as generously as the shade we sat in, and not only those of us who were living, but Old Ant'ny and Maw Proudfoot and

Uncle O. R. and Uncle Fowler and Aunt Belle and Lester and the rest whose bodies lay in their darkness nearby.

And I will never forget the ones who were still alive that day and how they looked: old Tol with his hands at rest in his lap, laughing until tears ran down his face, and the others around him laughing with him. It was Tol's benediction, as I grew to know, on that expectancy of good and surprising things that had kept Lester's eyes, and Tol's, too, wide open for so long.

And years later my grandmother would tell me that down among the women, hearing Tol laugh, Miss Minnie had smiled the prim, matronly smile with which she delighted in him. "Mr. Proudfoot," she said. "Mr. Proudfoot is amused."

Making It Home (1945)

He had crossed the wide ocean and many a river. Now not another river lay between him and home but only a few creeks that he knew by name. Arthur Rowanberry had come a long way, trusting somebody else to know where he was, and now he knew where he was himself. The great river, still raised somewhat from the flood of that spring and flowing swiftly, lay off across the fields to his left; to his right and farther away were the wooded slopes of the Kentucky side of the valley, and over it all, from the tops of the hills on one side to the tops of the hills on the other, stretched the gray sky. He was walking along the paved road that followed the river upstream to the county seat of Hargrave. On the higher ground to the right of the road stood fine brick farmhouses that had been built a hundred and more years ago from the earnings of the rich bottomland fields that lay around them. There had been a time when those houses had seemed as permanent to him as the land they stood on. But where he had been, they had the answer to such houses.

"We wouldn't let one of them stand long in our way," he thought.

Art Rowanberry walked like the first man to discover upright posture —as if, having been a creature no taller than a sheep or a pig, he had suddenly risen to the height of six feet and looked around. He walked too like a man who had been taught to march, and he wore a uniform. But whatever was military in his walk was an overlay, like the uniform, for he had been a man long before he had been a soldier, and a farmer long before he had been a man. An observer might have sensed in his walk and in the way he carried himself a reconciliation to the forms and distances of the land such as comes only to those who have from childhood been accustomed to the land's work.

The noises of the town were a long way behind him. It was too early for the evening chores, and the farmsteads that he passed were quiet. Birds sang. From time to time he heard a farmer call out to his team. Once he had heard a tractor off somewhere in the fields and once a towboat out on the river, but those sounds had faded away. No car had passed him, though he walked a paved road. There was no sound near him but the sound of his own footsteps falling steadily on the pavement.

Once it had seemed to him that he walked only on the place where he was. But now, having gone and returned from so far, he knew that he was walking on the whole round world. He felt the great, empty distance that the world was turning in, far from the sun and the moon and the stars.

"Here," he thought, "is where we do what we are going to do — the only chance we got. And if somebody was to be looking down from up there, it would all look a lot littler to him than it does to us."

He was talking carefully to himself in his thoughts, forming the words more deliberately than if he were saying them aloud, because he did not want to count his steps. He had a long way still to go, and he did not want to know how many steps it was going to take. Nor did he want to hear in his head the counted cadence of marching.

"I ain't marching," he thought. "I am going somewheres. I am going up the river towards Hargrave. And this side of Hargrave, before the bridge, at Ellville, I will turn up the Kentucky River, and go ten miles, and turn up Sand Ripple below Port William, and I will be at home."

He carried a duffel bag that contained his overcoat, a change of clothes, and a shaving kit. From time to time, he shifted the bag from one shoulder to the other.

"I reckon I am done marching, have marched my last step, and now I am walking. There is nobody in front of me and nobody behind. I have come here without a by-your-leave to anybody. Them that have known where I was, or was supposed to, for three years don't know where I am now. Nobody that I know knows where I am now."

He came from killing. He had felt the ground shaken by men and what they did. Where he was coming from, they thought about killing day after day, and feared it, and did it. And out of the unending, unrelenting great noise and tumult of the killing went little deaths that belonged to people one by one. Some had feared it and had died. Some had died without fearing it, lacking the time. They had fallen around him until he was amazed that he stood — men who in a little while had become his buddies, most of them younger than he, just boys.

The fighting had been like work, only a lot of people got killed and a lot of things got destroyed. It was not work that *made* much of anything. You and your people intended to go your way, if you could. And you wanted to stop the other people from going their way, if you could. And whatever interfered you destroyed. You had a thing on your mind that you wanted, or wanted to get to, and anything at all that stood in your way, you had the right to destroy. If what was in the way were women and little children, you would not even know it, and it was all the same. When your power is in a big gun, you don't have any small intentions. Whatever you want to hit, you want to make dust out of it. Farm buildings, houses, whole towns — things that people had made well and cared for a long time — you made nothing of.

"We blew them apart and scattered the pieces so they couldn't be put together again. And people, too. We blew them apart and scattered the pieces."

He had seen tatters of human flesh hanging in the limbs of trees along with pieces of machines. He had seen bodies without heads, arms and legs without bodies, strewn around indifferently as chips. He had seen the bodies of men hanging upside down from a tank turret, lifeless as dolls.

Once, when they were firing their gun, the man beside him — Eckstrom — began to dance. And Art thought, "This ain't no time to be dancing." But old Eckstrom was dancing because he was shot in the head, was killed, his body trying on its own to keep standing.

And others had gone down, near enough to Art almost that he could have touched them as they fell: Jones, Bitmer, Hirsch, Walters, Corelli.

He had seen attackers coming on, climbing over the bodies of those who had fallen ahead of them. A man who, in one moment, had been a helper, a friend, in the next moment was only a low mound of something in the way, and you stepped over him or stepped on him and came ahead.

Once while they were manning their gun and under fire themselves, old Eckstrom got mad, and he said, "I wish I had those sons of bitches lined up to where I could shoot every damned one of them."

And Art said, "Them fellers over there are doing about the same work we are, 'pears like to me."

There were nights when the sky and all the earth appeared to be on fire, and yet the ground was covered with snow and it was cold.

At Christmas he was among those trapped at Bastogne. He had expected to die, but he was spared as before though the ground shook and the town burned under a sky bright as day. They held their own, and others, fighting on the outside, broke through.

"We was mighty glad to see that day when it come," he thought. "That was a good day."

The fighting went on, the great tearing apart. People and everything else were torn into pieces. Everything was only pieces put together that were ready to fly apart, and nothing was whole. You got to where you could not look at a man without knowing how little it would take to kill him. For a man was nothing but just a little morsel of soft flesh and brittle bone inside of some clothes. And you could not look at a house or a schoolhouse or a church without knowing how, rightly hit, it would just shake down into a pile of stones and ashes. There was nothing you could look at that was whole—man or beast or house or tree—that had the right to stay whole very long. There was nothing above the ground that was whole but you had the measure of it and could separate its pieces and bring it down. You moved always in a landscape of death, wreckage, cinders, and snow.

And then, having escaped so far, he was sitting by his gun one afternoon, eating a piece of chocolate and talking to an old redheaded, freckle-faced boy named McBride, and a shell hit right where they were. McBride just disappeared. And a fragment came to Art as if it were his own and had known him from the beginning of the world, and it burrowed into him.

From a man in the light on the outside of the world, he was trans-formed in the twinkling of an eye into a man in the dark on the inside of himself, in pain, and he thought that he was dead. How long he was in that darkness he did not know. When he came out of it, he was in a place that was white and clean, a hospital, and he was in a long room with many beds. There was sunlight coming in the window.

A nurse who came by seemed glad to see him. "Well, hello, bright eyes," she said.

He said, "Why, howdy."

She said, "I think the war is over for you, soldier."

"Yes, mam," he said. "I reckon it is."

She patted his shoulder. "You almost got away from us, you know it?"

And he said, "Yes, mam, I expect I did."

The uniform he wore as he walked along the road between Jefferson and Hargrave was now too big for him. His shirt collar was loose on his neck, in spite of the neatly tied tie, and under his tightened belt the waistband of his pants gathered in pleats.

He stayed in hospitals while his life grew back around the wound, as a lightning-struck tree will sometimes heal over the scar, until finally they gave him his papers and let him go.

And now, though he walked strongly enough along the road, he was still newborn from his death, and inside himself he was tender and a little afraid.

The bus had brought him as far as the town of Jefferson on the north side of the river, letting him out in the middle of the afternoon in front of the hotel that served also as a bus station. From there, he could have taken another bus to Hargrave had he been willing to wait until the next morning. But now that he was in familiar country he did not have it in him to wait. He had known a many a man who would have waited, but he was old for a soldier; though he was coming from as far as progress had reached, he belonged to an older time. It did not occur to him, any more than it would have occurred to his grandfather, to wait upon a machine for something he could furnish for himself. And so he thanked the kind lady at the hotel desk, shouldered his bag, and set out for home on foot.

The muddy Ohio flowed beneath the bridge and a flock of pigeons wheeled out and back between the bridge and the water, causing him to sway as he walked, so that to steady himself he had to look at the hills that rose over the rooftops beyond the bridge. He went down the long southward arc of the bridge, and for a little while he was among houses again, and then he was outside the town, walking past farmsteads and fields in unobstructed day. The sky was overcast, but the clouds were high.

"It ought to clear off before morning," he thought. "Maybe it'll be one of them fine spring days. Maybe it'll do to work, for I have got to get started."

They would already have begun plowing, he thought — his father and his brother, Mart. Though they had begun the year without him, they would be expecting him. He could hear his father's voice saying, "Any day now. Any day."

But he was between lives. The war had been a life, such as it was, and now he was out of it. The other life, the one he had once had and would have again, was still ahead of him; he was not in it yet.

He was only free. He had not been out in the country or alone in a long time. Now that he had the open countryside around him again and was alone, he felt the expectations of other people fall away from him like a shed skin, and he came into himself.

"I am not under anybody's orders," he thought. "What I expect myself to do, I will do it. The government don't owe me, and I don't owe it. Except when I have something again that it wants, then I reckon I will owe it."

It pleased him to think that the government owed him nothing, that he needed nothing from it, and he was on his own. But the government seemed to think that it owed him praise. It wanted to speak of what he and the others had done as heroic and glorious. Now that the war was coming to an end, the government wanted to speak of their glorious victories. The government was made up of people who thought about fighting, not of those who did it. The men sitting behind desks — they spent other men to buy ground, and then they ruined the ground they had and more men to get the ground beyond. If they were on the right side, they did it the same as them that were on the wrong side.

"They talk about victory as if they know all them dead boys was glad to die. The dead boys ain't never been asked how glad they was. If they had it to do again, might be they wouldn't do it, or might be they would. But they ain't been asked."

Under the clouds, the country all around was quiet, except for birds singing in the trees, wherever there were trees, and now and then a human voice calling out to a team. He was glad to be alive.

He had been glad to be alive all the time he had been alive. When he was hit and thought he was dead, it had come to him how good it was to be alive even under the shelling, even when it was at its worst. And now he had lived through it all and was coming home. He was now a man who had seen far places and strange things, and he remembered them all. He had seen Kansas and Louisiana and Arizona. He had seen the ocean. He had seen the little farms and country towns of France and Belgium and Luxembourg—pretty, before they were ruined. For one night, he was in Paris.

"That Paris, now. We was there one day and one night. There was wine everywheres, and these friendly girls who said, 'Kees me.' And I don't know what happened after about ten o'clock. I come to the next morning in this hotel room, sick and broke, with lipstick from one end to the other. I reckon I must have had a right good time."

At first, before he was all the way in it, there was something he liked about the war, a reduction that in a way was pleasing. From a man used to doing and thinking for himself, he became a man who did what he was told.

"That laying around half a day, waiting for somebody else to think— that was something I had to *learn*."

It was fairly restful. Even basic training tired him less than what he would ordinarily have done at that time of year. He gained weight.

And from a man with a farm and crops and stock to worry about, he became a man who worried only about himself and the little bunch of stuff he needed to sleep, dress, eat, and fight.

He furnished only himself. The army furnished what little else it took to make the difference between a man and a beast. More than anything else, he liked his mess kit. It was all the dishes a man really needed. And

when you weren't cooking or eating with it, you could keep things in it
— a little extra tobacco, maybe.

"When I get to Ellville," he thought, "I won't be but mighty little
short of halfway. I know the miles and how they lay out end to end."

It had been evening for a while now. On the farmsteads that he
passed, people were busy with the chores. He could hear people calling
their stock, dogs barking, children shouting and laughing. On one farm
that he passed, a woman, a dog, and a small boy were bringing in the
cows; in the driveway of the barn he could see a man unharnessing a
team of mules. It was as familiar to him as his own breath, and because
he was outside it still, he yearned toward it as a ghost might. As he
passed by, the woman, perhaps because he was a soldier, raised her hand
to him, and he raised his own in return.

After a while, he could see ahead of him the houses and trees of Ellville, and over the trees the superstructure of the bridge arching into
Hargrave. All during his walk so far, he had been offering himself the
possibility that he would walk on home before he would sleep. But now
that he had come nearly halfway and Ellville was in sight, he knew he
would not go farther that day. He was tired, and with his tiredness had
come a sort of melancholy and a sort of aimlessness, as if, all his ties cut,
he might go right on past his home river and on and on, anywhere at all
in the world. The little cluster of buildings ahead of him now seemed
only accidentally there, and he himself there only accidentally. He had
arrived, as he had arrived again and again during the healing of his
wound, at the apprehension of a pure emptiness, as if at the center of an
explosion — as if, without changing at all, he and the town ahead of him
and all the long way behind him had been taken up into a dream in which
every creature and every thing sat, like that boy McBride, in the dead
center of the possibility of its disappearance.

In the little town a lane turned off the highway and went out beyond
the houses and across the river bottom for perhaps a quarter of a mile to
a barn and, beyond the barn, to a small weatherboarded church. It was
suppertime then; the road and the dooryards were deserted. Art entered
the lane and went back past the gardens and the clutter of outbuildings
that lay behind the houses. At the barn there was a cistern with a chain

pump. He set down his bag and pumped and drank from his cupped left hand held under the spout.

"Looks like I ought to be hungry," he thought. "But I ain't."

He was not hungry, and there was no longer anything much that he wanted to think. He was tired. He told himself to lift the bag again and put it on his shoulder. He told his feet to walk, and they carried him on to the church. The door was unlocked. He went in.

He shut the door behind him, not allowing the latch to click. The quiet inside the church was palpable; he came into it as into a different element, neither air nor water. He crossed the tiny vestibule where a bell rope dangled from a worn hole in the ceiling, went through another door that stood open, and sat down on the first bench to his left, leaving his duffel bag in the aisle, propped against the end of the bench. He let himself become still.

"I will eat a little," he thought, "'gainst I get hungry in the night."

After a while he took a bar of candy from the bag and slowly ate it. The church windows were glazed with an amber-colored glass that you could not see through, and though it was still light outdoors, in the church it was dusk. When he finished the candy, he folded the wrapper soundlessly and put it in his pocket. Taking his overcoat from the bag to use as a blanket, he lay down on the bench. Many thoughts fled by him, none stopping. And then he slept.

He woke several times in the night, listening, and, hearing no threat out in the darkness anywhere, slept again. The last time he woke, roosters were crowing, and he sat up. He sat still a while in the dark, allowing the waking quiet of the place to come over him, and then he took another bar of candy from his bag and ate it and folded the wrapper and put it in his pocket as before. The night chill had seeped into the church; standing, he put on the overcoat. He picked up his bag and felt his way to the door.

It had cleared and the sky was full of stars. To the east, upriver, he could see a faint brightening ahead of the coming day. All around him the dark treetops were throbbing with birdsong, and from the banks of the two rivers at their joining, from everywhere there was water, the voices of spring peepers rose as if in clouds. Art stood still and looked around him and listened. It was going to be the fine spring day that he had imagined it might be.

He thought, "If a fellow was to be dead now, and young, might be he would be missing this a long time."

There was a privy in back of the church and he went to it. And then, on his way out of the lane, he stopped at the barn and drank again at the cistern.

Back among the houses, still dark and silent among their trees, he took the road that led up into the smaller of the two river valleys. There was no light yet from the dawn, but by the little light of the stars he could see well enough. All he needed now was the general shape of the place given by various shadows and loomings.

"I have hoofed it home from here a many a night," he thought. "Might be I could do it if I was blind. But I can see."

He could see. And he walked along, feeling the joy of a man who sees, a joy that a man tends to forget in sufficient light. The quiet around him seemed wide as the whole country and deep as the sky, and the morning songs of the creatures and his own footsteps occurred distinctly and separately in it, making a kind of geography and a kind of story. As he walked the light slowly strengthened. As he more and more saw where he was, it seemed to him more and more that he was walking in his memory or that he had entered, awake, a dream that he had been dreaming for a long time.

He was hungry. The candy bar that he had eaten when he woke had hardly interrupted his hunger.

"My belly thinks my throat has been cut. It is laying right flat against my backbone."

It was a joy to him to be so hungry. Hunger had not bothered him much for many weeks, had not mattered, but now it was as vivid to him as a landmark. It was a tree that put its roots into the ground and spread its branches out against the sky.

The east brightened. The sun lit the edges of a few clouds on the horizon and then rose above them. He was walking full in its light. It had not shone on him long before he had to take off the overcoat, and he folded and rolled it neatly and stuffed it into his bag. By then he had come a long way up the road.

Now that it was light, he could see the marks of the flood that had recently covered the valley floor. He could see drift logs and mats of cornstalks that the river had left on the low fields. In places where the river ran near the road, he could see the small clumps of leaves and grasses that the currents had affixed to the tree limbs. Out in one of the bottoms he saw two men with a team and wagon clearing the scattered debris from their fields. They had set fire to a large heap of drift logs, from which the pale smoke rose straight up. Above the level of the flood, the sun shone on the small, still-opening leaves of the water maples and on the short new grass of the hillside pastures.

As he went along, Art began to be troubled in his mind: How would he present himself to the ones at home? He had not shaved. Since before his long ride on the bus he had not bathed. He did not want to come in, after his three-year absence, like a man coming in from work, unshaven and with his clothes mussed and soiled. He must appear to them as what he had been since they saw him last, a soldier. And then he would be at the end of his soldiering. He did not know yet what he would be when he had ceased to be a soldier, but when he had thought so far his confusion left him.

He came to the mouth of a small tributary valley. Where the stream of that valley passed under the road, he went down the embankment, making his way, first through trees and then through a patch of dead horseweed stalks, to the creek. A little way upstream he came to a place of large flat rocks that had been swept clean by the creek and were now in the sun and dry. Opening the duffel bag, he carefully laid its contents out on the rocks. He took out his razor and brush and soap and a small mirror, and knelt beside the stream and soaped his face and shaved. The water was cold, but he had shaved with cold water before. When he had shaved, he took off his clothes and, standing in flowing water that instantly made his feet ache, he bathed, quaking, breathing between his teeth as he raised the cold water again and again in his cupped hands.

Standing on the rocks in the sun, he dried himself with the shirt he had been wearing. He put on his clean, too-large clothes, tied his tie, and combed his hair. And then warmth came to him. It came from inside himself and from the sun outside; he felt suddenly radiant in every vein and fiber of his body. He was clean and warm and rested and hungry. He was well.

He was in his own country now, and he did not see anything around him that he did not know.

"I have been a stranger and have seen strange things," he thought. "And now I am where it is not strange, and I am not a stranger."

He was sitting on the rocks, resting after his bath. His bag, repacked, lay on the rock beside him and he propped his elbow on it.

"I am not a stranger, but I am changed. Now I know a mighty power that can pass over the earth and make it strange. There are people, where I have been, that won't know their places when they get back to them. Them that live to get back won't be where they were when they left."

He became sleepy and he lay down on the rock and slept. He slept more deeply than he had in the night. He dreamed he was where he was, and a great, warm light fell upon that place, and there was light within it and within him.

When he returned to the road after his bath and his sleep, it was past the middle of the morning. His steps fell into their old rhythm on the black-top.

"I know a mighty power," he thought. "A mighty power of death and fire. An anger beyond the power of any man, made big in machines equal to many men. And a little man who has passed through mighty death and fire and still lived, what is he going to think of himself when he is back again, walking the river road below Port William, that we would have blowed all to flinders as soon as look at it if it had got in our way?"

He walked, as before, the left side of the road, not meaning to ask for rides. But as on the afternoon before, there was little traffic. He had met two cars going down toward Hargrave and had been passed by only one coming up.

Where the road began to rise toward Port William up on the ridge, a lesser road branched off to the left and ran along the floor of the valley. As Art reached this intersection, he heard a truck engine backfiring, coming down the hill, and then the truck came into sight and he recognized it. It was an old green International driven, as he expected and soon saw, by a man wearing a trucker's cap and smoking a pipe. The truck was loaded with fat hogs, heading for the packing plant at Jefferson. As he went by, the old man waved to Art and Art waved back.

"Sam Hanks," he thought. "I have been gone over three years and have traveled a many a thousand miles over land and ocean, and in all that time and all them miles the first man I have seen that I have always known is Sam Hanks."

He tried to think what person he had seen last when he was leaving, but he could not remember. He took the lesser road and, after perhaps a mile, turned into a road still narrower, only a pair of graveled wheel tracks. A little later, when the trees were fully leaved, this would be almost a burrow, tunneling along between the creek and the hillside under the trees, but now the leaves were small and the sun cast the shadows of the branches in a close network onto the gravel.

Soon he was walking below the high-water line. He could see it clearly marked on the slope to his right: a line above which the fallen leaves of the year before were still bright and below which they were darkened by their long steeping in the flood. The slope under the trees was strewn with drift, and here and there a drift log was lodged in the branches high above his head. In the shadow of the flood the spring was late, the buds of the trees just opening, the white flowers of twinleaf and bloodroot just beginning to bloom. It was almost as if he were walking under water, so abrupt and vivid was the difference above and below the line that marked the crest of the flood. But somewhere high in the sunlit branches a redbird sang over and over in a clear, pealing voice, "Even so, even so."

And there was nothing around him that Art did not know. He knew the place in all the successions of the year: from the little blooms that came in the earliest spring to the fallen red leaves of October, from the songs of the nesting birds to the anxious wintering of the little things that left their tracks in snow, from the first furrow to the last load of the harvest.

Where the creek turned away from the road the valley suddenly widened and opened. The road still held up on the hillside among the trees, permitting him to see, through the intervening branches, the broad field that lay across the bottom. He could see that plowing had been started; a long strip had been back-furrowed out across the field, from the foot of the slope below the road to the trees that lined the creek bank. And then he saw, going away from him, almost out to the end of the strip, two mule teams with two plowmen walking in the opening furrows. The plowmen's heads were bent to their work, their hands riding easy on the handles of the plows. Some distance behind the second plowman was a little boy, also walking in the furrow and carrying a tin can; from time to time he bent and picked something up from the freshly turned earth and dropped it into the can. Walking behind the boy was a large hound. The first plowman was Art's father, the second his brother Mart. The boy was Art's sister's son, Roy Lee, who had been two years old when Art left and was now five. The hound was probably Old Bawler, who made it a part of his business to be always at work. Roy Lee was collecting fishing worms, and Art looked at the creek and saw, in an open place at the top of the bank, as he expected, three willow poles stuck into the ground, their lines in the water.

The first of the teams reached the end of the plowland, and Art heard his father's voice clear and quiet: "Gee, boys." And then Mart's team finished their furrow, and Mart said, "Gee, Sally." They went across the headland and started back.

Art stood as if looking out of his absence at them, who did not know he was there, and he had to shake his head. He had to shake his head twice to persuade himself that he did not hear, from somewhere off in the distance, the heavy footsteps of artillery rounds striding toward them.

He pressed down the barbed wire at the side of the road, straddled over it, and went down through the trees, stopping at the foot of the slope. They came toward him along the edge of the plowland, cutting it two furrows wider. Soon he could hear the soft footfalls of the mules, the trace ends jingling, the creaking of the doubletrees. Present to himself, still absent to them, he watched them come.

At the end of the furrow his father called, "Gee!" and leaned his plow over so that it could ride around the headland on the share and right handle. And then he saw Art. "Well now!" he said, as if only to himself.

"Whoa!" he said to the mules. And again: "Well now!" He came over to Art and put out his hand and Art gave him his.

Art saw that there were tears in his father's eyes, and he grinned and said, "Howdy."

Early Rowanberry stepped back and looked at his son and said again, "Well now!"

Mart came around onto the headland then and stopped his team. He and Art shook hands, grinning at each other.

"You reckon your foot'll still fit in a furrow?"

Art nodded. "I reckon it still will."

"Well, here's somebody you don't hardly know," Mart said, gesturing toward Roy Lee, "and who don't know you at all, I'll bet. Do you know who this fellow is, Roy Lee?"

Roy Lee probably did not know, though he knew he had an uncle who was a soldier. He knew about soldiers—he knew they fought in a war far away—and here was a great, tall, fine soldier in a soldier suit with shining buttons, and the shoes on his feet were shining. Roy Lee felt something akin to awe and something akin to love and something akin to fear. He shook his head and looked down at his bare right foot.

Mart laughed. "This here's your Uncle Art. You know about Uncle Art." To Art he said, "He's talked enough about you. He's been looking out the road to see if you was coming."

Art looked up the creek and across it at the house and outbuildings and barn. He looked at the half-plowed field on the valley floor with the wooded hillsides around it and the blinding blue sky over it. He looked again and again at his father and his young nephew and his brother. They stood up in their lives around him now in such a way that he could not imagine their deaths.

Early Rowanberry looked at his son, now and then reaching out to grasp his shoulder or his arm, as if to feel through the cloth of the uniform the flesh and bone of the man inside. "Well now!" he said again, and again, "Well now!"

Art reached down and picked up a handful of earth from the furrow nearest him. "You're plowing it just a little wet, ain't you?"

"Well, we've had a wet time," Mart said. "We felt like we had to go ahead. Maybe we'll get another hard frost. We could yet."

Art said, "Well, I reckon we might."

And then he heard his father's voice riding up in his throat as he had never heard it, and he saw that his father had turned to the boy and was speaking to him:

"Honey, run yonder to the house. Tell your granny to set on another plate. For we have our own that was gone and has come again."

Where Did They Go? (1947)

For every day he lived, my father could imagine two or three others that
he would like to live if he did not have to do what he had to do. "Your
father," my mother used to say to my brother and me, to explain him to
us, "has eyes bigger than his stomach." We understood that, and it did
not seem strange to us that most of our mornings, on school-year week-
ends and in summer, would begin with a summons to the bathroom
where our father would be shaving and thinking. "Andy!" he would say.
"Henry! Come here, boys."

As we stood at his elbows, he would describe for us in detail a day,
impossible for himself, that he nonetheless had in mind. Some would be
workdays, and he would talk his way through a set of little jobs at the
farm that he did not have time to do himself, anticipating problems,
solutions, and incidental satisfactions. Others were pleasure days, and he
would tell us how he thought a certain pond or the holes in a certain
creek might be successfully fished, or where there was a hickory tree
loaded with nuts, or where we might find a covey of birds. As he hurriedly applied the lather to his face, shaved, and dressed for his day at the
office, he would loiter over the details: from what direction to approach
the covey, how to manage the dog; what kind of pole and what kind of
bait to use, by the roots of which old tree we should drop in our lines.
The workday instructions were orders. The others were suggestions; he
was telling us what he would do if he were us and had the happiness of

living that day outside the demands of his particular life. We were to be his delegates to the great realm of possibility.

Of course, the world and the imagination being what they are, we often failed him—mismanaged his instructions, or refused to take his suggestions. But his was a practical imagination, and sometimes we succeeded. Even when we failed them, his imaginings remained with us, so that we inherited from him early his abounding sense of the possibilities of the countryside lying around our ancestral town of Port William. After forty years I can recollect, as vividly as if they had happened, a number of hunting and fishing jaunts that he imagined and none of us ever made.

Thus it was news but no surprise to me when he called me into the bathroom one May morning in 1947 to tell me that I was to work for Jake Branch that summer as a hired hand. My father had bought the old Mack Crayton place in 1940, and Jake and Minnie Branch had come there to do the farming and to shelter and feed their large and ever-larger family—"the multitude," as my father called it. The Crayton place had been badly run down; my father had bought it partly because of his vision of how it would look cleaned up and put to rights. It was a job of work that he would have loved to take part in, but had little time to take part in, and so was sending me to take part in, with his proxy, so to speak, not as the bearer of his authority, but as the heir of his imagined joy.

That this was to be a part of my education, I also understood. My father's strongest-held theory of education was that if Henry and I could learn the use of our hands, then, whatever might happen to us as a result of the use or misuse of our heads, we at least need not starve. From Jake Branch—and from Elton Penn, the Coulters, my grandfathers, my father himself—I did learn the use of my hands. But when he put me under the tutelage of Jake Branch, my father in effect abandoned me to a vast and chancy curriculum of which nobody was in charge.

This plan of my father's suited me as well as it did him, probably better, though for a different reason. My reason was that it would put me for the whole summer in the company of R. T., Minnie Branch's youngest son by her first marriage. From the neck down, R. T. looked as I, at the age of thirteen, would have died to look. He looked, from the neck down, like Michelangelo's *David*. From the neck up, he looked like nothing on earth but himself. He had a nose that appeared to have been pushed hard onto his face by God's thumb. His tongue lived in the corner of his mouth, hospitable to the occasional gnat or fly that lit there to drink. He was sixteen and had been, in body, a grown man for three or four years. I admired him without reservation. When he discovered my awe of him, there was virtually no limit to the stunts he undertook to amuse me: catch and ride bridleless an unbroke two-year-old mule, or run headfirst under a sizable rick of baled hay, or lift off the ground the hind legs of a Jersey cow that Jake Branch happened at the time to be milking. The latter feat earned him a lick over the head with the milking stool that would have felled an ordinary mortal, but not R. T., who merely staggered loose from the cow, and, crossing his eyes, donated his pain and suffering to the good cause of my amusement.

Besides R. T. and Minnie and Jake, there was also Ester, the youngest of Minnie's first family of six, she and R. T. being the only two still living at home. Ester was fifteen and a big girl, who seemed forever at work in the kitchen, where, heaven knows, there was an endless amount of work to do. She favored me, every time I looked at her, with a wild giggle, which made me feel that I was party to a conspiracy that I had not heard about, which made me blush, which made her giggle, until Minnie would tell her, "Shut up, girl! Leave him alone!"

And there were Lillybelle and Col Oaks, Lillybelle one of the five children of Jake's first set, and Col her husband, whose style she no longer even tried to live up to. Col was a dandy. His attention to himself—to what a more vulgar time would call his "image"—would have been almost ladylike, had it not been so clearly the result of a monopolizing male vanity. There was a precision of self-adulation in the way he rolled a smoke, the way he rolled his sleeves, the way he cocked his hat, the way he grinned around a matchstick held delicately always between the same pair of incisors, the way his voice quavered when he sang "Born to Lose." A hundred times a day, Col would lift his hat in a three-fingered pinch as exquisite as a jeweler's, toss back his languorous forelock, and replace the hat as though preparing to meet, if not his Maker, perhaps the press. This procedure required him to stop absolutely whatever he might be doing, and was almost routinely concluded by a curse from his father-in-law, who in the meantime might have been holding up one end

of a log. The smooth underside of Col's right forearm bore the tattoo of
a scantily clad lady who danced when Col flexed his muscles, and in the
midst of work he would sometimes spend long minutes studying it,
slowly doubling and relaxing his fist, whether entranced by the loveliness of his own arm or by the lady who danced there, I could not tell. For
these and other reasons, Jake had renamed him Noah. Noah Count.

With the same justice, he called Lillybelle Mrs. Noah Count. Lillybelle spent most of her time at odds with her father over his remarriage,
and consequently at odds with Minnie, and with all the rest of the house.
She stayed all day, when they would let her, in her and Col's upstairs
room where they did "light housekeeping." She was childless, bitterly
jolly, disappointed, lazy, and mean—mad at everybody, jealous of Col,
afraid of the dark. I used to visit her sometimes because she was always
nice to me and I liked to hear the things she would say about the others.
She would be sitting, fat and sad, in her yellow chenille bathrobe, her
hair in curlers, eating pear preserves out of the jar with a long spoon,
without benefit of bread, "just making it through to Saturday night." On
Saturday night, when she and Col would go down to Hargrave to the
double feature and other social attractions, she would emerge from their
room done up in lipstick and curls and high heels, smelling, Jake said,
"like two rose bushes and one honeysuckle."

There were also Jake's and Minnie's own children: Angeleen, Beureen,
Coreen, Delano (who had by fate of gender escaped being Doreen), the
twins, Eveleen and Franklin (alias Floreen), and one soon to be born,
already named Gloreen or Grover, as the case might be—"all of 'em the
same age," my father said, "or damn near it." To say that Minnie was
fertile would be an understatement. Her womb was the horn of plenty
itself, from which her babes leapt, as my father maintained, after only
five months, wide-eyed and yelling vigorously, ready, according to Jake,
to go to work, milking and spreading manure. Jake was awed by his
prowess as a sire. "They going to have to do something about me," he
would say gaily. "All I got to do is *look* at her."

That was the regular family membership. But in that spring of 1947
there was also Reenie, Jake's youngest child by his first wife, who still
lived with her mother at Hargrave, and who had come to visit and to
help set out the crop. Reenie was eighteen that spring, a small, beauti-

fully made, brash-talking girl with freckles across her nose and short brown curls that filled with red lights when the sun shone on them. R. T., I knew, was in love with her. "Reenie" was short for Irene, and it was Reenie's prettiness, I think, that had suggested to Minnie the ideal of a string of girl children, alphabetically ordered, all named something-een.

There was, finally, Leaf Trim, Jake's full-time hired hand — hired, Jake said, because he had to have *somebody* who both knew how to work and would. Leaf lived in the room above the kitchen, reached by a narrow, steep stair between the back porch and the kitchen wall. I went up there once with R. T., and I remember how that room astonished me. Its sole piece of furniture was a large wooden bedstead covered with a strawtick ripped down the side and leaking straw onto the floor. It was a room as unceremoniously occupied as a stall in the barn.

Leaf was a gaping stutterer and a veteran of World War I. He had been to Paris, and he told R. T. and me stories of French ladies who did a dance of couples called the jigjig — only Leaf, because of his speech impediment, sang the word and made it rather lyrical: "Ji-igjiig." That jigjigging in Paris, it seemed, had been the high point of his life, for the ladies there, he said, "di-id it be-etter than mm-ah-anything you e-ever sa-aw." The subject fascinated R. T., and embarrassed him, made him put his cap on crossways and grin and bite his tongue. I ingratiated myself with him by cross-examining Leaf closely on the subject of jigjigging. "Ask him what she done after that," R. T. would whisper, and I would ask, and Leaf would tell.

This had been a subject keenly interesting to me and my schoolmates for some time. We were aware of girls off yonder in their world, and we supposed that eventually there was going to be some sort of meeting between our kind and their kind. We had heard a good deal about jigjigging, under different names, and we talked about it a good deal. We knew that it happened among the animals. We assumed that it had happened among our parents, and that we were the results, but we had very little in the way of empirical evidence. One of the boys in our class had seen his parents performing the jigjig, or something like it, in a dry creek bed, but it is hard to establish common usage on the basis of a single instance. I had hoped that R. T. might be able to help, but if R. T. was better informed than I was, he would not admit it, and he was not of a speculative turn of mind. And so I was delighted to receive Leaf Trim's testimony, even if it did imply that jigjigging was an activity that went on mostly in foreign countries. I wondered if Leaf's own jigjigging days were not about over, in any case, for he had lost several front teeth and tobacco juice was usually glistening in the creases of his chin.

Though talking put Leaf to extreme effort, tightening the cords of his neck, when he sang his voice came sweet and free. To hear him stop talking, which he seldom did, and start to sing "The Wabash Cannonball" or "Footprints in the Snow" always seemed a sort of miracle to me, as if a groundhog had suddenly soared into the air like a swallow. "Leaf" was a merciful foreshortening of Lafayette, which would have been a fancy mouthful for poor Leaf, if he had ever said it.

There was a big weatherboarded frame house on the Crayton place then, burned down now, and Jake Branch's domestic enterprise had filled it to overflowing. There was not an empty or a quiet corner in it. It was always full of clatters, shouts, scrapes, laughs, cries, screams, songs, grunts, snores, blows, jars, and shocks of every kind. This wondrous commotion was, in a manner of speaking, overseen by a great spreading white oak, a member of the old original forest, that stood in the yard and shaded the porch and the front of the house in the afternoon. On fair days in warm weather much of the work and most of the social life of the household went on under it. I had not grown far enough from childhood to make much of coincidences; to me, it seemed merely appropriate that people named Oaks and Branch and Leaf should live under an oak tree.

When my father let me out of the car early in the morning, and I walked back the driveway past the house to the barn, I could usually hear Minnie talking in the house. She had a carrying voice — in its ordinary conversational range, if the weather was quiet, you could stand half a mile away and understand every word she said — and most of her household talk consisted of commands: "Delano, *get* that damned old nasty mop out of that baby's *face!* Angeleen, is *that* what you call *sweeping?* Ester, *hurry* up now and get them dishes done! Beureen! *Get* out of them ashes! I *told* you!" And then she might start whistling, as sweetly as if she were off somewhere in the woods by herself. She could whistle anything, trilling it out like a bird; you wanted to stop and listen. "Don't never go nowhere in the dark with a whistling woman," Jake liked to say to me in her presence, and wink and shake his head.

I would go on back to the barn where they would have the mules harnessed and ready to go to the field, usually, by the time I got there, and Jake would tell me what he wanted me to do. He made it a point of honor not to treat me as the boss's son. "Wheeler," he said to my father, "I'll treat him just like he was my own boy," a proposition to which I thought my father agreed too readily. Though Jake did not swing at me with whatever he happened to have in his hand, which was his way, frequently, of bringing R. T. back to reality, at times he did, as he put it, speak to me "pretty plain." "*Now* what in the hell are you doing, Andy?" he would say, or, "What you need for that is your little ass kicked." And once when I had taken off my shirt in imitation of R. T., Jake looked down at my physique from his seat on the tobacco-setter barrel, spat over the wheel, and pronounced: "*Mouse* tits!"

He could be kind too, and sometimes was, even to Col, and he was the first man who ever trusted me to work by myself. Later that same summer he sent me to the tobacco patch with a hoe and a file and a jug of water. "When you can step on the head of your shadow, Andy, come in for dinner." I found that I could not lengthen my leg, and that only the climb of the unhurriable sun toward meridian could shorten my shadow. And so I learned that I lived under law, as if my father had not already told me.

When I got out of school and began work for Jake that year, they were setting out the tobacco crop. It was a big crop, and Jake was in a sort of ecstasy compounded of pleasure over what he had got done, worry over what he had still to do, and outrage at what fate had given him in the way of help. We were as oddly assorted a crew as ever went to the field: Col full of persnickety self-regard; Lillybelle sulking, a scarf tied over her curlers; Leaf with his stutter; Reenie dressed, every day, as if it were Saturday night; R. T. with his cap on sideways, tongue in the corner of his mouth, eyes on Reenie; and I, who that summer weighed about ninety pounds, and was, as Jake plainly told me several times a day, "too short in the push-up."

It would have to be said for us, at least, that we worked. It would have to be said for Jake that he got it out of us somehow. We used the setter when the weather was good, and when it rained we set the plants in the muddy rows by hand. When it rained we went to the field barefooted, and stayed wet. Nothing except the occasional downpour stopped us, and then, having no shelter, we stood in the rain until it slacked up, and went back to work. We did not miss a day.

We worked, and we ate. There was never anything like the meals we sat down to at the big table in Minnie Branch's kitchen. The mornings would have begun there with a great commerce between kitchen and garden and smokehouse and chicken house and cellar. Even the young children would be put to picking and plucking and fixing. The result would be a quantity of food at which you would be surprised when you saw it laid out on the table, and surprised again to see how quickly it was eaten up. Minnie would put the biscuits on the table heaped up in a wash-pan, and they would vanish beneath a cascade of forks. The thought of reaching for one bare-handed was frightening. There would be thirteen or fourteen of us at the table, Ester standing at the stove to wait on us, Jake at the head of the table, Minnie at the foot with the baby on her lap, the rest of us sitting anywhere we could on everything from high chairs to beehives. The house's indigenous uproar of voices and noises did not stop. It did not stop for anything. We ate, straggled out to the barn, watered the mules, hitched them up again, and went back to work.

Jake's triumph that year was that he had Col and Lillybelle working on the setter. He had accomplished this by great practical and psychological cunning, which he acknowledged to me by many stealthy winks and grins, but he could not help saying to me, once, to their faces: "Damn, Andy, I got 'em where I want 'em now!" He had them where he wanted them because he had them in his power; because he drove the setter, he could see to it that they did not stop work for any frivolous reason, and he drove at a pace that nudged relentlessly at the limits of their speed and endurance. The big black mules drew the setter down one long row after another, and Col and Lillybelle rode the low seats with their laps full of plants, placing them one at a time into the ground, grumbling and muttering at Jake's heedless back.

Each morning, when we had got enough plants pulled from the bed to get the setter started, Jake and Col and Lillybelle would start setting, Leaf would take three mules and the disk and prepare the ground ahead of the setter, R. T. would take another team and keep the setter supplied with water and plants. And Reenie and I would continue pulling plants from the beds, helped out by Leaf and R. T. when they had time to spare.

It was pretty work when you had time to think about it, and weren't too tired to care. We drew the white-stemmed, green-leafed plants out of the moist ground of the beds, and laid them neatly in bushel baskets and old washtubs. R. T. hauled them to the patch where the setter crew spaced them out in the long rows. They would wilt in the heat that day, but by the next morning or the next, they would be sticking up again, pert and green and orderly, in the dew-darkened ground. Each night when we quit, Jake would say to me, fairly singing: "We're getting it done, Andy boy! We're leaving it behind!"

At the end of the day, my father would come to take me home. If we were working late, which we almost always did, he would drive back to where we were. If the ground was too wet for him to drive in the fields, he would stop at the barn and blow the horn, and I would quit and hurry to meet him.

As we got near the end of the tobacco setting and Jake's elation grew, he stepped the pace up on Col and Lillybelle a little dangerously, enjoying their complaints, his own silence deepening in response. And then one night he made an invention that he liked so well that he would tell about it for years afterwards. We were working late. It was well after sundown and everybody was tired. Nearing the end of a round, Jake said, "One more round, and then . . ."

As he came to the end of the next round, he said, "One more, and then . . ."

At the end of the next he said it again.

Col, unable to stand it any longer, said, "And then *what*, old man?"

His voice dancing on laughter, the trap sprung at last, Jake said, "And *then* do another'n."

That couldn't last, of course. It all blew up in a big fracas right before dinner the next day. We could hear it clear to the plantbeds: Col making a profane speech on the theme of insurrection, Lillybelle swearing and crying, Jake protesting in the voice of surprised reason: "Well, I didn't know you was upset. Why didn't you all *say* something?"

Too much had been said by then to permit things to be put back the way they had been. After dinner Jake told Lillybelle to stay at the house. He drafted Ester out of the kitchen, put her on the setter with Leaf, and sent Col to the plantbed with Reenie and me.

I was sorry to have Col at the plantbed, for I had been having a good time talking with Reenie. She was curious, I think, as to what manner of creature I might be, and she drew me out by soliciting my opinions. I was full of strong opinions, which became even stronger when I discovered that they amused her, and even inspired her sometimes to agree. She liked strong opinions. In return, she told me at length about herself. She was living with her mother and her two sisters, Trill and Juanita. Juanita was the oldest, and was engaged to a goofy old boy named Calvin Sweet-swing, a match that Reenie looked down upon from a great height: "She's going to *marry* that bug-eyed silly thing! I wouldn't sweep under his lazy feet for all the cows in Texas!" But she seemed to dismiss the matter, nevertheless, with a sort of approval: "Well, anyhow, it keeps her out of *my* hair." Trill was another matter. Trill was only a year older than Reenie, and pretty too, as Reenie was willing to admit, and her taste in young men was very close to Reenie's. In fact, it was not unusual for them to like the same young man, and then they did not get along. Reenie was beginning to be uneasy about being so long away from home. She reminded me frequently that she did not know what Trill might be up to.

"Do you like R. T.?" I asked her.

"*That* silly thing?" She stuck out her tongue and laughed. I laughed too, in eager disloyalty to R. T.

Being Reenie's confidant there in the plantbed was a fine pleasure, surprisingly satisfying, and I hated to give it up. I had to, of course, when Jake sent Col to work with us. Col clearly knew how to talk to beautiful young women better than I did. He knew just what to say, and just how to say it. Some of his opinions were even stronger than mine, and Reenie was even gladder to agree with them. They talked, facing one another across the bed, and I listened, admiring Reenie from afar. Grudgingly, I admired Col too. He did have his ways. If Reenie had not been there, I knew, he would have been killing time — making smokes, adjusting his hat, changing places, getting up to do little jobs that did not need to be done, groaning about the pain it gave him to work in a stoop, looking off for any help that might be coming down from the sky — Mr. Noah Count himself. But with Reenie there he worked quickly and well, putting grace into it, paying attention to what he was doing, and talking to her all the time, as if absentmindedly, as if she might be just anybody else. I would have given anything to be able to talk to her that way. He had style. His cuffs were turned back from his wrists as if to keep them from getting dirty, his hat was tilted just so, and he had a matchstick pinched between his front teeth. I couldn't figure *how* that matchstick worked, but it worked; it was the master touch.

Knowing that Col was there with Reenie made R. T. desperate. He would hurry off to take a new supply of plants to the people in the field, or get a load of water from the pond, and then hurry back and stay until Jake hollered to him to get the hell on over there with more plants. He would load the sled then and, with a lot of backward looks, hurry away again.

The weather turned fine, and after the blowup between Col and Jake, the work went smoothly. It got to be Friday afternoon, and we were going to try to finish up by Saturday night. Col and Reenie and R. T. and I were at the plantbed. Jake hollered for water, and R. T. left to bring a new load from the pond. As soon as he was gone, Col's and Reenie's way of talking to each other changed a little, as it had begun to do. It was not a big change, but when R. T. was out of the way they spoke as people do when they are alone. For all the attention they paid to me, I might as well have been a spirit.

Reenie got up and carried an armload of plants to a basket a little way up the bed and put them in it, and then returned to her place and stood with her hands on her hips, resting. I can see her now, across all the years, as plainly as if I were still looking up at her across only the plantbed. She wore a cotton dress, red with a pattern of tiny white and yellow flowers, full-skirted, tight in the bodice. She had rings on her fingers, silver bracelets on her wrists. She had taken off her shoes. The sun behind her, her hair was all a tangle of red lights. She gave you the nice warming impression that you get from certain women, at a certain brief time in their lives, that she perfectly filled her skin: there was nothing wanting anywhere, and nothing wasted. And then, without any invitation whatsoever, my mind informed me how excellent it would be to kiss her.

She gathered her skirt and lifted it a little as she knelt and went to work again. "I'm going to go home," she said. "If Daddy won't take me, I'm going to get a ride with Wheeler."

Col looked up at her quickly and studied her, but she was looking down.

"Tomorrow will be Saturday," she said. "I got to be home by dinnertime tomorrow."

"Aw," Col said, drawing the words out gently as if speaking to a child, "you don't want to go home yet."

"Oh, yes, I do. I'm worried about Trill. I'm scared she'll get something I won't."

Col was kneeling there across from her, his right hand holding a plant still rooted in the bed. But he had stopped. He had not pulled the plant. Perhaps he never did. He said, "Maybe you'll get something *she* won't."

While they looked at each other, time stopped. Or I suppose it did, for it is a moment that has not stopped happening yet in *my* mind, and whatever happened next never got into my mind at all. I knew that something powerful had passed, something strange to me, as from another world, and yet pertaining to all that I had ever known in this one.

I was not exactly transfixed, for I must have kept working, but it seems to me that nothing happened at all until R. T. pulled up beside the plantbed and said, "Whoa!" He was silent a moment, looking, standing on the sled with the lines in his hands, and then he said, "Where'd Col and Reenie go?"

I looked then, and they were gone. "I don't know."

He leapt off the sled then and started to run. I got up and pitched my handful of plants into a basket and started after him.

It was one of those brilliant late spring afternoons that make things look both substantial and translucent as if made entirely of light. The sun had got down into the last quarter of the day, and the light was stretching out across the hollows and ridges and woodlands of the farm. Jake's mules drew the setter across the patch slowly, as if its lengthening shadow made a friction on the ground, but all the rest was light. It gleams in my memory now, leaf and cloud, thicket and grassy ridge, as luminous almost as the great blue sky itself.

R. T. was running, it seemed to me, as fast as a horse, down off the ridge where the plantbeds were, on a long slant toward the woods in the hollow, and I did not catch up with him until he got in among the trees, where he had to slow down. By then it had come to me what we were running for: Col and Reenie had gone off to jigjig, though it came to me at the same time that jigjig was not the right name for it. Nor was any other word I knew. They had gone beyond all our words, somewhere beyond anywhere we knew. R. T. knew it as certainly as I did, I think, and that was why he was running so nearly out of his head. What he planned to do if he found them, I do not know. I doubt that he knew.

We sped over the ground like two young hawks. We looked into wooded hollows where the sunlight slanted in long girders, and little encampments of mayapples stood green and perfect among the heavy trunks. We searched the dry trashy floors of locust thickets. We looked into leafy rooms under the low drooping branches of sugar maples. We looked, as we leapt over them, into grassy coverts and nests in the pasture draws. We hunted over the whole farm, and though we did not find Reenie and Col in any of its receptive and secret places, all of them, the whole country, came alive for me with a possibility that I had not thought of before and have not ceased to think of since, beyond all the words that I have learned.

It wore us out finally. We gave up and started for the house, walking slow, upset because we could hear Jake calling R. T., who had not done his chores. We knew that R. T. was going to catch it. It was way after sundown, a star or two was shining, and we could smell the damp coming up out of the hollows.

I heard my father's horn. He had come to take me home, and I felt farther away than I had ever been.

The Discovery of Kentucky*

John T. McCallum said he just felt it was his patriotic duty to take part in the inaugural parade in Frankfort.

"Jayber Crow," John T. said, "I just feel like anybody that *can* do something *ought* to do something." He always called people by their whole names; he didn't want people to get the idea that they could expect favors from him. He was a trader.

"Why, sure," I said. "Now just hold still a minute. I want to see if I can shave around your ear without cutting it off."

John T. had no more humor than a bucket of ashes. He could not see the funny side of anything. If Burley Coulter came into the shop and announced that a certain creek had been so high he couldn't get over it but he had just waited until it got a little higher and went under it, John T. would just stare at him as if he was an affront to the scientific spirit. It followed that John T. was laughed at a good deal, which he did not know. That he did not know it made whatever was funny even funnier. Everybody observed him with a good deal of interest.

And so if John T. had determined that looking good with his team of four black Percherons in the inaugural parade was his patriotic duty, then it was his patriotic duty, and whatever feelings he had about it would be patriotic feelings, and he would feel them seriously.

*Records and surviving memories at Port William do not disclose the date of the events described herein. The best guess is "sometime in the fifties."

The real cause of John T.'s seizure of patriotism was an old black mare named McCallum's Polly C. and three of her daughters that John T. drove in public at every opportunity. Old Poll and her three daughters were jet black, of a like conformation, size, and style, and they were, as John T. said himself, "up and down good ones, every one of 'em." John T. and his horses lived on a river bottom farm closer to Hargrave than to Port William. By farming, stock breeding, and shrewd trading, he had made himself tolerably well off, accumulating his money both by making it and by keeping it. John T. was tight; you couldn't drive a flaxseed in his ass with a sledge-hammer, as Burley Coulter often said. Burley was one of those who observed John T. with interest. The utter predictability of John T.'s humorlessness and self-absorption was wonderful to Burley, who took the same satisfaction in it that he might have taken in a circus dog.

It would have stood to reason for John T. to get his hair cut at Hargrave, since he lived closer to there than to Port William, but he liked my price which was fifty cents cheaper than at Hargrave. A lot of people enjoy getting a haircut, having a comfortable seat in a pleasant place and doing nothing for a while. But not John T. He was always in a hurry, even when he had a proposition like the inaugural parade on his mind. It was a Tuesday morning and not another soul in the shop, but John T., being a horse trader, had a reputation for subtlety and confidentiality to keep up, and he told me his idea in a voice as sly and guarded as if it were a dangerous secret and the room full of people.

The theme of the parade this year, he said, was to be "Kentucky for Progress." The various floats would all be captioned: "Forward with Kentucky Agriculture"—or coal or timber, or whatever. "We," John T. said, were going to have a float that would be a covered wagon drawn, of course, by four splendid black mares, and surrounded by armed men dressed as pioneers who would represent the discovery of Kentucky.

"But what has that got to do with progress?" I asked.

"It was progress at one time," John T. said. "And how can you progress if you ain't ever been discovered?"

"I see. Kentucky Pioneers Look Into The Future—is that the idea?"

"That's it," he said. "We'll write that on the side."

But of course John T. wasn't telling me this just to let me in on his wonderful thought. He proposed to furnish the covered wagon, the four-horse team, and the ideas. He wanted me to furnish the crew of pioneers.

"Now you all grow out your hair and beards, see. Make some coonskin caps. Carry guns and shoot them, to make it lively and real. Carry liquor jugs — you know, with water in them — so you look like authentic Kentuckians."

As if we were not already authentic Kentuckians. As if Kentucky had been discovered by people who, before they came, were authentic Kentuckians.

"It'll be purely Christian," John T. said. "There ain't no profit in it."

"I don't know," I said. "I'll think about it."

Which I did, off and on, for the rest of the day, but I kept it to myself until evening, when Burley happened in, not for a haircut, but just to sit a while and visit, as he often did.

"Well," I said, "big doings are going to be done, this time, at the inauguration of our honorable new governor."

"How's that?" he said.

"John T.'s going to do them."

And then I told him the whole thing: the looking like authentic Kentuckians, the coonskin caps, the guns, the shooting of the guns, the liquor jugs with water in them. "He says it's our patriotic duty," I said.

Burley had not, to my knowledge, been involved in a celebration since the war's end. He was well past fifty then, and perhaps he was asking himself whether or not he any longer had within him the requisite celebratory spirit. While I was talking, he stared without expression at the wall. He did not move for some time after I had finished. And then he looked straight at me, and I saw something kindle way back in his eyes.

He said, "Jayber, I believe I hear my country calling."

"Well, remember, he wants it to be lively and real."

"It'll be that," he said.

It wasn't a thing I wanted to push — if it happened, it would happen and I didn't say anything more about it. Neither did Burley, who came and went as he always did. We didn't speak of the subject again for a couple of weeks.

And then one evening Burley came in and outwaited the other

loafers, and when the last one had gone he said, "Well, I've recruited a little party for the discovery of Kentucky."

"Who?"

"Well, for one, me."

"Fine."

"And you."

"All right."

"And Petey Tacker."

"Why?" Petey was the undertaker down at Hargrave. I wasn't sure how he fitted in.

"Petey's a big gun collector and shooter, you know. He loads his own shells. We're not going to employ live shot and ball on this expedition, I don't guess, are we?"

"No!" I said.

"So we need somebody who can load us a lot of blanks, and somebody who can furnish guns that can shoot blanks of the sizes he can load, in case we can't furnish them ourselves."

"All right. Petey Tacker. I reckon he will lend a certain dignity to the occasion."

"No question about it," Burley said. "And then we got Grinner Hample."

Frankie Lee Hample was known as Grinner because, even with his thick glasses, he could not see very far ahead, and so his face was set in a perpetual grimace as though he suspected that he was only a step or two from something that was going to hurt if he ran into it. A man of courage. "Splendid choice," I said.

"And we got Big Ellis."

Big Ellis was a man of large girth and small behind, who customarily did whatever he was doing with one hand while holding up his pants with the other.

"Ah, the element of suspense."

"And," Burley said, "we got Mushrat Cotman."

Mushrat was six and three-quarters feet tall, round of face, long of trunk, and short of leg. He was called Mushrat, Mush for short, because he eked out the income from his little hillside farm by trapping in the wintertime. "Brilliant," I said.

"Old Daniel Boone hisself," Burley said. "Well, what do you think?"

"That's just six of us. Is that enough to discover Kentucky? It's a big place."

"Well," Burley said, "we ain't going to discover but just a little of it."

When John T. came in again, I told him we had put together the most authentic band of pioneers to be found anywhere. I didn't tell him who.

"That's good, that's good," he said.

"I reckon you don't want a haircut, then."

He made his mouth little, as if it had a drawstring, while he let on to think the matter over. As almost anybody could have predicted, he didn't want to appear to be one of us. "I'm going to be the teamster," he said. "You all are going to be the pioneers."

But the rest of us turned out our hair and beards. Word soon got around that we were part of an authentic reenactment of history that was going to be put on at Frankfort. As if Frankfort's business were not the reenactment of history.

We grew a good deal of hair. Burley and Mush gathered up some coon hides and fashioned them into caps that were rough, smelly, and fairly greasy on the inside, but authentic. Petey Tacker inventoried our arsenal, supplemented it where necessary, and spent several nights in the manufacture of blank cartridges and shells. One night after I closed the shop Burley and I ripped up a sheet and painted two large banners, one for each side of John T.'s wagon, that said: KENTUCKY PIONEERS LOOK INTO THE FUTURE. And Burley found two white earthenware jugs and painted black X's around their outsides.

As we would have known if we had been interested in thinking about it, John T. could take us as pioneers or let us alone. It was roustabouts and horse grooms that he wanted. But we were good-humored about it. We went down to his place the afternoon before the parade and helped him.

He had hired Sam Hanks to haul the equipment on his truck, and Sam was not in a good mood. He had been hauling livestock and tobacco to market out of the Port William community for forty years. He had allowed himself to be hired by John T. in order to be a proper public servant, but he didn't especially like John T. He thought our project was frivolous, and he made his opinion plain by sitting on the driver's seat of his truck with the door open and his feet on the running board, smoking his pipe, while we worked. We loaded John T.'s wagon, which was a pretty authentic antique of some kind. We loaded its hoops and canvas cover. We cleaned the four mares' harness and loaded it. We found places for our firearms and ammunition, the two painted banners, and the two earthenware jugs now pleasantly weighted and guggly as we passed them up into the load. And we did this under the influence of a lizardly skepticism in the eyes of Sam Hanks, and under the strict and picky supervision of John T. McCallum.

"Boys," John T. said, "it may freeze tonight. Ain't you all afraid them jugs are going to bust?"

"John T.," Burley said, "them jugs ain't going to bust."

Down at John T.'s before daylight the next morning, we loaded the mares, standing them crossways and head-to-tail, in John T.'s truck, and then started for the seat of government — Burley and Grinner and I riding with Sam, Petey and Big Ellis and Mush with John T.

When we got to the place where the parade was being assembled it was full day, and we could see ourselves. John T. looked natty in a suit and overcoat and a snap-brim felt hat and a pair of kid gloves; it was clear that he had come to drive, not to work. Sam, in his trucker's cap and coveralls, looked the way he often did: displeased. The rest of us, as Burley said, didn't look like anybody you'd want to walk up on in a fog. If authentic beards had been wanted, they should have provided more time between election and inauguration. We didn't look bearded; we looked unshaven. We didn't look long-haired; we looked unbarbered and uncombed. And our coonskin caps just looked outlandish. We were an authentic version of something that John T. evidently had not quite foreseen, for he paused a long moment to look at us as he came around the truck.

And then he said, "Boys, we got to get these mares unloaded and ready, and we got to get all this equipment unloaded. It won't do to stand around."

But Burley, who had unloaded his jugs the first thing, said, "John T., you always ought to drink plenty of water early in the morning. It keeps you reg'lar."

What was in those jugs was not water, or not water entirely. Each of them held about a pint of water, which had been diluted with perhaps a quart of Kentucky Pride, a distilled essence of our homeland, of which the only notable virtue was cheapness. In its pure state, it would roll the skin off your tongue like a window blind — and, even as Burley had diluted it, would warm the throat a little more than pleasantly and bring a few sincere tears to the eyes.

Burley lifted one of the jugs, authentically stoppered with a corncob, withdrew the cob, and proffered the jug to John T. "John T.?" he said.

"No, thanks," said John T. politely, but looking at the jug for the first time with something like curiosity.

Burley raised the jug toward Sam Hanks, who was again sitting in his truck with his feet on the running board, smoking and not looking at us. "Sam?"

Sam withdrew his pipestem, said, "Naw," and replaced the pipestem without looking at it or at us.

Burley handed the jug to Petey Tacker, and then opened the other one and handed it to me. We each took two or three swallows, managing not to exclaim, and turned away from John T. to hide our tears.

We set to work then, and tried honestly to please John T., and did. We unloaded the mares, tied them to the racks, and groomed them until they shone. We put the harness on them. We rolled the wagon off Sam's truck, and fixed the hoops in place and stretched the canvas cover over it. We attached the lettered banners to the sides. We filled our pockets with ammunition and put an extra supply along with our firearms inside the tailgate of the wagon. The outfit actually did look authentic. We stood back and admired it.

"Here," Burley said, starting the jugs around again. "We got to keep our circulation circulating."

John T. waited politely until I had passed the jug to the next man, and then he crooked his forefinger at me and I followed him to the far side of the wagon.

"Jayber Crow," he said, "now here's the deal." He was standing practically on my toes, speaking right into my face in that confidential undertone of his. "You all walk *behind* the wagon, see. Because there are just a few of you, and we want the crowd to get the full force of you all being pioneers. If you all scatter out too much and get up alongside the wagon and all, it won't make no impression. Don't you see?" He stuck his forefinger into my breastbone three times to make sure I saw.

I saw. He didn't want the impression that he and his horses would make to be mixed with the impression that we would make.

But I thought, "Well, why not?" I said, "Why, sure, John T. I see exactly what you mean. You're the doctor."

"And listen," he said. "One more thing." He became even more confidential. "That Linda mare, the off mare in the wheel team? She might be just a little bit on the fractious side. Now she won't be no trouble, long as she's going. And I can hold her, of course, if I have to. But if we stop, I'd appreciate it if you'd just step up beside her, where you can take hold of her bit."

Well, John T. was an odd case, but in some ways he was as shrewd as he thought he was. I saw that he had made me his second-in-command, the person most eligible to be depended on, and I had enough Kentucky Pride in me by then to be proud.

"Why, sure," I said. "Just walk up to where I can hook my finger in her bit ring, right?"

"Right," John T. said, and he gave me a comradely pat on the elbow.

When we rejoined the other discoverers, who were having another authentic sip from the authentic jugs, John T. felt so good about his conquest of me that he decided to take offense at Sam Hanks's indifference.

"Sam Hanks," he said with a put-on affability that would have maddened a pig, "ain't you going to go with us?"

"Hell, no!" Sam said, still looking at the far horizon.

"Well, why not?" John T. said. His voice was now full of patriotic indignation.

"Because," Sam said.

"Because why?"

"Because I ain't a going to do it, that's why."

"Well, if you wasn't going to take part, why did you haul our stuff up here?"

"I'm a hauler," Sam said. "I ain't no inaugerater."

"Well, these other fellows here, they're taking part," John T. said. He was enjoying himself, just wonderfully gratified by the superiority of his sense and his patriotism.

"Well, these other fellows here ain't me, and I ain't them."

"But look here," John T. said. "Why would a fellow not want to help out to inaugerate his own governor of his own state?"

"The last thing this state needs is another damned governor. What good's a governor ever done us?"

"Why, roads! They build us roads."

"Roads' ass! You know what roads are for? To haul stuff out that sells for too little, and to haul stuff in that sells for too much. I've hauled enough livestock out of Port William community in my time to make us all well off, and what I've mostly done is put it where somebody can steal it." He was looking at John T. now, just furious.

And John T. was furious too. "The duly elected governor of your state," he said, "is being inaugerated today. And you're too contrary to help out."

"I'm right proud to say I am."

"Our duly elected governor . . ." John T. said, enjoying the phrase.

"Elected's ass! Auctioned! A governor gets elected by auctioning his-self off. Governors don't govern Kentucky — *companies* govern Kentucky. We'll see the day when some damned company will tear that capitol down and sell it off for doorstops."

I had heard it all before — most of us had — but John T. had never heard any of it, because he usually didn't listen to anybody but himself. He was shocked. For almost a full minute, Sam having spoken to his satisfaction and John T. unable to speak at all, they just looked at each other.

And then John T. turned around and walked off. "Well!" he said. "We got a governor to inaugerate."

"Go right ahead," Sam said. "Inaugerate a rangatang if you want to. It won't make no difference."

All of us frontiersmen looked at each other and grinned. The parade hadn't even started yet, and we were already having a good time. We took on a little more Kentucky Pride.

And then another blow fell on poor old John T. An official-looking group with a clipboard, who had been watching us from afar, came over

and informed John T. that the parade position of KENTUCKY PIO-
NEERS LOOK INTO THE FUTURE would be last.

And John T., whose face had just returned to a more or less normal
color, began to turn red again, starting with his ears. It was plain that
John T. had imagined his horses leading the parade, not following it. He
said, "Wuh . . . ," but the official group was already hurrying off, following its clipboard. John T. watched them go, and then he turned around
and looked at us. He had begun to regret that Kentucky was going to be
discovered by anybody he knew.

He was glad, all the same, to have our help in getting the mares
hitched to the wagon. And one of us stood by the head of each mare
until he was on the seat and Burley handed him the lines. Now that the
outfit was all put together, we felt a certain patriotic pride in being asso-
ciated with it. The four mares stood as if they knew they were being
watched, all as black and bright as buttons, and even John T., we had to
admit, looked good, sitting up there in his faultless suit with the reins in
his gloved hands.

And then a covey of breathless ladies robed all in white fluttered up to
the wagon, followed by the officials with the clipboard. Their float had
broken down, they said. Something had happened to the motor. And
would John T. mind, please, if they rode on his wagon, since it was
empty? They were a church choir, and it seemed so important to them
that a religious note should be sounded somewhere in the parade.

A very sweet-faced youngish lady, who appeared to be the leader of
the choir, looked up at John T. almost with tears in her eyes and said,
"Oh, won't you please let us ride with you?"

John T., who had removed his hat and was holding it against his breast
like a proper horseman, said, "Yes, mam, climb right on." He was, you
could see, just transported, having been granted, as if by divine intervention, a change of causes. Now Kentucky was going to have to look
out for its own discovery; John T. was rescuing ladies in distress.

While Grinner and Big Ellis stayed with the horses, John T. and Petey
and Mush helped the ladies into the wagon, and Burley and I loosened
the canvas cover and furled it neatly along one side.

As I happened to be going by him, John T. caught me firmly by the
elbow, gave me a straight look and said, "*Behind* the wagon, Jayber Crow."

"All right," I said. "Fine."

The wagon looked even better with the choir on it. We got ourselves behind it, and loitered about for a few minutes, having another infusion of Kentucky Pride. And then it came to us that, since the parade was not even ready to start and we were the tail end of it, we had time on our hands.

"If we're *in* the parade, we can't *see* it," Petey Tacker said. "Let's go *see* it before we have to get *in* it."

There was much sound sense in that, so we set off in a bunch. And then I thought of my responsibility, and I looked back at John T. "What about Linda?" I said.

John T. thought a minute and then said, "Well, let Grinner Hample stay with her."

So Grinner turned back to stand at Linda's head, and John T. waved the rest of us on. He was plainly glad to be shed of us, and our departure did add greatly to his dignity.

Petey was the most authentic one of us, for he had on an old leather coat of some kind that could have passed for buckskin. The rest of us, besides our coonskin caps, were wearing just whatever we worked or hunted in. But however authentic we looked, with our ringtailed hats and our old clothes and our hair and whiskers, we attracted a lot of notice and comment.

At some point in the proceedings, Petey had come to be deeply amused. As he walked along, he chuckled under his breath and scratched his stomach. At the sight of anything he thought remarkable, he said, "Well! What *about* that? *What* about *that*?"

Mush too was amused, but he was silent; he just had a broad, warm-hearted smile on his face. He looked as if he could not possibly have been more pleased. His pants and old hunting coat were rather smudgy in complexion, frazzled by briars, and his coat cuffs were slick with tallow. He looked like a tall broken-off tree stump on the top of which some-body had treed a coon.

Big Ellis, very happy also, appeared to be ascending out of his pants into his hat. His pants, loaded with cartridges, were requiring much assistance from his left hand, but he never raised them above his pelvis, and he had risen well past his eyebrows into his hat, so that he had to tilt his head back to see.

And Burley was wearing an expression of utter decorum, as if he was not impersonating John T.'s idea of a pioneer at all but was well-groomed and wearing a suit. Only when he looked straight at you could you see way back in his eyes the flicker of profound amusement. When I looked at him I could feel a grin stretching across my soul.

There were wonderful things to see in that parade. There were floats of every kind, decorated in various ways that had taken a lot of work. And the floats were separated by all manner of high school and college bands. There were drum majors in tall hats, majorettes in short skirts, actors and dancers and clowns, companies of soldiers, many flags and banners. We'd had no idea.

There was a float that said, FORWARD WITH KENTUCKY COAL. It had a lump of coal on it as big as a house, and on top of the lump of coal was a crown, and inside the crown were three fiddlers, for this was Old King Coal, don't you see?

And there was a float that said, FORWARD WITH KENTUCKY TIMBER; and one that said, FORWARD WITH KENTUCKY TOBACCO; and one that said, FORWARD WITH KENTUCKY WHISKEY; and one that said, FORWARD WITH KENTUCKY BASKETBALL. And every one of them was as clever as it could be.

There was a float that said, KENTUCKY — OPEN FOR BUSINESS. It showed a kind of cutout of the state, a sort of fancy candy box, with the lid propped up like a piano lid, and inside it were people at desks, paying and collecting money. Another float said, SELL KENTUCKY, and there was a man in a suit on it, sitting at a big desk. Behind the man's chair was a heap of coal and a stuffed sheep and a sawlog and a basket of tobacco, and in front of the desk a coal miner and a farmer and a logger were standing in line, waiting to receive their checks. Another float bore a living replica of the state seal: a man in buckskin handing a check to a gentleman in a cutaway coat; a legend arching over their heads said, THE COMMONWEALTH OF KENTUCKY; and along the side of the float was a banner that said, TO THEM THAT HAVE, IT SHALL BE GIVEN.

The last one we came to was a long float with a little log schoolhouse on one end, and on the other end a modern classroom with a lot of elec-

trical equipment and no books. The sign said, FORWARD WITH KEN-
TUCKY EDUCATION. We stopped at one end to look at the log school,
and I said, "Abraham Lincoln came of this." And then we walked to the
other end to look at the wonderful mechanical classroom, and I said,
"And what will come of this?"

The truth was upon me, as Kentucky Pride was within me, and I
made a gesture from the cabin to the classroom to the float that said,
KENTUCKY — OPEN FOR BUSINESS. "We've come a long way," I said,
"to be first in folly."

"Now, hold on!" Mush Cotman said, attentive to the Kentucky Pride
within himself. "Wait a damn minute! Ain't we supposed to be smarter
'n Alabama?"

"Arkansas, ain't it?" Burley said.

"Or Mississippi," Petey Tacker said. "As the case may be."

"Or *what?*" said Big Ellis, addressing, apparently, another personage
inside his hat.

"First in folly, *second* in ignorance," I said, making a phrase that I
should have regretted somewhat even then.

For Big Ellis patted me on the shoulder and said, "Now *that* was a
good one, Jayber. Now *that* was one I'm going to remember."

All of a sudden we realized that everything was moving except us. The
various parts of the parade were falling into place, and one of the bands
had struck up a march. Some of the floats were already in the street. It
hit us all at the same time that we might already be too late. We started
in a half run for where we thought we had left the wagon, but we'd come
farther than we thought, and we despaired two or three times before we
finally found it. The ladies were still standing together in the wagon, all
white and billowy like a choir of angels, and John T. was still on the seat
with the lines in his hands, and Grinner was still standing at the perhaps
fractious Linda's head, grinning as if he expected at any moment to be
hit with a two-by-four.

John T. began waving his arm. "Behind the wagon, boys," he said,
looking at me. "Behind the wagon."

I said, "Behind the wagon, boys," and we all bunched up behind the wagon, laughing with what breath we had left, and Petey hauled our guns out over the tailgate and handed them around.

Mush and Burley and Petey had furnished their own shotguns. And Petey had provided a shotgun for Grinner; for Big Ellis, in view of the previous engagement of his left hand, he had provided a .44 revolver; and for me he had brought an old-time army rifle of some kind with a bayonet, which made it altogether about as long as a fishing pole.

After we were armed and all set, it still took a while for our end of the parade to get started, and so we unstoppered the jugs and took on a little social armament in the form of Kentucky Pride, and then just stood around, not saying anything. Now that we saw that we were actually going to do what we were going to do, we were scared.

When the wagon started, we just walked along behind it, not knowing at all how to be lively and real. And then all of a sudden, it seemed like, we were in the street, our ladies in the wagon began to sing, and we were going by the crowd. As soon as we got well into sight, the people in the crowd began to laugh, and that got us over our stagefright. It inspired us, in fact.

Directly, right before our eyes, Mushrat Cotman transformed himself into Daniel Boone. Of course, he didn't look like Daniel Boone — or for that matter, like anybody else. He looked like himself, which is to say unprecedented. What I mean is he was inspired to assume the role and character of D. Boone. He struck an attitude like a man standing on an immense height, shading his eagle eyes with his hand and peering far, far into the distance. In a voice calculated to be heard by generations yet unborn, he announced the discovery of Kentucky: "Thaaaaaaare she is! As big as aaaaaaall outdoors!" And then Big Ellis, holding to his pants with one hand, waving his great pistol with the other, and looking up into his cap, said, "Firrrrst in folly! Seconnnnd in ignernce." And we all let out a whoop and shot off our guns.

Well, it was wonderful the way people laughed. They held to each other and they clapped and yelled. Our ladies sang right on. And now and again, up in front of the ladies, we caught a glimpse of John T. nodding his head proudly and gratefully to the crowd.

We were the star attraction of the parade, it looked like, and we repeated the discovery of Kentucky every few hundred feet. And after every fourth or fifth discovery of Kentucky, we opened our jugs and renewed our pride in our native state. The time just flew by. It seemed that we hadn't more than got started when we saw that we were coming up to the viewing stand that had been built for the new governor and the other dignitaries.

This was the moment we were waiting for. We refreshed ourselves once more, and prepared to put our best effort into one grand final discovery of Kentucky. The ladies on the wagon began singing "When They Ring the Golden Bells," the song they had saved for this climactic moment because they did so well on the high notes. And then we saw that the governor himself, with the first lady at his side, had come down to the roadside to be among the people. There is nothing like the democratic spirit of a Kentucky governor, after he has sold himself for enough to afford to be democratic. The governor looked all natty and dignified, and his wife looked pretty and beamy and overcome. A white corsage was pinned to the front of her coat. They stood right beside the road, smiling and waving at the floats and marchers as they passed.

And lo and behold, when we got abreast of the chosen pair, John T. stopped the team, just out of the goodness of his heart, to let all the dignitaries see what a good, well-matched four-horse team looked like. I remembered my commission and started up to take hold of the perhaps fractious Linda, and then, Heaven help me, I saw the sign on the side of the wagon. While we were gone looking at the floats, John T. had taken down our banners and put up his own, right at the knees of our choir of ladies. His banners proclaimed: ALL BRED BY JOHN T. McCALLUM. A horseman to the last, he had made fools of us all, including himself, and you couldn't have told him how he had done it if you had explained for a week.

I walked on by and took hold of Linda's bit, and from there I could see all the rest that happened. The people in the viewing stand were clapping and hollering and howling with laughter. The governor and his wife were trying not to laugh, but only to smile and look grateful. John T. sat straight up on the wagon seat, proud as a pigeon. The ladies in the wagon were singing about those golden bells as if they could already hear them ringing:

In that far-off sweet forever,
Just beyond the shining river,
When they ring the golden bells for you and me.

And our bunch, still innocent, were putting on their most inspired performance of the discovery of Kentucky.

Mush Cotman shaded his eyes and saw for the first time, far off in the hazy distance, our unharmed, unsold, beautiful and abounding land. "Thaaaaaaare she is!" he sang out. "As big as aaaaaaall outdoors!"

And Big Ellis said, "Firssst in folly! Seconnnnd in ignernce!" Blam! And the fool shot off his own cap.

No sooner had the shooting stopped than I saw Burley Coulter approaching the first lady, who was smiling at him bravely, seeing that he came in the guise of one of her forefathers. I could see the corsage quivering on her breast. There were tears in Burley's eyes, and he said in a voice husky with emotion: "Verily, madam, thou art an angel sent from Heaven, as I perceiveth by thy two noses and thy four starry shining eyes."

All of a sudden, there were police easing toward us from every direction.

I looked over my shoulder and saw that during our stop we had gained plenty of room ahead of us. I started back to the rear of the wagon, and as I walked by her singletree I just sort of, as if by accident, let old Linda feel the point of my bayonet. She squatted, clapped the pavement twice with all four feet, thus communicating to the other three the imminent danger to their glossy rumps, and they all set off at a brisk pace, as if they were just too modest for so much public acclaim and thought only of going home.

It Wasn't Me (1953)

The crowd in the courthouse square in Hargrave has not begun to assemble yet. The various pieces of it are now present, but scattered about: half a dozen bidders or potential bidders, a few who have come out of concern or interest or curiosity, a few who are on hand simply for whatever may happen, as if in loyalty to the present tense of the county's history. Wheeler Catlett has been studying the scene below him now for some minutes, its several components as telling to him as sentences written in his own hand. He stands motionless at the window, the room behind him as thoroughly forgotten as if he is not in it. He has been preparing himself for weeks for what is about to happen. And yet, since what is about to happen is still, so far as he can tell, unpredictable, he is not ready.

On the least busy side of the square Elton and Mary Penn are sitting in their car, watching the courthouse door, not moving, not talking. Their car is an old Plymouth coupe, black under the dust; along the side that Wheeler can see there is an elongated fan of dried mud. On the opposite side of the square, Clara and Gladston Pettit are standing on the sidewalk with their lawyer. The three of them have not moved beyond the pale blue aura of Glad's burnished Cadillac. Talking, they stand close together as if aware of their difference from everything else in sight. Clara is wearing a fur coat and hat and gloves. Glad has on a pearl-gray overcoat and hat. The lawyer, a man much younger than Glad, coatless as if by misunderstanding of the weather, stands with his hands in his pockets, his shoulders hunched, looking curiously around him as he listens to Clara, who, Wheeler imagines, is telling him that this was a familiar place to her in her girlhood. And he can imagine her tone of disparagement: "Well, *we* thought it quite a city. We were, you know, so *far* from everything." No one would know from looking at her that Clara ever rode into Hargrave behind a team of mules. She looks like a stranger—which, Wheeler guesses, is how she means to look. But from his window he can see too, beyond the cornices along Front Street, the wide slow-flowing river reaching westward, making its great difference that, as always, consoles him for lesser ones. Now the wind has roughened it, and under the brilliant sky its surface blinks with whitecaps.

Wheeler watches the triad of the two Pettits and their lawyer with distaste, but mainly out of curiosity now, for they are no longer the problem. The problem is now in the intentions and the eligibility of certain would-be buyers of a certain farm in whose fate Wheeler is urgently involved. And he is involved, now, as the agent of a dead man.

Clara Pettit's father, Old Jack Beechum, was Wheeler's client, his kinsman by marriage, and his friend. Old Jack was one of that venerable school of farmers and stockmen whose life was regulated by the knowledge of what "a good one" was and meant. Horses, mules, cattle, sheep, hogs, and people all submitted in his mind to the measure of that height of excellence represented by the known, proved, and remembered good ones of their respective kinds. Old Jack knew a good one when he saw one, and Elton Penn was a good one, and so was Mary, Elton's wife.

The Penns moved to Old Jack's farm as his tenants at the time Old Jack finally gave up his lonely independence and moved to a room in the hotel in Port William, eight years before he died. The Penns proved satisfactory. They proved, in fact, far more than satisfactory. They were good, they were Old Jack's kind, they listened to him and cared about him, they were the chief pleasure of his final years. Old Jack wanted them to have the farm after his death—and wanted the farm to have them after his death—and to that purpose he willed them what he thought would be half the purchase price.

As Wheeler told Elton on the afternoon Old Jack was buried, Old Jack also *set* the purchase price. But he did not do that in his will. He should have done so, but he did not. At that time he had hesitated to state so finally and formally what he knew: that Clara cared nothing for the place and would sell it as soon as it was hers. The father and daughter were irreconcilably different, irreconcilably divided, and yet he loved her, and he was torn. So he left the farm to Clara and the empowering sum of money to Elton and Mary. He set the price several years later in a letter to Wheeler in the little notebook that he kept in the bib pocket of his overalls, where they found it after he died. By the time he wrote the note, Old Jack was often absent from himself; he apparently wrote it in some passing moment of realization and anxiety, and then forgot it — for how long before he died, Wheeler does not know. The note, the pencil scrawl trenched deeply into the tiny page, read:

> *Wheeler see the*
> *boy has his place*
> *200 $ acre be*
> *about right she*
> *ought to not*
> *complain Wheeler*
> *see to it*

The slow, crooked legend of that page fell upon Wheeler's conscience with a palpable gravity, as if the old man had reached out from beyond the grave and laid a hand on him. The letter, of course, was of no legal worth whatsoever. In the eyes of a court it would answer no pertinent question. Who was "the boy"? What was "his place"? Who was "she"? Who was "Wheeler"? Who, for that matter, wrote the letter? But Wheeler, had he been the one to be held, would have been held tighter by that letter, that outcry, than by the will itself. He himself had no question as to the intention or the authenticity of the letter, and he assumed that Clara, understanding what was obviously her father's dying wish, would be bound by it as a matter of course.

He was mistaken. He had done his assuming, as he often did, in a world that he assumed was ruled by instinctive decency. That Clara and Glad

Pettit did not inhabit that particular world, they let him know fast. After the reading of Old Jack's will, Wheeler asked them to remain in his office to speak privately with him. He thereupon showed them the letter in the notebook, explained what it meant, and suggested that they proceed with the sale of the farm to Elton and Mary Penn at the stipulated price.

Clara quickly glanced at her husband in a way that alone ought to have informed Wheeler that he had driven his ducks to the wrong pond.

"No," Glad Pettit said.

And then Clara herself said, "No."

That was not a reply calculated to please Wheeler, and it certainly did not. It surprised him too. He was surprised at Clara, and surprised at the extent of his own innocence, which had left him now without a plan. He had begun the conversation leaning back in his chair; now he sat forward, lacing his fingers in front of him. Making an effort to suppress his irritation, he said, "Excuse me, Clara, but are you sure you understand the reasons for what I just proposed?"

"Yes," she said, looking at Glad and then back at Wheeler. "I understand. Of course I do."

Wheeler studied her—a plumpish lady, now beyond her middle years, opulently dressed, her perfectly manicured hands resting on her purse in her lap. She was wearing a smart little pillbox hat with a veil, and behind the veil her eyes were looking straight at Wheeler. She did understand. She knew exactly what she was doing. And yet he was not ready to give up.

"Surely you can't feel that you're being deceived. The letter there in the notebook—no court would honor it, of course, but among us there can be no doubt."

"I have no doubt."

"And this is a most deserving young couple. I don't have to tell you how well and honorably they've taken care of the place, and how kindly and hospitably they treated your father."

Seeing the embarrassment that Wheeler intended for Clara, Gladston Pettit stepped in. "Wheeler, you as a lawyer and I as a banker know that this is purely a matter of law—of principle, I would say. The kindness of this young couple was undoubtedly great. We don't question it. They have our gratitude. But their kindness was not to Clara, it was to her father, and it has been amply, some would say extravagantly, repaid. As for their farming, it was done in fulfillment of their half of a contract, of which the other half was also well and honorably fulfilled. All Clara is asking for, Wheeler, is what is rightly hers. She has the right to fair market value for her property."

Glad's voice had an unction in it that implied what he scrupled to say: that poor Clara would not, in fact, receive fair market value for her property, because her father's too-generous bequest to the Penns must be seen as, in effect, a deduction from that value. And his tone conveyed as well the implicit accusation that Wheeler, as Old Jack's lawyer, being obviously of sounder mind, should have counseled him against such overgenerosity. Neither the speech nor any of its implications suited Wheeler, who never had liked Glad's way of reducing things to their barest (usually monetary) essentials — his habitual reduction of principle to his own interest — and he disliked too to be put in the position, an odd one for a lawyer, of both knowing and resenting Clara's rights.

He knew, anyhow, that he was licked, and in spite of himself his exasperation had begun to show. While Glad talked, Wheeler had regarded him with a look suggestive that human discourse had not been expectable from that quarter. And then he swiveled his chair away from Glad in a movement that seemed not merely to dismiss him but to forget him as well. He made himself smile and addressed his final plea to Clara:

"It's not a question of what was owed and what was paid, Clara. That wasn't what Uncle Jack had on his mind. There were other questions that he put ahead of that one. What would be best for this good pair of young people? What would be best for this good farm? What should be done here for the good of the world? — Uncle Jack would have put it that way, and I hope you don't mind if I do. He thought it over a lot of times, and he concluded that the best thing would be to put the good people and the good farm together — to bind their fates together, so to speak. I know he thought about it that way. I heard him talk about it that way. It's not an old man's senile foolishness. He knew what he was doing." He paused, looking at Clara, and then he said, "Clara, I don't know anybody more worthy to walk in your daddy's tracks than Elton Penn. And your daddy loved him."

And that failed too, for Clara said, "My father's loves are not mine."

After that, the Pettits communicated with Wheeler by way of the young Louisville lawyer, and they had little enough to communicate. Old associations, family ties, the dead man's wishes were left to blow as the wind listed. But Old Jack's letter, failing to hold Clara, held Wheeler. His duties as executor of Old Jack's will were soon fulfilled, but disemployment brought him none of the freedom of the disemployed. There was no rest in it for him, no possibility that he and the problem of the dishonored letter might leave one another alone. The farm, according to the Pettits' wishes, was to be sold at the courthouse door early in January, and until that day had passed the problem was Wheeler's as much as it was Elton and Mary Penn's. It was not a problem appointed to him, but one that he inherited, a part of his own legacy from his deceased client and friend. Jack Beechum came back to haunt him, and often in the small hours of the night Wheeler would find himself talking and arguing with the old man face-to-face. Trying to end these encounters, he would cry out in his thoughts: "But I *did* try! I can't, damn it, *make* 'em do it!" And then he would think, no longer arguing but only mourning, that the Pettits were playing a different game from any that Old Jack had ever played, and living in a different world from the one that he had lived in. The letter in the notebook was written in a language the Pettits did not speak; they had forgot the tongue in which an old man might cry out from his grave in love and in defense of a possibility no longer his own in this world.

But it was not merely that the old man would not take no for an answer; Wheeler could not bring himself to offer it for an answer. The truth is that Wheeler is a seer of visions — not the heavenly visions of saints and mystics, but the earthly ones of a mainly practical man who sees the good that has been possible in this world, and, beyond that, the good that is desirable in it. Wheeler has known the hundred and fifty acres called, until now, the Beechum Place all his life. It is a good farm, a third or so of it rough enough, but the rest of it plenty good, and all of it well kept for a long time. It is a pretty place too. The fences and buildings are in good repair. The yard in front of the old house is full of low-spreading maples. And behind the house there is an ample garden plot with a grape arbor and a dozen old pear and apple trees. It is a place with good human life already begun in it, where the right sort of young man and woman could do well. Knowing all this, knowing the farm, knowing Elton and Mary Penn, Wheeler has irresistibly imagined the life they might live there. He does not think of it, of course, as the life they *will* live there, for he is aware of chance and human nature and mortality, but it is a life that they could hope to live, and a life that, Wheeler believes, a certain number of people in every generation *must* hope to live and try to live. He wants Elton and Mary to have that hope and make that effort there on Old Jack's place where they have, in fact, already begun. And so Wheeler has a reason of his own not to take no for an answer.

Though the direct way was now lost, and the only available route appeared to wander in thicket and hollow without a plan, he would not give up. He did not give up when he learned for certain that there would be one strong contending bidder, or when he learned that there would be at least two. He did not know what could be done, but he did not give up. And he found it necessary to exercise his stubbornness on Elton's behalf as well as his own.

In addition to the good judgment and good sense that Old Jack and Wheeler have admired in him, Elton has pride enough to overpower sense and judgment both — such pride that, as Wheeler understands, puts him more in need of a friend than it will let him admit. Being Old Jack's heir was a nervous business for Elton in the first place. Nothing in his experience had prepared him for a benefit that was unasked, unearned, and unexpected. Nothing in his character prepared him to be comfortable with an obligation he could not repay. His election, both public and unexpected, to sonship to a man already dead took more getting used to than he'd had time for, and then he learned of the opposition between himself and the other heir.

His impulse, on hearing of that, was to declare his own independence at any cost, to renounce his share in Old Jack's estate along with whatever chance he had to buy the farm, and simply walk off, flinging defiance behind him like a handful of ashes.

"Whoa!" Wheeler said. "Wait a minute, now."

And Mary said, "Oh, Elton!"

Wheeler was standing with his hat and raincoat on in the middle of the kitchen floor, having just told them the outcome of his discussion with the Pettits. When he entered in response to their call, Elton and

Mary had just sat down to supper. Though he had expected it, Wheeler was distressed by the intensity of Elton's embarrassment.

"Wait, Elton," he said. "You can't do that."

"Well, I'd like to know why in the hell I can't!"

Wheeler went to the table then and pulled out a chair and sat down.

"Here, Wheeler," Mary said, starting to get up. "Let me get you a plate."

"No. Don't, Mary. I have to go home."

But he sat on with them while they ate, patiently explaining—though he knew that Elton knew—that there could now be no backing out. To go ahead was best in Elton's own interest, best in Mary's interest, best in the interest of any children they might have.

"You've got to try for it, Elton," Mary said.

"That's right," Wheeler said. "You're in a fix, I admit, that I didn't want to see you in, and didn't think you'd be in. I know it won't be easy for you to try for it and lose it. And you could do that. But you could come out with the farm too."

He hushed and sat with his head down, looking at his hands at rest on his lap, thinking. Elton and Mary sat watching him, no longer eating. And then Wheeler raised his head and looked at them. "Listen," he said. "Think about Jack Beechum getting his start here—way back yonder, seventy or seventy-five years ago. He was young and strong, excited by what he could do, demanding a lot of himself and of the place. And some things he asked were wrong. You've heard him tell it. He made mistakes that damaged him and the farm too, and that delayed and hampered him a long time. But he had the grace and the intelligence to learn and to keep on. And Ben Feltner, who was, you know, his brother-in-law, but a second father to him too, stood by him and put in a word when it would help, and helped in other ways.

"And those years changed him. He learned to do what his place asked of him. He became the man it asked him to be. He knew what it had cost him to become that kind of farmer, he knew he'd become his farm's belonging, necessary to it, and he knew he was getting old.

"He was getting old, and he had no successor. He had an heir, but no successor. As his own workdays were coming to an end, he saw his farm going into a kind of widowhood. He'd talk about it sometimes.

"And then you and Mary came along. He saw right away what the two of you and the old farm could mean to each other, and what you meant to him. He saw that you could be the man and woman the place was asking for, and his life's work might not go to waste, after all."

"We've got to try it for Mr. Beechum's sake, Elton."

"Well," Elton said, and cleared his throat. "Well, of course, *that's* why we've got to try."

Wheeler sat on with them for a while, talking of other things. When he got up to go he laid his hand on Elton's shoulder and said, "Don't worry." He knew it was useless to say that to Elton, but he meant it. His own determination had grown, for he was in the presence of what he desired. "I don't know what we'll do, but we'll do something."

That there was plenty to worry about was soon evident. Earl Benson, who lived on one of the farms adjoining the Beechum Place, had bought two neighboring farms, the first of which joined his own original farm, the second being divided from it by the Beechum Place. It was a pattern that did not leave much to guess. Earl Benson was expected to be a bidder, and gossip soon confirmed that he would be. Wheeler knew the man, had done legal work for him in fact, and liked him. But meeting him on the street one afternoon, he said to him: "Earl, if Elton Penn can buy the Beechum Place, and he wants to, you'll have a good neighbor."

To which Earl replied, around his cigar, pleasantly enough: "And if *I* buy it, I'll have a good farm."

That didn't surprise Elton any more than it did Wheeler.

"I figured that," Elton said. "If I was in his place, I reckon I'd try to buy it too."

Wheeler was sitting in his car with the motor running, Elton leaning down to talk to him through the window. A few feet away Elton's tractor was standing with its motor running.

Wheeler had begun to make these visits almost daily, not because he had news for Elton that often, but because he was anxious and could not stay away.

"With Earl in it," Wheeler said, "you'll have to bid higher than you want to. You might as well get ready for that."

"I'm ready to go a little bit higher."

Wheeler thought it would have to be more than a little bit, but he didn't say so. He said, "Well, I'll see you."

Two days later, Wheeler was stopped in the post office by Dr. Stedman.

"Just the man I want to see," the doctor said, taking hold of Wheeler's elbow.

"Wheeler," he said in the low, confidential voice with which some people talk to lawyers about serious matters, "I've got a little backlog of cash that I'm thinking of investing in land."

"Well, do it," Wheeler said. He was in a hurry, and he was impatient anyhow with the doctor's persistent raids on him for free advice, legal and other.

When the doctor starts with his questions, Wheeler always wants to say, "While we're standing here, Doc, would you mind taking my pulse?" But so far he has never said it. He merely saves himself as much time and trouble as possible by discovering what the doctor wants to do and advising him to do it. Even so, he always has to suffer an explanation.

"Well now," the doctor said, "that old Beechum place up by Port William, I hear it's going to be sold at auction."

"That's right."

"I hear it's a good one."

"Yessir. It's a good one." There was more, Wheeler knew, and he did not want to hear it. He shifted his weight to turn away, but the grip on his elbow tightened.

"That young fellow who lives there, Elton Penn, I understand he made the old man a good tenant."

"That's right."

"Well," the doctor said, pursing his lips, looking down and looking up, "my thinking is this. If I bought the farm, he'd make *me* a good tenant. With my obligations, you know, I'd need somebody there who wouldn't require a lot of seeing to. Do you see what I mean?"

"I do."

"So if I could get the place and a good man on it at the same time, it would solve my problems, don't you see? It would kill two birds with one stone."

Wheeler knew very well the history of those two birds, the wish to own land, and the wish to have somebody else worry about it, and there were certain things that he was prepared to say on the subject. But he gently freed his elbow, and just as gently took hold of the doctor's arm.

"Doctor, do you know that Elton Penn wants to buy that farm for himself?"

"No, sir, I didn't."

"Well, he does. Listen. If you want to do a public service, get out of his way and let him have it."

Wheeler turned away then, leaving the doctor's reply floating in the air.

And so there was another bad possibility to warn Elton about.

"I don't know how far he'll go," Wheeler said, "I don't know how much money he's got."

"More than I got," Elton said.

That Elton himself made the farm attractive to at least one of his competitors, Wheeler decided not to tell him.

Standing at the window, looking down, Wheeler thinks again, as he has many times, of the terms of a possible surrender. If the farm goes too high, why should Elton not just let it go? He would have his money still. He could take his time and find another place to buy — one that maybe, in the long run, would suit him just as well. And that was all right, as far as it went. But it left out Old Jack. It left the letter in the little notebook unanswered. It failed to answer Old Jack's, and Wheeler's, notion of what the farm itself needed and deserved. No more than the dead man could the living one bear to see the little farm's boundaries dissolved in Earl Benson's adding of house to house and field to field. And if the doctor bought it? Wheeler knows that story as well as if it had already happened. Elton would not stay, and the doctor was right in supposing that he needed Elton along with the farm. He needed somebody who knew how to farm it, for he did not know how to farm it himself. When Elton and Mary left, they would be followed by a procession of other tenants who would also leave, worse following worse, while the farm ran down.

"No," Wheeler says. "Hell, no."

The sound of his own voice seems to move him. He glances at the clock on the courthouse tower, and then looks at his watch. He turns, walks slowly, looking at the floor, to the hat rack in the corner of the room, puts on his hat and coat, and returns to the window.

Clara is talking animatedly with Gladston and the lawyer, her coat collar turned up against the wind. As he watches her, it seems to Wheeler that she is elated, and he realizes with the sudden astonishment that one feels in looking into a life beyond the possibilities of one's own, that for her the sale of the farm is a freedom, her own connection with it, her own early life there, being merely an encumbrance, probably an embarrassment. This whole passage of time has been burdened for Wheeler by his dislike of the Pettits, and he feels it now. He feels it, exults in it a little, for he knows that it defines his true allegiance, and yet is sorry for it. How much better it would be to be at peace with them, fellow mortals as they are, kindred as they are. And yet he feels, as he knows Old Jack felt, the irreconcilable division between his kind and their kind, between the things of this world and their value in money.

Now the courthouse door opens. The auctioneer crosses the porch, takes his stand at the top of the steps, begins to summon the crowd. Buttoning his coat, Wheeler hurriedly crosses the room and goes out. "Back in a minute," he says to Miss Julia, his secretary, as he strides through the outer office. She widens her eyes by way of comment as the door slams and his steps quicken going down the stairs.

Outside, the unblemished winter sunlight and the strong wind fill the square. Wheeler comes out into it with a relief and a pleasure that are familiar to him. This is the sort of day that makes an active man working inside feel that he is missing something. The year is starting. The weather is busy. Out over the river he sees a flock of birds fly up into the face of the wind and then turn, as one, away from it.

Once he is in the street, with the square in sight again, he slows down, looking, pausing, speaking to passersby as he makes his way toward the little crowd collecting at the foot of the courthouse steps. He lets the crowd shape itself before he gets there, and then he stops on its outer edge.

The crowd is hollow-centered, a kind of diffidence making everybody stay back a little, not wanting to appear too interested. The Penns are standing in front of Wheeler on the inside of the ring. Wheeler sees Mary looking around for him. He catches her eye, gives her a quick nod. She whispers to Elton then, her lips forming the words: "Wheeler's here." Elton nods, but does not look back. Mary is holding to Elton's arm, huddled against him, more from nervousness, Wheeler knows, than from the chill in the wind. There is something in the set of Elton's head and shoulders that denies the crowd and sets him aside from it even though he is in it.

Dr. Stedman is standing close to the foot of the steps. He looks away when Wheeler looks at him, and carefully does not look back. And then Wheeler catches Earl Benson's eye and nods, and Earl throws his head back, grinning on both sides of his cigar, and gives him a wave. The Pettits and their lawyer have moved closer to the crowd. They see Wheeler and nod, and he tips his hat. Though the day is brilliant and the sun in sheltered places gives some warmth, in the open square the wind presses upon them with an irrestistible chill; people stand with their hands in their pockets and their shoulders hunched.

The auctioneer gives a little introductory speech, welcoming everybody, describing the property to be sold, explaining the terms of the sale. And then, starting into his spiel, he calls for a bid of $175 an acre. The figure is hardly named before Wheeler sees Elton nod.

"Well, that's aggressive enough," Wheeler thinks. He would have been a little slower than that himself, maybe, but he sees that Elton is performing in the way proper to him, and he is pleased. "Be careful, now," he thinks.

The doctor gives a little wave of his hand at $200, and at $225 Earl Benson says loudly, "Yeah!" And so they've gone beyond Old Jack's price at a run. The auctioneer asks for $250.

"Two thirty-five," Elton says, slowing it down, and Wheeler thinks, "That's right."

Earl Benson comes in quickly at $245. The spiel continues for some time after that without a bid. Elton and Mary are talking in whispers. The doctor shakes his head, turns away, and then changes his mind and bids again: $255. Earl Benson bids $265 as quickly as before. The doctor, finished, puts his hand back in his pocket and sidles into the crowd.

Wheeler is watching only Elton now, but Elton is shaking his head at Mary, ready to quit. And then, making one of the sudden shifts from stillness to haste that is characteristic of him, Wheeler steps through the crowd just as Elton is turning away and the auctioneer's hand is raised in the air. He stops at Elton's left shoulder, a little behind him, and takes hold of his arm. He says, "Go on!" and when Elton hesitates, "It'll be all right! Go on!" And Wheeler knows, he can feel in his hand, when Elton yields himself to his struggle again — can feel him settling onto his feet.

"Two seventy-five," Elton says.

The auctioneer looks at Earl Benson. His tone has grown quiet now and personal, the public auction reduced to a conversation among three men. He is asking Earl if he will pay $285.

For a long time Earl does not give any sign that he knows he is where he is. He is looking down, thinking, and Wheeler knows within a guess or two what he is thinking about. He has a mortgage against his home place. He has the bank to account to. He has interest and wages to pay. He has bills for fuel and fertilizer and seed and parts and supplies. He has something to gain, and perhaps more to lose. He stands with his head down while desire and pride argue with chance, mortality, and arithmetic. Finally he raises his head, looks at the auctioneer, looks away, and nods.

Before the auctioneer can begin his spiel again, Wheeler's hand has tightened on Elton's arm and Elton has said, "Two ninety."

"That's right," Wheeler says.

And there is another pause, and Earl Benson bids $295.

"Go on," Wheeler says, and Elton says, "Three hundred."

They wait then while the auctioneer speaks to Earl, who shakes his head once, and again, and turns away.

The auctioneer brings his hand down. "Sold! To Elton Penn here, for three hundred dollars an acre."

Elton, shaken, still shaking, looks at Wheeler and grins. "Is that me?"

And the auctioneer, overhearing, laughs and says, "You Elton Penn, ain't you, honey?"

Wheeler leaves Elton and Mary to complete their purchase, and goes back to his office. In the privacy of the dark stairway, he allows himself to grin at last, in relief and triumph, and in his mind he says to Old Jack, "How's *that*?" And to himself he says, "And what's next?" He pretty well knows what is next. He is still hurrying.

He shuts his office door and, without taking off his overcoat and hat, picks up a yellow pad with some figures on it, reads them over, and then sits down and rapidly works his way through another set of figures.

Elton and Mary have paid a hundred dollars an acre more than the two hundred stipulated by Old Jack's letter. And so Clara's dishonoring of that letter has earned her, and cost the Penns, $15,000. The place has cost $45,000, of which Old Jack's legacy to the Penns will cover a third, and Wheeler assumes that they will have savings that will increase that by somewhat. By Wheeler's own estimate, the farm would have been worth its price to anybody at $250 an acre, which puts Elton above the mark by $7,500. Going beyond $250, Wheeler thought beforehand and still thinks, might be justifiable for Earl Benson, who owns adjoining land, or for Elton, whose occupation of the place and whose familiarity with it, both from his own experience and Old Jack's instruction, would have a practical worth. Whether or not that worth would reach $7,500, Wheeler does not know. But at that point he would, anyhow, shift the ground of justification: Elton and Mary ought to have the farm because they are worthy of it.

Studying his figures, considering all that he knows to consider, Wheeler concludes that the Penns are safe enough. Assuming that they can continue to do as well as they have done, they will own their farm — which is perhaps as good a chance as anybody could ask.

But Wheeler is not done assuming yet. If he assumes, as he must, that if left alone Elton would have stopped bidding at $235, then Wheeler must consider himself in some manner responsible for $9,750 of the Penns' debt. He cannot come up with that kind of money without selling something that he ought to keep, and he does not need it now, anyway; he may not need it ever, but he knows that he must regard it as one of the possible prices of his own freedom.

He does another brief computation, and picks up the telephone. He calls the cashier of the Hargrave Farmers' Bank and finds that he can spare a thousand dollars, and he arranges for the transfer of that sum to a savings account in the name of Beechum, Catlett, and Penn. "I'll send the check right over," he says. "Yes. That's right. That's the name of the company." He hangs up, takes a check pad from the drawer of his desk, writes out a check, and seals it in an envelope.

He has been sitting upright on the edge of his chair, and now he leans back, pushes his hat off his forehead, and lapses into stillness. But even still, he remains expectant, listening, and soon he hears the street door open and shut and then footsteps coming up the stairs. Miss Julia opens the door. "Elton Penn is here."

"Tell him to come in," Wheeler says, and then, himself, calls, "Come in, Elton." As Miss Julia goes out, he hands her the envelope. "Take that to the bank, please."

When Elton comes in, Wheeler grins at him. "Well. You've come out all right, I think."

"I don't know, Wheeler. I might have made one hell of a mistake." Elton is as tightly strung as a banjo, and there is a little glistening in his eyes.

"Sit down," Wheeler says, and Elton does.

"Where's Mary?"

"The grocery store," Elton says. That is not what he has come to talk about.

"Well, it could have been better," Wheeler says. "No doubt about that." And then he grins again and says, "And it could have been worse."

"This was bad enough, maybe. What do you think?"

"I think it was a shame it had to happen the way it did. A damned shame. I don't understand—" Wheeler stops then and shakes his head. "But I suppose we mustn't say everything we think."

He picks up the pad with his figures on it and looks at it, thinking, for a minute, and then pitches it back onto the desk. "I know you're worried about the price, Elton. But it's an amount I think you can manage—if you live, of course, and stay on your feet."

"I could get sick or die too," Elton says.

Wheeler laughs. "Of course you could. But I don't see how we can depend on that. I'm afraid we'll just have to assume that you won't. It's a risky business." He swivels his chair toward the window and looks at the sky a moment, recovering his thought, and then turns back to Elton. "In other words, I think you did what you should have done. You have the farm, and I believe you're going to be glad of it. And *I'm* glad of it. It's a great relief to me."

"Well, of course, if I'd lost it, I'd have been sick. But I can still lose it."

"No, my boy. You're not going to lose it. Not if we *both* can help it. I told you to go ahead because it would be all right. You must understand that I meant that. If you need help, I'm going to help you."

"But, damn it, Wheeler, don't you think I *ought* to lose it if I can't make it on my own?"

"No," Wheeler says. "I *don't* think that. I can see how a person *might* think that. It seems to me I thought something like that myself once. But I don't think it anymore."

"It's the obligation, Wheeler." Elton looks up at Wheeler and his eyes glisten again. "If it hadn't been for you, Wheeler, I'd have lost that farm today. I know it, and I appreciate it. But why should you have done that? Why should you have felt obliged to help me get into a problem that now you feel obliged to help me get out of?"

Wheeler knows this longing for independence in Elton because he knows it in himself. He knows that he is a trespasser, and he feels suddenly heavy with the complexity and difficulty of what he has begun. But he is amused too and is trying not to show it. Like any young man who has won his heart's desire, Elton wishes he had won it by himself, wishes to possess it on his own terms, its first and only lover.

"It wasn't me," Wheeler says, and is at once startled by his words and filled with a sort of glee by them. "It wasn't me. If I had stood back and let you lose that farm, or let it lose you, that old man would have talked to me in the dark for the rest of my life."

"You did it out of loyalty to Mr. Beechum?"

"Partly." Wheeler studies the man sitting in front of him, who is sitting there studying him, puzzled by him at the moment, Wheeler guesses, and waiting courteously for him to say what he is talking about. And Wheeler again feels his great liking for this Elton Penn — a young man, as Old Jack would say, with a good head on his shoulders. An orderly man, who makes order around him.

"The place," Wheeler says, "is not its price. Its price stands for it for just a minute or two while it's bought and sold, and may hang over it a while after that and have an influence on it, but the place has been here since the evening and the morning were the third day. The figures are like us — here and gone."

"The figures make it mine," Elton says, "if I can be equal to 'em."

"The figures give you the right to call it yours for a little while."

"They give me the right to do a hell of a lot more than that."

For some time now they do not say anything. There is more feeling in what Elton has said than he has found words for, and more than Wheeler wants to deal with in a hurry. Wheeler is amused by Elton's predicament, and yet is moved and troubled by it. Here is a young man whose experience has taught him the meaning of debt, who wants above all to be paid up and in the clear, and who has become first the inheritor of a bequest that he did not ask for and did not expect, and next the beneficiary of an act of friendship that he did not ask for and, with part of his mind, does not want. Wheeler sits and looks at Elton while Elton sits and looks at the palm of his right hand, oppressed between gratitude and resentment. Watching him struggle, Wheeler realizes again the fatality of what he has undertaken. He has started something that he will have to finish. And how long will that be?

The office has faded away around them. They might as well be in a barn, or in an open field. They are meeting in the world, Wheeler thinks, striving to determine how they will continue in it. Both of them are still wearing their hats and coats.

"People have been exercising those rights here for a hundred and seventy-five years or so," he says finally, "and in general they've wasted more than they've saved. One of the rights the figures give is the right to ruin."

"You're talking about something you learned out of a book, Wheeler."

"I'm talking about something that I learned from Jack Beechum, among others, and something you'll learn too, if you stay put and pay attention, whether I tell it to you or not."

"Do you know what I want, Wheeler?"

"I expect I do. But tell me."

"I want to make it on my own. I don't want a soul to thank."

Wheeler thinks, "Too late," but he does not say it. He grins. That he knows the futility of that particular program does not prevent him from liking it. "Well," he says, "putting aside whatever Mary Penn might have to say about that, and putting aside what it means in the first place just to be a living human, I don't think your old friend has left you in shape to live thankless."

He sees that Elton sees, or is beginning to. This man who longs to be independent cannot bear to be ungrateful. Wheeler knows that. But the suffering of obligation is still on Elton, and he says, "What do you mean?"

"I mean you're a man indebted to a dead man. So am I. So was he. That's the story of it. Back of you is Jack Beechum. Back of him was Ben Feltner. Back of him was, I think, his own daddy. And back of him somebody else, and on back that way, who knows how far? And I'm back of you because Jack Beechum is, and because he's back of me, along with some others.

"It's no use to want to make it on your own, because you can't. Oh, Glad Pettit, I reckon, would say you can, but Glad Pettit deals in a kind of property you can put in your pocket. Or he thinks he does. But when you quit living in the price and start living in the place, you're in a different line of succession."

Elton laughs. "The line of succession I'm in says you've got to make it on your own. I'm in the line of succession of root, hog, or die."

"That may have been the line of succession you *were* in, but it's not the one you're in now. The one you're in now is different."

"Well, how did I get in it?" Elton says almost in a sigh, as if longing to be out of it.

"The way you got in it, I guess, was by being chosen. The way you stay in it is by choice."

"And I got in because Mr. Beechum chose me."

"And Mary. He chose you and Mary. He thought you two were a good match, and that mattered to him. His own marriage, you know, was not good. Yes, you could say he chose you. But there's more to it. He chose you, we'd have to say too, because he'd been chosen. The line is long, and not straight."

Wheeler pauses for a minute. He's leaning a little forward now, his elbows resting on the chair arms, his hands loosely joined in front of him.

"And then we'd have to say that, through him, the farm chose you."

Elton looks straight at him. "The *farm* did."

Wheeler smiles. "The land expects something from us. The line of succession, the true line, is the membership of people who know it does. Uncle Jack knew it, and he knew you would learn it."

"Now wait a minute," Elton says. "Hold on."

But Wheeler sees a little of the way ahead now, and he keeps going. "We start out expecting things of it. All of us do, I think. And then some of us, if we stay put and pay attention, see that expectations are going the other way too. Demands are being made of us, whether we know it or know what they are or not. The place is crying out to us to do better, to be worthy of it. Uncle Jack knew that."

Wheeler stops again and looks at Elton. "He thought you were worthy. Do you remember that spring day when he first came to visit, after you and Mary moved in?"

"In May 1945," Elton says. "The day Germany surrendered."

"Well, right then he started hoping that you and Mary would own the farm. He mentioned it to me that same evening. I remember it very well. I said, 'Well, what do you think of Elton Penn?' And he said, 'I think he's a good one.'"

"But, Wheeler," Elton says, and there is a catch of tenderness in his voice now, and there is some fear in it. "Maybe he was wrong about me."

"Maybe," Wheeler says. "But he didn't think so — he didn't change his mind in seven years — and I don't think so."

Wheeler is remembering the first time he ever saw Elton. It was March of 1944, and Wheeler was trying to persuade Old Jack to leave his farm and take up residence in the hotel in Port William. Since his wife's death Old Jack had lived alone and had done, as he said, a good job of it. But now everybody who cared about him was worried about him. He was too old, they thought, to be living by himself, and Wheeler had begun his argument, which he soon saw would have to be improved. If Old Jack was ever to be persuaded to move out, somebody Wheeler could *vouch* for would have to be ready to move in.

Because of the war, suitable people were even less available than usual, but finally Wheeler heard of a tenant on a rough farm on Cotman Ridge, a young fellow by the name of Elton Penn, who was looking for a better place.

When Wheeler stopped in Goforth to ask directions — it was a bright, warm, windy morning — his sometime client, Braymer Hardy, was sitting on a keg in front of the store.

Elton Penn was not at home, Braymer said. He was plowing some corn ground he had rented from Mrs. Cotman over across the creek, in the bottom over there.

Having got his directions, Wheeler asked, "What about this boy, Braymer?"

"He'll do!"

"Well, what do you know about him?"

"He's been on his own ever since he was fourteen, Wheeler. He's sort of a half orphan, you might say. He's made a crop every year since he was fourteen, and every damn one of 'em's been a good one."

"Can you depend on him?"

Braymer nodded. "Yessir. You can depend on him."

Wheeler started his car.

"I'd a thought you'd a knowed this boy, Wheeler. Didn't he sprout over about Port William?"

"I don't know."

"His daddy was Albert Penn. You knowed him."

"Yes. I knew Albert. So this is Albert's boy."

"I expect Albert was dead and they was gone from over there before Elton got growed up enough for a fellow to know."

"I expect so," Wheeler said.

He followed the gravel road across the Katy's Branch valley toward the farm he had been directed to, but before he reached the turnoff to the house he found his man.

Elton was plowing a field in the bottom that began level along the creek and then rose gradually up toward the steeper slope of the valley side. Wheeler saw that the plowlands were laid out correctly. He saw the quality of the thought that had gone ahead of the work, the design of the year's usage laid neatly and considerately upon the natural shape of the field. Elton was working a team of black horses. He had them stepping, urging them and himself, and yet there was an appearance of ease in their work that to Wheeler bespoke the accomplishment of the workman: the horses were fitted and harnessed and hitched right; the plow was running right.

Having already stopped his car, Wheeler turned off the engine, and in the quiet that followed, in which he could hear the wind, he sat and looked. Watching Elton, he might, he felt, have been watching his own father as a young man, or Old Jack himself as a young man. He felt himself in the presence of a rare and passionate excellence belonging to his history and his country, and he was moved. He sat there a long time, watching, forgetting the year he was in.

"Maybe we were wrong about you," he says to Elton. "You've still got time to prove us wrong. But it's too late now for me to believe you will."

Elton sits with his head down, thinking. The question they have come to now requires a long proof. The burden of time is on him. When he dies, somebody will answer.

And then he looks up again at Wheeler. "So this has happened now because of all these things coming together—because Mr. Beechum wanted it to happen, and because the farm, as you say, wanted it to, and because you wanted it to."

"And because you and Mary wanted it to," Wheeler says.

Elton looks at him and slowly nods.

"And because what has happened has been desirable to a lot of people we never knew, who lived before us."

Elton nods, looks down, thinks again, and again looks up. "And you're saying you're going to be my friend because of all that?"

"Yes. Because of you yourself, and because of all that."

Elton laughs. "You're going to be my friend, it sounds pret' near like, because you can't get out of it."

"If I was his friend, given what that meant, I can't get out of it."

"But, Wheeler, that's pretty tough."

"It's tough. It's not as tough as being nobody's friend."

"You're saying there's not any way to get out of this friendship."

"No. You can get out of it. By not accepting it. I'm the one, so far, who can't escape it. You have it because I've given it to you, and you don't have to accept. I gave it to you because it was given to me, and I accepted."

Elton draws a long breath, and holds it, looking out the window, and then breathes it out and looks at Wheeler. "I can't repay him, Wheeler. And now you've helped me, and I can't repay you."

"Well, that's the rest of it," Wheeler says. "It's not accountable. If the place was its price, or you thought it was, maybe you could consider such debts payable—but then some of those debts you wouldn't have contracted, and the rest you wouldn't recognize as debts. Your debt to Jack Beechum *is* a debt, and it's *not* payable—not to him, anyhow. Your debt to me is smaller than your debt to him, not much at all, and it may or may not be payable to me. This is only human friendship. I could need a friend too, you know. I could get sick or die too."

Elton says, "Well, I—"

But Wheeler raises a hand, and goes on. "It's not accountable, because we're dealing in goods and services that we didn't make, that can't exist at all except as gifts. Everything about a place that's different from its price is a gift. Everything about a man or woman that's different from their price is a gift. The life of a neighborhood is a gift. I know that if you bought a calf from Nathan Coulter you'd pay him for it, and that's right. But aside from that, you're friends and neighbors, you work together, and so there's lots of giving and taking without a price — some that you don't remember, some that you never knew about. You don't send a bill. You don't, if you can help it, keep an account. Once the account is kept and the bill presented, the friendship ends, the neighborhood is finished, and you're back to where you started. The starting place doesn't have anybody in it but you."

"It's before the line of succession," Elton says.

"That's right."

Wheeler leans back in his chair now and spreads his hands and lets them hang relaxed over the ends of the chair arms. "So." He thinks of Old Jack again, at ease with that imperious ghost at last.

He looks at Elton. "So. There is to be no repayment. Because there is to be no bill. Do you see what I mean?"

"Maybe." Elton grins, at ease now too, looking at Wheeler, his hand fishing in his shirt pocket for his cigarettes. "Probably."

Wheeler laughs. "Well, give me one of your smokes."

The Boundary (1965)

He can hear Margaret at work in the kitchen. That she knows well what she is doing and takes comfort in it, one might tell from the sounds alone as her measured, quiet steps move about the room. It is all again as it has been during the going on twenty years that only the two of them have lived in the old house. Sitting in the split-hickory rocking chair on the back porch, Mat listens; he watches the smoke from his pipe drift up and out past the foliage of the plants in their hanging pots. He has finished his morning stint in the garden, and brought in a half-bushel of peas that he set down on the drainboard of the sink, telling Margaret, "There you are, mam." He heard with pleasure her approval, "Oh! They're nice!" and then he came out onto the shady porch to rest.

Since winter he has not been well. Through the spring, while Nathan and Elton and the others went about the work of the fields, Mat, for the first time, confined himself to the house and barn lot and yard and garden, working a little and resting a little, finding it easier than he expected to leave the worry of the rest of it to Nathan. But slowed down as he is, he has managed to make a difference. He has made the barn his business, and it is cleaner and in better order than it has been for years. And the garden, so far, is nearly perfect, the best he can remember. By now, in the first week of June, in all its green rows abundance is straining against order. There is not a weed in it. Though he has worked every day, he has had to measure the work out in little stints, and between stints he has had to rest.

But rest, this morning, has not come to him. When he went out after breakfast he saw Nathan turning the cows and calves into the Shade Field, so called for the woods that grows there on the slope above the stream called Shade Branch. He did not worry about it then, or while he worked through his morning jobs. But when he came out onto the porch and sat down and lit his pipe, a thought that had been on its way toward him for several hours finally reached him. He does not know how good the line fence is down Shade Branch; he would bet that Nathan, who is still rushing to get his crops out, has not looked at it. The panic of a realized neglect came upon him. It has been years since he walked that fence himself, and he can see in his mind, as clearly as if he were there, perhaps five places where the winter spates of Shade Branch might have torn out the wire.

He sits, listening to Margaret, looking at pipe smoke, anxiously working his way down along that boundary in his mind.

"Mat," Margaret says at the screen door, "dinner's ready."

"All right," he says, though for perhaps a minute after that he does not move. And then he gets up, steps to the edge of the porch to knock out his pipe, and goes in.

When he has eaten, seeing him pick up his hat again from the chair by the door, Margaret says, "You're not going to take your nap?"

"No," he says, for he has decided to walk that length of the boundary line that runs down Shade Branch. And he has stepped beyond the feeling that he is going to do it because he should. He is going to do it because he wants to. "I've got something yet I have to do."

He means to go on out the door without looking back. But he knows that she is watching him, worried about him, and he goes back to her and gives her a hug. "It's all right, my old girl," he says. He stands with his arms around her, who seems to him to have changed almost while he has held her from girl to wife to mother to grandmother to great-grandmother. There in the old room where they have been together so long, ready again to leave it, he thinks, "I am an old man now."

"Don't worry," he says. "I'm feeling good."

He does feel good, for an old man, and once outside, he puts the house behind him and his journey ahead of him. At the barn he takes from its nail in the old harness room a stout stockman's cane. He does not need a cane yet, and he is proud of it, but as a concession to Margaret he has decided to carry one today.

When he lets himself out through the lot gate and into the open, past the barn and the other buildings, he can see the country lying under the sun. Nearby, on his own ridges, the crops are young and growing, the pastures are lush, a field of hay has been raked into curving windrows. Inlets of the woods, in the perfect foliage of the early season, reach up the hollows between the ridges. Lower down, these various inlets join in the larger woods embayed in the little valley of Shade Branch. Beyond the ridges and hollows of the farm he can see the opening of the river valley, and beyond that the hills on the far side, blue in the distance.

He has it all before him, this place that has been his life, and how lightly and happily now he walks out again into it! It seems to him that he has cast off all restraint, left all encumbrances behind, taking only himself and his direction. He is feeling good. There has been plenty of rain, and the year is full of promise. The country *looks* promising. He thinks of the men he knows who are at work in it: the Coulter brothers and Nathan, Nathan's boy, Mattie, Elton Penn, and Mat's grandson, Bess's and Wheeler's boy, Andy Catlett. They are at Elton's now, he thinks, but by midafternoon they should be back here, baling the hay.

Carrying the cane over his shoulder, he crosses two fields, and then, letting himself through a third gate, turns right along the fencerow that will lead him down to Shade Branch. Soon he is walking steeply downward among the trunks of trees, and the shifting green sea of their foliage has closed over him.

He comes into the deeper shade of the older part of the woods where there is little browse and the cattle seldom come, and here he sits down at the root of an old white oak to rest. As many times before, he feels coming to him the freedom of the woods, where he has no work to do. He feels coming to him such rest as, bound to house and barn and garden for so long, he had forgot. In body, now, he is an old man, but mind and eye look out of his old body into the shifting leafy lights and shadows among the still trunks with a recognition that is without age, the return of an ageless joy. He needs the rest, for he has walked in his gladness at a faster pace than he is used to, and he is sweating. But he is in no hurry, and he sits and grows quiet among the sights and sounds of the place. The time of the most abundant blooming of the woods flowers is past now, but the tent villages of mayapple are still perfect, there are ferns and stonecrop, and near him he can see the candle-like white flowers of black cohosh. Below, but still out of sight, he can hear the water in Shade Branch passing down over the rocks in a hundred little rapids and falls. When he feels the sweat beginning to dry on his face he gets up, braces himself against the gray trunk of the oak until he is steady, and stands free. The descent beckons and he yields eagerly to it, going on down into the tireless chanting of the stream.

He reaches the edge of the stream at a point where the boundary, coming down the slope facing him, turns at a right angle and follows Shade Branch in its fall toward the creek known as Sand Ripple. Here the fence that Mat has been following crosses the branch over the top of a rock wall that was built in the notch of the stream long before Mat was born. The water coming down, slowed by the wall, has filled the notch above it with rock and silt, and then, in freshet, leaping over it, has scooped out a shallow pool below it, where water stands most of the year. All this, given the continuous little changes of growth and wear in the woods and the stream, is as it was when Mat first knew it: the wall gray and mossy, the water, only a spout now, pouring over the wall into the little pool, covering the face of it with concentric wrinkles sliding outward.

Here, seventy-five years ago, Mat came with a fencing crew: his father, Ben, his uncle, Jack Beechum, Joe Banion, a boy then, not much older than Mat, and Joe's grandfather, Smoke, who had been a slave. And Mat remembers Jack Beechum coming down through the woods, as Mat himself has just come, carrying on his shoulder two of the long light rams they used to tamp the dirt into postholes. As he approached the pool he took a ram in each hand, holding them high, made three long approaching strides, planted the rams in the middle of the pool, and vaulted over. Mat, delighted, said, "Do it again!" And without breaking rhythm, Jack turned, made the three swinging strides, and did it again — *does* it again in Mat's memory, so clearly that Mat's presence there, so long after, fades away, and he hears their old laughter, and hears Joe Banion say, "Mistah Jack, he might nigh a *bird*!"

Forty-some years later, coming down the same way to build that same fence again, Mat and Joe Banion and Virgil, Mat's son, grown then and full of the newness of his man's strength, Mat remembered what Jack had done and told Virgil; Virgil took the two rams, made the same three strides that Jack had made, vaulted the pool, and turned back and grinned. Mat and Joe Banion laughed again, and this time Joe looked at Mat and said only "Damn."

Now a voice in Mat's mind that he did not want to hear says, "Gone. All of them are gone." And they *are* gone. Mat is standing by the pool, and all the others are gone, and all that time has passed. And still the stream pours into the pool and the circles slide across its face.

He shrugs as a man would shake snow from his shoulders and steps away. He finds a good place to cross the branch, and picks his way carefully from rock to rock to the other side, using the cane for that and glad he brought it. Now he gives attention to the fence. Soon he comes upon signs—new wire spliced into the old, a staple newly driven into a sycamore—that tell him his fears were unfounded. Nathan has been here. For a while now Mat walks in the way he knows that Nathan went. Nathan is forty-one this year, a quiet, careful man, as attentive to Mat as Virgil might have been if Virgil had lived to return from the war. Usually, when Nathan has done such a piece of work as this, he will tell Mat so that Mat can have the satisfaction of knowing that the job is done. Sometimes, though, when he is hurried, he forgets, and Mat will think of the job and worry about it and finally go to see to it himself, almost always to find, as now, that Nathan has been there ahead of him and has done what needed to be done. Mat praises Nathan in his mind and calls him son. He has never called Nathan son aloud, to his face, for he does not wish to impose or intrude. But Nathan, who is not his son, has become his son, just as Hannah, Nathan's wife, Virgil's widow, who is not Mat's daughter, has become his daughter.

"I am blessed," he thinks. He walks in the way Nathan walked down along the fence, between the fence and the stream, seeing Nathan in his mind as clearly as if he were following close behind him, watching. He can see Nathan with axe and hammer and pliers and pail of staples and wire stretcher and coil of wire, making his way down along the fence, stopping now to chop a windfall off the wire and retighten it, stopping again to staple the fence to a young sycamore that has grown up in the line opportunely to serve as a post. Mat can imagine every move Nathan made, and in his old body, a little tired now, needing to be coaxed and instructed in the passing of obstacles, he remembers the strength of the body of a man of forty-one, unregarding of its own effort.

Now, trusting the fence to Nathan, Mat's mind turns away from it. He allows himself to drift down the course of the stream, passing through it as the water passes, drawn by gravity, bemused by its little chutes and falls. He stops beside one tiny quiet backwater and watches a family of water striders conducting their daily business, their feet dimpling the surface. He eases the end of his cane into the pool, and makes a crawfish spurt suddenly backward beneath a rock.

A water thrush moves down along the rocks of the streambed ahead of him, teetering and singing. He stops and stands to watch while a large striped woodpecker works its way up the trunk of a big sycamore, putting its eye close to peer under the loose scales of the bark. And then the bird flies to its nesting hole in a hollow snag still nearer by to feed its young, paying Mat no mind. He has become still as a tree, and now a hawk suddenly stands on a limb close over his head. The hawk loosens his feathers and shrugs, looking around him with his fierce eyes. And it comes to Mat that once more, by stillness, he has passed across into the wild inward presence of the place.

"Wonders," he thinks. "Little wonders of a great wonder." He feels the sweetness of time. If a man eighty-two years old has not seen enough, then nobody will ever see enough. Such a little piece of the world as he has before him now would be worth a man's long life, watching and listening. And then he could go two hundred feet and live again another life, listening and watching, and his eyes would never be satisfied with seeing, or his ears filled with hearing. Whatever he saw could be seen only by looking away from something else equally worth seeing. For a second he feels and then loses some urging of the delight in a mind that could see and comprehend it all, all at once. "I could stay here a long time," he thinks. "I could stay here a long time."

He is standing at the head of a larger pool, another made by the plunging of the water over a rock wall. This one he built himself, he and Virgil, in the terribly dry summer of 1930. By the latter part of that summer, because of the shortage of both rain and money, they had little enough to do, and they had water on their minds. Mat remembered this place, where a strong vein of water opened under the roots of a huge old sycamore and flowed only a few feet before it sank uselessly among the dry stones of the streambed. "We'll make a pool," he said. He and Virgil worked several days in the August of that year, building the wall and filling in behind it so that the stream, when it ran full again, would not tear out the stones. The work there in the depth of the woods took their minds off their parched fields and comforted them. It was a kind of work that Mat loved and taught Virgil to love, requiring only the simplest tools: a large sledgehammer, a small one, and two heavy crowbars with which they moved the big, thick rocks that were in that place. Once their tools were there, they left them until the job was done. When they came down to work they brought only a jug of water from the cistern at the barn.

"We could drink out of the spring," Virgil said.

"Of course we could," Mat said. "It's dog days now. Do you want to get sick?"

In a shady place near the creek, Virgil tilted a flagstone up against a small sycamore, wedging it between trunk and root, to make a place for the water jug. There was not much reason for that. It was a thing a boy would do, making a little domestic nook like that, so far off in the woods, but Mat shared his pleasure in it, and that was where they kept the jug.

When they finished the work and carried their tools away, they left the jug, forgot it, and did not go back to get it. Mat did not think of it again until, years later, he happened to notice the rock still leaning against the tree, which had grown over it, top and bottom, fastening the rock to itself by a kind of natural mortise. Looking under the rock, Mat found the earthen jug still there, though it had been broken by the force of the tree trunk growing against it. He left it as it was. By then Virgil was dead, and the stream, rushing over the wall they had made, had scooped out a sizable pool that had been a faithful water source in dry years.

Remembering, Mat goes to the place and looks and again finds the stone and finds the broken jug beneath it. He has never touched rock or jug, and he does not do so now. He stands, looking, thinking of his son, dead twenty years, a stranger to his daughter, now a grown woman, who never saw him, and he says aloud, "Poor fellow!" He does not know he is weeping until he feels his tears cool on his face.

Deliberately, he turns away. Deliberately, he gives his mind back to the day and the stream. He goes on down beside the flowing water, loitering, listening to the changes in its voice as he walks along it. He silences his mind now and lets the stream speak for him, going on, descending with it, only to prolong his deep peaceable attention to that voice that speaks always only of where it is, remembering nothing, fearing and desiring nothing.

Farther down, the woods thinning somewhat, he can see ahead of him where the Shade Branch hollow opens into the Sand Ripple valley. He can see the crest of the wooded slope on the far side of the creek valley. He stops. For a minute or so his mind continues on beyond him, charmed by the juncture he has come to. He imagines the succession of them, openings on openings: Sand Ripple opening to the Kentucky River, the Kentucky to the Ohio, the Ohio to the Mississippi, the Mississippi to the Gulf of Mexico, the Gulf to the boundless sky. He walks in old memory out into the river, carrying a heavy rock in each hand, out and down, until the water closes over his head and then the light shudders above him and disappears, and he walks in the dark cold water, down the slant of the bottom, to the limit of breath, and then drops his weights and cleaves upward into light and air again.

He turns around and faces the way he has come. "*Well*, old man!" he thinks. "*Now* what are you going to do?" For he has come down a long way, and now, looking back, he feels the whole country tilted against him. He feels the weight of it and the hot light over it. He hears himself say aloud, "Why, you've got to get back out of here."

But he is tired. It has been a year since he has walked even so far as he has already come. He feels the heaviness of his body, a burden that, his hand tells him, he has begun to try to shift off his legs and onto the cane. He thinks of Margaret, who, he knows as well as he knows anything, already wonders where he is and is worrying about him. Fear and exasperation hold him for a moment, but he pushes them off; he forces himself to be patient with himself. "Well," he says, as if joking with Virgil, for Virgil has come back into his thoughts now as a small boy, "going up ain't the same as coming down. It's going to be different."

It would be possible to go on down, and he considers that. He could follow the branch on down to the Sand Ripple road where it passes through the Rowanberry place. That would be downhill, and if he could find Mart Rowanberry near the house, Mart would give him a ride home. But the creek road is little traveled these days; if he goes down there and Mart is up on the ridge at work, which he probably is, then Mat will be farther from home than he is now, and will have a long walk, at least as far as the blacktop, maybe farther. Of course, he could go down there and just wait until Mart comes to the house at quitting time. There is sense in that, and for a moment Mat stands balanced between ways. What finally decides him is that he is unsure what lies between him and the creek road. If he goes down much farther he will cross the line fence onto the Rowanberry place. He knows that he would be all right for a while, going on down along the branch, but once in the creek bottom he would have to make his way to the road through dense, undergrowthy thicket, made worse maybe by piles of drift left by the winter's high water. He might have trouble getting through there, he thinks, and the strangeness of that place seems to forbid him. It has begun to trouble him that no other soul on earth knows where he is. He does not want to go where he will not know where he is himself.

He chooses the difficult familiar way, and steps back into it, helping himself with the cane now. He does immediately feel the difference between coming down and going up, and he wanders this way and that across the line of his direction, searching for the easiest steps. Windfalls that he went around or stepped over thoughtlessly, coming down, now require him to stop and study and choose. He is tired. He moves by choice.

He and his father have come down the branch, looking for a heifer due to calve; they have found her and are going back. Mat is tired. He wants to be home, but he does not want to *go* home. He is hot and a scratch on his face stings with sweat. He would just as soon cry as not, and his father, walking way up ahead of him, has not even slowed down. Mat cries, "*Wait*, Papa!" And his father does turn and wait, a man taller than he looks because of the breadth of his shoulders, whom Mat would

never see in a hurry and rarely see at rest. He has turned, smiling in the
heavy bush of his beard, looking much as he will always look in Mat's
memory of him, for Mat was born too late to know him young and he
would be dead before he was as old as Mat is now. "Come on, Mat," Ben
says. "Come on, my boy." As Mat comes up to him, he reaches down
with a big hand that Mat puts his hand into. "It's all right. It ain't that far."
They go on up the branch then. When they come to a windfall across
the branch, Ben says, "This one we go under." And when they come to
another, he says, "This one we go around."

Mat, who came down late in the afternoon to fix the fence, has fixed
it, and is hurrying back, past chore time, and he can hear Virgil behind
him, calling to him, "Wait, Daddy!" He brought Virgil against his better
judgment, because Virgil would not be persuaded not to come. "You
need me," he said. "I do need you," Mat said, won over. "You're my right-
hand man. Come on." But now, irritated with himself and with Virgil
too, he knows that Virgil needs to be carried, but his hands are loaded
with tools and he can't carry him. Or so he tells himself, and he walks on.
He stretches the distance out between them until Virgil feels that he has
been left alone in the darkening woods; he sits down on a rock and gives
himself up to grief. Hearing him cry, Mat puts his tools down where he
can find them in the morning, and goes back for Virgil. "Well, it's all
right, old boy," he says, picking him up. "It's all right. It's all right."

He is all right, but he is sitting down on a tree trunk lying across the
branch, and he has not been able to persuade himself to get up. He came
up to the fallen tree, and, to his surprise, instead of stepping over it, he
sat down on it. At first that seemed to him the proper thing to do. He
needed to sit down. He was tired. But now a protest begins in his mind.
He needs to be on his way. He ought to be home by now. He knows that
Margaret has been listening for him. He knows that several times by
now she has paused in her work and listened, and gone to the windows
to look out. She is hulling the peas he brought her before dinner. If he
were there, he would be helping her. He thinks of the two of them
sitting in the kitchen, hulling peas, and talking. Such a sense of luxury
has come into their talk, now that they are old and in no hurry. They talk
of what they know in common and do not need to talk about, and so talk
about only for pleasure.

They would talk about where everybody is today and what each one is doing. They would talk about the stock and the crops. They would talk about how nice the peas are this year, and how good the garden is.

He thought, once, that maybe they would not have a garden. There were reasons not to have one.

"We don't need a garden this year," he said to Margaret, wanting to spare her the work that would be in it for her.

"Yes," she said, wanting to spare him the loss of the garden, "of course we do!"

"Margaret, we'll go to all that work, and can all that food, and neither one of us may live to eat it."

She gave him her smile, then, the same smile she had always given him, that always seemed to him to have survived already the worst he could think of. She said, "Somebody will."

She pleased him, and the garden pleased him. After even so many years, he still needed to be bringing something to her.

His command to get up seems to prop itself against his body and stay there like a brace until finally, in its own good time and again to his surprise, his body obeys. He gets up, steps over the tree, and goes on. He keeps himself on his feet for some time now, herding himself along like a recalcitrant animal, searching for the easy steps, reconciling himself to the hard steps when there are no easy ones. He is sweating heavily. So deep in that cleft of the hill, the air is hot and close. He feels that he must stretch upward to breathe. It is as though his body has come to belong in a different element, and the mere air of that place now hardly sustains it.

He comes to the pool, the wall that he and Virgil made, and pauses there. "Now you must drink," he says. He goes to where the spring comes up among the roots of the sycamore. There is a smooth clear pool there, no bigger than his hat. He lies down to drink, and drinks, looking down into the tiny pool cupped among the roots, surrounded with stonecrop and moss. The loveliness of it holds him: the cool water in that pretty place in the shade, the great tree rising and spreading its white limbs overhead. "I am blessed," he thinks, "I could stay here." He rests where he lies, turned away from his drinking, more comfortable on the roots and rocks than he expected to be. Through the foliage he can see white clouds moving along as if mindful where they are going. A chipmunk comes in quick starts and stops across the rocks and crouches a long time not far from Mat's face, watching him, as if perhaps it would like a drink from the little pool that Mat just drank from. "Come on," Mat says to it. "There ain't any harm in me." He would like to sleep. There is a weariness beyond weariness in him that sleep would answer. He can remember a time when he could have let himself sleep in such a place, but he cannot do that now. "Get up," he says aloud. "Get up, get up."

But for a while yet he does not move. He and the chipmunk watch each other. Now and again their minds seem to wander apart, and then they look again and find each other still there. There is a sound of wings, like a sudden dash of rain, and the chipmunk tumbles off its rock and does not appear again. Mat laughs. "You'd *better* hide." And now he does get up.

He stands, his left hand propped against the trunk of the sycamore. Darkness draws across his vision and he sinks back down onto his knees, his right hand finding purchase in the cold cup of the spring. The darkness wraps closely around him for a time, and then withdraws, and he stands again. "*That* won't do," he says to Virgil. "We got to do better than that, boy." And then he sees his father too standing with Virgil on the other side of the stream. They recognize him, even though he is so much older now than when they knew him—older than either of them ever lived to be. "Well," he says, "looks like we got plenty of help." He reaches down and lets his right hand feel its way to the cane, picks it up, and straightens again. "*Yessir.*"

The world clears, steadies, and levels itself again in the light. He looks around him at the place: the wall, the pool, the spring mossy and clear in the roots of the white tree. "I am not going to come back here," he thinks. "I will never be in this place again."

Instructing his steps, he leaves. He moves with the utmost care and the utmost patience. For some time he does not think of where he is going. He is merely going up along the stream, asking first for one step and then for the next, moving by little plans that he carefully makes, and by choice. When he pauses to catch his breath or consider his way, he can feel his heart beating; at each of its beats the world seems to dilate and spring away from him.

His father and Virgil are with him, moving along up the opposite side of the branch as he moves up his side. He cannot always see them, but he knows they are there. First he does not see them, and then he sees one or the other of them appear among the trees and stand looking at him. They do not speak, though now and again he speaks to them. And then Jack Beechum, Joe Banion, and old Smoke are with them. He sees them sometimes separately, sometimes together. The dead who were here with him before are here with him again. He is not afraid. "I could stay here," he thinks. But ahead of him there is a reason he should not do that, and he goes on.

He seems to be walking in and out of his mind. Or it is time, perhaps, that he is walking in and out of. Sometimes he is with the dead as they were, and he is as he was, and all of them together are walking upward through the woods toward home. Sometimes he is alone, an old man in a later time than any of the dead have known, going the one way that he alone is going, among all the ways he has gone before, among all the ways he has never gone and will never go.

He does not remember falling. He is lying on the rocks beside the branch, and there is such disorder and discomfort in the way he is lying as he could not have intended. And so he must have fallen. He wonders if he is going to get up. After a while he does at least sit up. He shifts around so that his back can rest against the trunk of a tree. His movements cause little lurches in the world, and he waits for it to be steady. "Now you have got to stop and think," he says. And then he says, "Well, you have stopped. Now you had better think."

He does begin to think, forcing his vision and his thoughts out away from him into the place around him, his mind making little articulations of recognition. The place and his memory of it begin to speak to one another. He has come back almost to the upper wall and pool, where he first came down to the branch. When he gets there he will have a choice to make between two hard ways to go.

But his mind, having thought of those choices, now leaves him, like an undisciplined pup, and goes to the house, and goes back in time to the house the way it was when he and Margaret were still young.

About this time in the afternoon, about this time in the year, having come to the house for something, he cannot remember what, he pushes open the kitchen door, leans his shoulder on the jamb, and looks at Margaret, who stands with her back to him, icing a cake.

"Now nobody's asked for my opinion," he says, "and nobody's likely to, but if anybody ever was to, I'd say *that* is a huggable woman."

"Don't you come near me, Mat Feltner."

"And a spirited woman."

"If you so much as lay a hand on me, I'm going to hit you with this cake."

"And a dangerous, mean woman."

"Go back to work."

"Who is, still and all, a huggable woman. Which is only my opinion. A smarter man might think different."

She turns around, laughing, and comes to get her hug. "I could never have married a smart man."

"She didn't marry *too* smart a one," he thinks. He is getting up, the effort requiring the attendance of his mind, and once he is standing he puts his mind back on his problem. That is not where it wants to be, but this time he makes it stay. If he leaves the branch and goes back up onto the ridge by the way he came down, that will require a long slanting climb up across the face of a steep slope. "And it has got steeper since I came down it," he thinks. If he goes on up Shade Branch, which would be the easiest, surest route, he will have, somehow, to get over or through the fence that crosses the branch above the wall. He does not believe that he can climb the fence. Where the fence crosses the stream it is of barbed wire, and in that place a stronger man might go through or under it. But he does not want to risk hooking his clothes on the barbs.

But now he thinks of a third possibility: the ravine that comes into Shade Branch just above him to his right hand. The dry, rocky streambed in the ravine would go up more gently than the slope, the rocks would afford him stairsteps of a sort for at least some of the way, and it would be the shortest way out of the woods. It would bring him out farther from home than the other ways, but he must not let that bother him. It is the most possible of the three ways, and the most important thing now, he knows, is to get up onto the open land of the ridge where he can be seen if somebody comes looking for him. Somebody will be looking for him, he hopes, for he has to admit that he is not going very fast, and once he starts up the ravine he will be going slower than ever.

For a while he kept up the belief, and then the hope, that he could make it home in a reasonable time and walk into the house as if nothing had happened.

"Where on earth have you been?" Margaret would ask.

He would go to the sink to wash up, and then he would say, drying his hands, "Oh, I went to see about the line fence down the branch, but Nathan had already fixed it."

He would sit down then to help her with the peas.

"Mat Feltner," she would say, "surely you didn't go away off down there."

But it is too late now, for something *has* happened. He has been gone too long, and is going to be gone longer.

Margaret has got up from her work and gone to the windows and looked out, and gone to the door onto the back porch and spoken his name, and walked on out to the garden gate and then to the gate to the barn lot.

He can see her and hear her calling as plainly as if he were haunting her. "Mat! Oh, Mat!"

He can hear her, and he makes his way on up the branch to the mouth of the ravine. He turns up the bed of the smaller stream. The climb is steeper here, the hard steps closer together. The ascent asks him now really to climb, and in places, where the rocks of the streambed bulge outward in a wall, he must help himself with his hands. He must stoop under and climb over the trunks of fallen trees. When he stops after each of these efforts the heavy beating of his heart keeps on. He can feel it shaking him, and darkness throbs in his eyes. His breaths come too far between and too small. Sometimes he has roots along the side of the ravine for a banister, and that helps. Sometimes the cane helps; sometimes, when he needs both hands, it is in the way. And always he is in the company of the dead.

Ahead of him the way is closed by the branchy top of a young maple, blown down in a storm, and he must climb up the side of the ravine to get around it. At the top of the climb, when the slope has gentled and he stops and his heart plunges on and his vision darkens, it seems to him that he is going to fall; he decides instead to sit down, and he does. Slowly he steadies again within himself. His heart slows and his vision brightens again. He tells himself again to get up. "It ain't as far as it has been," he says to Virgil. "I'm going to be all right now. I'm going to make it."

But now his will presses against his body, as if caught within it, in bewilderment. It will not move. There was a time when his body had strength enough in it to carry him running up such a place as this, with breath left over to shout. There was a time when it had barely enough strength in it to carry it this far. There is a time when his body is too heavy for his strength. He longs to lie down. To Jack Beechum, the young man, Jack Beechum, who is watching him now, he says, "You and I were here once."

The dead come near him, and he is among them. They come and go, appear and disappear, like feeding birds. They are there and gone. He is among them, and then he is alone. To one who is not going any farther, it is a pretty place, the leaves new and perfect, a bird singing out of sight among them somewhere over his head, and the softening light slanting in long beams from the west. "I could stay here," he thinks. It is the thought of going on that turns that steep place into an agony. His own stillness pacifies it and makes it lovely. He thinks of dying, secretly, by himself, in the woods. No one now knows where he is. Perhaps it would be possible to hide and die, and never be found. It would be a clean, clear way for that business to be done, and the thought, in his weariness, comforts him, for he has feared that he might die a nuisance to Margaret and the others. He might, perhaps, hide himself in a little cave or sink hole if one were nearby, here where the dead already are, and be one of them, and enter directly into the peaceableness of this place, and turn with it through the seasons, his body grown easy in its weight.

But there is no hiding place. He would be missed and hunted for and found. He would die a nuisance, for he could not hide from all the reasons that he would be missed and worried about and hunted for. He has an appointment that must be kept, and between him and it the climb rises on above him.

He has an accounting he must come to, and it is not with the dead, for

Margaret has not sat down again, but is walking. She is walking from room to room and from window to window. She has not called Bess, because she does not want Bess to drive all the way up from Hargrave, perhaps for nothing. Though she has thought about it, she has not even called Hannah, who is nearer by. She does not want to alarm anybody. But she is alarmed. She walks from room to room and from window to window, pausing to look out, and walking again. She walks with her arms tightly folded, as she has walked all her life when she has been troubled, until Mat, watching her, has imagined that he thinks as she thinks and feels as she feels, so moved by her at times that he has been startled to realize again his separateness from her.

He remembers the smile of assent that she gave him once: "Why, Mat, I thought you did. And I love you." Everything that has happened to him since has come from that—and leads to that, for it is not a moment that has ever stopped happening; he has gone toward it and aspired to it all his life, a time that he has not surpassed.

Now she is an old woman, walking in his mind in the rooms of their house. She has called no one and told no one. She is the only one who knows that she does not know where he is. The men are in the hayfield, and she is waiting for one of them or some of them to come to the barn. Or Wheeler might come by. It is the time of day when he sometimes does. She walks slowly from room to room, her arms folded tightly, and she watches the windows.

Mat, sitting in his heaviness among the trees, she does not know where, yearns for her as from beyond the grave. "Don't worry," he says. "It's going to be all right." He gets up.

And now an overmastering prayer that he did not think to pray rushes upon him out of the air and seizes him and grapples him to itself: an absolute offering of himself to his return. It is an offer, involuntary as his breath, voluntary as the new steps he has already taken up the hill, to give up his life in order to have it. The prayer does not move him beyond weariness and weakness, it moves him merely beyond all other thoughts.

He gives no more regard to death or to the dead. The dead do not appear again. Now he is walking in this world, walking in time, going home. A shadowless love moves him now, not his, but a love that he belongs to, as he belongs to the place and to the light over it. He is thinking of Margaret and of all that his plighting with her has led to. He is thinking of the membership of the fields that he has belonged to all his life, and will belong to while he breathes, and afterward. He is thinking of the living ones of that membership—at work today in the fields that the dead were at work in before them.

"I am blessed," he thinks. "I am blessed."

He is crawling now, the cane lost and forgotten. He crawls a little, and he rests a lot. The slope has gentled somewhat. The big woods has given way to thicket. He has turned away from the stream, taking the straightest way to the open slope that he can see not far above him. The cattle are up there grazing, the calves starting to play a little, now that the cool of the day is here.

When he comes out, clear of the trees, onto the grassed hillside, he seems again to have used up all his strength. "Now," he thinks, "you have got to rest." Once he has rested he will go on to the top of the ridge. Once he gets there, he can make it to the road. He crawls on up the slope a few feet to where a large walnut tree stands alone outside the woods, and sits against it so that he will have a prop for his back. He wipes his face, brushes at the dirt on his knees and then subsides. Not meaning to, he sleeps.

The sun is going down when he wakes, the air cold on his damp clothes. Except for opening his eyes, he does not move. His body is still as a stone.

Now he knows what woke him. It is the murmur of an automobile engine up on the ridge—Wheeler's automobile, by the sound of it. And when it comes into sight he sees that it is Wheeler's; Wheeler is driving and Elton Penn and Nathan are with him. They are not looking for him. They have not seen Margaret. Perhaps they did not bale the hay. Or they may have finished and got away early. But he knows that Wheeler found Nathan and Elton, wherever they were, after he shut his office and drove up from Hargrave, and they have been driving from field to field ever since, at Elton's place or at Nathan's or at Wheeler's, and now here. This is something they do, Mat knows, for he is often with them when they do it. Wheeler drives the car slowly, and they look and worry and admire and remember and plan. They have come to look at the cattle now, to see them on the new grass. They move among the cows and calves, looking and stopping. Now and then an arm reaches out of one of the car windows and points. For a long time they do not turn toward Mat. It is as though he is only part of the field, like the tree he is leaning against. He feels the strangeness of his stillness, but he does not move.

And then, still a considerable distance away, Wheeler turns the car straight toward the tree where Mat is sitting. He sees their heads go up when they see him, and he raises his right hand and gives them what, for all his eagerness, is only an ordinary little wave.

Wheeler accelerates, and the car comes tilting and rocking down the slope. Where the slope steepens, forcing the car to slow down, Mat sees Nathan leap out of it and come running toward him, Elton out too, then, while Wheeler is still maneuvering the car down the hill. Seeing that they are running to help him, Mat despises his stillness. He forces himself to his knees and then to his feet. He turns to face Nathan, who has almost reached him. He lets go of the tree and stands, and sees the ground rising against him like a blow. He feels himself caught strongly, steadied, and held. He hears himself say, "Papa?"

That night, when Margaret finds him wandering in the darkened house, he does not know where he is.

That Distant Land (1965)

For several days after the onset of his decline, my grandfather's mind seemed to leave him to go wandering, lost, in some foreign place. It was a dream he was in, we thought, that he could not escape. He was looking for the way home, and he could not find anyone who knew how to get there.

"No," he would say. "Port William. Port William is the name of the place."

Or he would ask, "Would you happen to know a nice lady by the name of Margaret Feltner? She lives in Port William. Now, which way would I take to get there?"

But it was not us he was asking. He was not looking at us and mistaking us for other people. He was not looking at us at all. He was talking to people he was meeting in his dream. From the way he spoke to them, they seemed to be nice people. They treated him politely and were kind, but they did not know any of the things that he knew, and they could not help him.

When his mind returned, it did so quietly. It had never been a mind that made a lot of commotion around itself. One morning when my grandmother went in to wake him and he opened his eyes, they were looking again. He looked at my grandmother and said, "Margaret, I'll declare." He looked around him at the bright room and out the window at the ridges and the woods, and said, "You got a nice place here, ma'am."

My grandmother, as joyful as if he had indeed been gone far away and had come home, said, "Oh, Mat, are you all right?"

And he said, "I seem to be a man who has been all right before, and I'm all right now."

That was the middle of June, and having come back from wherever it had been, his mind stayed with him and with us, a peaceable, pleasant guest, until he died.

He did not get out of bed again. What troubled us, and then grieved us, and finally consoled us, was that he made no effort to get up. It appeared to us that he felt his time of struggle to be past, and that he agreed to its end. He who had lived by ceaseless effort now lived simply as his life was given to him, day by day. During the time his mind had wandered he ate little or nothing, and though his mind returned his appetite did not. He ate to please my grandmother, but he could not eat much. She would offer the food, he would eat the few bites that were enough, and she would take the plate away. None of us had the heart to go beyond her gentle offering. No one insisted. No one begged. He asked almost nothing of us, only to be there with us, and we asked only to be with him.

He lay in a room from which he could look out across the ridges toward the river valley. And he did often lie there looking out. Now that he felt his own claims removed from it, the place seemed to have become more than ever interesting to him, and he watched it as the dark lifted from it and the sun rose and moved above it and set and the dark returned. Now and then he would speak of what he saw—the valley brimming with fog in the early morning, a hawk circling high over the ridges, somebody at work in one of the fields—and we would know that he watched with understanding and affection. But the character of his watching had changed. We all felt it. We had known him as a man who watched, but then his watching had been purposeful. He had watched as a man preparing for what he knew he must do, and what he wanted to do. Now it had become the watching, almost, of one who was absent.

The room was bright in the mornings, and in the afternoons dim and cool. It was always clean and orderly. My grandfather, who had no wants, made no clutter around him, and any clutter that the rest of us made did not last long. His room became the center of the house, where we came to rest. He would welcome us, raising his hand to us as we came in, listening to all that was said, now and again saying something himself.

Because, wherever we were, we kept him in our minds, he kept us together in the world as we knew he kept us in his mind. Until the night of his death we were never all in the house at the same time, yet no day passed that he did not see most of us. In the morning, my mother, his only surviving child, or Hannah Coulter, who had been his daughter-in-law and was, in all but blood, his daughter, or Flora, my wife, or Sara, my brother Henry's wife, would come in to spend the day with my grandmother to keep her company and help with the work. And at evening my father or Henry or I or Nathan Coulter, who now farmed my grandfather's farm and was, in all but blood, his son, would come, turn about, to spend the night, to give whatever help would be needed.

And others who were not family came: Burley Coulter, Burley's brother Jarrat, Elton and Mary Penn, Arthur and Martin Rowanberry. They would happen by for a few minutes in the daytime, or come after supper and sit and talk an hour or two. We were a membership. We belonged together, and my grandfather's illness made us feel it.

But "illness," now that I have said it, seems the wrong word. It was not like other illnesses that I had seen — it was quieter and more peaceable. It was, it would be truer to say, a great weariness that had come upon him, like the lesser weariness that comes with the day's end — a weariness that had been earned, and was therefore accepted.

I had lived away, working in the city, for several years, and had returned home only that spring. I was thirty years old, I had a wife and children, and my return had given a sudden sharp clarity to my understanding of my home country. Every fold of the land, every grass blade and leaf of it gave me joy, for I saw how my own place in it had been prepared, along with its failures and its losses. Though I knew that I had returned to difficulties — not the least of which were the deaths that I could see coming — I was joyful.

The nights I spent, taking my turn, on the cot in a corner of my grandfather's room gave me a strong, sweet pleasure. At first, usually, visitors would be there, neighbors or family stopping by. Toward bedtime, they would go. I would sit on a while with my grandmother and grandfather, and we would talk. Or rather, if I could arrange it so, they would talk and I would listen. I loved to start them talking about old times — my mother's girlhood, their own young years, stories told them by their parents and grandparents, memories of memories. In their talk the history of Port William went back and back along one of its lineages until it ended in silence and conjecture, for Port William was older than its memories. That it had begun we knew because it had continued, but we did not know when or how it had begun.

It was usually easy enough to get them started, for they enjoyed the remembering, and they knew that I liked to hear. "Grandad," I would say, "who was George Washington Coulter's mother?" Or: "Granny, tell about Aunt Maude Wheeler hailing the steamboat." And they would enter the endlessly varying pattern of remembering. A name would remind them of a story; one story would remind them of another. Sometimes my grandmother would get out a box of old photographs and we would sit close to the bed so that my grandfather could see them too, and then the memories and names moved and hovered over the transfixed old sights. The picture that most moved and troubled me was the only consciously photographed "scene": a look down the one street of Port William at the time of my grandparents' childhood — 1890 or thereabouts. What so impressed me about it was that the town had then been both more prosperous and more the center of its own attention than I had ever known it to be. The business buildings all had upper stories, the church had a steeple, there was a row of trees, planted at regular intervals, along either side of the road. Now the steeple and most of the upper stories were gone — by wind or fire or decay — and many of the trees were gone. For a long time, in Port William, what had gone had not been replaced. Its own attention had turned away from itself toward what it could not be. And I understood how, in his dream, my grandfather had suffered his absence from the town; through much of his life it had grown increasingly absent from itself.

After a while, my grandmother would leave us. She would go to my grandfather's side and take his hand. "Mat, is there anything you want before I go?"

"Ma'am," he would say, "I've got everything I want." He would be teasing her a little, as he was always apt to do.

She would hesitate, wishing, I think, that he did want something. "Well, good night. I'll see you in the morning."

And he would pat her hand and say very agreeably, as if he were altogether willing for that to happen, if it should happen, "All right."

She would go and we would hear her stirring about in her room, preparing for bed. I would do everything necessary to make my grandfather comfortable for the night, help him to relieve himself, help him to turn onto his side, straighten the bedclothes, see that the flashlight was in reach in case he wanted to look at the clock, which he sometimes did. I was moved by his willingness to let me help him. We had always been collaborators. When I was little, he had been the one in the family who would help me with whatever I was trying to make. And now he accepted help as cheerfully as he had given it. We were partners yet.

I was still a young man, with a young man's prejudice in favor of young bodies. I would have been sorry but I would not have been surprised if I had found it unpleasant to have to handle him as I did — his old flesh slackened and dwindling on the bones — but I did not find it so. I touched him gratefully. I would put one knee on the bed and gather him in my arms and move him toward me and turn him. I liked to do it. The comfort I gave him I felt. He would say, "Thanks, son."

When he was settled, I would turn on the dim little bedlamp by the cot and go to bed myself.

"Sleep tight," I would tell him.

"Well," he would say, amused, "I will part of the time."

I would read a while, letting the remembered dear stillness of the old house come around me, and then I would sleep.

My grandfather did only sleep part of the time. Mostly, when he was awake, he lay quietly with his thoughts, but sometimes he would have to call me, and I would get up to bring him a drink (he would want only two or three swallows), or help him to use the bedpan, or help him to turn over.

Once he woke me to recite me the Twenty-third Psalm. "Andy," he said. "Andy. Listen." He said the psalm to me. I lay listening to his old, slow voice coming through the dark to me, saying that he walked through the valley of the shadow of death and was not afraid. It stood my hair up. I had known that psalm all my life. I had heard it and said it a thousand times. But until then I had always felt that it came from a long way off, some place I had not lived. Now, hearing him speak it, it seemed to me for the first time to utter itself in our tongue and to wear our dust. My grandfather slept again after that, but I did not.

Another night, again, I heard him call me. "Andy. Listen." His voice exultant then at having recovered the words, he recited:

> *There entertain him all the saints above,*
> *In solemn troops and sweet societies*
> *That sing, and singing in their glory move,*
> *And wipe the tears forever from his eyes.*

After he spoke them, the words stood above us in the dark and the quiet, sounding and luminous. And then they faded.

After a while I said, "Who taught you that?"

"My mother. She was a great hand to improve your mind."

And after a while, again, I asked, "Do you know who wrote it?"

"No," he said. "But wasn't he a fine one!"

As the summer went along, he weakened, but so slowly we could hardly see it happening. There was never any sudden change. He remained quiet, mainly comfortable, and alert. We stayed in our routine of caring for him; it had become the ordinary way of things.

In the latter part of August we started into the tobacco cutting. For us, that is the great divider of the year. It ends the summer, and makes safe the season's growth. After it, our minds are lightened, and we look ahead to winter and the coming year. It is a sort of ritual of remembrance, too, when we speak of other years and remember our younger selves and the absent and the dead — all those we have, as we say, "gone down the row with."

We had a big crew that year — eight men working every day: Jarrat and Burley and Nathan Coulter, Arthur and Martin Rowanberry, Elton Penn, Danny Branch, and me. Hannah Coulter and Mary Penn and Lyda Branch kept us fed and helped with the hauling and housing. And Nathan and Hannah's and the Penns' children were with us until school started, and then they worked after school and on Saturdays. We worked back and forth among the various farms as the successive plantings became ready for harvest.

"What every tobacco cutting needs," Art Rowanberry said, "is a bunch of eighteen-year-old boys wanting to show how fast they are."

He was right, but we did not have them. We were not living in a time that was going to furnish many such boys for such work. Except for the children, we were all old enough to be resigned to the speed we could stand. And so, when we cut, we would be strung out along the field in a pattern that never varied from the first day to the last. First would be Elton and Nathan and Danny, all working along together. Elton, I think, would have proved the fastest if anybody had challenged him, but nobody did. Then came Mart Rowanberry, who was always ahead of me, though he was nearly twice my age, and then, some distance behind me, would come Art Rowanberry, and then Burley Coulter, and then, far back, Burley's brother Jarrat, whose judgment and justification of himself were unswerving: "I'm old and wore out and not worth a damn. But every row I cut is a cut row."

In my grandfather's absence Jarrat was the oldest of us, a long-enduring, solitary, mostly silent man, slowed by age and much hard work. His brushy eyes could stare upon you as if you had no more ability to stare back than a post. When he had something to say, his way was simply to begin to say it, no matter who else was talking or what else was happening, his slow, hard-edged voice boring in upon us like his stare — and the result, invariably, was that whatever was happening stopped, and whoever was talking listened.

I never caught up with Elton and Nathan and Danny, or came anywhere near it, but at least when the rows were straight I always had them in sight, and I loved to watch them. Though they kept an even, steady pace, it was not a slow one. They drove into the work, maintaining the same pressing rhythm from one end of the row to the other, and yet they worked well, as smoothly and precisely as dancers. To see them moving side by side against the standing crop, leaving it fallen, the field changed, behind them, was maybe like watching Homeric soldiers going into battle. It was momentous and beautiful, and touchingly, touchingly mortal. They were spending themselves as they worked, giving up their time; they would not return by the way they went.

The good crew men among us were Burley and Elton. When the sun was hot and the going hard, it would put heart into us to hear Burley singing out down the row some scrap of human sorrow that his flat, exuberant voice both expressed and mocked:

Allll *our sins and griefs to* bear — *oh!*

—that much only, raised abruptly out of the silence like the howl of some solitary dog. Or he would sing with a lovelorn quaver in his voice:

Darlin', fool yourself and love me one more time.

And when we were unloading the wagons in the barn, he would start his interminable tale about his life as a circus teamster. It was not meant to be believed, and yet in our misery we listened to his extravagant wonderful lies as if he had been Marco Polo returned from Cathay.

Elton had as much gab as Burley, when he wanted to, but he served us as the teller of the tale of our own work. He told and retold everything that happened that was funny. That we already knew what he was telling, that he was telling us what we ourselves had done, did not matter. He told it well, he told it the way we would tell it when we told it, and every time he told it he told it better. He told us, also, how much of our work we had got done, and how much we had left to do, and how we might form the tasks still ahead in order to do them. His head, of course, was not the only one involved, and not the only good one, but his was indeed a good one, and his use of it pleased him and comforted us. Though we had a lot of work still to do, we were going to be able to do it, and these were the ways we could get it done. The whole of it stayed in his mind. He shaped it for us and gave it a comeliness greater than its difficulty.

That we were together now kept us reminded of my grandfather, who had always been with us before. We often spoke of him, because we missed him, or because he belonged to our stories, and we could not tell them without speaking of him.

One morning, perhaps to acknowledge to herself that he would not wear them again, my grandmother gave me a pair of my grandfather's shoes.

It was a gift not easy to accept. I said, "Thanks, Granny," and put them under my arm.

"No," she said. "Put them on. See if they fit."

They fit, and I started, embarrassedly, to take them off.

"No," she said. "Wear them."

And so I wore them to the field.

"New shoes!" Burley said, recognizing them, and I saw tears start to his eyes.

"Yes," I said.

Burley studied them, and then me. And then he smiled and put his arm around me, making the truth plain and bearable to us both: "You can wear 'em, honey. But you can't fill 'em."

It got to be September, and the fall feeling came into the air. The days would get as hot as ever, but now when the sun got low the chill would come. It was not going to frost for a while yet, but we could feel it coming. It was the time of year, Elton said, when a man begins to remember his long underwear.

We were cutting a patch at Elton's place where the rows were longer than any we had cut before, bending around the shoulder of a ridge and rising a little over it. They were rows to break a man's heart, for, shaped as they were, you could not see the end, and those of us who were strung out behind the leaders could not see each other. All that we could see ahead of us was the cloudless blue sky. Each row was a long, lonely journey that, somewhere in the middle, in our weariness, we believed would never end.

Once when I had cut my row and was walking back to start another, Art Rowanberry wiped the sweat from his nose on the cuff of his sleeve and called out cheerfully to me, "Well, have you been across? Have you seen the other side?"

That became the ceremony of that day and the next. When one of us younger ones finished a row and came walking back, Art would ask us, "Have you seen the other side?"

Burley would take it up then, mourning and mocking: "Have you reached the other shore, dear brother? Have you seen that distant land?" And he would sing,

Oh, pilgrim, have you seen that distant land?

On the evening of the second day we had the field nearly cut. There was just enough of the crop left standing to make an easy job of finishing up—something to look forward to. We had finished cutting for the day and were sitting in the rich, still light under a walnut tree at the edge of the field, resting a little, before loading the wagons. We would load them the last thing every evening, to unload the next morning while the dew was on.

We saw my father's car easing back along the fencerow, rocking a little over the rough spots in the ground. It was a gray car, all dusty, and scratched along the sides where he had driven it through the weeds and briars. He still had on his suit and tie.

"Ah, here he comes," Burley said, for we were used to seeing him at that time of day, when he would leave his office at Hargrave and drive up to help us a little or to see how we had got along.

He drove up beside us and stopped, and killed the engine. But he did not look at us. He looked straight ahead as if he had not quit driving, his hands still on the wheel.

"Boys," he said, "Mr. Feltner died this afternoon. About an hour ago."

And then, after he seemed to have finished, he said as though to himself, "And now that's over."

I heard Burley clear his throat, but nobody said anything. We sat in the cooling light in my grandfather's new absence, letting it come upon us.

And then the silence shifted and became our own. Nobody spoke.

Nobody yet knew what to say. We did not know what we were going to do. We were, I finally realized, waiting on Jarrat. It was Elton's farm, but Jarrat was now the oldest man, and we were waiting on him.

He must have felt it too, for he stood, and stood still, looking at us, and then turned away from us toward the wagons.

"Let's load 'em up."

A Friend of Mine (1967)

During the three weeks they had been in the tobacco cutting so far, Elton Penn had accumulated several errands that he had put off almost too long. And so on Friday morning, instead of going to the Rowanberry Place where the crew was now at work, he drove first to Port William and then to Hargrave. His several duties in those places needed to be done, but his doing of them was dogged by the guilty knowledge that he was glad to have them to do.

He was tired. He was forty-seven years old that summer — this was almost thirty years ago — and he was beginning to know what the older men meant when they told the young ones, "you don't know what tired is." Elton did not rest as well at night as he once did, and he had got so, in the times of hardest work, he was always sore in the morning. And so it was pleasant to see to his brief business at the bank in Port William and purchase a hundred pounds of stock salt at Jasper Lathrop's store, and then drive down the river road to the farm equipment place at Hargrave.

But he was mindful that his friends were at work, and he did not linger anywhere. He was back at home an hour and a half before noon. He changed into his soiled clothes and used the rest of the morning in straightening up his barn. They had been at work in his crop the first of the week and would return again in a few days, and so he made ready.

When Mary called him to dinner, he ate, and then filled his water jug. He drove back through Port William and down the Sand Ripple road into the creek bottom. As he crossed the creek on the graveled lane that went by the Rowanberrys' house, he came up behind Mart Rowanberry, who was on his way to the tobacco patch with a tractor and wagon. Elton tooted the horn, and Mart looked back and waved.

Beyond the house, Mart stopped. Elton pulled his truck out of the lane into the shade of the great chinquapin oak that stood well below the house and yet reached its top branches higher than the roof. A dozen feet above Elton's head a railroad spike had been driven into the trunk to mark the crest of the 1937 flood.

"Yessir!" Mart said. "Reckon you'll ever get anywhere without changing jobs? How's this one for a fine day?"

"It's the one the doctor ordered!"

Elton tossed his cutting tools onto the wagon and hoisted himself on, setting his jug on his lap.

Mart drove on up the steep road into the woods and then finally out again onto the open ridgetop.

They came to a gap in a fence beyond which was a tobacco patch, the ripe leaves golden in the strong light. Mart stopped the tractor again.

"How about if I leave you here?" he said. "We got all the hands we need to haul in and house. Me and Art thought, if you didn't mind, you could start cutting on this piece."

"I don't mind," Elton said, telling the truth. It would please him to work alone. He stood beside the wagon, holding his tools and his jug.

"Sticks are dropped in maybe half the rows," Mart said.

"All right."

"And listen. There's a patch of little watermelons yonder on the far end. They're just about dead ripe and sweet as sugar. Whatever you do, don't eat any of them."

"Well, you know I don't like watermelon."

Mart drove on then, drawing the rattling wagon out of sight. Elton straddled over the gap, walked to the far end of the patch, and set his jug in the shade of an old pear tree. The watermelon vines were in two short rows alongside the tobacco; he went back and picked three ripe melons and carried them to the tree and put them down in the deep grass in the shade.

From where he stood he could see out over the treetops on the bluff and down the river valley almost to Hargrave. For a moment he let his mind go out into that reach of bright air, longingly, for now the dread of the hard afternoon of work was on him. The clear free light over the green slopes and the fields of the bottomlands offered an invitation that he felt it hard to refuse and yet would have needed wings to accept.

And then, without mercy to himself, which was the only way to do it, he entered into the work. He went to the first two rows on the right-hand side of the patch, picked up a stick, jobbed it upright into the ground at the end of the outside row, and clapped his spear onto it. He leaned and cut the first plant and speared it, and then a second and then a third. After he had cut five plants from the two rows, he stabbed the second stick into the ground and filled it as he had the first.

Though he did not begin slowly, for a while because of the stiffness of his muscles and joints he seemed to work in harness that was too tight. And then he began to sweat, and his body loosened into its motion. He worked easier, becoming gradually less conscious of himself, his mind beginning to wander among thoughts.

It was a fine day for work — in comparison, anyhow, with the days preceding. For two weeks the weather had been punishingly hot and humid; not a whiff of air had stirred. They had worked from morning to night in sweat-soaked clothes that bound and galled. And then during the night a little rain had come. This morning the air had tasted of the coming fall. And so the thought of what they had to do had become more tolerable. It was hot again by noon, but it was not so humid as it had been, and Elton's mind had changed.

Though he was known as a man passionate in his work, willing to spend himself in long days, Elton was a man also who knew the dread of work. He had sometimes, in moments of candor, spoken of himself as a lazy man.

"You're lazy," Mart would say, "and I reckon I'm that feller that scratches his ass with his big toe."

And Elton would insist: "I dread it as much as anybody!"

He was telling the truth; when he had the work still ahead of him, there would always come a time when he dreaded it. The tobacco harvest always came upon him that way, and followed the same course, at once surprising and familiar, from seeming impossibility to obvious possibility to eventual completion, when almost strangely the great effort would be behind him, and he would become again farsighted in his thoughts, desiring the coming year. He had not changed in this since his boyhood; he had not outgrown his reluctance. Beforehand he could not imagine how he would get the work done, how he would find in his mortal back and arms the strength to do it. And then, once it was begun, the work elaborating itself in the familiar sequence of motions and days, he would again become able to imagine it. He would feel coming into him each morning the necessary strength and will.

As he worked now he thought of the older men he had known — men of another time and kind, perhaps — who seemed always reconciled to the hardship of their work. Maybe they did not imagine the whole effort, Elton thought. Maybe they did not think of it at all the way he did, making it dreadful by adding it up, but just worked it out day by day, living each day for itself.

Art Rowanberry was one of that old kind. When the work piled up or did not go right, Elton fretted. But Art, no matter the difficulty or the urgency, always had something cheerful to say. Art was getting old and he had worked hard from childhood, yet he would still run like a boy to get in on a lift. The important thing, Art said, was for a man to feel good and be satisfied with what he had.

Elton was a strong man who felt good often enough. He was a man too of satisfactions. But his satisfactions were discontinuous, often interrupted, often not even remembered, for he was a man of dread too, and a man of desire. He wanted things he did not have, and he longed for the time when he would have them. He remembered his mother telling him, when he was wishing for Christmas to come, wishing for spring to come, wishing for school to let out, wishing for hunting season to begin, "Child, you're wishing your life away."

He was, and he knew it. He was wishing it away. When he put the bucks in with the ewes, he would be already wanting to see the lambs that would be born; he could hardly wait. And yet he knew that the price of seeing them would be a hundred and forty-five more of his days that would have to pass and be gone. He was wishing his life away. In his eagerness to live it, he was wishing it away.

Even before he was a man, he had wanted his own crop, his own team of horses. He had wanted to be on his own, a tenant, independent of family help. And then he had wanted to own the good farm that he had been a tenant on. And then, when his and Mary's names were on the deed, he had wanted it freed from debt; he longed for the day when they would pay the last dollar and bring home the canceled note. They had done that, and sooner even than they had expected. They freed the farm from debt and from their fear that they would not be able to pay the debt. And still Elton looked forward with the alternation of joy and dread that was characteristic of him. He longed to see the farm as it would look after each of his improvements. He saw visions and hurried to make the visions real. He longed to accumulate savings that would assure an education for his children; he longed to see them well-started in the world, and he feared that they would not be.

He thought, "I am wishing my life away, wishing it away." But he had come into satisfaction, too, for he was working well. Beyond the desire and the dread was the work itself. Beyond the dread, always, was a new world, intimately present, satisfying moment by moment.

Now half the row was behind him. He straightened, took off his hat and mopped the sweat from his forehead and eyes. He looked forward and back, and then went at his work again, feeling a sort of joy now in the expenditure of his strength. If he had done half, he could do all, and half and then all again, and yet again and again. When the day was done, he would have something to show for it. He felt the heat and the beginning of thirst. He thought of the watermelons.

The year would be cooling now. Before long they would notice the shortening of the days. The nights would be getting cool, and good for sleep. In the mornings then, going out before breakfast, he would need to reach for his jacket. There would come a morning when the ground would be white with frost. The leaves would turn. Persimmons and wild grapes and black haws would ripen in the woods. The great force of winter would be approaching, recognizable from other years, feelable in the bones.

Elton was gone now almost completely into the rhythm of his work, carried along by it. In the stifling heat of recent days, though they had gone ahead and not stopped—they had not stopped even their storytelling and their laughter—the work had been oppressive. Half-smothered in the heavy air, bound in clothes that stayed wet with sweat, the body insisted constantly on its misery. But now, the weather changed so that he felt the turning of the year, his body went freely to its work, his mind to its thoughts.

He reached the other end of the patch and walked back, carrying his tools. He laid his tools down at the end of the next row. If he had been at home, with the crew on hand and the order of the work his own to worry about, he might have pushed a little at this point, not wanting to appear to favor himself. But here, where the worry belonged to the Rowanberrys and he was working alone, a little margin of ease surrounded him. Entering the shade of the pear tree, he lifted one of the small melons from its nest in the grass. He sat down, leaning his back against the trunk of the tree, and placed the melon on the ground between his spread legs. He took out his pocket knife, opened the longest blade, and inserted the point into the melon at the blossom-end. The melon cracked ahead of the blade as he drew it toward him. If Mart had been there, he would have said, "Green as a gourd, boys. Green as a gourd."

Elton turned the melon and drew the cut the rest of the way around. The knife had not penetrated all the way through, and he had to strike the melon lightly against the ground to open it. And then he took one of the halves and sliced it twice. The flesh was dark red, juicy, and sweet. He ate it in huge bites, not bothering to spit out the seeds. He sat, eagerly eating the melon, looking out and down where the Sand Ripple valley opened into the wider valley of the river. The second half of the melon he ate more slowly, working the seeds free of the pulp and spitting them out. He had a gift for such moments and he was having a good time. When he had eaten the melon he took a drink from his jug, and then he lit a cigarette and got up.

He had rested for no more than five minutes, and now he went back to his work before its momentum left him. The dread was long past. He did not even remember it. He liked where he was and what he was doing. He had fallen, there on the Rowanberry Place, into a happiness he recognized as Art Rowanberry's: feeling good and satisfied with what he had. The long row lay before him, almost as if he had never stopped, almost as if it joined all the other rows of his life, behind and ahead, and he had never stopped and there was nothing else in the world. And now, way behind him, across years, and still somehow ahead of him yet, he could hear his father crying out in mockery, in self-mockery, and yet in earnest: "All I want is a good day and a long row! Follow me, boys—you'll wear diamonds!"

He was in it now. It was as though his motion through the field was not made by him, but he by it, and it was carrying him. It would carry him to the row's end, and to the end of the next and the next, to the day's end, and then it would release him to his rest. And yet there was a momentum that went beyond tiredness and sleep. It would carry him on and on, through the fall days and into the cold, and into the spring again, and on to other years. He could feel it moving in him like the flow of blood, and through him like a wind.

When the tobacco harvest was over and they would separate to work alone or in pairs again on their own farms, he would sow the bared ground in wheat. And then he would gather his corn. He looked forward to that: the sight of the yellow ears, once dispersed in the wide field, now compact and deep within the crib. With the barns full of hay and the corn in the crib, he would feel relief, his responsibility to his animals fulfilled: they would make it through to spring. As the days shortened and the nights grew, the last of the garden would come in. On a cold morning in December, they would kill their meat hogs, and so would end the gathering of the year. Between them, he and Mary would have made kitchen and smokehouse and cellar as rich as the cribs and barns.

That provisioning was what he loved. The things that he and Mary brought together brought them together. In their parting and returning ways, out of their two lives that diverged and gathered in, they brought good things and offered them to each other in the same place.

He loved the thought of the year gathered in around them—food for themselves, feed for the stock, fuel for the stoves—and the winter coming. He loved to think ahead of time of his winter clothes: warm underwear and socks, coveralls and jacket, good shoes and overshoes, his cap with earflaps. He loved to think of them and then when the time came, he loved to put them on.

He had known winters when he had not had enough clothes. His father had died just as the country was tilting over into the Depression,

and for a long time after that they had lived lean. His mother had been a
thrifty woman and a doer. She scavenged and scrimped and saved. Every
dime they earned had the distinction of rarity and a hard history that she
knew. She was always busy. She knew every art by which the landscape
could be made to yield food, and they were never hungry. Elton took
from her and from that time his love of provisioning. Her garden, her
cow and meat hogs, her beans and squashes from the cornfield, her
buckets of wild fruit were virtual organs of her body; she would not
have known herself, she could not have lived, without them. But even
she had limits, and of what they had to buy they often did not have
enough. Going about his chores on winter mornings and then walking
across the ridge to school, Elton had felt the icy wind lay itself against
him as if he wore no clothes at all.

He and his brothers were hard on clothes. Their mother complained
and patched, and Elton was proud of his patches because her stitching
was precise and, he thought, beautiful. Because Elton was the youngest,
his clothes were rarely new. But she did buy him one new pair of brown
jersey gloves every fall, and those had to last him until spring. She would
mend and patch them endlessly, but if he lost them he got no more.

His thoughts about his mother were always divided. He admired her
industry and her saving ways, but too soon after his father's death she
had married a man named Corbin Crane, who still was a bad taste in
Elton's mouth.

Corbin Crane was always encumbered by unpaid debts and half-done
work, by delays and clumsy deceptions and lies that he told even to himself; he was always behind. He lived by shifting and conniving, depending without shame on what other people would let him talk them out of.
He used his neighbors by a brash and talky craftiness that they were only
briefly susceptible to, and so he was always looking for a better place. At
home he was a bully, exacting obedience from his wife's boys by force,
and so inciting them to rebellion, which he was forever in the process of
quelling by force.

For Elton, this stepfather was not just an enemy but a condition, one
that he felt he had to get out of or die. He was still only a boy, but he
fought his way out, in a sort of panic of suffocation, to confront the
world in the open where, as he told himself, he could at least breathe.

Until Corbin's shiftings carried his family out of the Sand Ripple neighborhood where Elton was born and spent most of his childhood, Elton was often underfoot at the Rowanberrys'. During the years of his absence, he held them in mind. They belonged to the part of his childhood that he liked to remember, and they were what Corbin Crane was not: honest, orderly, kind, and quiet.

When Elton returned, newly married, to the Port William vicinity, having moved as his mother's tenant to her small, rough farm on Cotman Ridge, he presented himself at the Rowanberrys' back door one night just as they were finishing up supper.

Mart pushed open the screen, and Elton, grinning, said, "You don't know me, do you?"

Mart looked him up and down carefully as if he were perhaps a horse or mule that was for sale. "Well," he said, "I reckon I do. Ain't you Elton?"

They were friends after that. Working and hunting together, they found that they were alike in mind and in readiness. They enjoyed working together because they did not have to waste time in explanations.

When you need somebody at the other end of something, Elton thought, Mart is already there.

He did not even pause in the second row until he reached the end. He was working at a pace he knew he could sustain until quitting time; he was hitting his lick. The difficulty had come to be balanced by his being equal to it. He seemed almost to be gliding, as if drawn on now not by will but by gravity.

Only when he had stopped and straightened up at the row end, did he let himself stand still. Around him as he had worked he had felt the stillness of all but himself: the field, the woods on the slopes, the clear sky. And now the stillness came to him. He felt the presence of the country; it formed around him, under his feet; it seemed to press upward within him. It seemed to him a great beauty that he at once saw and felt and breathed. The work of the afternoon had reached its summit. Now he would be going down.

From that end of the field, he could see out the ridge in the direction Mart had gone with the tractor, past the decaying log house of Rowanberrys dead and gone, to the tobacco patch that the crew had finished cutting the day before and the barn where they were housing the tobacco. Elton knew who was at work there, and he named their names to himself: Arthur and Martin Rowanberry, known as Art and Mart, Burley and Nathan Coulter, Danny Branch. As he watched, a tractor drawing a load of tobacco made its way slowly out of the patch toward the barn. And again he thought of Art Rowanberry, seeing that movement from field to barn as he thought Art might have seen it: the continuation of a movement begun before anybody remembered. The tractor was driven by a woman Elton recognized as Lyda Branch, Danny's wife, who had been there also the afternoon before. Though the men spared them all they could, one or more of their wives would often be with them, especially in the afternoons.

No living Rowanberry knew the name of the forefather who had built the log house where every Rowanberry down to Art and Mart had been born. The early ones had cleared and cropped the slopes, which, under the returned trees, still bore the scars. Now Art and Mart cropped only the ridges that rose above the woods, a gently rounded crest so bent and branched that they thought of it not as one ridge but several. And the several still bore the names given by bygone and unremembered Rowanberrys. The ridge where Elton was at work was the Locust Ridge. Almost opposite, a long grass field pointing out on the upriver side of the main ridge, was the Peach Orchard Ridge, though nobody remembered the peach trees for which it had been named. On beyond was the old house with its three surviving apple trees whose fruit Art and Mart still ate. The tobacco patch and the barn where the crew was at work was on the Hollow Tree Ridge. Beyond that, there was a narrow wooded backbone called the Gold Mine Ridge, named for an immense hole dug there long ago by Uncle Jackson Jones in his search, not in fact for a gold vein but for a trove of minted money, which he believed was buried somewhere near Port William—on what evidence, if any, nobody remembered. To search for it, Art remembered that his grandfather had remembered that Uncle Jackson used an instrument of some sort that he called his "needle." Guided, or misguided, by his needle, Uncle Jackson had pocked the whole countryside with holes, and in some of them you could have buried a henhouse.

The load disappeared into the dark yawn of the barn door, and presently a small flash in the air that Elton knew to be a melon rind came flying out. They would be taking a rest over there now. Mart probably had sliced the melons before the tractor got to the barn. Now they would be sitting on whatever came handy with their elbows on their knees, or sitting on the ground, leaning back against the posts of the driveway, eating and talking, enjoying the melon and their stillness, as they could do only in the midst of work. Some taunt or joke or funny story would probably be going among them now, and they would be laughing. The wish to be there with them passed through Elton and went away, for he felt also the pleasure of his own quiet and the simplicity, the lightness, of working alone.

He walked back to the other end of the patch. He went into the shade of the pear tree as into a shelter, leaving the blast of the sun and feeling his sweated shirt suddenly begin to cool. He picked up the second of the little melons and sat down as before against the tree with his legs stretched out in front of him on the grass. He sliced the melon and ate it slowly, relishing it, in big bites. The light had changed on the two valleys; now it was the light of midafternoon. The changes of the light from early to late to darkness and starlight or moonlight, he thought, were things you had, as you had other changing and passing things, water or food or love, as you had thirst or hunger or desire. And having had them, you were those things. You were the having them and the not-having them, and so you knew their worth. He tossed away the last rind, drank from the jug, smoked, and got up again.

As before, he had not rested long, but he had rested happily. The goodness of his rest seemed added to him now. He had cut his way twice across the long patch, and he would do so twice more. Now, starting again, with half the afternoon's work behind him, he felt lightened, pressed on by the force of what he had done.

What he had done was there to be seen. He could imagine the rest that he would do. He could imagine what they all would have done by evening. When they quit in the evening the last loads of the patch on the Hollow Tree Ridge would be on the wagons. The work there would be behind them. Leaving a harvested patch, he thought, is like leaving a house where you have lived. For you *have* lived there, and suffered and rejoiced, and looking back, you see that it was after all a good time, and you like to remember it.

One by one, they would clear the patches and leave them behind. It was a long job, an ordeal in a way, making them sore and tired — tireder even than they could imagine when they were dreading it beforehand. And yet, he thought, it was a job they needed. They needed the feeling they would have when at last they would be done, the feeling of having done it and of being done. They needed their being together and all the talk that passed between them. They needed even what they dreaded, the difficulty of their work and their hard pride in being equal to it.

They needed the feeling of the completion of work and the feeling of going free again. The time was coming soon when the same ones, or some of them, who had worked so many hard days together would be together again in the country at night, following their hounds to who could tell where over the ridges and along the wooded slopes. They would go and stay late, and be up again early in the morning to work all day. Beginning work on such a morning, groggy for want of sleep, they could not imagine why they had hunted the night before or why they would ever want to hunt again. They would work all day, thinking that they would not go again, and then as evening approached and they saw that it would be another thawing night when the ground would hold a scent, what Mart Rowanberry called "the fever" would come upon them again. And they would go again.

There was something lovely in their going. It was as though they simply gave themselves over to the pull of a gravity by which the countryside drew them to itself. They did not go, certainly, for the coon hides that would never bring enough, Mart said, to pay for shoe leather and lost sleep. Nor did they go for the music of the hounds trailing out beyond, somewhere in the dark, which yet did compensate them for something. They went to be at large in the country grown immense in the dark, their own places in it shrunk to the reach of the little lights they carried. On the heights of the ridges as they crossed them, they would know securely where they were by the geography of houselights flung out around them. And then they would go down into the folds and creases of the wooded slopes and the multiple branchings of the hollows, where from time to time they would know the strange pleasure of being lost in places that in daylight would have been familiar. Half their stories of these nights dealt with the recurring comedy of getting lost.

"Well, where you reckon we are?" Mart asked.

"Well, we're right here by this sycamore tree by this creek," Burley Coulter said.

"Well, anybody would have known that."

"Well, *you* didn't."

On those nights their minds held two geographies: one of the daylight and their history, signified at night by the houselights pinpricking the dark landscape, and the other described by the one line, ever changing, that connected only themselves to only the hounds crying "This way! This way!" out somewhere beyond them. Wandering at their end of that ever-changing line, boundaryless and timeless in the dark woods, it sometimes seemed to them that the first of their forebears had not yet arrived, or that the last of their successors had departed.

You could have much joy from an able dog with a keen nose and heart enough and a good mouth. It was a feeling strong and unspeakable that you felt when your reach was extended into the countryside by a willing animal who would call to you out of the dark. The feeling came to you already old, bearing almost the memory of all the ones who had felt it before.

He was getting well along now toward the far end of the patch. He had a hard way to travel, but he was getting on. If all the rows of his life had been laid end to end, he wondered, how far would he have gone? It would have been a many a mile. He thought of all that distance, and of himself back there on the far end of it, a big boy just starting out, believing the world would always be as he knew it then.

He thought of himself as he was now, having come so far, and of the changes he had seen. On the long ridge, reaching out under the waning day to the log house of the old Rowanberrys and the barn beyond, which he could now see again, he felt the quietness with which the country had submitted to all the changes that had passed over it since the first Rowanberry had arrived and struck the first axe-stroke.

For a long time it had been a story of flesh alone, the flesh of horses and mules and people, doing the work and bearing the hardship. Elton had grown up in that old way of farming, and he had liked it. He had owned good teams that had answered to his need and will almost as his own hand and feet had done. It had put tears in his eyes sometimes to see what his horses could do, and how willingly they went to it. The tractor, when he finally bought a second-hand one after the war, had satisfied two of his wants: it increased the amount of work he could accomplish and it lengthened his days to the limit of his endurance. Now he could work at night. A man such as he was, who was ambitious and who loved the changes his work made, was bound to be excited by this sudden enlargement. And yet there were times that brought the old ways back full-fleshed into his memory, and he missed his horses and the lost brotherly tie of mutual effort and mutual weariness.

The machines had come, as irresistibly as the hunters and land speculators who had come earlier — and not just tractors but machines of all kinds, shortening distances, shifting attention and people too from country to city. And now this crop that they had depended on from the beginning was in disrepute and under threat.

"It *all* could change," Wheeler Catlett said.

On a Sunday afternoon Elton and Wheeler were sitting in Wheeler's car on a ridgetop, looking at Elton's steers that were grazing around them. The sun was almost down. They had been together all afternoon, doing what they were still doing, driving through the fields and looking and talking. They had looked at everything and talked about everything. And several times Wheeler had been reminded and brought back to the question of the crop and the life and the people that the crop supported.

"It all could change," he said. "It might be that if we should come back from the dead in the time to come, we wouldn't know where we were."

And they fell quiet, for it was really the end of time that they thought of then, foreseeing not only their own absence from that place, but the earth silent, the heavens empty of light, the whole story over and done.

"Ah!" Elton said. "Ah!" He finished the row and stepped free of it.

Without pausing this time, he turned and walked back to the starting end. The afternoon, by his reckoning, was now three-quarters gone. One more row, he thought. One more. But he was tired now. This time, when he returned to the pear tree, he did not sit down. He knew that if he sat down this time he would need willpower to get up, and he did not want the rest of the day to become a matter of willpower. He picked up the third melon, knelt on one knee to slice it, and then ate it standing with his left shoulder propped against the tree, his back to the patch, looking again out over the valleys of Sand Ripple and the river.

He finished the melon, drank from his jug, and smoked. He did not turn to look again at the patch. He watched the light over and within the two valleys, now slowly becoming the light of evening. When he had finished his smoke he picked up his tools.

One more row, he thought. One more, and now every plant I cut will make it that much less than one. While he rested he had preserved in his body the momentum of his work, as one might hold in mind the tune of a song, and now he gave himself back to it again. He needed to keep the momentum, find his rhythm, stay with it to the end. If he kept to his lick, he would be accurate; the plants would seem just to float free of the ground and onto the spear. But if he faltered, if he acknowledged his tiredness, the plants would grow heavy and clumsy in his hands. It would come to willpower then. His weariness would descend on him like a heavy load. He would not finish the row; the day would feel incomplete, and he would not be free of it. It was the difference between grace and force that he had to bear in mind now. Going the way he was going was a hard way to travel, but he was moving like a dancer in his dance, momentum carrying him across the downfalling of the day.

Momentum and desire. For now hunger was returning to him. Between his belt buckle and his backbone a hollow place was opening that asked to be filled with something more substantial than watermelon, something dense and weighty, meat and bread. He could imagine his supper now, and he gave some care to it, allowing his hunger to take its full dimension, anticipating his satisfaction.

When he got home, Mary would have done the milking and the other chores. If she had found the time, she would have his supper warm. Or, if not, he would eat it cold. She was a good cook; it would be good, hot or cold.

For the nearly thirty years of their marriage, they had worked hard every day. At night they would be tired. Maybe they would be occupied with their thoughts and worries. And maybe they would go from supper on through the little duties of the evening and then to bed, paying no more attention to each other than any two people who were used to living together.

Sometimes it seemed to Elton that they had come so far from the boy and girl they had been when they married that, looking back, they could hardly see themselves. At those times they would be apart, and all their differences stood between them, a dark thicket. They were like two horses working together. They did not walk the same; they were not always in step.

But that they walked differently meant that they would be in step from time to time. There would come another time, always unforeseen, as if approaching out of the apparently vacant sky, when all that had happened between them, the landscape of all their years, became a bond that joined them together. Almost only by their having waited, the approach would be open, with signs of Welcome! Welcome! all the way. And then he would become a man without history or memory, fear or hope — a man only lost in the world, who found it good. The burden of living and dying rested lightly on his shoulders then, he waited with so great a longing for the night to fall.

He heard a tractor engine and looked up. Mart Rowanberry was heading down the hill with a load. It was late in the day. The air was beginning to cool. Seeing that Elton had seen him, Mart drew his right arm through the air in three long strokes, meaning "We're going down now. Quit, and come on." Mart did not stop. Other loads were coming; Elton could catch one of them.

But Elton did not stop cutting, and he did not look up as the other loads went by. He wanted to finish the row, and there was not much left. With the end of the row and the day in sight, he worked easily, easily, and fast, as if he were going downhill. He worked swiftly and accurately to the end of the row, cutting and spearing plant after plant until there were no more ahead of him, and he was done. Weariness then seemed to flow downward through his body, and with it came an old elation.

He did not leave the field to follow the loads down the graveled track to the barn, but instead turned and walked again to the other side of the patch, looking at the rows he had cut. There were four of them — long ones — the sticks of cut tobacco standing like little tents, perfectly aligned. It was all his own work, done in a quietness that extended over the whole afternoon and that seemed still present. In that quietness, and now complete, his work was lovely to him, and he walked along beside it, to be near it, reluctant to leave.

When he got back to the pear tree, he laid his tools down at the base of the trunk and set his water jug beside them. They would be there tomorrow and so would he, but at the moment he had no more need for tomorrow than he had for his tools. The sun was down now, and all around him the countryside was still. The backwash of the sunset seemed to concentrate and glow in the two valleys, and the ridgetops, like hens on a roost, had hushed and settled for the night. He heard a bobwhite call brightly above the edge of the woods.

He looked another moment back at the cut rows, the place of his long journey, where he had traveled hard only to stay in place, and then he went to the melon patch and picked three more ripe melons. He sliced the smallest, and nested the other two in the crooks of his arms. Eating the sweet fragile flesh of the melon, he headed straight down over the wooded bluff toward the barn.

When his shortcut brought him out of the woods and into the open again at the foot of the hill, Mart and the others had drawn the three wagons into the driveway of the barn for the night. In the morning, while the standing tobacco was still wet with dew, they would be at work there, housing the loads. Now they loitered a little while in the barn door, speaking of what they had done, of what they would do tomorrow.

And now Elton came walking out of the woods, eating one melon and carrying two. They hushed and watched him as he came in among them.

"Four rows," Mart said. "You were dogging on! And I see you laid off of them watermelons."

They were grinning at him, and he grinned back, his mouth full, a drop of juice clinging to his chin. "Boys," he said, "all I want is a good day and a long row."

In seven years from that day he would be in his grave, and in the pauses of their work the ones who were left would be remembering him, along with the others who were gone. Often, when they spoke of him, Mart Rowanberry would tell again how Elton had worked that long half day alone on the ridgetop, going hard and eating a watermelon at the end of every row, and still eating when he came down the hill. Thinking of Elton as he had stood there with them in the barn door in the long shadow, sweaty and soiled, exultant and graceful, eating that sugary little melon, Mart would laugh with satisfaction and delight.

And then, leaning forward, his elbows on his knees, his hands at rest, one within the other, he would shake his head. "He was a friend of mine," he would say, accenting lightly the final word. "A friend of mine."

The Wild Birds (1967)

"Where have they gone?" Wheeler thinks. But he knows. Gone to the cities, forever or for the day. Gone to the shopping center. Gone to the golf course. Gone to the grave.

He can remember Saturday afternoons when you could hardly find space in Hargrave to hitch a horse, and later ones when an automobile could not move through the crowd on Front Street as fast as a man could walk.

Wheeler is standing at his office window, whose lower pane announces Wheeler Catlett & Son, Attorneys-at-Law; he is looking out diagonally across the courthouse square and the roofs of the stores along Front Street at the shining reach of the Ohio, where a white towboat is shoving an island of coal barges against the current, its screws roiling the water in a long fan behind it. The barges are empty, coming up from the power plant at Jefferson, whose dark plume of smoke Wheeler can also see, stretching out eastward, upriver, under the gray sky.

Below him, the square and the streets around it are deserted. Even the loafers are gone from the courthouse where, the offices shut, they are barred from the weekday diversions of the public interest, and it is too cold to sit on the benches under the Social Security trees, now leafless, in the yard. The stores are shut also, for whatever shoppers may be at large are out at La Belle Riviere Shopping Plaza, which has lately overborne a farm in the bottomland back of town. Only a few automobiles stand widely dispersed around the square, nosed to the curbs, Wheeler's own and half a dozen more, to suggest the presence, somewhere, of living human beings — others like himself, Wheeler supposes, here because here is where they have usually been on Saturday afternoon.

But he knows too that he is *signifying* something by being here, as if here is where he agreed to be when he took his law school diploma and came home, or as near home as he could get and still practice law, forty-one years ago. He is here as if to prove "to all to whom these presents may come" his willingness to be here.

And yet if he is here by agreement, he is here also in fidelity to what is gone: the old-time Saturday to which the country people once deferred all their business, when his old clients, most of them now dead, would climb the stairs to his office as often as not for no business at all, but to sit and speak in deference to their mutual trust, reassuring both to them and to him. For along with the strictly business or legal clientele such as any lawyer anywhere might have had, Wheeler started out with a clientele that he may be said to have inherited — farmers mostly, friends of his father and his father-in-law, kinsmen, kinsmen's friends, with whom he thought of himself as a lawyer as little as they thought of themselves as clients. Between them and himself the technical connection was swallowed up in friendship, in mutual regard and loyalty. Such men, like as not, would not need a dime's worth of legal assistance between the settling of their parents' estates and the writing of their own wills, and not again after that. Wheeler served them as their defender against the law itself, before which they were ciphers, and so felt themselves — and he could do this only as their friend.

"What do I have to do about that, Wheeler?" they would ask, handing him a document or a letter.

And he would tell them. Or he would say, "Leave it here. I'll see to it."

"What I owe you, Wheeler?"

And he would name a figure sometimes to protect himself against the presumptuousness and long-windedness of some of them, or to protect the pride of others. Or he would say, "Nothing," deeming the work already repaid by "other good and valuable considerations."

So Wheeler is here by prior agreement and pursuant history — survivor, so far, of all that the agreement has led to. The office has changed little over the years, less by far than the town and the country around it. It contains an embankment of file cabinets, a small safe, a large desk, Wheeler's swivel chair, and a few more chairs, some more comfortable than others. The top of the desk is covered with books and file folders neatly stacked. On the blotter in the center is a ruled yellow tablet on which Wheeler has been writing, the top page nearly covered with his impatient blue script. By way of decoration, there are only a few photographs of Wheeler's children and grandchildren. Though the room is dim, he has not turned on a light.

A more compliant, less idealistic man than Wheeler might have been happier here than he has been, for this has been a place necessarily where people have revealed their greed, arrogance, meanness, cowardice, and sometimes their inviolable stupidity. And yet, though he has known these things, Wheeler has not believed in them. In loyalty to his clients, or to their Maker, in whose image he has supposed them made, he has believed in their generosity, goodness, courage, and intelligence. Mere fact has never been enough for him. He has pled and reasoned, cajoled, bullied, and preached, pushing events always toward a better end than he knew they could reach, resisting always the disappointment that he knew he should expect, and when the disappointment has come, as it too often has, never settling for it in his own heart or looking upon it as a conclusion.

Wheeler has been sketching at a speech. In that restless hand of his, that fairly pounces on each word as it comes to him, he has refined his understanding of the points to be made and has worked out the connections. What he was struggling to make clear is the process by which unbridled economic forces draw life, wealth, and intelligence off the farms and out of the country towns and set them into conflict with their sources. Farm produce leaves the farm to nourish an economy that has thrived by the ruin of land. In this way, in the terms of Wheeler's speech, *price* wars against *value*.

"Thus," he wrote, "to increase the *price* of their industrial products, they depress the *value* of goods — a process not indefinitely extendable," and his hand rose from the page and hovered over it, the pen aimed at the end of his sentence like a dart. The last phrase had something in it, maybe, but it would not do. At that failure, his mind abruptly refused the page. A fidelity older than his fidelity to word and page began to work on him. He picked up another pad on which he had drawn with a ruler the design of a shed to be built onto a feed barn. The new shed would require changes in the dimensions of the barn lot and in the positions of two gates, and those changes he had drawn out also. His mind, like a boy let out of school, returned to those things with relief, with elation. His thoughts leapt from his speech to its sources in place and memory, the generations of his kin and kind.

For the barn is the work of Wheeler's father, Marcellus, who built it to replace an older barn on the same spot. So methodical and clever a carpenter was Marcellus that he built the new barn while the old one stood, incorporating the old into the new, his mules never absent a night from their stalls, and he did virtually all the work alone. The building of the barn was one of the crests of the life of Marce Catlett, a pride and a comfort to him to the end of his days. Adding a new shed to it now is not something that Wheeler can afford to intend lightly or do badly.

Why at his age — when most of his generation are in retirement, and many are in the grave — he should be planning a new shed is a question he has entertained dutifully and answered perhaps a trifle belligerently: Because he *wants* to.

But his mind had begun a movement that would not stop yet. His mind's movement, characteristically, was homeward. What he hungered for was the place itself. He saw that his afternoon's work in the office was over, and that was when he got up and went to the window, as if to set eyesight and mind free of the room. He would go soon. By going so early, he would have time to salt his cattle.

This sudden shift of his attention is so familiar to him as almost to have been expected, for in its fundamental structure, its loyalties and preoccupations, Wheeler's mind has changed as little in forty years as his office. If change happens, it happens; Wheeler can recognize a change when he sees one, but change is not on his program. Difference is. His business, indoors and out, has been the making of differences. And not the least of these has been this shift that he is about to make again from office to farm.

But for a moment longer he allows himself to be held at the window by the almost solemn stillness of the square and the business streets of the little town, considering again the increasing number of empty buildings, the empty spaces where buildings have been burned or torn down and not replaced, hating again the hopeless expenditure of its decay.

And now, directly across from his office door, a pickup truck eases in to the curb; two men and a woman get out. Wheeler recognizes his cousin, Burley Coulter, Burley's nephew Nathan, and Hannah, Nathan's wife. The three come together at the rear of the truck, the woman between the two men, and start across the street.

"What are *they* doing here?" Wheeler wonders. And then from their direction he understands that they have come to see him. He smiles, glad of it, and presently he hears their footsteps on the stairs.

The footsteps ascend slowly, for Burley is past seventy now and, though still vigorous, no longer nimble.

Wheeler goes through the outer office, where his secretary's typewriter sits hooded on its desk, and meets them in the dim hallway at the top of the stairs, reaching his hand to them as they come up.

"Hello, Hannah. Go right on in there in the office, honey. How're you, Nathan? Hello, Burley."

"How you making it, Wheeler?" Burley says in his hearty way, as if speaking to him perhaps across a wide creek. "I told them you'd be here."

"You were right," Wheeler says, glad to feel his presence justified by that expectation. It is as though he has been waiting for them. Burley's hand is hard and dry, its grip quick on his own. And then Wheeler lays his hand on the shoulder of the older man, pressing him toward the door, and follows him through into the greater light of the windowed rooms.

In his office he positions chairs for them in a close arc facing his chair. "Sit down. I'm glad to see you."

They take chairs and he returns to his own. He *is* glad to see them, and yet seeing them here, where they regard him with a certain unaccustomed deference, is awkward for him. He sees them often, Burley and Nathan especially, but rarely indoors, and today they have made a formal occasion of their visit by dressing up. Hannah is wearing a gray suit, and looks lovely in it, not to Wheeler's surprise, for she is still a beautiful woman, her beauty now less what she has than what she is. Nathan is wearing a plaid shirt, slacks, and a suede jacket. Burley, true to custom, has put on his newest work clothes, tan pants and shirt, starched and ironed to creases stiff as wire, the shirt buttoned at the throat but without a tie, a dark, coarse wool sweater, which he has now unbuttoned, and he holds on his lap, as delicately as if it is made of eggshell, his Sunday hat. Only the hat looks the worse for wear, but any hat of Burley's will look the worse for wear two hours after he has put it on; the delicacy of his hold on it now, Wheeler knows, is a formality that will not last, a sign of his uneasiness within his own sense of the place and the occasion. In his square-cut, blunt hand, so demanding or quieting upon hound or mule or the shoulder of another man, he holds the hat so that it touches without weight the creased cloth of his pants.

"Kind of dreary out, Wheeler," he says.

"Yes. It is, Burley. Or it looks dreary since it clouded up. I haven't been out. I was *going* out, though, pretty soon."

"Well, we won't keep you very long."

But Wheeler didn't mean to be hinting, and to make up for it, though he knows they have come on business, he says, "You're caught up in your work, I reckon."

Nathan laughs and shakes his head. "No."

"None of us, these times, will live to be caught up," Burley says. "We finished gathering corn yesterday. Monday morning, I reckon, we'll take a load of calves to the market. After that we'll be in the stripping room."

But Burley is waiting, Wheeler sees, for permission to begin his business. "Well," he says, "what have you got on your mind?"

"Wheeler," Burley says, "I want you to write my will."

"You do?" Wheeler is surprised and embarrassed. One does not normally write a person's will point-blank in the presence of his heirs. For Burley to bequeath his farm to Nathan right under Nathan's nose strikes Wheeler as a public intimacy of a sort. He is amazed to hear himself ask, "What for?"

"Well, Wheeler, I'm old enough to die, ain't I?"

Wheeler grins. "You always have been." He leans back in his chair as if to make the occasion more ordinary than he can feel it becoming. "Well then, Nathan, you and Hannah should let Burley and me talk this over alone."

"But Hannah and Nathan ain't in it, Wheeler. They ain't going to be in it."

Wheeler sits up. He says, "Oh," though that is not what he meant to say. And then, deliberately, he says, "Then who is in it?"

"Danny Branch."

"Danny." Though he was determined not to be, Wheeler is again surprised. The springs of his chair sing as he leans slowly back. For a long moment he and Burley sit and look at each other, Burley smiling, Wheeler frowning and staring as if Burley is surrounded by a mist.

"Danny? You're going to leave your daddy's place, Dave Coulter's place, old George Coulter's place, to Danny Branch?"

"That's right."

"Why?"

"He's my boy, Wheeler. My son."

"Who said he is?"

"Well, Wheeler, for one, I did. I just said it."

"Do you have any proof?"

Burley has not perceptibly moved, but his thumb and middle finger, which at first pinched just the brim of his hat, have now worked their way to the base of the crown, the brim rolled in his hand. "I ain't *looking* for proof, Wheeler. Don't want any. It's done too late for proof. If there's a mistake in this, it has been my life, or a whole lot of it."

"Did Kate Helen say he was yours?"

Burley shakes his head, not going to answer that one. "Now Wheeler, I know you know the talk that has said he was my boy, my son, ever since he was born."

Wheeler does know it. He has known it all along. But it is irregular knowledge, irregularly known. He does not want to know it, or to admit that he knows it. "Talk's talk," he says. "Talk will be talk. To hell with talk. What we're dealing with now is the future of a good farm and the family that belongs to it, or ought to."

"Yes indeed."

"I don't think you ought to take a step like this, Burley, until you know for sure."

"I know all I want to know, more than I need to know."

Wheeler says, "*Well* . . . ," ready to say that *he*, anyhow, can think of several questions he would like to know the answers to, but Burley raises the hand with the hat in it and stops him.

"It finally don't have anything to do with anything, Wheeler, except just honesty. If he's my boy, I've got to treat him like he is."

"But you do treat him like he is, and you have. You gave him half his upbringing, or three-quarters. Right up to Kate Helen's death you saw that he raised a crop and went to school and had what he needed. You've taken him to live with you, him and Lyda and their children, and you've . . ." Wheeler stops, realizing that he is saying nothing that all four of them do not already know.

"But now it's time to go beyond all that. Now I have to say that what belongs to me will belong to him, so he can belong to what I belong to. If he's my boy, I owe that to him free and clear."

"Suppose he's not."

"Suppose he is."

Wheeler is slouched low in his chair now, in the attitude, nearly, of a man asleep, except that his fingers are splayed out stiffly where they hang over the ends of his chair arms, and his eyes are widened, set on Burley in a look that would scour off rust. It is not a look easily met.

But Burley is looking back at him, still smiling, confidently and just a little indulgently smiling, having thought beyond where they have got to so far.

"It's wayward, Wheeler. I knowed you'd say what you've said. Or anyhow think it. I know it seems wayward to you. But wayward is the way it is. And always has been. The way a place in this world is passed on in time is not regular or plain, Wheeler. It goes pretty close to accidental. But how else *could* it go? Neither a deed or a will, no writing at all, can tell you much about it. Even when it looks regular and plain, you know that somewhere it has been chancy, and just slipped by. All I see that I'm certain of is that it has got to be turned loose — loose is the way it is — to who knows what. I can say in a will, and I'm going to, that I leave it to Danny, but I don't know how it's going to him, if it will, or past him, or what it's coming to, or what will come to it. I'm just the one whose time has come to turn it loose."

Now it seems that they are no longer looking at each other, but at a cloud between them, a difference, that they have never before come so close to making or admitting. Whatever there may have been of lawyer and client in this conversation is long gone now, and Wheeler feels and regrets that departure, for he knows that something dark and unwieldy has impinged upon them, that they will not get past except by going through.

It is Burley's word *wayward* that names the difference that they are going to have to reckon with. Wheeler's mind makes one final, despairing swerve toward the field where his cattle are grazing. For a moment he sees it as he knows it will look now in the wind of late November, in the gray light under the swift clouds. And then he lets it go.

Wayward — a word that Burley says easily. If the things of this world are wayward, then he will say so, and love them as they are. But as his friends all know, it is hard to be a friend of Wheeler's and settle for things as they are. You will be lucky if he will let you settle for the possible, the faults of which he can tell you. The wayward is possible, but there must be a better way than wayward. Wheeler can remember Burley's grandfather, George Washington Coulter. He wrote his father's, Dave Coulter's, will here in this very room. He does not remember not knowing Burley, whom he has accompanied as younger kinsman, onlooker, and friend through all his transformations, from the wildness of his young years, through his years of devotion in kinship and friendship, to his succession as presiding elder of a company of friends that includes Wheeler himself. It has a pattern clear enough, that life, and yet, as Wheeler has long known without exactly admitting, it is a clear pattern that includes the unclear, the wayward. The wayward and the dark.

Almost as suddenly as his mind abandons its vision of the daylit field, Wheeler recalls Burley as a night hunter. Back in his own boyhood and young manhood, he used to go hunting with Burley, and so he knows the utter simplicity of Burley's entrances into the woods.

He gets out of his car at the yard gate and walks across the dark yard and back porch to the kitchen door, to find Burley waiting for him. *"Here* you are! I was about to go ahead."

Burley is at the door, ready to go, his Smith and Wesson twenty-two in its shoulder holster, hat and coat already on. He pulls on his overshoes, takes his lantern from its nail and lights it, steps off the porch, calls the dogs, and walks down over the brow of the hill. Within two hundred steps they are enclosed in the woods along the river bluff, the damp of the night cold on their faces. Along that margin of steep wild ground between the ridges and the gentler slopes lower down, where the woods has stood unmolested from before memory, they walk in the swaying room of yellow lantern light, their huge tapering shadows leaping from tree to tree beside them. And soon, from off in the dark, beyond time, the voice of a hound opens.

It was another world they went to. Wheeler, as often as he went, always went as a stranger and a guest. Or so it seemed to him, as it seemed to him that Burley went always as a native, his entrance into the wild darkness always a homecoming.

One night when they have made a fire and sat down to wait while the dogs make sense of a cold trail, Burley goes to sleep, lying on his back on a pile of rocks, the driest bed available, and wakes an hour later, intently listening. "Dinah's treed. Let's go."

Sometimes Nathan would be with them or Nathan's brother, Tom, before he went to the war and was killed, or, rarely, Old Jack Beechum or, later, Elton Penn, and nearly always the brothers, Arthur and Martin Rowanberry.

On a moonless, starless night, late, in the quiet after a kill, the dogs lying on the leaves around them, they realize that they are lost. Intent upon a course flagged through the dark by the hounds' cries, they have neglected the landmarks. Now they stand around the lanterns under a beech in a little draw on a steep, wooded hillside, debating which way they may have come. Below them they can hear water running, but they cannot be sure in which branch.

"Naw," Arthur Rowanberry says to his brother, "we come by that little barn on the Merchant place and down through the locust thicket."

"Yes, and *then* we went up the Stillhouse Run, that's what we all know, but how many hollers did we pass before we turned up this one?"

"Well, I don't know."

That is what it keeps coming back to and they all laugh. The debate is being conducted partly for pleasure, for they are not *much* lost, but they are tired now and would rather not risk finding themselves by going in the wrong direction.

Finally Burley, who has said nothing, but has stood outside the light, looking and thinking, says, "*I* know where we are."

And they all turn to him.

"Where?"

"Where?"

"Right here."

Though Wheeler is now long past any yen he ever had to roam the woods at night, he knows that Burley is still a hunter, and, with Danny Branch and the Rowanberrys, still a breeder of hounds. At Burley's house at this moment, probably asleep in their stall in the barn, there is a blue-tick hound named Rock, another much older one named Sputnik, and a bitch by the name of Queen. And now Wheeler's son, Andy, is apt to be in the company of the hunters on the thawing or the rainy winter nights, and that is the way Wheeler has learned some of the things he knows.

He knows, he has always known, that as often as he has hunted with companions, Burley has hunted alone. The thought of Burley solitary in the woods at night has beguiled Wheeler's imagination and held it, more strongly perhaps than anything else outside the reach of his own life. For he knows — or from his own memory and from hearsay he is able to infer — that at those times Burley has passed over into a freedom that is old and, because it is strenuous and solitary, also rare. Those solitary hunts of his have always begun by chance or impulse. He may be out of the house already when they begin — on his way afoot to visit a neighbor after supper, maybe, followed by the dogs, who pick up a trail, and he is off. Or he will wake in the night, hearing his dogs treed away on the bluff below his house or in a thicketed slue hollow in the river bottom, and he will get up and go to them, leaving the warm bed, and so begin a route through the dark that may not bring him home again until the sun is up. Or the fever, as he calls it, will hit him while he is eating supper, and he will go, pausing only to strap on the pistol, light the lantern, and stick into the game pocket of his canvas hunting coat an apple or two, a handful of cold biscuits, perhaps a half-pint "against the chill." They start almost accidentally, these hunts, and they proceed according to the ways of coon and hound, or if the hunting is slow, according to the curiosity of a night traveler over his dark-estranged homeland. If he goes past their house, he may call to the Rowanberrys to join him or at least turn loose their dogs. In his young manhood, before responsibilities began to call him home, these solitary hunts might carry him away two days and nights, across long stretches of the country and back again, ignoring the roads except to cross them, not seen by a human eye, as though in the dark traverses of his own silence he walked again the country as it was before Finley and the Boones, at home in it time out of time.

He has been a man of two loves, not always compatible: of the dark woods, and of the daylit membership of kin and friends and households that has cohered in one of its lineages through nearly a century of living memory, and surely longer, around Ben Feltner, and then Jack Beechum, and then Mat Feltner, and then Burley's brother, Jarrat, and now around himself. So Wheeler has known him. But it has made him more complex than Wheeler knows, or knows yet, that double love. He has never learned anything until he has had to — as he willingly says, as perhaps is so — but he has had to learn a good deal.

For Wheeler, behind this neatly, somewhat uncomfortably dressed Burley Coulter here in his office, there stands another and yet another: the Burley of the barns and fields of all their lives and of his own loyally kept place and household, and then the Burley of the nighttime woods and the wayward ways through the dark.

In Wheeler's mind the symbol of Burley's readiness to take to the woods at nightfall is the tan canvas hunting coat — or, he must suppose, the succession of them, though he does not remember seeing Burley in a new one — that he has worn through all the winters that Wheeler has known him, on all occasions except funerals, tobacco or livestock sales, or trips to Hargrave on business, such as this. The coat, as Wheeler remembers it, is always so worn that it seems more a creature than an artifact, ripped, frazzled, crudely patched, short a button or two, black at the edges. As a farmer, Burley seems, or has come to seem, constant enough, and yet, even as such, to Wheeler he has something of the aspect of a visitor from the dark and the wild—human, friendly to humans, but apt to disappear into the woods.

If Burley has walked the marginal daylight of their world, crossing often between the open fields and the dark woods, faithful to the wayward routes that alone can join them, Wheeler's fidelity has been given to the human homesteads and neighborhoods and the known ways that preserve them. Through dark time and bad history, he has been keeper of the names that bear hope of light to the human clearings, and an orderly handing down. He is a preserver and defender of the dead, the more so, the more passionately so, as his acquaintance among the dead has increased, and as he has better understood the dangers to their living heirs. How, as a man of law, could he have been otherwise, or less? How, thinking of his own children and grandchildren, could he not insist on an orderly passage of these frail human parcels through time?

It is not as though he is unacquainted with the wayward. He has, God knows, spent his life trying to straighten it out. The wayward is a possible way—because, for lack of a better, it has had to be. But a better way is thinkable, is imaginable, and Wheeler, against all evidence and all odds, is an advocate of the better way. To plead the possibility of the merely possible, losing in the process all right to insist on the desirability of what would be better, is finally to lose even the possible — or so, in one way or another, Wheeler has argued time and again, and against opponents of larger repute than Burley Coulter. If he is set now to do battle with his friend, his purpose is not entirely self-defense, though it is that.

He does not forget — it has been a long time since he has been able to forget — that he is making his stand in the middle of a dying town in the midst of a wasting country, from which many have departed and much has been sent away, a land wasting and dying for want of the human names and knowledge that could give it life. It has been a comfort to Wheeler to think that the Coulter Place, past Burley's death, would live on under that name, belonging first to Nathan, whom Wheeler loves as he loves Burley, and then to one of Nathan's boys. That is what he longs for, that passing on of the land, in the clear, from love to love, and it is in grief for that loss that he is opposing Burley. But this grief has touched and waked up a larger one. How many times in the last twenty years has Wheeler risen to speak, to realize that the speech he has prepared is a defense of the dead and the absent, and he is pleading with strangers for a hope that, he is afraid, has no chance?

"It was wayward when it come to me," Burley is saying. "Looked like to me I was there, born there and not someplace else, just by accident. I never took to it by nature the way Jarrat did, the way Nathan here, I think, has. I just turned up here, take it or leave it. I might have gone somewhere else when I got mustered out in 1919, but I come back, and looked like I was in the habit of staying, so I stayed. I thought of leaving, but the times was hard and Pap needed me — or needed somebody better, to tell the truth — and I stayed. I stayed to help bring up Tom and Nathan after their mother died. And then Pap died and Mam was old, and I stayed on with her. And when she died I stayed on and done my part with Jarrat; the boys was gone then, and he needed me. And somehow or other along the way, I began to stay because I wanted to. I wanted to be with Jarrat, and Nathan and Hannah here, and Mat and you and the others. And somewhere or other I realized that being here was the life I had because I'd never had another one any place else, and never would have.

"And that was all right, and is, and is going to be. But it looks like a bunch of intentions made out of accidents. I think of a night now, Wheeler — I lie awake. I've thought this over and over, from one end to the other, and I can't see that the way it has been is in line with what anybody planned or the way anybody thought it ought to be."

"But they did plan. They hoped. They started hoping and planning as soon as they got here — way back yonder."

"It missed. Or they did. Partly, they were planning and hoping about what they'd just finished stealing from the ones who had it before, and were already quarreling over themselves. You know it. And partly they were wrong. How could they be right about what hadn't happened? And partly it was wayward."

"But what if they *hadn't* planned and hoped — the ones that did anyhow — the good ones."

"Then we wouldn't know how far it missed, or how far we did, or *what* we missed. I ain't disowning them old ones, Wheeler."

"But now it's your time to plan and hope and carry it on. That we missed doesn't make any difference."

"No. That time's gone for me now, and I've missed probably as bad as the worst of the others. Now it's my time to turn it loose. You're talking to an old man, Wheeler, damn it!"

"Well, you're talking to an old man too, damn it, but I've still got some plans and hopes! I still know what would be best for my place!"

"I know the same as you, Wheeler. I know what would be best for my place too—somebody to live on it and care about it and do the work. And I know what it would look like if somebody did. But I come here today to turn it loose. And I've got good reason to do it."

"You've got a better reason than you've told me?"

Burley has been sitting upright on his chair as if it were a stool. Now he sags back, and for a moment sits staring at Wheeler without paying any particular attention to him, as if he doesn't notice or it doesn't matter that Wheeler is staring back at him. And then he says, "Cleanse thou me from secret faults."

"*What?*"

"Cleanse thou me from secret faults." As always when he quotes Scripture, Burley is grinning, unwilling, as Wheeler knows, to be entirely serious about any part of it that he can understand, even though, once he has understood it, he may be entirely willing to act on it.

Recognizing the passage now, Wheeler grins too, and then laughs and says what otherwise he would not say, "Well, Burley, mighty few of *your* faults have been secret."

And that is pretty much a fact. Burley Coulter's faults have been public entertainment in the town and neighborhood of Port William ever since he was a boy, most of his transgressions having been committed flagrantly in the public eye, and those that were not, if they had any conceivable public interest, having been duly recounted to the public by Burley Coulter himself. His escapades have now, by retelling, worn themselves as deeply into that countryside as its backroads.

Wheeler himself has loved to tell the story of Burley's exit from the back door of Grover Gibbs's house, having paid his compliments to

Beulah Gibbs, as Grover returned unexpectedly through the front door. Carrying his clothes in his arms through a night black as the inside of a gourd, Burley ran through the stock pond behind the barn, and then, heading downhill into the woods, got behind a big calf who was going slower than he was, whereupon, according to him, he cried, "Calf, get out of the way! Let somebody run that knows how!"

"All that's past," Wheeler says. "Whatever was wrong in it can be forgiven in the regular way. When the psalmist said 'thou,' he didn't mean anybody in Port William or Hargrave. That account's not to be settled here."

"But some of it is." Burley's smile is now gone altogether. "Listen, Wheeler. I didn't come to take up a lot of your time, but we've done got this started now. I'm not telling you what you need to know to be my lawyer. I'm telling you what you need to know to be my friend. If a lawyer was all I wanted, I reckon I wouldn't have to hire a friend."

"You're not hiring a friend. You *have* one. Go on."

"Well, Kate Helen was an accommodating woman, too accommodating some would say, but she was good to me, Wheeler. We had what passed with me then for some good times. When I look back at them now, they still pass with me for good, though they come up with more results than I expected. I ain't going to go back on them, or on her, though I'm sorry, Lord knows, for some of the results."

There is a tenderness in Burley's voice now that Wheeler did not expect, that confesses more than he is yet prepared to understand, but it gives Kate Helen a standing, a presence, there in the room, one among them now, who will not lightly be dismissed. And Wheeler is carried back to a day in his own life when he passed along the lane in front of Kate Helen's house, and saw her sitting on the porch in a rocking chair, barefooted, a guitar forgotten on her lap, a red ribbon in her hair. He has never forgotten. And the Kate Helen who attends them now, in Wheeler's mind as perhaps in Burley's, is Kate Helen as she was then— a woman, as Burley used to say, who could take up a lot of room in a man's mind. In Wheeler's opposition to Burley there is no uncertainty as to what Burley saw when he looked at Kate Helen; Wheeler saw too, and he remembers. But now she has come back to him with something added to her: all that was said or implied in the gentleness with which

Burley spoke of her. If she is with them now, Burley is now with them as her protector, and there are some things that Wheeler might have said about her that he is not going to say, and will never say again. He feels under his breastbone the first pain of a change.

But he turns to Nathan. "Is this what you want? If it wasn't to be Danny Branch's, it would be yours — your children's." He is holding out against what he sees he will have to give in to, still determinedly doubting what he knows he is going to have to believe, and his voice has the edge of challenge in it. He will not settle easily for the truth just because it happens to be the truth. He wants a truth he can like, and they are not surprised.

As his way is, Nathan has been sitting without moving, staring down at the toe of his shoe, as if he is shy perhaps, and now he makes only the small movement that brings his gaze up to meet Wheeler's. It is the look of a man utterly resolved to mean what he says, and Wheeler feels the force of it.

"I know what Uncle Burley wants, Wheeler, and it's all right. And I aim to stick to Danny."

Burley passes his hand through the air, the hat still in it, but forgotten now; it is just along for the ride. "I've not asked that of him, Wheeler. I don't ask anything. If Nathan sticks to Danny after I'm dead, that'll be fine, but my ghost won't trouble him if he don't."

Wheeler turns to look at Hannah, knowing what to expect, but his eyes tax her nevertheless, making it difficult.

"Yes," she says, nodding once and smiling at him, being as nice to him as she can be, though he can sense how much she is forbearing. "It's what we all want. It's best." And without looking away from Wheeler, she reaches for Burley's left hand, and drawing it over into her lap holds it in both of her own. To Wheeler's surprise then, her eyes suddenly fill with tears.

And then his own do. He looks down at his hands. "Well."

"Wheeler," Burley says, "Nathan and Hannah are going to have enough land, and their children too —"

"What if they weren't?"

"— and Danny's a good boy, a good young man."

"What if he wasn't?"

"There's no use in coming with them what-ifs, Wheeler. I ain't responsible for them. They dried up and blowed away long years ago. What if I had been a better man?

"If Nathan needed what I've got, I'd have to think of that. He don't. Besides what he has got on his own, he's his daddy's heir, and in the right way. You might say that he has come, as far as he has got anyhow, by the main road, the way you have, Wheeler, and has been regular. I haven't been regular. I've come by a kind of back path — through the woods, you might say, and along the bluffs. Whatever I've come to, I've mostly got there too late, and mostly by surprise.

"I don't say everybody *has* to be regular. Being out of regular may be all right — I liked it mostly. It may be in your nature. Maybe it's even useful in a way. But it finally gets to be a question of what you can recommend. I never recommended to Jarrat's boys or Danny or your boys that they ought to be careless with anything, or get limber-legged and lay out all night in a hayrick. Your way has been different from mine, but by my way I've come here where you are, and now I've got to know it and act like it. I know you can't make the irregular regular, but when you have rambled out of sight, you have got to come back into the clear and show yourself."

"Wait now," Wheeler says. "I didn't —"

But Burley raises his hand and silences him. It is as if they recognize only now a change that has been established for some time: Burley has quietly, without gesture, assumed the role of the oldest man — the first time he has ever done this with Wheeler — and has begun to speak for Wheeler's sake as well as his own.

"I know how you think it ought to be, Wheeler. I think the same as you. I even thought once that the way things ought to be was pretty much the way they were. I thought things would go on here always the way they had been. The old ones would die when their time came, and the young ones would learn and come on. And the crops would be put out and got in, and the stock looked after, and things took care of. I thought, even, that the longer it went on the better it would get. People would learn; they would see what had been done wrong, and they would make it right.

"And then, about the end of the last world war, I reckon, I seen it go wayward. Probably it had been wayward all along. But it got more wayward then, and I seen it then. They began to go and not come back — or a lot more did than had before. And now look at how many are gone — the old ones dead and gone that won't ever be replaced, the mold they were made in done throwed away, and the young ones dead in wars or killed in damned automobiles, or gone off to college and made too smart ever to come back, or gone off to easy money and bright lights and ain't going to work in the sun ever again if they can help it. I see them come back here to funerals — people who belong here, or did once, looking down into coffins at people they don't have anything left in common with except a name. They come from another world. They might as well come from that outer space the governments are wanting to get to now.

"When I think of a night, Wheeler, my mind sometimes slants off into that outer space, and I'm sorry the ones that knowed about it ever brought it up — all them lonesome stars and things up there so far apart. And they tell about these little atoms and the other little pieces that things are made out of, all whirling and jiggling around and not touching, as if a man could reach his hand right through himself. I know they know those things to blow them up.

"I lay my hand on me and quiet me down. And I say to myself that all that separateness, outside and inside, that don't matter. It's not here and not there. Then I think of all the good people I've known, not as good as they could have been, much less ought to have been, none of them, but good for the good that was in them along with the rest — Mam and Pap and Old Jack, and Aunt Dorie and Uncle Marce, and Mat and Mrs. Feltner, and Jarrat and Tom and Kate Helen, all of them dead, and you three here and the others still living. And I think of this country around here, not purely good either, but good enough for us, better than we deserve. And I think of what I've done here, all of it, all I'm glad I did, and all I wish had been done different or better, but wasn't."

"You're saying you're sorry for what you've done wrong? And by what you're proposing to do now you hope to make it right?"

"No! God damn it, Wheeler — excuse me, Hannah — no! What is done is done forever. I know that. I'm saying that the ones who have been here have been the way they were, and the ones of us who are here now are the way we are, and to *know* that is the only chance we've got, dead and living, to be here together. I ain't saying we don't have to know what we ought to have been and ought to be, but we oughtn't to let that stand between us. That ain't the way we are. The way we are, we are members of each other. All of us. Everything. The difference ain't in who is a member and who is not, but in who knows it and who don't. What has been here, not what ought to have been, is what I have to claim. I have to be what I've been, and own up to it, no secret faults. Because before long I'm going to have to look the Old Marster in the face, and when He says, 'Burley Coulter?' I hope to say 'Yes, Sir. Such as I am, that's me.'"

And now he leans forward and, the hat brim clenched in the outer three fingers of his right hand, hooks his forefinger into Wheeler's vest. He does not pull, but only holds, as gently as possible given the hand's forthrightness and the rigor in the crook of the old finger.

"And, Wheeler, one thing I am is the man who cared about Kate Helen Branch — all her life, you might say."

"You loved her," Wheeler says.

"That's right."

"You were a husband to her — in all but name."

"That's right."

"And you're her widower — in all but name."

"That's right."

Burley unhooks his finger and leans back. He is smiling again.

And finally the direction of this meeting declares itself to Wheeler. What Burley is performing, asking him to assist in, too late but nonetheless necessarily, is a kind of wedding between himself and Kate Helen Branch. It is the secrecy of that all-but-marriage of his that has been his great fault, for its secrecy prevented its being taken seriously, perhaps even by himself, and denied it a proper standing in the world.

"And so that secret fault you've been talking about — that didn't have anything to do with the things we've always known."

"No."

"It was secret love."

"That's right. In a way I don't think I even knowed it myself, Wheeler. Anyhow, not for a long time. Not till too late."

Wheeler is smiling too now, asking and listening, helping him along. "Why didn't you clear all this up any sooner?"

"I've never learned anything until I had to, Wheeler. That's the kind of head I've got."

"And you've been learning this a long time?"

"Years and years. Pret' near all my life I've been figuring out where I am and what I'm responsible for—and, as I said, pret' near always too slow and too late. Some things haven't got my attention until they knocked me in the head."

"But you and Kate Helen were involved in this friendly connection for a long time. She must not have minded."

"That had a lot to do with it. We *were* friends, and she *didn't* mind— or didn't seem to."

Burley crosses his arms over his lap, going ahead now on his own.

"You know the little paper-sided house in Thad Spellman's thicket field that she and her mother moved into after her daddy died—there by the creek at the foot of the hill. I could get there from town you might say by gravity, and at first that was usually how I got there.

"This is how it went. I want you to know.

"On Saturday night I'd walk to Port William and loaf around in one place and another a few hours, visiting, maybe shoot a game or two of pool. And after while I'd get me a pint from Alice Whodat and stroll out across the ridge, drinking along the way, listening to the sounds and looking all around at whatever there was light enough to see—free as a bird, as they say, and, as far as I can remember, nothing on my mind at all. Sometimes if the night was warm and dry, I'd sit down somewhere and sing a while. None of the real things that have happened to me had happened then. My head might as well have been a cabbage, except I could eat and drink with it. And after while I'd tumble down through the woods and the bushes to Kate Helen's house.

"And maybe the first real thing that ever happened to me was that I started going down there because I *liked* to. I liked Kate Helen. I liked to sit and jaw with old Mrs. Branch. Sometimes I would go there in broad daylight, just to visit, if you know what I mean, and we would sit and talk and laugh. Part of it, I guess, was what you said. Kate Helen didn't mind. Or up to a point she didn't, however far that was. She liked me and her mother did too. And they wasn't *at* me all the time — which for a while I thought was pretty low class of them, I will admit.

"They were poor, of course, which anybody could see, and so it come about that whenever I went there I would gather up a few groceries, things I knew they needed, and bring them along, or if we'd killed hogs I'd bring a middling or a sack or two of sausage. And I'd always try to save out a head or two for them. The old woman was a great one to make souse, and made the best, too, that ever I ate. And then I got so I'd help them make a garden. And then in the winter I took to getting up their firewood. They needed those things to be done, and I was the only soul they had to do them. I liked being of use to them better than anything.

"But oftentimes, I'd go there just to sit a while and visit. We'd talk, maybe pop some corn. Sometimes we'd play and sing a little."

Wheeler might never have remembered it again. He had forgot that he remembered. But now in thought he comes again down through the steep fields along the side of the little creek valley. He is hunting, supposedly, his shotgun lying in the crook of his arm, and busily quartering the slope ahead of him is his good English setter by the name of Romney; but the weather is dry, they have found no birds, and, submitting to the charm of the warm, bright, still afternoon, he has ceased to pay attention to the dog. He has idled down along the fall of the valley, pausing to look, watching the little fields and the patches of woodland open ahead of him with the intense, pleased curiosity that idleness on such an afternoon can sometimes allow. And now, climbing over a rock fence at the edge of a strip of woodland into a pasture, he pauses again, and hears in the distance a few muted, dispersed notes that it takes him a minute or two to recognize as human singing.

The curve of the slope presently brings him around to where he can see the square of tin roof within the square of yard and garden within the close network of leafless thicket overgrowing Thad Spellman's abandoned field. And now the voices are carried clearly up to him, rising and braiding themselves together over the sweet pacing of a fiddle and guitar:

> *Oh, he taught me to love him and called me his flower,*
> *A blossom to cheer him through life's dreary hour,*
> *But now he has gone and left me alone,*
> *The wildflowers to weep, the wild birds to mourn.*

Wheeler knows who they are. Burley he has heard play before at a dance or two, a little embarrassedly "filling a gap" in a band, and has even heard him sing, though only emblematic scraps of songs sung out raucously at work. Now he realizes that Burley is better at both than he thought, though in both playing and singing his manner is straightforward and declarative, almost a speaking in support of the melody, which is carried by Kate Helen. It is Kate Helen's voice that takes Wheeler by surprise — by a kind of shock, in fact; he expected nothing like it — for it is so pure, and so feelingly intelligent in its singing of the words.

They finish the song and laugh at the end of it and speak a little, words that he cannot hear, and begin another — and another and another. The dog finally comes back and lies down at Wheeler's feet, and still he stands and listens — until it comes to him that they play and sing so well because they believe that nobody is listening. He turns away then, embarrassed for himself, and makes his way back up the long hollow onto the upland and to his father's place again, the country remaining bemused around him in the hovering late warmth and light, and the two voices seeming to stay with him a long part of the way, as if they too hung and hovered in the air:

> *I'll dance and I'll sing and my heart shall be gay. . . .*

"My lord," he thinks, "that was forty years ago!"

It was forty years ago almost to the day, he thinks, and remembering the clarity of that voice lifted into the bright air that carried it away, he says,

"And Kate Helen never did say anything? Never did suggest maybe that you two ought to get married?"

"Fact is, she never did. And you'll wonder why, Wheeler, and I can't tell you. I could give you some guesses, I've thought about it enough. But as for knowing, I don't. I don't know, and won't ever."

"She thought you were a lucky catch any way she could get you," Hannah says to him, patting his hand. It is something Wheeler can tell that she has said to him before. And then she says, more seriously, "She thought you were better than she deserved. So did her mother, I'll bet."

"Well, I wasn't. But whatever her reason was, not to know it is wrong. It's the very thing that's wrong."

They pause at that failure, allowing it its being. And then Burley speaks on, describing his long odd-times domestic companionship with Kate Helen. He tells of Danny's birth: "I purely did not think of that ahead of time, Wheeler. It was a plumb surprise. And yet it tickled me." He tells of the death of old Mrs. Branch; and of how, as Danny grew, time and usage grew on him and Kate Helen; how he depended on her and was dependable, took her and was taken for granted, liking the world too well as it was, "laying aside wars and such," to think how it might be improved, usually, until after his chance to improve it had gone by; how in time she became sick and died; how at her death, seeing it all then, he would have liked to have been openly and formally her mourner, but, faithful to appearances, he had shown himself only an interested bystander, acting a great deal more like himself than he felt. Behind appearances, he paid the doctor, paid the hospital, paid the under-taker, bought a lot in the cemetery; he saw to everything — as Wheeler knew pretty well at the time, and attributed to guilt of conscience — as quietly as he has done for the others who have been his declared dependents.

Danny, grown by then, was still living with his mother at the time of her death.

"You just as well come on, now," Burley said, "and live with me." For then he saw it the way it should have been — though he let Danny go on calling him "Uncle Burley," as he acknowledges now to Wheeler, and is shaken once by a silent laugh.

"Well, now that Mammy's gone, I want to get married."

"Well, bring the gal. I got a big house."

As though he has now finally lived in his own life up to that time when Danny came to live with Burley, Wheeler admits him into his mind. Or, anyhow, Danny Branch now turns up in Wheeler's mind, admitted or not, put there by the words of his would-be lawful father, after the failure of all events so far to put him there, and his face now takes its place among the faces that belong there.

Danny, Wheeler would bet, is not as smart as Burley, but he does look like him in a way; he has Burley's way of looking at you and grinning and nodding his head once before saying what he has to say — a fact that Wheeler now allows to underwrite Burley's supposition and his intent. He allows Burley's argument to make sense — not all the sense there is, but enough.

And so with Wheeler's consent Danny comes into their membership and also is one there with them, Wheeler already supposing that Nathan will not be the only one who will stick to Danny, and looking forward to the possibility of his own usefulness to that young man.

As often, the defeat of his better judgment has left him only with a job to do, a job that he *can* do, and he feels a sudden infusion of good humor. If Danny is Burley's son and heir, and if that is less than might have been hoped, it is what they are left with, what they have, and Wheeler will be as glad as the rest of them to make the most of it.

He feels preparing in himself the friendship for Danny Branch that these three, after all, have come to ask him for — and which, all three know, probably better than Wheeler, will be a gift and a blessing to the younger man, and also undoubtedly something of a burden, for once Wheeler has Danny on his mind he will be full of advice for him that Danny will not easily ignore.

As soon as he has a chance, Wheeler thinks, he will stop by for a visit with Burley and Danny and Lyda and the little ones. He would like, for one thing, to see if there is any resemblance to Burley or the other Coulters showing up in Danny's children.

"*So,*" he says. "You just want to leave everything to Danny. That won't take but a few words. I'll get it typed up first thing Monday morning, and you can come in and sign it." He smiles at Hannah and Nathan. "You all can come with him and be witnesses."

He leans back in his chair, having, as he thinks, brought the meeting to an end. He is ready for them to go, ready to go himself. He allows the wind and the gray sky back into mind.

Burley is busy restoring the shape of his hat, as though he might be about to put it on, but he does not. He looks up at Wheeler again and studies him a moment before he speaks.

"Wheeler, do you know why we've been friends?"

"I've thought so," Wheeler says. He has thought so because of that company of friends to which they both belong, which has been so largely the pleasure and meaning of both their lives. "But why?"

"Because we ain't brothers."

"What are you talking about?" Wheeler says.

But he is afraid he knows, and his discomfort is apparent to them all. Nathan and Hannah obviously feel it too, and are as surprised as he is.

"If we'd been brothers, you wouldn't have put up with me. Or anyhow you partly wouldn't have, because a lot of my doings haven't been your kind of doings. As it was, they could be tolerable or even funny to you because they wasn't done close enough to you to matter. You could laugh."

Wheeler sits forward now, comfortless, straight up in his chair, openly bearing the difficulty he knows it is useless to hide. Though this has never occurred to him before, because nobody has said it to him before, he knows with a seizure of conviction that Burley is right. He knows they all know, and again under his breastbone he feels the pain of a change that he thought completed, but is not completed yet. A great cavity has opened at the heart of a friendship, a membership, that not only they here in the office and the others who are living but men and women now dead belong to, going far back, dear as life. Dearer. It is a cavity larger than all they know, a cavity that somebody — their silence so testifies — is going to have to step into, or all will be lost.

If things were going slower, if he had the presence of mind he had even a minute ago, Wheeler would pray for the strength to step into it, for the *knowledge* to step into it. As it is, he does not know how. He sits as if paralyzed in his loss, without a word to his name, as if suddenly pushed stark naked into a courtroom, history and attainment stripped from him, become as a little child.

But Burley is smiling, and not with the vengeful pleasure that Wheeler feared, but with understanding. He knows that what he has given Wheeler is pain, his to give, but Wheeler's own. He sees.

"Wheeler, if we're going to get this will made out, not to mention all else we've got to do while there's breath in us, I think you've got to forgive me as if I was a brother to you." He laughs, asserting for the last time the seniority now indisputably his, and casting it aside. "And I reckon I've got to forgive you for taking so long to do it."

He has spoken out of that cavity, out of that dark abyss.

It is as if some deep dividing valley has been stepped across. There can be no further tarrying, no turning back. To Wheeler, it seems that all their lives have begun again — lives dead, living, yet to be. As if feeling himself simply carried forward by that change, for another moment yet he does not move.

And then he reaches out and grips Burley's shoulder, recognizing almost by surprise, with relief, the familiar flesh and bone. "Burley, it's all right."

And Burley lays his own hand on Wheeler's shoulder. "Thank you, Wheeler. Shore it is."

Wheeler's vision is obscured by a lens of quivering light. When it steadies and clears, his sight has changed. Now, it seems to him, he is looking through or past his idea of Burley, and can see him at last, the fine, clear, calm, generous, amused eyes looking back at him out of the old face.

And Hannah, smiling again too, though she has averted her eyes, is digging in her purse for her handkerchief. "Well!" she says.

The office is crowded now with all that they have loved, the living remembered, the dead brought back to mind, and a gentle, forceless light seems to have come with them. There in the plain, penumbral old room, that light gathers the four of them into its shadowless embrace. For a time without speaking they sit together in it.

Wheeler stands looking down into the street over the top of the reversed painted legend: WHEELER CATLETT & SON, ATTORNEYS-AT-LAW. The day remains as it was, the intensity of the clouded light the same. Except that the towboat is gone now, the world seems hardly to have moved, the smoke from the power plant still tainting the sky.

In a little while Wheeler will leave the office and leave town. The room he stands in is driven out of his mind by the thought of the raw, free wind over the open fields. But he does not go yet. He thinks of the fields, how all we know of them lies over them, taking their shape, for a little while, like a fall of snow.

He watches Burley and Hannah and Nathan walk back to their truck, waiting for their departure to complete itself before he will begin his own.

Are You All Right? (1973)

The spring work had started, and I needed a long night's rest, or that was my opinion, and I was about to go to bed, but then the telephone rang. It was Elton. He had been getting ready for bed, too, I think, and it had occurred to him then that he was worried.

"Andy, when did you see the Rowanberrys?"

I knew what he had on his mind. The river was in flood. The backwater was over the bottoms, and Art and Mart would not be able to get out except by boat or on foot.

"Not since the river came up."

"Well, neither have I. And their phone's out. Mary, when did Mart call up here?"

I heard Mary telling him, "Monday night," and then, "It was Monday night," Elton said to me. "I've tried to call every day since, and I can't get anybody. That's four days."

"Well, surely they're all right."

"Well, that's what Mary and I have been saying. Surely they are. They've been taking care of themselves a long time. But, then, you never know."

"The thing is, we *don't* know."

We knew what we were doing, and both of us were a little embarrassed about it. The Rowanberry Place had carried that name since the first deeds were recorded in the log cabin that was the first courthouse at

Hargrave. Rowanberrys had been taking care of themselves there for the better part of two hundred years. We knew that Arthur and Martin Rowanberry required as little worrying about as anybody alive. But now, in venturing to worry about them, we had put them, so to speak, under the sign of mortality. They were, after all, the last of the Rowanberrys, and they were getting old. We were uneasy in being divided from them by the risen water and out of touch. It caused us to think of things that could happen.

Elton said, "It's not hard, you know, to think of things that could happen."

"Well," I said, "do you think we'd better go see about them?"

He laughed. "Well, we've thought, haven't we? I guess we'd better go."

"All right. I'll meet you at the mailbox."

I hung up and went to get my cap and jacket.

"Nobody's heard from Art and Mart for four days," I said to Flora. "Their phone's out."

"And you and Elton are going to see about them," Flora said. She had been eavesdropping.

"I guess we are."

Flora was inclined to be amused at the way Elton and I imagined the worst. She did not imagine the worst. She just dealt with mortality as it happened.

I picked up a flashlight as I went out the door, but it was not much needed. The moon was big, bright enough to put out most of the stars. I walked out to the mailbox and made myself comfortable, leaning against it. Elton and I had obliged ourselves to worry about the Rowanberrys, but I was glad all the same for the excuse to be out. The night was still, the country all silvery with moonlight, inlaid with bottomless shadows, and the air shimmered with the trilling of peepers from every stream and pond margin for miles, one full-throated sound filling the ears so that it seemed impossible that you could hear anything else.

And yet I heard Elton's pickup while it was still a long way off, and then light glowed in the air, and then I could see his headlights. He turned into the lane and stopped and pushed the door open for me. I made room for myself among a bundle of empty feed sacks, two buckets, and a chain saw.

"Fine night," he said. He had lit a cigarette, and the cab was fragrant with smoke.

"It couldn't be better, could it?"

"Well, the moon could be just a little brighter, and it could be a teensy bit warmer."

I could hear that he was grinning. He was in one of his companionable moods, making fun of himself.

I laughed, and we rode without talking down the Katy's Branch road and turned onto the blacktop.

"It's awful the things that can get into your mind," Elton said. "I'd hate it if anything was to happen to them."

Elton had known the Rowanberrys ever since he was just a little half-orphan boy, living with his mother and older brothers. He had got a lot of his raising by being underfoot and in the way at the Rowanberrys'. And in the time of his manhood, the Rowanberry Place had been one of his resting places.

Elton worked hard and worried hard, and he was often in need of rest. But he had a restless mind, which meant that he could not rest on his own place in the presence of his own work. If he rested there, first he would begin to think about what he had to do, and then he would begin to do it.

To rest, he needed to be in somebody else's place. We spent a lot of Sunday afternoons down at the Rowanberrys', on the porch looking out into the little valley in the summertime, inside by the stove if it was winter. Art and Mart batched there together after their mother died, and in spite of the electric lights and telephone and a few machines, they lived a life that would have been recognizable to Elias Rowanberry, who had marked his X in the county's first deed book—a life that involved hunting and fishing and foraging as conventionally as it involved farming. They practiced an old-fashioned independence, an old-fashioned generosity, and an old-fashioned fidelity to their word and their friends. And they were hound men of the old correct school. They would not let a dog tree anywhere in earshot, day or night, workday or Sunday, without going to him. "It can be a nuisance," Art said, "but it don't hardly seem right to disappoint 'em."

Mart was the one Elton liked best to work with. Mart was not only a fine hand but had a gift for accommodating himself to the rhythms and ways of his partner. "He can think your thoughts," Elton said. Between the two of them was a sympathy of body and mind that they had worked out and that they trusted with an unshaken, unspoken trust. And so Elton was always at ease and quiet in Mart's company when they were at rest.

Art was the rememberer. He knew what he knew and what had been known by a lot of dead kinfolks and neighbors. They lived on in his mind and spoke there, reminding him and us of things that needed to be remembered. Art had a compound mind, as a daisy has a compound flower, and his mind had something of the unwary comeliness of a daisy. Something that happened would remind him of something that he remembered, which would remind him of something that his grandfather remembered. It was not that he "lived in his mind." He lived in the place, but the place was where the memories were, and he walked among them, tracing them out over the living ground. That was why we loved him.

We followed the state road along the ridges toward Port William and then at the edge of town turned down the Sand Ripple Road. We went down the hill through the woods, and as we came near the floor of the valley, Elton went more carefully and we began to watch. We crossed a little board culvert that rattled under the wheels, eased around a bend, and there was the backwater, the headlights glancing off it into the treetops, the road disappearing into it.

Elton stopped the truck. He turned off his headlights and the engine, and the quietness of the moonlight and the woods came down around us. I could hear the peepers again. It was wonderful what the road going under the water did to that place. It was not only that we could not go where we were used to going; it was as if a thought that we were used to thinking could not be thought.

"Listen!" Elton said. He had heard a barred owl off in the woods. He quietly rolled the window down.

And then, right overhead, an owl answered: "HOOOOOAWWW!"

And the far one said, "Hoo hoo hoohooaw!"

"Listen!" Elton said again. He was whispering.

The owls went through their whole repertory of hoots and clucks and cackles and gobbles.

"Listen to them!" Elton said. "They've got a lot on their minds." Being in the woods at night excited him. He was a hunter. And we were excited by the flood's interruption of the road. The rising of the wild water had moved us back in time.

Elton quietly opened his door and got out and then, instead of slamming the door, just pushed it to. I did the same and came around and followed him as he walked slowly down the road, looking for a place to climb out of the cut.

Once we had climbed the bank and stepped over the fence and were walking among the big trees, we seemed already miles from the truck. The water gleamed over the bottomlands below us on our right; you could not see that there had ever been a road in that place. I followed Elton along the slope through the trees. Neither of us thought to use a flashlight, though we each had one, nor did we talk. The moon gave plenty of light. We could see everything—underfoot the blooms of twin-leaf, bloodroot, rue anemone, the little stars of spring beauties, and overhead the littlest branches, even the blooms on the sugar maples. The ground was soft from the rain, and we hardly made a sound. The flowers around us seemed to float in the shadows so that we walked like waders among stars, uncertain how far down to put our feet. And over the broad shine of the backwater, the calling of the peepers rose like another flood, higher than the water flood, and thrilled and trembled in the air.

It was a long walk because we had to go around the inlets of the backwater that lay in every swag and hollow. Way off, now and again, we could hear the owls. Once we startled a deer and stood still while it plunged away into the shadows. And always we were walking among flowers. I wanted to keep thinking that they were like stars, but after a while I could not think so. They were not like stars. They did not have that hard, distant glitter. And yet in their pale, peaceful way, they shone. They collected their little share of light and gave it back. Now and then, when we came to an especially thick patch of them, Elton would point. Or he would raise his hand and we would stop a minute and listen to the owls.

I was wider awake than I had been since morning. I would have been glad to go on walking all night long. Around us we could feel the year coming, as strong and wide and irresistible as a wind.

But we were thinking, too, of the Rowanberrys. That we were in a mood to loiter and did not loiter would have reminded us of them, if we had needed reminding. To go to their house, with the water up, would have required a long walk from any place we could have started. We were taking the shortest way, which left us with the problem that it was going to be a little too short. The best we could do, this way, would be to come down the valley until we would be across from the house but still divided from it by a quarter mile or more of backwater. We could call to them from there. But what if we got no answer? What if the answer was trouble? Well, they had a boat over there. If they needed us, one of them could set us over in the boat. But what if we got no answer? What if, to put the best construction upon silence, they could not hear us? Well, we could only go as near as we could get and call.

So if our walk had the feeling of a ramble, it was not one. We were going as straight to the Rowanberrys' house as the water and the lay of the land would allow. After a while we began to expect to see a light. And then we began to wonder if there was a light to see.

Elton stopped. "I thought we'd have seen their light by now."

I said, "They're probably asleep."

Those were the first words we had spoken since we left the truck. After so long, in so much quiet, our voices sounded small.

Elton went on among the trees and the shadows, and I followed him. We climbed over a little shoulder of the slope then and saw one window shining. It was the light of an oil lamp, so their electricity was out, too.

"And now we're found," Elton said. He sang it, just that much of the old hymn, almost in a whisper.

We went through a little more of the woods and climbed the fence into the Rowanberrys' hill pasture. We could see their big barn standing up black now against the moonlight on the other side of the road, which was on high ground at that place, clear of the backwater.

When we were on the gravel we could hear our steps. We walked side by side, Elton in one wheel track, I in the other, until the road went under the water again. We were as close to the house then as we could get without a boat. We stopped and considered the distance. It was only a quarter of a mile, but at night, with the water dividing us, it seemed almost hopelessly far.

And then Elton cupped his hands around his mouth, and called, "Ohhhhh, Mart! Ohhhhh, Art!"

We waited, it seemed, while Art had time to say, "Did you hear some-body?" and Mart to answer, "Well, I *thought* so." We saw light come to another window, as somebody picked up a lamp and opened the hall door. We heard the front door open. And then Art's voice came across the water: "Yeeeaaah?"

And Elton called back, "Are you aaalll riiight?"

I knew they were. They were all right, and we were free to go back through the woods and home to sleep.

But now I know that it was neither of the Rowanberrys who was under the sign of mortality that night. It was Elton. Before another April came he would be in his grave on the hill at Port William. Old Art Rowanberry, who had held him on his lap, would survive him a dozen years.

And now that both of them are dead, I love to think of them standing with the shining backwater between them, while Elton's voice goes out across the distance, is heard and answered, and the other voice travels back: "Yeeeaaah!"

Fidelity (1977)

For Carol and John Berry,
with love and thanks.

Lyda had not slept, and she knew that Danny had not either. It was close to midnight. They had turned out the light two hours earlier, and since then they had lain side by side, not moving, not touching, disturbed beyond the power to think by the thought of the old man who was lying slack and still in the mechanical room, in the merciless light, with a tube in his nose and a tube needled into his arm and a tube draining his bladder into a plastic bag that hung beneath the bed. The old man had not answered to his name, "Uncle Burley." He did not, in fact, appear to belong to his name at all, for his eyes were shut, he breathed with the help of a machine, and an unearthly pallor shone on his forehead and temples. His hands did not move. From time to time, unable to look any longer at him or at the strange, resistant objects around him in the room, they looked at each other, and their eyes met in confusion, as if they had come to the wrong place.

They had gone after supper to the hospital in Louisville to enact again the strange rite of offering themselves where they could not be received. They were brought back as if by mere habit into the presence of a life that had once included them and now did not, for it was a life that, so far as they could see, no longer included even itself. And so they stood around the image on the bed and waited for whatever completion would let them go.

There were four of them: Nathan Coulter, Burley's nephew, who might as well have been his son; Danny Branch, his son in fact, who had until recent years passed more or less as his nephew and who called him "Uncle Burley" like the others; and there were Nathan's wife, Hannah, and Lyda, Danny's wife, who might as well have been his daughters.

After a while, Hannah rested her purse on the bed, and opened it, and took out a handkerchief with which she touched the corners of her eyes. She put the handkerchief back into her purse and slowly shut the clasp, watching her hands with care as if she were sewing. And then she looked up at Nathan with a look that acknowledged everything, and Nathan turned and went out, and the others followed.

All through the latter part of the summer Burley had been, as he said himself, "as no-account as a cut cat." But he had stayed with them, helping as he could, through the tobacco harvest, and they were glad to have him with them, to listen to his stories, and to work around him when he got in their way. He had begun to lose the use of himself, his body only falteringly answerable to his will. He blamed it on arthritis. "There's a whole family of them Ritis boys," he would say, "and that Arthur's the meanest one of the bunch." But the problem was not arthritis. Burley was only saying what he knew that other old men had said before him; he was too inexperienced in illness himself to guess what might be wrong with him.

They had a fence to build before corn gathering, and they kept him with them at that. "We'll need you to line the posts," they told him. But by then they could not keep him awake. They would find him asleep wherever they left him, in his chair at home, or in the cab of a pickup, or hunched in his old hunting coat against a post or the trunk of a tree. One day, laying a hand on Burley's shoulder to wake him, Danny felt what his eyes had already told him but what he had forborne to know with his hand: that where muscle had once piled and rounded under the cloth, there was now little more than hide and bone.

"We've got to do something for him," Danny said then, partly because Lyda had been saying it insistently to him.

Nathan stared straight at him as only Nathan could do. "What?"

"Take him to the doctor, I reckon. He's going to die."

"Damn right. He's eighty-two years old, and he's sick."

They were getting ready to go in to dinner, facing each other across the bed of Danny's pickup where they had come to put their tools. Burley, who had not responded to the gentle shake that Danny had given him, was still asleep in the cab.

Nathan lifted over the side of the truck a bucket containing staples and pliers and a hammer, and then, as he would not ordinarily have done, he pitched in his axe. "He's never been to a doctor since I've known him. He said he wouldn't go. You going to knock him in the head before you take him?"

"We'll just take him."

Nathan stood a moment with his head down. When he looked up again, he said, "Well."

So they took him. They took him because they wanted to do more for him than they could do, and doctors exist, and they could think of nothing else. Nathan held out the longest, and he gave in only because he was uncertain.

"Are you — are we — just going to let him die like an old animal?" Hannah asked.

And Nathan, resistant and grouchy in his discomfort, said, "An old animal is maybe what he wants to die like."

"But don't we need to help him?"

"Yes. And we don't know what to do, and we're not going to know until after we've done it. Whatever it is. What better can we wish him than to die in his sleep out at work with us or under a tree somewhere?"

"Oh," Hannah said, "if only he already had!"

Nathan and Danny took him to the doctor in Nathan's pickup, Nathan's being more presentable and dependable than Danny's, which anyhow had their fencing tools in it. The doctor pronounced Burley "a very sick man"; he wanted him admitted to the hospital. And so, the doctor having called ahead, with Burley asleep between them, Danny and Nathan took him on to Louisville, submitted to the long interrogation required for admission, saw him undressed and gowned and put to bed by a jolly nurse, and left him. As they were going out, he said, "Boys, why don't you all wait for me yonder by the gate. I've got just this one last round to make, and then we'll all go in together." They did not know from what field or what year he was talking.

Burley was too weak for surgery, the doctor told them the next day. It would be necessary to build up his strength. In the meantime tests would be performed. Danny and Lyda, Nathan and Hannah stood with the doctor in the corridor outside Burley's room. The doctor held his glasses in one hand and a clipboard in the other. "We hope to have him on his feet again very soon," he said.

And that day, when he was awake, Burley was plainly disoriented and talking out of his head—"saying some things," as Nathan later told Wheeler Catlett, "that he never thought of before and some that nobody ever thought of before." He was no longer in his right mind, they thought, because he was no longer in his right place. When they could bring him home again, he would be himself.

Those who loved him came to see him: Hannah and Nathan, Lyda and Danny, Jack Penn, Andy and Flora Catlett, Arthur and Martin Rowanberry, Wheeler and his other son and law partner, Henry, and their wives. They sat or stood around Burley's bed, reconstructing their membership around him in that place that hummed, in the lapses of their talk, with the sound of many engines. Burley knew them all, was pleased to have them there with him, and appeared to understand where he was and what was happening. But in the course of his talk with them, he spoke also to their dead, whom he seemed to see standing with them. Or he would raise his hand and ask them to listen to the hounds that had been running day and night in the bottom on the other side of the river. Once he said, "It's right outlandish what we've got started in this country, big political vats and tubs on every roost."

And then, in the midst of the building of strength and the testing, Burley slipped away toward death. But the people of the hospital did not call it dying; they called it a coma. They spoke of curing him. They spoke of his recovery.

A coma, the doctor explained, was certainly not beyond expectation. It was not hopeless, he said. They must wait and see.

And they said little in reply, for what he knew was not what they knew, and his hope was not theirs.

"Well, then," Nathan said to the doctor, "we'll wait and see."

Burley remained attached to the devices of breathing and feeding and voiding, and he did not wake up. The doctor stood before them again, explaining confidently and with many large words, that Mr. Coulter soon would be well, that there were yet other measures that could be taken, that they should not give up hope, that there were places well-equipped to care for patients in Mr. Coulter's condition, that they should not worry. And then he said that if he and his colleagues could not help Mr. Coulter, they could at least make him comfortable. He spoke fluently from within the bright orderly enclosure of his explanation, like a man in a glass booth. And Nathan and Hannah, Danny and Lyda stood looking in at him from the larger, looser, darker order of their merely human love.

When they returned on yet another visit and found the old body still as it had been, a mere passive addition to the complicated machines that kept it minimally alive, they saw finally that in their attempt to help they had not helped but only complicated his disease beyond their power to help. And they thought with regret of the time when the thing that was wrong with him had been simply unknown, and there had been only it and him and them in the place they had known together. Loving him, wanting to help him, they had given him over to "the best of modern medical care"—which meant, as they now saw, that they had abandoned him.

If Lyda was wakeful, then, it was because she, like the others, was shaken by the remorse of a kind of treason.

Lyda must have dozed finally, because she did not hear Danny get up. When she opened her eyes, the light was on, and he was standing at the foot of the bed, buttoning his shirt. The clock on the dresser said a quarter after twelve.

"What are you doing?"

"Go back to sleep, Lyda. I'm going to get him."

She did not ask who. She said "Good," which made him look at her, but he did not say more.

And she did not ask. He suited her, and moreover she was used to him. He was the kind, and it was not a strange kind to her, who might leave the bed in the middle of the night if he heard his hounds treed somewhere and not come back for hours. Like Burley, Danny belonged half to the woods. Lyda knew this and it did not disturb her, for he also belonged to her, in the woods as at home.

He finished dressing, turned the light off, and went out. She heard him in Burley's room and then in the kitchen. She heard the scrape of the latchpin at the smokehouse door. He was being quiet; she would not have heard him if she had not listened. But then the hounds complained aloud when he shut them in a stall in the barn.

Presently he came back, and she seemed to feel rather than hear or see him as he moved into the doorway and stopped. "I don't know how long I'll be gone. You and the kids'll have to do the chores and look after things."

"All right."

"I fastened up the dogs."

"I heard you."

"Well, don't let them out. And listen, Lyda. If somebody wants to know, I've said something about Indiana."

She listened until she heard the old pickup start and go out the lane. And then she slept.

Danny's preparations were swift and scant but sufficient for several days. He stripped the bedclothes from Burley's bed, laid them out neatly on the kitchen floor, and then rolled them up around a slab of cured jowl from the smokehouse, a small iron skillet, and a partly emptied bag of cornmeal. He tied the bundle with baling twine, making a sling by which it could hang from his shoulder. From behind the back hall door he took his hunting coat with his flashlight in one pocket and his old long-barreled .22 pistol in the other. He removed the pistol and laid it on top of the dish cabinet.

His pickup truck was sitting in front of the barn, and the confined hounds wailed again at the sound of his footsteps.

"Hush!" he said, and they hushed.

He pitched his bundle onto the seat and unlatched and raised the hood. He had filled the tank with gas that afternoon but had not checked the oil and water. By both principle and necessity, he had never owned a new motor vehicle in his life. The present pickup was a third-hand

Dodge, which Burley had liked to describe as "a loose association of semiretired parts, like me." But Danny was, in self-defense, a good mechanic, and he and the old truck and the box of tools that he always kept on the floorboard made a working unit that mostly worked.

The oil was all right. He poured a little water into the radiator, relatched the hood, set the bucket back on the well-top, and got into the truck. He started the engine, backed around in front of the corncrib, turned on the headlights, headed out the lane — and so committed himself to the succession of ever wider and faster roads that led to the seasonless, sunless, and moonless world where Burley lay in his bonds.

The old truck roaring in outlandish disproportion to its speed, he drove through Port William and down the long slant into the river bottoms where the headlights showed the ripening fields of corn. After a while he slowed and turned left onto the interstate, gaining speed again as he went down the ramp. The traffic on the great road was thinner than in the daytime but constant nevertheless. As he entered the flow of it, he accelerated until the vibrating needle of the speedometer stood at sixty miles an hour — twenty miles faster than he usually drove. If at the crescendo of this acceleration the truck had blown up, it would not altogether have surprised him. Nor would it altogether have displeased him. He hated the interstate and the reeking stream of traffic that poured along it day and night, and he liked the old truck only insofar as it was a salvage job and his own. "If she blows," he thought, "I'll try to stop her crosswise of both lanes."

But though she roared and groaned and panted and complained, she did not blow.

Danny's mother, Kate Helen Branch, had been the love of Burley Coulter's life. They were careless lovers, those two, and Danny came as a surprise — albeit a far greater surprise to Burley than to Kate Helen. Danny was born to his mother's name, a certified branch of the Branches, and he grew up in the care of his mother and his mother's mother in a small tin-roofed, paper-sided house on an abandoned corner of Thad Spellman's farm, not far from town by a shortcut up through the woods. As the sole child in that womanly household, Danny was more than amply mothered. And he did not go fatherless, for Burley was that household's faithful visitor, its pillar and provider. He took a hand in Danny's upbringing from the start, although, since the boy was nominally a Branch, Danny always knew his father as "Uncle Burley."

If Danny became a more domestic man than his father, that is because he loved the frugal, ample household run by his mother and grandmother and later by his mother and himself. He loved his mother's ability to pinch and mend and make things last. He was secretly proud of her small stitches in the patches of his clothes. They kept a big garden and a small flock of hens. They kept a pig in a pen to eat scraps and make meat, and they kept a Jersey cow that picked a living in the green months out of Thad Spellman's thickety pasture. The necessary corn for the pig and chickens and the corn and hay for the cow were provided by Burley and soon enough by Burley and Danny.

If Danny became a better farmer than his father that is because, through Burley, he came under the influence of Burley's brother, Jarrat, and of Jarrat's son, Nathan, and of Burley's and Nathan's friend, Mat Feltner, all of whom were farmers by calling and by devotion. From them he learned the ways that people lived by the soil and their care of it, by the bounty of crops and animals, and by the power of horses and mules.

But if Danny became more a man of the woods and the streams than nearly anybody else of his place and time, that was because of Burley himself. For Burley was by calling and by devotion a man of the woods and streams. When duty did not keep him in the fields, he would be hunting or fishing or roaming about in search of herbs or wild fruit, or merely roaming about to see what he could see; and from the time Danny was old enough to want to go along, Burley took him. He taught him to be quiet, to watch and not complain, to hunt, to trap, to fish and swim. He taught him the names of the trees and of all the wild plants of the woods. Danny's first providings on his own to his mother's household were of wild goods: fish and game, nuts and berries that grew by no human effort but furnished themselves to him in response only to his growing intimacy with the place. Such providing pleased him and made him proud. Soon he augmented it with wages and produce from the farmwork he did with Burley and the others.

The world that Danny was born into during the tobacco harvest of 1932 suited him well. That the nation was poor was hardly noticeable to him, whose people had never been rich except in the things that they continued to be rich in though they were poor. He loved his half-wooded native country of ridge and hillside and hollow and creek and river bottom. And he loved the horse- and mule-powered independent farming of that place and time.

When Danny had finished the eighth grade at the Port William school, he was growing a crop of his own and was nearly as big as he was going to get, a little taller and somewhat broader than his father. He was a trapper of mink and muskrat, a hunter and fisherman. He farmed for himself or for wages every day that he was out of school and in the mornings and evenings before and after school. If Burley had not continued to be Kate Helen's main provider, Danny could and would have been.

When he began to ride the bus to the high school at Hargrave, the coaches, gathering around him and feeling his arms and shoulders admiringly as if he had been a horse, invited him to go out for basketball. He gave them the smile, direct and a little merry, by which he reserved himself to himself, and said, "I reckon I already got about all I can do."

He quit school the day he was sixteen and never thought of it again. By then he was growing a bigger crop, and he owned a good team of mules, enough tools of his own to do his work, and two hounds. When he married Lyda two years later, he had, except for a farm of his own, everything he had thought of to want.

By then the old way of farming was coming to an end. But Danny never gave it up.

"Don't you reckon you ought to go ahead and get you a tractor, like everybody else?" Burley asked him.

And Danny looked up at him from the hoof of the mule he was at that moment shoeing and smiled his merry smile. "I ain't a-going to pay a company," he said, "to go and get what is already here."

"Well," Burley said, though he knew far better than the Hargrave basketball coach the meaning of that smile, "tractors don't eat when they ain't working."

Danny drove in a nail, bent over the point, and reached for another nail. He did not look up this time when he spoke, and it was the last he would say on the matter: "They don't eat grass when they ain't working."

That was as much as Burley had wanted to say. He liked mules better than tractors himself and had only gone along with the change to accommodate his brother, Jarrat, who, tireless himself, wanted something to work that did not get tired. Burley loved to be in the woods with the hounds at night, and Danny inherited that love early and fully. They hunted sometimes with their neighbors, Arthur and Martin Rowanberry, sometimes with Elton Penn, but as often as not there would be just the two of them—man and little boy, and then man and big boy, and at last two men—out together in the dark-mystified woods of the hollows and slopes and bottomlands, hunting sometimes all night, but enacting too their general approval of the weather and the world. Sometimes, when the hunting was slow, they would stop in a sheltered place and build a fire. Sometimes, while their fire burned and the stars or the clouds moved slowly over them, they lay down and slept.

There was another kind of hunting that Burley did alone. Danny did not know of this until after Kate Helen died, when he and Lyda got married and, at Burley's invitation, moved into the old weatherboarded log house on the Coulter home place where Burley had been living alone. There were times—though never when he was needed at work—when Burley just disappeared, and Danny and Lyda would know where he had gone only because the hounds would disappear at the same time. Little by little, Danny came to understand.

In love Burley had assumed many responsibilities. In love and responsibility, as everyone must, he had acquired his griefs and losses, guilts and sorrows. Sometimes, under the burden of these, he sought the freedom of solitude in the woods. He might be gone for two or three days or more, living off the land and whatever leftovers of biscuits or cornbread he might be carrying in his pockets, sleeping in barns or in the open by the side of a fire. If the dogs became baffled and gave up or went home, Burley went on, walking slowly hour after hour along the steep rims of the valleys where the trees were old. When he returned, he would be smiling, at ease and quiet, as if his mind just fit within his body.

"Don't quit," Danny said to the truck, joking with it as he sometimes did with his children or his animals. "It's going to be downhill all the way home."

He was making an uproar, and uproar gathered around him as he came to the outskirts of the city. The trailer trucks, sleek automobiles, and other competent vehicles now pressing around him made him aware of the disproportion between his shuddering, smoking old pickup and the job he had put it to, and he began to grin. He came to his exit and roared down into the grid of lighted streets. He continued to drive aggressively. Though he had no plan to speak of, it yet seemed to him that what he had to do required him to keep up a good deal of momentum.

At the hospital, he drove to the emergency entrance, parked as close to the door as he could without being too much in the light, got out, and walked to the door as a man walks who knows exactly what he is doing and is already a little late. His cap, which usually sat well to the back of his head, he had now pulled forward until the bill was nearly parallel with his nose. Only when he was out of the truck and felt the air around him again, did he realize that it was making up to rain.

The emergency rooms and corridors were filled with the bloodied and the bewildered, for it was now the tail end of another Friday night of the Great American Spare-Time Civil War. Danny walked through the carnage like a man who was used to it.

Past a set of propped-open double doors, an empty gurney was standing against the corridor wall, its sheets neatly folded upon it. Without breaking stride, he took hold of it and went rapidly on down the corridor, pushing the gurney ahead of him. When he came to an elevator, he thumbed the "up" button and waited.

When the doors opened, he saw that a small young nurse was already in the elevator, standing beside the control panel. He pushed the gurney carefully past her, nodding to her and smiling. He said, "Four, please."

She pushed the button. The doors closed. She looked at him, sighed, and shook her head. "It's been a long night."

"Well," he said, "it ain't as long as it has been."

At the fourth floor the doors slid open. He pushed the gurney off the elevator.

"Good night," the nurse said.

He said, "Good night."

He had to go by the fourth floor nurse's station, but there was only one nurse there and she was talking vehemently into the telephone. She did not look up.

The door of Burley's room was shut. Danny pushed the gurney in and reshut the door. Now he was frightened, and yet there was no caution in him; he did not give himself time to think or to hesitate. Burley was lying white and still in the pallid light. Danny took a pair of rubber gloves from the container affixed to the wall and put them on. Wetting a rag at the wash basin, he carefully washed the handle of the gurney. He then pushed the gurney up near the bed and removed the folded sheet from it. Leaning over the bed, he spoke in a low voice to Burley. "Listen. I'm going to take you home. Don't worry. It's me. It's Danny."

Gently he withdrew the tube from Burley's nose. Gently he pulled away the adhesive tapes and took the needle out of Burley's arm. He took hold of the tube of the bladder catheter as if to pull it out also and then, thinking again, took out his pocketknife and cut the tube in two.

He gathered Burley into his arms and held him a moment, surprised by his lightness, and then gently he laid him onto the gurney. He unfolded the sheet and covered the sleeper entirely from head to foot. He opened the door, pushed the gurney through, and closed the door.

The nurse at the nurse's station was still on the phone. "I told you no," she was saying. "N, O, period. You have just got to understand, when I say no, I *mean* no."

Near the elevator two janitors were leaning against the wall, mops in hand, as stupefied, apparently, as the soldiers at the Tomb.

When the elevator arrived, the same nurse was on it. She gave him a smile of recognition. "My goodness, I believe we must be on the same schedule tonight."

"Yes, mam," he said.

She hardly glanced at the still figure on the gurney. "She's used to it," he thought. But he was careful, nonetheless, to stand in such a way as to make it hard for her to see, if she looked, that this corpse was breathing.

"One?" she asked.

"Yes, mam," he said. "If you please."

Once out of the elevator, he rolled the gurney rapidly down the corridor and through the place of emergency.

A man with a bandaged eye stood aside as Danny approached and went without stopping out through the automatic doors.

A slow rain had begun to fall, and now the pavement was shining.

The Coulter lane turned off the blacktop a mile or so beyond Port William. Danny drove past the lane, following the blacktop on down again into the Katy's Branch valley. Presently he turned left onto a gravel road, and after a mile or so turned left again into the lower end of the Coulter lane, passable now for not much more than a hundred yards. Where a deep gulley had been washed across the road, he stopped the truck. He was in a kind of burrow, deep under the trees in a narrow crease of the hill: Stepstone Hollow.

He switched off the engine and sat still, letting the quiet and the good darkness settle around him. He had been gone perhaps two hours and a half, and not for a minute during that time had he ceased to hurry. So resolutely had he kept up the momentum of his haste that his going and his coming back had been as much one motion as a leap. And now, that motion completed, he began to take his time. In the quiet he could hear Burley's breathing, slow and shallow but still regular. He heard, too, the slow rain falling on the woods and the trees dripping steadily onto the roof of the truck. "Well," he said quietly to Burley, "here's someplace you've been before."

The shallow breathing merely continued out of the dark where Burley, wrapped in his sheet, slumped against the door.

"Listen," Danny said. "We're in Stepstone Hollow. It's raining just a little drizzling rain, and the trees are dripping. That's what you hear. You can pret' near just listen and tell where you are. In a minute I'm going to take you up to the old barn. You don't have a thing to worry about anymore."

He got out and stood a moment, accepting the dark and the rain. There was, in spite of the overcast, some brightness in the sky. He could see a little. He took his flashlight from the pocket of his coat and blinked it once. The bundle of bedclothes and food that he had brought from the house lay with the coat on the seat beside Burley. Danny dragged the bundle out and suspended it from his right shoulder, shortening the string to make the load more manageable. Taking the flashlight, he then went around the truck and gently opened the door on the other side. He tucked the sheet snugly around Burley and then covered his head and chest with the coat.

"Now," he said, "I'm going to pick you up and carry you a ways."

Keeping the flashlight in his right hand, he gathered Burley up into his arms, kneed the door shut, and started up the hollow through the rain. He used the light to cross the gulley. Beyond there, he needed only to blink the light occasionally to show himself the lay of things. Though his burden was awkward and the wet and drooping foliage brushed him on both sides, he could walk without trouble. He made almost no sound and was grateful for the silence and slowness and effort after his loud passage out from the city. It occurred to him then that this was a season-changing rain. Tomorrow would be clear and cool, the first fall day.

It was a quarter of a mile or more up to the barn, and his arms were aching well before he got there, but having once taken this burden up, he dared not set it down. The barn, doorless and sagging, stood on a tiny shelf of bottomland beside the branch. It was built in the young man-hood of Dave Coulter, Burley's father, to house the tobacco crops from the fields, now long abandoned and overgrown, on the north slopes above it. Abandoned along with its fields, the barn had been used for many years only by groundhogs and other wild creatures and by Burley and Danny, who had sheltered there many a rainy day or night. Danny knew the place in the dark as well as if he could see it. On the old north-ward-facing slopes on one side of the branch was a thicket of forty-year-old trees: redbud, elm, box elder, walnut, locust, ash—the trees of the "pioneer generation," returning the fields to the forest. On the south slope, where the soil was rockier and shallower, stood the uninterrupted forest of white and red oaks and chinquapins, hickories, ashes, and maples, many of them two or three hundred years old.

Needing the light now that they were in the cavern of the barn, Danny carried Burley the length of the driveway, stepping around a dere-lict wagon and then into a stripping room attached at one corner. This was a small shed that was tighter and better preserved than the barn. A bench ran the length of the north side under a row of windows. Danny propped Burley against the wall at the near end of the bench, which he then swept clean with an old burlap sack. He made a pallet of the bed-clothes and laid Burley on it and covered him.

"Now," he said, "I've got to go back to the truck for some things. You're in the old barn on Stepstone, and you're all right. I won't be gone but a few minutes."

He shone the light a moment on the still face. In its profound sleep, it wore a solemnity that Burley, in his waking life, would never have allowed. And yet it was, as it had not been in the hospital, unmistakably the face of the man who for eighty-two years had been Burley Coulter. Here, where it belonged, the face thus identified itself and assumed a power that kept Danny standing there, shining the light on it, and that made him say to himself with care, "Now these are the last things. Now what happens will not happen again in his life."

He hurried back along the road to the truck and removed an axe, a spade, and a heavy steel spud bar from among the fencing tools in the back. The rain continued, falling steadily as it had fallen since it began. He shouldered the bar and spade and, carrying the axe in his left hand, returned to the barn.

Burley had not moved. He breathed on, as steadily and forcelessly as the falling rain.

"You're in a good place," Danny said. "You've slept here before and you're all right. Now I've got to sleep a little myself. I'll be close by."

He was tired at last. There were several sheets of old tin roofing stacked in the barn, and he took two of these, laying one on the floor just inside the open door nearest to the shed where Burley slept and propping the other as a shield from the draft that was pulling up the driveway. He lay down on his back and folded his arms on his chest. His clothes were damp, but with his hunting coat snug around him he was warm enough.

Though in his coming and going he had hardly made a sound, once he lay still the woods around the barn reassembled a quiet that was larger and older than his own. It was as though the woods had permitted itself to be distracted by him and his burden and his task, and now that he had ceased to move it went back to its ancient preoccupations. The rain went on with its steady patter on the barn roof and on the leafy woods.

Danny lay still and thought of all that had happened since nightfall and of what he might yet have ahead of him. For a while he continued to feel in all his nerves the swaying of the old truck as it sped along the curves of the highway. And then he ceased to think either of the past or of what was to come. The rain continued to fall. The flowing branch made a varying little song in his mind. His mind went slowly to and fro with a dark treetop in the wind. And then he slept.

Lyda had the telephone put in when they closed the school in Port William and began to haul even the littlest children all the way to the consolidated grade school at Hargrave. This required a bus ride of an hour and a half each way for the Branch children and took them much farther out of reach than they had ever been.

"They'll be gone from before daylight to after dark in the winter, who with we don't know, doing what we don't know," Lyda said, "and they've got to be able to call home if they need to."

"All right," Danny said. "And there won't anybody call us up on it but the kids — is that right?"

When it rang at night, it just scared Lyda to death, even when the kids were home. If Danny was gone, she always started worrying about him when she heard the phone ring.

She hurried down to the kitchen in her nightgown. She made a swipe at the light switch beside the kitchen door, but missed and went ahead anyhow. There was no trouble in finding the telephone in the dark; it went right on ringing as if she weren't rushing to answer it.

"Hello?" she said.

"Hello. May I speak to Mr. Daniel Branch, please?" It was a woman's voice, precise and correct.

"Danny's not here. I'm his wife. Can I help you?"

"Can you tell us how to get in touch with Mr. Branch?"

"No. He said something about Indiana, but I don't know where."

There was a pause, as though the voice at the other end were preparing itself.

"Mrs. Branch, this is the hospital. I'm afraid I have some very disturbing news. Mr. Coulter — Mr. Burley Coulter — has disappeared."

"Oh!" Lyda said. She was grinning and starting to cry, and there had been a tremor of relief in her voice that she trusted might have passed for dismay.

"Oh, my goodness!" she said finally.

"Let me assure you, Mrs. Branch, that the entire hospital staff is deeply concerned about this. We have, of course, notified the police —"

"Oh!" Lyda said.

"— and all other necessary steps will be taken. Please have your husband contact us as soon as he returns."

"I will," Lyda said.

After she hung up, Lyda stood a moment, thinking in the dark. And then she turned on the light and called Henry Catlett, whose phone rang a long time before he answered. She was not sure yet that she needed a lawyer, but she could call Henry as a friend.

"Henry, it's Lyda. I'm sorry to get you up in the middle of the night."

"It's all right," Henry said.

"The hospital just called. Uncle Burley has disappeared."

"Disappeared?"

"That's what the lady said."

There was a pause.

"Where's Danny?"

"He's gone."

"I see."

There was another pause.

"Did he say where he was going?"

"He said something about Indiana, Henry. That's all he said."

"He said that, and that's all?"

"About."

"Did you tell that to the lady from the hospital?"

"Yes."

"Did she want to know anything else?"

"No."

"And you didn't tell her anything else?"

"No."

"Did *she* say anything else?"

"She said the police had been notified."

There was another pause.

"What time is it, Lyda?"

"Three o'clock. A little after."

"And you and the kids will have the morning chores to do, and you'll have to get the kids fed and off to school."

"That's right."

"So you'll have to be there for a while. Maybe that's all right. But you'll have to expect a call or maybe a visit from the police, Lyda. When you talk to them, tell them exactly what you told the lady at the hospital.

Tell the truth, but don't tell any more than you've already told. If they want to know more, tell them I'm your lawyer and they must talk to me."

"I will."

"Are you worried about Burley and Danny?"

"No."

"Are you worried about talking to the police?"

"I'm scared, but I'm not worried."

"All right. Let's try to sleep some more. Tomorrow might be a busy day."

Danny woke up cold and hungry. He was lying on his back with his arms folded on his chest; he had slept perhaps two hours, and he had not moved. Nor had anything moved in the barn or in the wooded hollow around it, so far as he could tell, except the little stream of Stepstone, which continued to make the same steady song it had been making when he fell asleep. A few crickets sang. The air was still, and in openings of mist that had gathered in the hollow he could see the stars.

Though he was cold, for several minutes he did not move. He loved the stillness and was reluctant to break it. An owl trilled nearby and another answered some distance away. Danny turned onto his side to face the opening of the doorway, pillowed his head on his left forearm, and, taking off his cap, ran the fingers of his right hand slowly through his hair.

He yawned, stretched, and got up. Taking the flashlight, he went in to where Burley lay and shone the light on him. Nothing had changed. The old body breathed on with the same steady yet forceless and shallow breaths. Danny saw at once all he needed to see, and yet he remained for a few moments, shining the light. And he said again in his mind, "These are the last things now. Everything that happens now happens for the last time in his life." He reached out with his hand and took hold of Burley's shoulder and shook it gently, as if to wake him, but he did not wake.

"It'll soon be morning," he said aloud. "I'm hungry now. I need to make a fire and fix a little breakfast before the light comes. We can't send up any smoke after daylight. I'll be close by."

He gathered dry scraps of wood from the barn floor, and then he pried loose a locust tierpole with the bark still on it and rapidly cut it into short lengths with the axe. Just outside the doorway, he made a small fire between two rocks on which he set his skillet. By the light of the flashlight he sliced a dozen thick slices from the jowl and started several of them frying. He crossed the creek to where a walled spring flowed out of the hillside. He found the rusted coffee can that he kept there, dipped it full and drank, and then dipped it full again. Carrying the filled can, he went back to his fire, where he knelt on one knee and attended to the skillet. The birds had begun to sing, and the sky was turning pale above the eastward trees.

When all the meat was fried, he set the skillet off the fire. With water from the spring and grease from the fried meat, he moistened some cornmeal and made six hoecakes, each the size of the skillet. When he was finished with his cooking, he took the pair of surgical gloves from his pocket and stirred them in the fire until they were burned. He brought water from the creek then and put out the fire. He divided the food carefully and ate half. He ate slowly and with pleasure, watching the light come. Movement, fire, and now the food in his belly had taken the chill out of his flesh, but fall was in the air that morning, and he welcomed it. The day would be clear and fine. And more would come — brisk, bright, dark-shadowed days colored by the turning leaves, days that would call up the hunter feeling in him. He remembered Elton Penn walking into the woods under the stars of a bright frosty night, half singing, as his way was, "Clear as a bell, cold as hell, and smells like old cheese." Now Elton was three years dead.

As Danny watched, the light reddened and warmed in the sky. The last of the stars disappeared. Above him, on both sides of the hollow, the wet leaves of the treetops began to shine among the fading strands and shelves of mist. Eastward, the mist took a stain of pink from the rising sun and glowed. And Danny felt a happiness that he knew was not his at all, that did not exist because he felt it but because it was here and he had returned to it.

He carried his skillet to the creek, scoured it out with handfuls of fine gravel and left it on a rock to dry.

He picked his way through the young thicket growth closing around the barn and entered the stand of old trees that covered the south slope.

There the great trees stood around him, the thready night mists caught in their branches, and every leaf was still. When the first white man in this place — the first Coulter or Catlett or Feltner or whoever it was — had passed through this crease of the hill, these trees were here, and the stillness in which they stood and grew had been here forever.

Timber cutters, in recent years, had had their eye on these trees and had approached Burley about "harvesting" them. "I reckon you had better talk to Danny here," Burley said. And Danny smiled that completely friendly, totally impenetrable smile of his, and merely shook his head.

Now Danny was looking for a place well in among the big trees and yet not too far from the creek or too readily accessible to the eye. His study took him a while, but finally he saw what he was looking for. Under a tall, straight chinquapin that was sound and not too old, a tree that would be standing a long time, there was a shallow trough in the ground, left perhaps by the uprooting of another tree a long time ago; the place was open and clear of undergrowth but hard to see because of a patch of thicket around a windfall. Danny stood and thought again to test his satisfaction, and was satisfied.

As he turned away he noticed, strung between two saplings, the dew-beaded orb of a large orange spider. He stopped to look at it and soon found the spider's home, a sort of tube fashioned of two leaves and so not easy to see, where the spider could withdraw to sleep or take shelter from the rain. It would not be long, Danny thought, before the spiders would have to go out of business for the winter. Soon there would be hard frosts, and the webs would be cumbered and torn by the falling leaves.

Sunlight now filled the sky above the shadowy woods. He went back to the barn, preoccupied with his thoughts, and so he was startled, on entering the stripping room, by Burley's opened eyes, looking at him.

He stopped, for the force of his surprise was almost that of fright. And then he went over to the bench and laid his hand on Burley's. Burley's eyes were perfectly calm; he was smiling. Slowly, pausing to breathe between phrases, he said, "I allowed you'd get here about the same time I did."

"Well, you were right," Danny said. "We made it. Do you know where you are?"

Again, smiling, Burley spoke, his voice so halting and weak as to seem not uttered by bodily strength at all but by some pure presence of recollection and will: "Right here."

"You're right again," Danny said, knowing that Burley did know where he was. "Are you comfortable? Is there anything you want?"

This time Burley said only, "Drink." He turned his head a little and looked at the treetops beyond the window.

Danny said, "I'll go to the spring."

At the spring, he drank and then dipped up a drink for Burley. When he returned, Burley's eyes were closed again, and he looked more deeply sunk within himself than before. It was as though his ghost, like a circling hawk, had swung back into this world on a wide curve, to look once more out of his eyes at what he had always known and to speak with his voice, and then had swung out of it again, the curve widening. Danny stood still, holding the can of water. He could hear Burley's breaths coming slower than before, tentative and unsteady. Danny listened. He picked up Burley's wrist and held it. And then he shouldered his tools and went up into the woods and began to dig.

Henry Catlett tried hard to take his own advice, but one thought ran on to another and he could not sleep. There was too much he needed to know that he did not know. Within twenty minutes he saw that he was not going to sleep again. He got up in the dark and, taking care not to disturb Sarah, who had gone back to sleep after the phone rang, went downstairs, turned on a light and called the hospital. After some trial and error, he was transferred to the supervisor who had talked to Lyda.

"This is Henry Catlett. I have a little law practice up the river at Hargrave. I hear you've mislaid one of your patients."

The voice in the receiver became extremely businesslike: "The patient would be—?"

"Coulter. Burley Coulter."

"Yes. Well, as you no doubt have heard, Mr. Catlett, Mr. Coulter was reported missing from his room at a little before two o'clock this morning. Such a thing has never happened here before, Mr. Catlett. Let me assure you, sir, that we're doing everything possible on behalf of the victim and his family."

"Of course," Henry said. "I can imagine. Well, I'm calling on behalf of the family. Have you any clues as to what happened?"

"Um. For that, I think I had better have you talk with the investigating officer who was here from the police. Let me find his number. Please hold one minute."

She gave him a name and a number, which Henry proceeded to dial.

"Officer Bush," he said, "I'm Henry Catlett, a country lawyer of sorts up at Hargrave. I'm calling on behalf of the family of Mr. Burley Coulter, who seems to have disappeared from his hospital room."

"Yes, Mr. Catlett."

"I understand that you were the investigating officer. What did you find out?"

"Not much, I'm afraid, sir. Mr. Coulter was definitely kidnapped. His attacker disconnected him from the life-support system and wheeled him out, we assume, by way of the emergency entrance. We have one witness, a nurse, who may have seen the kidnapper. She described him as a huge man in a blue shirt; she didn't get a good look at his face. She saw him on an elevator, going up with an empty gurney and down with what she took to be a corpse. Aside from that, we have only the coincidental disappearance of the victim's next of kin, Danny Branch, who his wife says may have gone to Indiana."

"Anything solid? Any fingerprints?"

"Nothing, Mr. Catlett. The man smeared everything he touched, and he didn't touch more than he had to. He may have used a pair of surgical gloves from the room."

"Would you let me know as soon as you have anything more to report?"

"Be glad to."

Henry gave him his phone numbers at home and at the office, thanked him, and hung up. He turned the light off then, felt his way to his easy chair, and sat down in the dark to think.

He knew several things. For one, he knew that Danny Branch, though by no means a small man, would not be described by most people as "huge." So far as he could see at present, all they had to worry about was the blue shirt, and that might be plenty.

He sat thinking until the shapes of the trees outside the window emerged into the first daylight, and then he went back to the phone and called Lyda.

Lyda called Nathan after she had talked to Henry the second time. Nathan, as was his way, said "Hello" and then simply listened. When she had told him of Burley's disappearance and of Danny's, Nathan said, "All right. Do you need anything?"

"No. We'll be fine," she said. "But listen. Henry called back while ago. He said the police didn't find any fingerprints at the hospital. The only witness they found was somebody who saw a man in a blue shirt. Henry wants you and Hannah and me to come to his office as soon as we get our chores done and all. When the police find us, he said, he'd just as soon they'd find us there. He said to tell you, and he'd call Jack and Andy and Flora and the Rowanberrys. He wants everybody who's closest to Burley to be there."

"All right," Nathan said. "It'll be a little while."

He hung up, and having told Lyda's message to Hannah, he put one of his shirts into a paper sack and went out. He had his chores to do, but he would do them later. He got into his pickup and drove out to the Coulter lane and turned, and turned again into the farm that had been his father's and was now his, divided by a steep, wooded hollow from Burley's place, where Danny and Lyda and their children had lived with Burley since Danny's mother's death. Beyond the two houses in the dawn light, he could see the morning cloud of fog shining in the river valley.

He pulled the truck in behind the house, got out, and started down the hill. Soon he was out of sight among the trees, and he went level along the slope around the point beyond Burley's house, turning gradually out of the river valley into the smaller valley of Katy's Branch. He went straight down the hill then to the creek road, turned into the lower end of the Coulter lane, and soon came to Danny's truck. He saw that Danny's axe and the digging tools were gone.

For several minutes he stood beside the truck, looking up the hollow toward the old barn. And then he took the switch key from where Danny always hid it under a loose flap of floor mat, started the truck and eased it backward along its incoming tracks until it stood on the gravel of the county road. There were a few bald patches of fresh mud that he had had to drive over, and he walked back to these and tramped out the tire tracks, taking care to leave no shoe track of his own.

When he returned to the truck, he drove back down the creek road toward the river and before long turned right under a huge sycamore into another lane. He forded the branch, went up by a stone chimney standing solitary on a little bench where a house had burned, and then down again to the disused barn of that place, and drove in. As before, he erased the few tire tracks that he had left in the lane. He stepped across the Katy's Branch Road and again disappeared into the woods.

While he did all this he had never ceased to whistle a barely audible whisper of a song, passing his breath in and out over the tip of his tongue.

The detective came walking out to the barn as if he were not sure where to put his feet. He was wearing shiny shoes with perforated toes, a tallish man, softening in the middle. He looked a little like somebody Lyda might have seen before. His dark hair was combed straight over his forehead in bangs. He walked with his left hand in his pocket, the jacket of his blue suit held back on that side.

Lyda herself was wearing a pair of rubber boots, but in expectation of company she had put on her best everyday dress. She was carrying two five-gallon buckets of corn that, as the detective approached, she emptied over the fence to the sows.

"Good morning. Mrs. Branch?" the detective said.

"Yes. Good morning."

The children were in the barn, doing the milking and the other chores, and Lyda, as she greeted the detective, started walking back toward the house.

He was showing her a badge. "Detective Kyle Bode of the state police, Mrs. Branch. I hope you'll be willing to answer a few questions."

Lyda laughed, looking out over the white cloud of fog that lay in the river valley. "I reckon I'll have to know what questions," she said.

"Well, you're Mrs. Danny Branch? And Danny Branch is Mr. Burley Coulter's next of kin?"

"That's right."

"And you're aware that Mr. Coulter has disappeared from his hospital room?"

"Yes."

"Is Mr. Branch at home?"

"No."

"Can you tell me where he went?"

"Well, he said something about Indiana."

"You don't know where?"

"Well, he sometimes goes up there to the Amish. You know, we farm with horses, and Danny has to depend on the Amish for harness and other things."

"Hmmm. Horses. Well," the detective said. "When did Mr. Branch leave?"

"I couldn't say."

"You don't know, or you don't remember?"

"I can't say that I do."

Lyda had not ceased to walk, nor he to walk with her, and now, as they were approaching the yard gate, the detective stopped. "Mrs. Branch, I have the distinct feeling that you are playing a little game with me. I think your husband has Mr. Coulter with him in Indiana — or wherever he is — and I think you know he does, and you're protecting him. Your husband, I would like to remind you, may be in very serious trouble with the law, and unless you cooperate you may be, too."

Lyda looked straight at him. Her eyes were an intense, surprising blue, and sometimes when she looked suddenly at you they seemed to leave little flashes of blue light dancing in the air. And the detective saw her then: a big woman, good-looking for her age, which was maybe forty or forty-five, and possessed of great practical strength (he remembered her tossing the contents of those heavy buckets over the fence), but her eyes, now that he looked at her, were what impressed him most. They were eyes not at all in the habit of concealment, but they certainly were in the habit of withstanding. They withstood him. They made him feel like explaining that he was only doing his duty.

"Mister," she said without any trace of fear that he could detect, "it scares me to be talking to the police. I never talked to the police before in my life. If you want to know any more, you'll have to talk to Henry Catlett down at Hargrave."

"Is Henry Catlett your lawyer?"

"Henry's our friend," she said.

"Yes," the detective said. "I'll go see him. Thank you very much for your time."

When Detective Bode walked away from Lyda, he already felt the mire of failure pulling at his feet. He had felt it before. Long ago, it seemed, he had studied to be a policeman because he wanted to become the kind of man who solved things. He had imagined himself becoming a man who — insightful, alert, and knowing — stepped into the midst of confusion and made clarity and order that people would be grateful for. So far, it had not turned out that way. He was thirty-two years old already, and he had been confused as much as most people. In spite of the law and the government and the police, it seemed, people went right on and did whatever they were going to do. They had motives that were confusing, and they left evidence that was confusing. Sometimes they left no evidence. The science of crime solving was much clumsier than he had expected. Many criminals and many noncriminals were smarter than Kyle Bode — or, anyhow, smarter than Kyle Bode had been able to prove himself to be so far. He had begun to believe he might end up as some kind of paper shuffler, had even begun to think that might be a relief.

He had understood all too well, anyhow, the rather cynical grin with which his friend, Rich Ferris, had handed him this case. "Here's one that'll make you famous."

And what a case it was! Here was an old guy resting easy in the best medical facility money could buy. And what happened? This damned redneck, Danny Branch, who was his nephew or something, came and kidnapped him out of his hospital bed in the middle of the night. And took him off where? To Indiana? Not likely, Detective Bode thought. He would bet that Mr. Burley Coulter, alive or dead, and his kidnapper, Mr. Danny Branch, were somewhere just out of sight in these god-forsaken hills and hollows.

Kyle Bode objected to hills and hollows. He objected to them especially if they were overgrown with trees. That the government of

the streets and highways persisted in having business in wooded hills
and hollows in every kind of weather was no small part of his dis-
illusionment.

And that big woman with her boots and her unimpressed blue eyes—
it pleased him to believe that she was looking him straight in the eye and
lying. In fact, he had wished a little that she would admire him, and he
knew that she had not.

Traveling at a contemplative speed down the river road toward Hargrave, he glanced up at his image in the rearview mirror and patted down
his hair.

Kyle Bode's father had originated in the broad bottomlands of a
community called Nowhere, two counties west of Louisville. Under
pressure from birth to "get out of here and make something out of yourself," Kyle's father had come to Louisville and worked his way into a
farm equipment dealership. Kyle was the dealer's third child and second
son. He might have succeeded to the dealership—"You boys can be partners," their father had said—but the older brother possessed an invinci-
ble practicality and a head start, and besides Kyle did not want to spend
his life dealing with farmers. He had higher aims, which made him dangerous to those he considered to be below him. Unlike his brother, Kyle
was an idealist, with a little bit of an ambition to be a hero. Perhaps by
the same token, he was also a man given to lethargy and to sudden onsets
of violence by which he attempted to drive back whatever circumstances
his lethargy had allowed to close in on him. Sagged and silent in his chair
at a party or beer joint, he would suddenly thrust himself, with fists flying, at some spontaneously elected opponent. This did not happen often
enough to damage him much, and it remained surprising to his friends.

Soon after graduation, he married his high school sweetheart. And
then while he was beginning his career as a policeman, they, and especially he, began to dabble in some of the recreational sidelines of the
countercultural revolution. He became sexually liberated. He suspected
that his wife had experienced this liberation as well, but he did not catch
her, and perhaps this was an ill omen for his police career. On the contrary, as it happened, she caught him in the very inflorescence of ecstasy
on the floor of the carport of a house where they were attending a party.
He was afraid for a while that she would divorce him, but when it

became clear to him that she would not, he began to feel that she was limiting his development, and he divorced her in order to be free to be himself.

He cut quite a figure at parties after that. One festive night a young lady said, "Kyle, do you know who you really look like?" And he said, "No." And she said, "Ringo Starr." That was when he began to comb down his bangs. Girls and young women were always saying to him after that, "Do you know who you look like?" And he would say, "No. Who?" as if he had no notion what they were talking about.

His second wife — whom he married when he made her pregnant, for he really was a conscientious young man who wanted to do the right thing — was proud of that resemblance, at first seriously and then jokingly, for a while. And then he ceased to remind her of anyone but himself, whereupon she divorced him.

He knew that she had not left him because she was dissatisfied with him but because she was not able to be satisfied for very long with anything. He disliked and feared this in her at the same time that he recognized it in himself. He, too, was dissatisfied; he could not see what he had because he was always looking around for something else that he thought he wanted. And so perhaps it was out of mutual dissatisfaction that their divorce had come, and now they were free. Perhaps even their little daughter was free, who was tied down no more than her parents were, for they sent her flying back and forth between them like a shuttlecock, and spoiled her in vying for her allegiance, and gave her more freedom of choice than she could have used well at twice her age. They were all free, he supposed. But finally he had had to ask if they were, any of them, better off than they had been and if they could hope to be better off than they were. For they were not satisfied. And by now he had to suppose, and to fear, that they were not going to be satisfied.

Surely there must be someplace to stop. In lieu of a more final place, though it was too early in the day to be thinking about it, he would take the lounge of the Outside Inn, the comers and goers shadowy between him and the neon, a filled and frosted glass in front of him, a slow broken-hearted song on the jukebox.

And maybe the mood would hit him to ask one of the women to dance. Angela, maybe, who admitted to being lonesome and liked to dance close. They would dance, they would move as one, and after a while he would let his right hand slide down, as if by accident, onto her hip.

But his car, as though mindful of his duty when he was not, had taken him into Hargrave. He stopped for the first light and then turned to drive around the courthouse square; he was looking for a place to eat breakfast. The futility of this day insinuated itself into his thoughts, as unignorable as if it crawled palpably on his skin. Here he was, looking for a comatose old geezer who (if Detective Bode mistook not) had been abducted by his next of kin, who, if the old geezer died, would be guilty of a crime that probably had not even been named yet. Maybe he was about to turn up something totally new in the annals of crime, though he would just as soon turn it up someplace else. In fact, he would just as soon somebody else turned it up. It ought, he told himself, to be easy enough to turn up, for it was clearly the work of an amateur. And yet this amateur, who had had the gall or stupidity or whatever it took to kidnap his victim right out of the middle of a busy hospital, had managed to be seen, and not clearly seen at that, by only one witness and had left no evidence. So Detective Bode was working from a coincidence, a good guess, and no evidence. His success, he supposed, depended on the improbable occurrence of a lucky moment in which he would be able to outsmart the self-styled "country lawyer of sorts," Henry Catlett.

"Later for that," Kyle Bode thought.

Among the dilapidating storefronts he found the place he thought he remembered, the Front Street Grill, and he parked and went in.

When Lyda called, Nathan and Hannah were just waking up. Before Nathan turned the light on by the bed, they could see the gray early daylight out the window. After Nathan went to the phone, Hannah lay still and listened, but from Nathan's brief responses she could not make out who had called.

She heard Nathan hang up the phone. He came back into the bedroom and told her carefully everything that Lyda had told him.

"But wait," she said. "What's happening? Where *is* Danny?"

"We'd better not help each other answer those questions, Hannah—not for a while, anyhow."

He opened a drawer of the bureau and took out one of his shirts, a green one.

"Where are you going?"

He smiled at her. "I'll be back before long."

Though Nathan was a quiet man, he was not usually a secretive one. But she asked no more.

He went out. She heard him go through the kitchen and out the back door. She heard the pickup start and go out the driveway. And then the sound of it was gone.

Usually, after Nathan got up, there would be a few minutes when she could stay in bed, sometimes rolling over into the warmth where he had slept, before she got up to start breakfast. She loved that time. She would lie still, listening, as the night ended and the day began. She heard the first birdsongs of the morning. She heard Nathan leave the house, the milk bucket ringing a little as he took it down from its nail on the back porch. She heard the barn door slide open, and then Nathan's voice calling the cows, and then the cowbells coming up through the pale light. If she got up when the cows reached the barn, she could have breakfast ready by the time Nathan came back to the house.

But this morning, as soon as the truck was out of earshot, she got up. For there was much to think about, much to do and to be prepared for. Now that she was fully awake, she had, like the others, caught the drift of what was happening.

She took the milk bucket and went to the barn and milked and did the chores, the things that Nathan usually did, and then she went to open the henhouse and put out feed and water for the hens — her work. At the house, she strained the milk, set the table for breakfast, and got out the food. But Nathan was not back. She sat down by the kitchen window where she could see him when he came in. She kept her sewing basket there and the clothes that needed mending. But now, though she took a piece of sewing onto her lap, she did not work. She sat with her hands at rest, looking out the window as the mists of the hollows turned whiter under the growing light. She wanted to be thinking of Burley, but amongst all the knowing and unknowing of this strangely begun day she could not think of him. Who was most on her mind now was Nathan, and she wished him home.

It was home to her, this house, though once it had not been, nor had this neighborhood been. She had come to Port William thirty-six years ago. She had married Virgil Feltner as war spread across the world, and had lived with him for a little while in the household of his parents, before he was called into the service. When he left, because her mother was dead and replaced long ago by an unkind stepmother, Mat and Margaret Feltner had made her welcome. She stayed on with them, and they were mother and father to her. In the summer of 1944, Virgil came home on leave; he and Hannah were together a little while again, and when he went back to his unit she was with child.

The life that Hannah had begun to live came to an end when her young husband was killed, and for a while it seemed that she had no life except in the child that she had borne into the world of one death and of many. And then Nathan had called her out of that world into the living world again, and a new life had come to her; she and Nathan had made and shaped it, welcomed its additions and borne its losses, together. They moved to this place that Nathan had bought not long before they married. Run-down and thicket-grown as it was, its possibility had beckoned to him and then to her. They had moved into the old house, restored it while they lived in it and while they restored the farm; they had raised their children here. And they were son and daughter both to Margaret and Mat Feltner and to Nathan's father, whose oldest son, Tom, had also been killed in the war.

They had raised their children, sent them to college, seen them go away to work in cities, and, though wishing they might have stayed, wished them well. Their children had gone, and over the years, one by one, so had their elders. And each one of these departures had left them with more work to do and, as Hannah sometimes thought, less reason to do it.

They were in their fifties now, farming three farms simply because there was no one else to do the work. In addition to the Feltner Place and their own, they were also farming Nathan's home place, which he had inherited from his father. Like everybody else still farming, they were spread too thin, and help was hard to find. The Port William neighborhood had as many people, probably, as it had ever had, but it did not have them where it needed them. It had a good many of them now on little city lots carved out of farms, from which they commuted to city jobs. Nathan and Hannah were overburdened, too tired at the end of every day, and with no relief in sight. And yet they did not think of quitting. Nathan worked through his long days steadily and quietly. Some days Hannah worked with him; when she needed help, he helped her. They had two jersey cows for milk and butter; they raised and slaughtered their meat hogs; they kept a flock of hens; they raised a garden. And still, in spite of all, there were quietnesses that they came to, in which they rested and were together and were glad to be.

And though their loneliness had increased, they were not alone. Of the membership of kin and friends that had held them always, some had died and some had gone, but some remained. There were Lyda and Danny Branch and their children. There were Arthur and Martin Rowanberry. After Elton Penn's death, his son Jack had continued to farm their place, and Mary Penn was living in Hargrave, still a friend. There were the various Catletts, who, whatever else they were, were still farmers and still of the membership: Bess and Wheeler who were now old, Sarah and Henry and their children, Flora and Andy and theirs.

When she thought of their neighborhood, Hannah wondered whether or not to count the children. Like the old, the young were leaving. The old were dying without successors, and Hannah was aware how anxiously those who remained had begun to look into the eyes of the children. They were watching not just their own children now but anybody's children. For as the burden of keeping the land increased for the always fewer who remained, as the difference continued to increase between the price of what they had to sell and the cost of what they had to buy, they knew that they had less and less to offer the children, and fewer arguments to make.

They held on, she and those others, who might be the last. They held on, and they held out, and they were seeing, perhaps, a little more clearly what they had to hold out against. Every year, it seemed to her, they were living more from what they could do for themselves and each other and less from what they had to buy. Nathan's refusals to buy things, she had noticed, were becoming firmer as well as more frequent. "No," he would say, "I guess we can get along without that." "No. Not at that price." "No. I reckon the old one will run a while longer." And though he spoke these answers kindly enough, there was no doubting their finality. Nobody ever asked twice.

Maybe, she thought, this was Danny's influence. Danny was eight years younger than Nathan, and it was strange to think that Nathan could have been influenced by him, but maybe he had been. Danny never had belonged much to the modern world, and every year he appeared to belong to it less. Of them all, Danny most clearly saw that world as his enemy — as *their* enemy — and most forthrightly and cheerfully repudiated it. He reserved his allegiance to his friends and his place.

Danny was the right one for the rescue that Hannah did not doubt was being accomplished, though she did not know quite how. He had some grace about him that would permit him to accomplish it with joy. She smiled, for she knew, too, that Danny was a true son to Burley, not only in loyalty but in nature — that he had shared fully in that half of Burley's life that had belonged to the woods and the darkness. Nathan, she thought, had understood that side of Burley and been friendly to it without so much taking part in it. Nathan would wander out with Burley and Danny occasionally and would enjoy it, but he was more completely a farmer than they were, more content to be bound within the cycle of the farmer's year. You never felt, looking at him, that he had left something somewhere beyond the cleared fields that he would be bound to go back and get. He did not have that air that so often hung about Danny and Burley, suggesting that they might suddenly look back, grin and wave, and disappear among the trees. He was as solid, as frankly and fully present as the doorstep, a man given to work and to quiet — like, she thought, his father.

They were her study, those Coulter men. Figuring them out was her need, her way of loving them, and sometimes her amusement. The one who most troubled her had been Nathan's father, Jarrat — a driven, work-brittle, weather-hardened, lonely, and nearly wordless man, who went to his grave without completing his sorrow for his young wife who had died when their sons were small, whom he never mentioned and never forgot. His death had left in Hannah an unused and yearning tenderness.

Burley lived in a larger world than his brother, and not just because, as a hunter and a woods walker, he readily crossed boundaries that had confined Jarrat. Burley was a man freely in love with freedom and with pleasures, who watched the world with an amused, alert eye to see what it would do next, and if the world did not seem inclined to get on very soon to anything of interest, he gave it his help. Hannah's world had been made dearer to her by Burley's laughter, his sometimes love of talk (his own and other people's), and his delight in outrageous behavior (his own and other people's). She knew that Burley did not forget the dead, whom he mourned and missed. She knew he grieved that he had not married Kate Helen Branch, Danny's mother, and that he regretted his late acknowledgment of Danny as his son. But she knew, too, how little he had halted in grief and regret, how readily and cheerfully he had gone on, however burdened, to whatever had come next. And because he was never completely of her world, she had the measure of his generosity to her and the others. Though gifted for disappearance, he had never entirely disappeared but had been with them to the end.

Now the thought of him did return to her. As he had grown sicker and weaker, the thought of him had come more and more into her keeping, and she had received it with her love and her thanks as she had received her children when they were newborn.

She thought it strange and wonderful that she had been given these to love. She thought it a blessing that she had loved them to the limit of her grief at parting with them, and that grief had only deepened and clarified her love. Since her first grief had brought her fully to birth and wakefulness in this world, an unstinting compassion had moved in her, like a live stream flowing deep underground, by which she knew herself and others and the world. It was her truest self, that stream always astir inside her that was at once pity and love, knowledge and faith, forgiveness, grief, and joy. It made her fearful, and it made her unafraid.

Like the others, she had mourned her uselessness to Burley in his sickness. Like the others, she had been persuaded and had helped to persuade that they should get help for him. Like the others, once they had given him into the power of the doctors and into the hard light of that way and place in which he did not belong, she had wanted him back. And she had held him to her in her thoughts, loving the old, failed flesh and bone of him as never before, as if she could feel, in thought, in nerve, and through all intervening time and distance, the little helpless child that he had been and had become again. Knowing now that he was with Danny, hidden away, somewhere at home, joy shook her and the window blurred in her sight.

She heard, after a while, the tires of Nathan's truck on the gravel, and then the truck came into sight, stopped in its usual place, and Nathan got out. She watched him as he walked to the house, not so light-stepping as he used to be. She knew that as he walked, looking alertly around, he would be whistling over and over a barely audible little thread of a tune.

When he came in and she looked at him from the stove, where she had gone to start their breakfast, he smiled at her. "Don't ask," he said.

She said, "I will only ask one question. Are you worried about Burley?"

"No," he said, and he smiled at her again.

Henry hurried up the steps to the office, knowing that his father would already be there. Wheeler came to the office early, an hour maybe before Henry and the secretary, because, as Henry supposed, he liked to be there by himself. It was a place of haste and sometimes of turmoil, that office, where they worked at one problem knowing that another was waiting and sometimes that several others were waiting. Wheeler would come there in the quiet of the early morning to meet the day on his own terms. He would sit down at his desk covered with opened books, thick folders of papers and letters, ruled yellow pads covered with his impulsive blue script, and with one of those pads on his lap and a pen in his hand he would call the coming day to order in his mind.

He had been at work there for more than fifty years. In all that time the look of the place had changed more by accretion than by alteration. There were three rooms: Wheeler's office in the front, overlooking the courthouse square; Henry's in the back, overlooking an alley and some backyards; and, between the two, a waiting room full of bookcases and chairs where the secretary, Hilda Roe, had her desk.

Wheeler was sitting at his desk with his hat on, his back to the door. He was leaning back in his chair, his right ankle crossed over his left knee, and he was writing in fitful jabs on a yellow pad. Henry tapped on the facing of the door.

"Come in," Wheeler said without looking up.

Henry came in.

"Sit down," Wheeler said.

Henry did not sit down.

"What you got on your mind?" Wheeler asked.

"Burley Coulter disappeared from the hospital last night."

Wheeler swiveled his chair around and gave Henry a look that it had taken Henry thirty years to meet with composure. "Where's Danny Branch?"

Henry grinned. "Danny's away from home. Lyda said he said something about Indiana."

"You've talked to the police?"

"Yes. And a state police detective, Mr. Kyle Bode, has already been to see Lyda."

Wheeler wrote Kyle Bode's name on the yellow pad. "What did you find out?"

"Somebody went into Burley's room sometime around two o'clock. Whoever it was disconnected him from the life machines, loaded him onto a gurney, and escaped with him 'into the night,' as they say. They found no fingerprints or other evidence. They have found one witness, a nurse, who saw 'a huge man' wearing a blue shirt going up on an elevator with an empty gurney and then down with what she thought was a dead person."

"We don't know anybody huge, do we?" Wheeler said. "What about the blue shirt?"

"Don't know," Henry said.

"Do you know this Detective Bode?"

"I had a little talk with him once, over in the courtroom."

"You're expecting him?"

"Yes."

Wheeler spread his hands palm-down on his lap, studied them a moment, and then looked up again. "Well, what are you going to do?"

"Don't know," Henry said. "I guess I'll wait to find out. I've told Lyda and everybody else concerned to come here as soon as they can. And I think you ought to call Mother and Mary Penn and tell them to come. I don't want the police to talk to any more of them alone."

This time it was Wheeler who grinned. He reached for the phone. "All right, my boy."

Working with the spade, Danny cut into the ground the long outline of the grave. It was hard digging, the gentle rain of the night not having penetrated very far, and there were tree roots and rocks. Danny soon settled into a rhythm in keeping with the length and difficulty of the job. He used the spud bar to loosen the dirt, cut the roots, and pry out the rocks. With the spade he piled the loosened dirt on one side of the grave; with his hands he laid the rocks out on the other side. He worked steadily, stopping only to return to the barn to verify that the sleeper there had not awakened. On each visit he stood by Burley only long enough to touch him and to say, "You're all right. You don't have to worry about a thing." Each time, he saw that Burley's breath came more shallow and more slow.

And finally, on one of these trips to the barn, he knew as he entered the doorway that the breaths had stopped, and he stopped, and then went soundlessly in where the body lay. It looked unaccountably small. Now of its long life in this place there remained only this small relic of flesh and bone. In the hospital, Burley's body had seemed to Danny to be off in another world; he had not been able to rid himself of the feeling that he was looking at it through a lens or a window. Here, the old body seemed to belong to this world absolutely, it was so accepting now of all that had come to it, even its death. Burley had died as he had slept—he had not moved. Danny leaned and picked up the still hands and laid them together.

He went back to his digging and worked on as before. As he accepted again the burden of the work and measured his thoughts to it, Burley returned to his mind, and he knew him again as he had been when his life was full. He saw again the stance and demeanor of the man, the amused eyes, the lips pressed together while speech waited upon thought, an almost inviolable patience in the set of the shoulders. It was as though Burley stood in full view nearby, at ease and well at home—as though Danny could see him, but only on the condition that he not look.

When Detective Bode climbed the stairs to the office of Wheeler Catlett & Son, the waiting room was deserted. Through the open door at the rear of the room, he could see Henry with his feet propped on his desk, reading the morning paper. Kyle Bode closed the waiting room door somewhat loudly.

Henry looked up. "Come in," he called. He got up to greet his visitor, who shook his hand and then produced a badge.

"Kyle Bode, state police."

Henry gave him a warm and friendly smile. "Sure," he said. "I remember you. Have a seat. What can I do for you?"

The detective sat down in the chair that Henry positioned for him. He had not smiled. He waited for Henry, too, to sit down. "I'm here in connection with what I suppose would be called a kidnapping. A man named Burley Coulter, of Port William, was removed from his hospital room without authorization at about two o'clock this morning."

"So I heard!" Henry said. "Lyda Branch called me about it. I figured you fellows would have made history of this case by now. You mean you haven't?"

"Not yet," Kyle Bode said. "It's not all that clear-cut, probably due to the unprecedented nature of the crime."

"You show me an unprecedented crime," Henry said, falling in with the detective's philosophical tone. "Kidnapping, you said?"

"It's a crime involving the new medical technology. I mean, some of this stuff is unheard of. We're living in the future right now. I figure this crime is partly motivated by anxiety about this new stuff. Like maybe the guy that did it is some kind of religious nut."

Henry put his dark-rimmed reading glasses back on and made his face long and solemn, tilting his head back, as he was apt to do when amused in exalted circumstances. "In the past, too," he said.

"What?"

"If we're living in the future, then surely we're living in the past, too, and the dead and the unborn are right here in our midst. Wouldn't you say so?"

"I guess so," Kyle Bode said.

"Well," Henry said, "do you have any clues as to the possible identity of the perpetrator of this crime?"

"Yes, as a matter of fact, we do. We have a good set of fingerprints."

Kyle Bode spoke casually, looking at the fingernails of his right hand, which he held in his left. When he looked up to gauge the effect, not the Henry of their recent philosophical exchange but an altogether different Henry, one he had encountered before, was looking at him point-blank, the glasses off.

"Mr. Bode," Henry said, "that was a lie you just told. As a matter of fact, you don't have any evidence. If we are going to get along, you had better assume that I know as much about this case as you do. Now, what do you want?"

Kyle Bode felt a sort of chill crawl up the back of his neck and over the top of his head, settling for an exquisite moment among the hair roots. He maintained his poise, however, and was pleased to note that he was returning Henry's look. And the right question came to him.

"I want to find the victim's nephew, Danny Branch. Do you know where he is?"

"Son," Henry said. "The victim's son. I only know what his wife told me."

"What did she tell you?"

"She said he said something about Indiana."

"We have an APB on him in Indiana." Detective Bode said this with the air of one who leaves no stone unturned. "But we really think—*I* think—the solution is to be found right here."

But looking at Henry and remembering Lyda, he felt unmistakably the intimation that he and his purpose were not trusted. These people did not trust him, and they were not going to trust him. He felt his purpose unraveling in his failure to have their trust. In default of that trust, *every* stone must be turned. And it was a rocky country. He knew he had already failed—unless, by some fluke of luck, he could find somebody to outsmart. Or, maybe, unless this Danny Branch should appear wearing a blue shirt.

"Maybe you can tell me," he said, "if Danny Branch is Mr. Coulter's heir."

"Burley was—is—my father's client," Henry said. "You ought to ask him about that. Danny, I reckon, is my client."

The detective made his tone more reasonable, presuming somewhat upon his and Henry's brotherhood in the law: "Mr. Catlett, I'd like to be assured of your cooperation in this case. After all, it will be in your client's best interest to keep this from going as far as it may go."

"Can't help you," Henry said.

"You mean that you, a lawyer, won't cooperate with the law of the state in the solution of a crime?"

"Well, you see, it's a matter of patriotism."

"Patriotism? You can't mean that."

"I mean patriotism—love for your country and your neighbors. There's a difference, Mr. Bode, between the government and the country. I'm not going to cooperate with you in this case because I don't like what you represent in this case."

"What I represent? What do you think I represent?"

"The organization of the world."

"And what does that mean?" In spite of himself, and not very coolly, Detective Bode was lapsing into the tone of mere argument, perhaps of mere self-defense.

"It means," Henry said, "that you want whatever you know to serve power. You want knowledge to *be* power. And you'll make your ignorance count, too, if you can be deceitful and clever enough. You think everything has to be explained to your superiors and concealed from your inferiors. For instance, you just lied to me with a clear conscience, as a way of serving justice. What I stand for can't survive in the world you're helping to make, Mr. Bode." Henry was grinning, enjoying himself, and allowing the detective to see that he was.

"Are you some kind of anarchist?" the detective said. "Just what the hell are you, anyway?"

"I'm a patriot, like I said. I'm a man who's not going to cooperate with you on this case. You're here to represent the right of the government and other large organizations to decide for us and come between us. The people you represent will come out here, without asking our opinion, and shut down a barbershop or a little slaughterhouse because it's not sanitary enough for us, and then let other businesses—richer ones—poison the air and water."

"What's *that* got to do with it?"

"Listen," Henry said. "I'm trying to explain something to you. I'm not the only one who won't cooperate with you in your search for Danny Branch. There are several of us here who aren't reconciled to the loss of *any* good thing."

"I'm just doing my duty," Kyle Bode said.

"And you're here now to tell us that a person who is sick and unconscious, or even a person who is conscious and well, is ultimately the property of the medical industry and the government. Aren't you?" Henry was still grinning.

"It wasn't authorized. He asked nobody's permission. He told nobody.

He signed no papers. It was a crime. You can't let people just walk around and do what they want to like that. He didn't even settle the bill."

"Some of us think people belong to each other and to God," Henry said. "Are you going to let a hospital keep a patient hostage until he settles his account? You were *against* kidnapping a while ago."

Detective Bode was resting his brow in the palm of his hand. He was shaking his head. When it became clear that Henry was finished, the detective looked up. "Mr. Catlett, if I may, I would like to talk to your father."

"Sure," Henry said, getting up. "You going to tell on me?"

And only then, finally, did Detective Bode smile.

Danny dug the grave down until he stood hip deep in it. And then he dug again until it was well past waist deep. And then, putting his hands on the ground beside it, he leapt out of it, and stood looking down into it, and thought. The grave was somewhat longer than Burley had been tall; it was widened at the middle to permit Danny to stand in it to lay the body down; it was deep enough.

Using the larger flagstones that he had taken from the grave and bringing more from the creek, Danny shaped a long, narrow box in the bottom of the grave. He was making such a grave as he knew the Indians of that place had made long before Port William was Port William. Digging to varying depths to seat the stones upright with their straightest edges aligned at the top, he worked his way from the head of the grave to the foot and back again, tamping each stone tightly into place. The day grew warmer, and Danny paused now and again to wipe the sweat from his face. The light beams that came through the heavy foliage shifted slowly from one opening to another, and slowly they became perpendicular. Again he went to the spring and drank, and returned to his work. The crickets sang steadily, and the creek made its constant little song over the rocks. Within those sounds and the larger quiet that included them, now and then a woodpecker drummed or called or a jay screamed or a squirrel barked. In the stillness a few leaves let go and floated down. And always Danny could smell the fresh, moist earth of the grave.

When he had finished placing the upright stones, he paved the floor of the grave, laying the broad slabs level and filling the openings that remained with smaller stones. He made good work of it, though it would be seen in all the time of the world only by him and only for a little while. He put the shape of the stone casket together as if the stones had made a casket once before and had been scattered, and now he had found them and pieced them together again.

He carried up more stones from the creek, the biggest he could handle. These would be the capstones, and he laid them in stacks at the head and foot of the grave. It was ready now. He went down to the barn and removed the blankets that covered Burley and withdrew the pillow from under his head. He folded the blankets into a pallet on the paved floor of the grave and placed the pillow at its head.

When he carried Burley to the grave, he went up by the gentlest, most open way so that there need be no haste or struggle or roughness, for now they had come to the last of the last things. A heavy pressure of finality swelled in his heart and throat as if he might have wept aloud, but as he walked he made no sound. He stepped into the grave and laid the body down. He composed it like a sleeper, laying the hands together as before. And the body seemed to accept again its stillness and its deep sleep, submissive to the motion of the world until the world's end. Danny brought up the rest of the bedclothes and laid them over Burley, covering, at last, his face.

As before, the thought returned to him that he was not acting only for himself. He thought of Lyda and Hannah and Nathan and the others, and he went down along the creek and then up across the thickety north slope on the other side, gathering flowers as he went. He picked spires of goldenrod, sprays of farewell-summer and of lavender, gold-centered asters; he picked yellow late sunflowers, the white-starred flower heads of snakeroot with their faint odor of warm honey, and finally, near the creek, the triple-lobed, deep blue flowers of lobelia. Stepping into the grave again, he covered the shrouded body with these, their bright colors and their weedy scent warm from the sun, laying them down in shingle fashion so that the blossoms were always uppermost, until the grave seemed at last to contain a small garden in bloom. And then, having touched Burley for the last time, he laid across the upright sides of the coffin the broad covering stones, first one layer, and then another over the cracks in the first.

He lifted himself out of the grave and stood at the foot of it. He let the quiet reassemble itself around him, the quiet of the place now one with that of the old body sleeping in its grave. Into that great quiet he said aloud, "Be with him, as he has been with us." And then he began to fill the grave.

Henry rapped on his father's door and then pushed it open. Wheeler was still wearing his hat, but now he was holding the telephone receiver in his right hand. His right arm was extended at full length, propped on the arm of his chair. Both Henry and Kyle Bode could hear somebody insistently and plaintively explaining something through the phone. When the door opened, Wheeler looked around.

"Detective Bode would like to talk with you."

Wheeler acknowledged Henry with a wave of his left hand. To Kyle Bode he said, "Come in, sir," and gestured toward an empty chair.

Kyle Bode came in and sat down.

Wheeler put the receiver to his mouth and ear and said, "But I *know* what your problem is, Mr. Hernshaw. You've told me several times . . ." The voice never stopped talking. Wheeler shifted the receiver to his left hand, clamping his palm over the mouthpiece, and, smiling, offered his right hand to the detective. "I'm glad to know you, Mr. Bode. I'll get done here in a minute." He dangled the receiver out over his chair arm again while he and Kyle Bode listened to it, its tone of injury and wearied explanation as plain as if they could make out the words. And then they heard it say distinctly, "So. Here is what I think."

In the portentous pause that followed, Wheeler quickly raised the receiver and said into it with an almost gentle patience, "But, Mr. Hernshaw, as I have explained to you a number of times, what you think is of no account, because you are not going to get anybody else on the face of the earth to think it."

Something was said then that Wheeler interrupted: "No. A verbal agreement is *not* a contract if there were no witnesses and you are the only one who can remember it. Now you think about it. I can't talk to you anymore this morning because I've got a young fellow waiting to see me."

He paused again, listening, and then said, "Yessir. Thank you. It's always good to talk with you too." He hung up.

"That was Walter Hernshaw," he said to Kyle Bode. "Like many of my friends, he has got old. I've had that very conversation with him the last four Saturdays. And I'll tell you something: If I sent him a bill for my time — which, of course, I won't, because he hasn't hired me, and because I won't be hired by him — he would be amazed. Because he thinks that if he conducts his business on Saturday by telephone, it's not work. Now what can I do for you?"

The detective cleared his throat. "I assume you're aware, Mr. Catlett, that Mr. Burley Coulter was taken from his hospital room early this morning by some unauthorized person."

"Yes," Wheeler said. "Henry told me, and I'm greatly concerned about it. Burley is a cousin of mine, you know."

"No," the detective said, feeling another downward swerve of anxiety. "I didn't."

"Yes," Wheeler said, "his father and my father were first cousins. They were the grandsons of Jonas T. Coulter, who was the son of the first Nathan Coulter, who was, I reckon, one of the first white people to come into this country. Well, have you people figured out how Burley was taken by this unauthorized person?"

"He just went in with a gurney," Kyle Bode said, "and loaded Mr. Coulter onto it, and covered him up to look like a corpse, and took him away — right through the middle of a busy hospital. Can you believe the audacity of it?"

"Sure, I believe it," Wheeler said. "But I've seen a lot of audacity in my time. Do you know who did this? Do you have clear evidence?"

"As a matter of fact, we don't. But we have a good idea who did it."

"Who?"

"Danny Branch — who is, I'm told, Mr. Coulter's son?"

"That's right," Wheeler said. "And you're wondering why he doesn't have his father's name." Wheeler then told why Danny went by the name of Branch, his mother's name, rather than Coulter, which was a long and somewhat complicated story to which the detective ceased to listen.

"Anyhow," Kyle Bode said, "Danny Branch seems also to have disappeared. I wonder, Mr. Catlett, if you have any idea where he might have gone."

"I only know what Henry says Danny's wife told him."

"And what did she tell him?"

"He said she said he said something about Indiana."

"The Indiana police are watching for him," Kyle Bode said. "But a much likelier possibility is that he's somewhere around here — and that his father, alive or dead, is with him."

"You're assuming, I see, that Danny Branch is the guilty party." Wheeler smiled at the detective as he would perhaps have smiled at a grandson. "And what are you going to charge him with — impersonating an undertaker?"

Kyle Bode did not smile back. "Kidnapping, to start with. And, after that, if Mr. Coulter dies, maybe manslaughter."

"Well," Wheeler said. "That's serious."

"Mr. Catlett, is Danny Branch Mr. Coulter's heir?" The detective was now leaning forward somewhat aggressively in his seat.

Wheeler smiled again, seeing (and, Kyle Bode thought, appreciating) the direction of the detective's thinking. "Yes," he said. "He is."

"That makes it more likely, doesn't it?" Kyle Bode was getting the feeling that Wheeler was talking to him at such length because he liked his company. He corrected that by wondering if Wheeler, elderly as he was, knew that he was talking to a detective. He corrected that by glancing at the writing pad that Wheeler had tossed onto his desk. On one blue line of the pad he saw, inscribed without a quiver, "Det. Kyle Bode."

"Now your logic is pretty good there, Mr. Bode," Wheeler said. "You've got something there that you certainly will want to think about. A man sick and unconscious, dependent on life-prolonging machinery, surely is a pretty opportunity for the medical people. 'For wheresoever the carcase is, there will the eagles be gathered together.' You suspect Danny Branch of experiencing a coincidence of compassion and greed in this case. And of course that suspicion exactly mirrors the suspicion that attaches to the medical industry."

"But they were keeping him alive," Kyle Bode said. "Isn't that something?"

"It's something," Wheeler said. "It's not enough. There are many degrees and kinds of being alive. And some are worse than death."

"But they were doing their duty."

"Oh, yes," Wheeler said, "they were doing their solemn duty, as defined by themselves. And they were getting luxuriously paid. They were being merciful and they were getting rich. Let us not forget that one of the subjects of our conversation is money — the money to be spent and made in the art of medical mercy. Once the machinery gets into it, then the money gets into it. Once the money is there, then come the damned managers and the damned insurers and (I am embarrassed to say) the damned lawyers, not to mention the damned doctors who were there for the money before anybody. Before long the patient is hostage to his own cure. The beneficiary is the chattel of his benefactors.

"And first thing you know, you've got some poor sufferer all trussed up in a hospital, tied and tubed and doped and pierced, who will never draw another breath for his own benefit and who may breathe on for years. It's a bad thing to get paid for, Mr. Bode, especially if you're in the business of mercy and healing and the relief of suffering.

"So there certainly is room for greed and mercy of another kind. I don't doubt that Danny, assuming he is the guilty party, has considered the cost; he's an intelligent man. Even so, I venture to say to you that you're wrong about him, insofar as you suspect him of acting out of greed. I'll give you two reasons that you had better consider. In the first place, he loves Burley. In the second place, he's not alone, and he knows it. You're thinking of a world in which legatee stands all alone, facing legator who has now become a mere obstruction between legatee and legacy. But you have thought up the wrong world. There are several of us here who belong to Danny and to whom he belongs, and we'll stand by him, whatever happens. After money, you know, we are talking about the question of the ownership of people. To whom and to what does Burley Coulter belong? If, as you allege, Danny Branch has taken Burley Coulter out of the hospital, he has done it because Burley belongs to him."

Wheeler was no longer making any attempt to speak to the point of Kyle Bode's visit, or if he was Kyle Bode no longer saw the point. And he had begun to hear, while Wheeler talked, the sounds of the gathering of several people in the adjoining room: the opening and shutting of the outer door, the scraping of feet and of chair legs, the murmur of conscientiously subdued voices.

Kyle Bode waved his hand at Wheeler and interrupted. "But he can't just carry him off without the hospital staff's permission."

"Why not?" Wheeler said. "A fellow would need their permission, I reckon, to get in. If he needs their permission to get out, he's in jail. Would you grant a proprietary right, or even a guardianship, to a hospital that you would not grant to a man's own son? I would oppose that, whatever the law said."

"Well, anyway," Detective Bode said, "all I know is that the law has been broken, and I am here to serve the law."

"But, my dear boy, you don't eat or drink the law, or sit in the shade of it or warm yourself by it, or wear it, or have your being in it. The law exists only to serve."

"Serve what?"

"Why, all the many things that are above it. Love."

Danny stood in the grave as he filled it, tamping the dirt in. The day in its sounding brightness stood around him. He kept to the rhythm he had established at the beginning, stopping only one more time to go to the spring for a drink. Though he sweated at his work, the day was comfortable, the suggestion of autumn palpable in the air, and he made good time.

As he filled the grave and thus slowly rose out of it, he felt again that the living man, Burley Coulter, was near him, watching and visible, except where he looked. The intimation of Burley's presence was constantly with him, at once troubling and consoling; in its newness, it kept him close to tears.

When the grave was filled, he spread and leveled the surplus dirt. He gathered leaves and scattered them over the dirt and brushed over them lightly with a leafy branch. From twenty feet, only a practiced and expectant eye would have noticed the disturbance. After the dewfall or frost of one night, it would be harder to see. After the leaves fell, there would be no trace.

He carried his tools down to the barn, folded the pot and skillet and the piece of jowl and the cornmeal into his hunting coat, making a bundle that he could sling over his shoulder as before. Again using a leafy branch, he brushed out his tracks in the dust of the barn floor. He sprinkled dust and then water over the ashes of his fire. When his departure was fully prepared, he brought water from the spring and sat down and ate quickly the rest of the food he had prepared at breakfast.

By the time he left, the place had again resumed its quiet. He walked away without disturbing it.

The absence of his truck startled Danny when he got back to where he had left it, but he stood still only for a moment before he imagined what had happened. If the wrong people had found the truck, they would have come on up the branch and found him and Burley. The right person could only have been Nathan, who would have known where the key was hidden and who would have taken the truck to the nearest unlikely place where he could put it out of sight. And so Danny shouldered his tools and his bundle again and went to the road.

The road was not much traveled. Only one car passed, and Danny avoided it by stepping in among the tall horseweeds that grew between the roadside and the creek. When he came to the lane that branched off under the big sycamore, he turned without hesitation into it, knowing he was right when he got to the first muddy patch where Nathan had scuffed out the tire tracks. And yet he smiled when he stepped through the door of the old barn and saw his truck. He laid his tools in with the other fencing tools in the back, and then, opening the passenger door to toss in his bundle, he saw Nathan's green shirt lying on the seat. He smiled again and took off the blue shirt he was wearing and put the green one on. He thought of burning the blue shirt, but he did not want to burn it. It was a good shirt. A derelict washing machine was leaning against the wall of the barn just inside the upper doorway, and he tossed the shirt into it. He would come back for it in a few days.

When he got home and went into the kitchen, he found Lyda's note on the table.

"We are all at Henry's and Wheeler's office," she had written. "Henry says for you to come, too, if you get back." And then she had crossed out the last phrase and added, "I reckon you are back."

Wheeler talked at ease, leaning back in his chair, his fingers laced over his vest, telling stories of the influence of the medical industry upon the local economy. He spoke with care, forming his sentences as if he were writing them down and looking at Kyle Bode all the time, with the apparent intent to instruct him.

"And so it has become possible," Wheeler said, "for one of our people

to spend a long life accumulating a few thousand dollars by the hardest
kind of work, only to have it entirely taken away by two or three hours
in an operating room and a week or two in a hospital."

Listening, the detective became more and more anxious to regain
control at least of his own participation in whatever it was that was
going on. But he was finding the conversation difficult to interrupt not
only because of the peculiar force that Wheeler's look and words put
into it but because he did not much want to interrupt it. There was a
kind of charm in the old man's earnest wish that the young man should
be instructed. And when the young man did from time to time break
into the conversation, it was to ask a question relative only to the old
man's talk—questions that the young man, to his consternation, actually wanted to know the old man's answers to.

Finally the conversation was interrupted by Wheeler himself. "I
believe we have some people here whom you'll want to see. They are
Burley's close kin and close friends, the people who know him best.
Come and meet them."

Kyle Bode had not been able to see where he was going for some
time, and now suddenly he did see, and he saw that *they* had seen where
he was going all along and had got there ahead of him. His mind
digressed into relief that he was assigned to this case alone, that none of
his colleagues could see his confusion. Conscientiously—though surely
not conscientiously enough—he had sought the order that the facts of
the case would make. And not only had he failed so far to achieve that
clear and explainable order but he had been tempted over and over again
into the weakness of self-justification. Worse than that, he had been
tempted over and over again to leave, with Wheeler, the small, clear
world of the law and its explanations and to enter the larger, darker
world not ordered by human reasons or subject to them, in which he
sensed obscurely that something might live that he, too, might be glad to
have alive.

Standing with his right arm outstretched and then with his hand
spread hospitably on Kyle Bode's back, Wheeler gathered him toward
the door, which he opened onto a room now full of people, all of whom
fell silent and looked expectantly at the detective as though he might
have been a long-awaited guest of honor.

Guided still by Wheeler's hand on his back, Kyle Bode turned toward the desk to the left of the stairway door, at which sat a smiling young woman who held a stenographer's pad and pencil on her lap.

"This is Detective Kyle Bode, ladies and gentlemen," Wheeler said. "Mr. Bode, this is Hilda Roe, our secretary."

Hilda extended her hand to Kyle Bode, who shook it cordially.

Wheeler pressed him on to the left. "This is Sarah Catlett, Henry's wife.

"This is my wife, Bess.

"This is Mary Penn.

"This is Art Rowanberry.

"This is his brother, Mart.

"This is Jack Penn, Jack Beechum Penn.

"This is my son, Andy.

"This is Flora Catlett, Andy's wife.

"You know Henry.

"This is Lyda Branch, Danny's wife.

"This is Hannah Coulter.

"And this is Hannah's husband, Nathan."

One by one, they silently held out their hands to Kyle Bode, who silently shook them.

He and Wheeler had come almost all the way around the room. There was a single chair against the wall to the left of the door to Wheeler's office. Wheeler offered this chair, with a gesture, to Kyle Bode, who thanked him and sat down. Wheeler then seated himself in the chair between Hilda Roe's desk and the stair door.

"Mr. Bode," Wheeler said. "All of us here are relatives or friends of Burley Coulter."

The secretary, Kyle Bode noticed, now began to write in shorthand on her pad. It was noon and past, and he had learned nothing that he could tell to any superior or any reporter who might ask.

"Nathan," Wheeler went on, "is Burley's nephew."

"Nephew?" Kyle Bode said, turning to Nathan, who looked back at him with a look that was utterly direct and impenetrable.

"That's right."

"I assume you know him well."

"I've known him for fifty-three years."

"You've been neighbors that long?"

"We've been neighbors all my life, except for a while back there in the forties when I was away."

"You were in the service?"

"Yes."

The detective coughed. "Mr. Coulter, my job, I guess, is to find your uncle. Do you know where he is? Or where Danny Branch is?"

The eyes that confronted him did not look down, nor did they change. And there was no apparent animosity in the reply: "I couldn't rightly say I do."

"Now them two was a pair," Mart Rowanberry said, as though he were not interrupting but merely contributing to the conversation. "There's been a many a time when nobody knew where them two was."

"I see. And why was that?"

"They're hunters!" Art Rowanberry said, a little impatiently, in the tone of one explaining the obvious. "They'd be off somewheres in the woods."

"A many a time," Mart said, "he has called me out after bedtime to go with him, and I would get up and go. A many a time."

"You are friends, then, you and Mr. Coulter?"

"We been friends, you might as well say, all along. Course, now, he's older than I am. Fifteen years or so, wouldn't it be, Andy?"

The Catlett by the name of Andy nodded, and Lyda said, "Yes."

And then she said, "You knew him all your life, and then finally he didn't know you, did he, Mart?"

"He didn't know you?" said Kyle Bode.

"Well, sir," Mart said, "I come up on him and Danny and Nathan while they was fencing. Burley was asleep, propped up against the end post. I shook him a little, and he looked up. He says, 'Howdy, old bud.' I seen he was bewildered. I says, 'You don't know me, do you?' He says, 'I know I ought to, but I don't.' I says, 'Well, if you was to hear old Bet open up on a track, who'd you say it was?' And he says, 'Why, hello, Mart!'"

There was a moment then in which nobody spoke, as if everybody there was seeing what Mart had told.

Kyle Bode waited for that moment to pass, and then he said, "This Bet you spoke of"—he knew he was a fool, but he wanted to know—"was she a dog?" It was not his conversation he was in; he could hardly think by what right he was in it.

"She was a blue tick mostly," Mart said. "A light, sort of cloudy-colored dog, with black ears and a white tip to her tail. And a good one." He paused, perhaps seeing the dog again. "I bought her from Braymer Hardy over by Goforth. But I expect," he said, smiling at Kyle Bode, "that was before your time." And then, as if conscious of having strayed from the subject, he said, "But, now, Burley Coulter. They never come no finer than Burley Coulter."

Another small silence followed, in which everybody assented to Mart's tribute.

"Burley Coulter," Wheeler said, "was born in 1895. He was the son of Dave and Zelma Coulter. He had one older brother, Jarrat, who died in the July of 1967.

"Burley attended the Goforth School as long as he could be kept there —not long enough for him to finish the eighth grade, which he thought might have taken him forever. His fame at Willow Hole was not for scholarship but for being able to fight as well on the bottom as on the top."

Wheeler spoke at first to Kyle Bode. And then he looked down at his hands and thought a minute. When he spoke again, he spoke to and for them all.

"He was wild, Burley was, as a young fellow. For me, he had all the charm of an older boy who was fine looking and wild and friendly to a younger cousin. I loved him and would have followed him anywhere. Though he was wild, he didn't steal or lie or misrepresent himself.

"He never was a gambler. Once I said to him, 'Burley, I know you've drunk and fought and laid out at night in the woods. How come you've never gambled?' And he said, 'No son of a bitch is going to snap his fingers and pick up *my* money.'

"His wildness was in his refusal, or his inability, to live within other people's expectations. He would be hunting sometimes when his daddy wanted him at work. He would dance all night and neglect to sober up before he came home.

"He was called into the army during the First World War. By then he was past twenty, long past being a boy, and he had his limits. He hit an officer for calling him a stupid, briar-jumping Kentucky bastard. He might have suffered any one of those insults singly. But he felt that, given all together, they paid off any obligation he had to the officer, and he hit him. He hit him, as he said, 'thoroughly.' I asked him, 'How thoroughly?' And he said, 'Thoroughly enough.' They locked him up a while for that.

"He was acting, by then, as a man of conscious principle. He didn't believe that anybody had the right, by birth or appointment, to lord it over anybody else.

"He broke his mother's heart, as she would sometimes say—as a young man of that kind is apt to do. But when she was old and only the two of them were left at home, he was devoted to her and took dutiful care of her, and she learned to depend on him.

"Though he never gave up his love of roaming about, he had become a different man from the one he started out to be. I'm not sure when that change began. Maybe it was when Nathan and Tom started following him around when they were little boys, after their mother died. And then, when Danny came along, Burley took his proper part in raising him. He took care of his mother until she died. He was a good and loyal partner to his brother. He was a true friend to all his friends.

"He was too late, as he thought and said, in acknowledging Danny as his son. But he did acknowledge him, and made him his heir, and brought him and Lyda home with him to live. And so at last he fully honored his marriage in all but name to Kate Helen.

"He was sometimes, but never much in a public way, a fiddler. And he was always a singer. His head was full of scraps and bits of songs that he sang out at work to say how he felt or to make himself feel better. Some of them, I think, he made up himself.

"From some morning a long time ago, I remember standing beside a field where Burley was plowing with a team of mules and hearing his voice all of a sudden lift up into the quiet:

> *Ain't going to be much longer, boys,*
> *Ain't going to be much longer.*
> *Soon it will be dinnertime*
> *And we will feed our hunger.*

"And he had another song he sometimes sang up in the afternoon, when the day had got long and he was getting tired:

Look down that row;
See how far we've got to go.
It's a long time to sundown, boys,
Long time to sundown.

"What was best in him, maybe, was the pleasure he took in pleasurable things. We'll not forget his laughter. He looked at the world and found it good.

"'I've never learned anything until I had to,' he often said, and so confessed himself a man like other men. But he learned what he had to, and he changed, and so he made himself exceptional.

"He was, I will say, a faithful man."

It was a lonely gathering for Henry Catlett. He was riding as a mere passenger in a vehicle that he ought to have been guiding — that would not be guided if he did not guide it — and yet he had no better idea than the others where it might be going.

So far, he thought, he had done pretty well. He had gathered all parties to the case — except, of course, for the principals — here under his eye for the time being. How long he would need to keep them here or how long the various ones of them would stay, he did not know. He knew that Lyda had left a note for Danny where he would see it when he came home, telling him to join them here. But when Danny might come home, Henry did not know. Nobody, anyhow, had said anything about eating dinner, though it was past noon. He was grateful for that.

Either he would be able to keep them there long enough, or he would not. Either Danny would show up, or he would not — wearing, or not wearing, that very regrettable blue shirt. At moments, as in a bad dream, he had wondered what it would portend if Danny showed up with fresh earth caked on his shoes. He wondered what concatenation of circumstances and lucky guesses might give Detective Bode some purchase on his case. It occurred to Henry to wish that Danny had given somebody a little notice of what he was going to do. But if Danny had been the kind of man to give such notice, he would not have done what he had done. It did not occur to Henry to regret that Danny had done what he had done.

As Wheeler spoke, his auditors sat looking at him, or down at their hands, or at the floor. From time to time, tears shone in the eyes of one or another of them. But no tear fell, no hand was lifted, no sound was uttered. And Henry was grateful to them all—grateful to his father, who was presuming on his seniority to keep them there; grateful to the others for their disciplined and decorous silence.

Out the corner of his eye, Henry could see his brother, Andy, slouched in his chair in the corner and watching also. Henry would have given a lot for a few minutes of talk with Andy. They would not need to say much.

Henry would have liked, too, to know what Lyda thought, and Hannah and Nathan. But all he could do was wait and watch.

And without looking directly at him, he watched Kyle Bode, partly with amusement. The detective's questions to Nathan and to Mart and now his attention to Wheeler so obviously exceeded his professional interest in the case that something like a grin occurred in Henry's mind, though his face remained solemn.

"He was, I will say, a faithful man," Wheeler said.

And then Henry heard the street door open and footsteps start slowly up the stairs.

Wheeler heard them, too, and stopped. Kyle Bode heard them; glancing around the room, he saw that all of them were listening. He saw that Lyda and Hannah were holding hands. Silence went over the whole room now and sealed them under it, as under a stone.

The footsteps rose slowly up the stairs, crossed the narrow hallway, hesitated a moment at the door. And then the knob turned, the door opened, and Danny Branch stepped into the room, wearing a shirt green as the woods, his well-oiled shoes as clean as his cap. He was smiling. To those seated around the book-lined old walls, he had the aspect and the brightness of one who had borne the dead to the grave, and filled the grave to the brim, and received the dead back into life again. The knuckles of Lyda's and Hannah's interlaced fingers were white; nobody made a sound.

And then Henry, whose mind seemed to him to have been racing a long time to arrive again there in the room, which now was changed, said quietly, "Well, looks like you made it home from Indiana."

And suddenly Kyle Bode was on his feet, shouting at Danny, as if from somewhere far outside that quiet room. "Where *have* you been? What have you done with him? He's dead, isn't he, and you have buried him somewhere in these end-of-nowhere, godforsaken hills and hollows?"

"I had an account to settle with one of my creditors," Danny said, still smiling, to Kyle Bode.

"Sit down, Mr. Bode," Henry said, still quietly. "You don't have the right to ask him anything. For that, you have got to have evidence. And you haven't got a nickel's worth. You haven't got any."

The room was all ashimmer now with its quiet. There was a strangely burdening weight in Kyle Bode that swayed him toward that room and what had happened in it. He saw his defeat, and he was not even sorry. He felt small and lost, somewhere beyond the law. He sat down.

"And so, " Wheeler said, "peace to our neighbor, Burley Coulter. May God rest his soul."

The Inheritors (1986)

There came a time in Wheeler Catlett's old age when the darkness that surrounds all our life in this world began to close in on him. Slowly, as the cloud drew in, it hid the things he knew, until at last we could not tell by any sign he gave that he knew who he was.

One morning toward the beginning of that time, while he still remained in charge of his life, though we could see that his departure had begun, Wheeler left his law office at Hargrave, drove up the river, through Port William, and turned into the lane to Danny Branch's place. As he drove he looked around as he always did to see the condition of the animals and the fields.

The first frosts had come and gone, the sky was overcast, the wind was in the north; that night, if the weather cleared, there would be a freeze. Danny had plenty of pasture, it looked like, to carry his stock until Christmas, and maybe past, but no more grass would grow until the first warm days in March or April.

Wheeler drove slowly, following the lane along the backbone of the ridge, and then went past the house where Lyda, mopping the back porch, gave him a wave. Lyda was a large woman with blue eyes that had a way of looking at you so that after she had looked away you could still see them. She was a woman full of intelligence and energy, who could get things done, and Wheeler liked her. He waved back and went on into the barn lot where he let the car roll to a stop in front of the barn. He looked around. Not seeing Danny anywhere, or any sign of him, he tooted the horn. There was no answer. Wheeler turned the engine off and just sat there, erect in the seat, still looking around, and waited. But it had never been in Wheeler's nature to wait very long. If he felt that what he was waiting for was coming to him, he went to meet it. If he felt that it was not coming, he went to see what was the matter.

He waited, listening intently in the silence, for perhaps two minutes, and then he started the engine again, getting ready to go back to the house to see if Lyda knew where Danny was. Before he could put the car into reverse, a little motion down at the edge of the woods caught his eye. It was one of Danny's hounds, and then Danny himself appeared, driving a pair of three-year-old mules to a wagonload of firewood.

"Ah!" Wheeler said. He turned the engine off again, and watched the team make the pull. He thought of his father. He knew what his father would have thought of the team and of Danny, and what he would have said. He would have said, "They're good ones! And they've got a good man ahold of 'em!" Sometimes, now, Wheeler could not tell who was thinking his thoughts.

Danny pulled right up beside the car. "Whoa!" he said. "Whoa, girls."

He sat on top of the load, grinning down at Wheeler, who was grinning up at him. "Morning!"

Wheeler said, "Come on. I want you to go with me."

Danny sat still and continued to grin. "Where we going?"

"Louisville. My calves sell this morning. I thought you might like to go." Wheeler hesitated. "You could drive."

Danny noted that. He did not remember anybody else ever driving Wheeler's car — not with Wheeler in it. For a moment Danny sat there, looking down at his clothes. He did not think they looked very presentable: a pair of coveralls with one knee torn; a hunting coat, not clean, and frayed at the cuffs. He took off his cap and studied it; it was a corduroy cap, very old, which looked at once dusty, greasy, and damp. He knew he had not shaved. But when he had put his cap back on he looked again at Wheeler and said, "Well. All right."

Lyda was still on the porch. She had quit mopping and was watching them, waiting to learn what they were up to. Danny hoped she had not started dinner.

"Lyda," he called, "I'm going to drive Wheeler to Louisville. I'll be back after while."

She gave him a wave as if flinging a cobweb away from her face, and went back to mopping.

Danny pulled the wagon over to the side of the lot and unhitched the mules. He unbridled them, offered them water at the trough and tied them in their stalls, leaving their harness on. He would be back, he thought, by the middle of the afternoon.

Wheeler had followed him, urged out of the car and away from himself into the presence of the open daylight and its demands. He had studied the team of mules in all their movements, and he asked, when Danny had shut their stall doors, "Have they got plenty of hay?"

It was, Danny knew, a compliment to his team. "Yes," he said. "They've got a plenty."

"Ay, Lord! They're good ones!" Wheeler said, as his father, Marce Catlett, would have said. Again, because of the mules, he felt his mind converge with his father's, so that, standing in his tracks, he seemed to sway out of time. He gathered his coat about him briskly against the wind and turned toward the car. "Let's go," he said.

Danny got under the wheel. They drove to the interstate highway and plunged into the flow of traffic, heading for Louisville. To Danny's surprise and somewhat to his discomfort, for it made him feel odd, Wheeler sat in the passenger seat in his own car as if that had been his habit all his life.

For a while Wheeler talked about mules. He remembered how, when he was just a little bit of a boy on a pony, he had helped his father to take a drove of twenty-some yearling mules through the lanes to the railroad. His father had a white horse he always kept with the young mules, and that helped to hold them in a bunch when they were moved from place to place. For some reason, mules love a light-colored horse.

And then Wheeler talked about his calves. He thought they were excellent that year, and he was looking forward to a good price.

"How many is it you've got?" Danny asked.

"Thirty-seven. Seventeen heifers and twenty bulls."

"What'll they weigh?"

"I would say the heifers'll average about four hundred and seventy-five pounds, and the bulls a little better than five hundred."

But Danny did not have to ask many questions or say much. Wheeler was in an easy companionable mood. Letting his mind run among his memories, he talked as much for his own benefit as for Danny's, or he sat and thought. When he was sitting and thinking, he clearly was not waiting for Danny to say something.

They found a parking place, Danny gave Wheeler the car keys, and they went into the stockyards, a place not as thriving as it once had been. Wheeler and Danny both remembered when it had been the gathering point for the grass-fed slaughter steers and fat hogs and spring lambs from thousands of farms. And now many of the little farms had become part of bigger ones or had disappeared under urban developments, most of the stockmen of the earlier time were dead, and a fine old zest and excitement had gone from the air. The stockyards had lost the powerful sense of gathering-up that it had when hundreds of small farmers would come there, proud of their animals, to submit them to judgment and then wait for their checks in the commissioners' offices along the marbled corridors. Wheeler and Danny could remember when the truckloads of spring lambs lined up for blocks down Market Street, waiting their turn at the chutes, and the sheep pens were full to overflowing —a time gone as if it had never been.

But Wheeler remembered, and he talked, describing animals, naming prices and years, walking all the while in a hurry to find where his calves were penned. Wheeler was a tall man who all his life had walked in a hurry. And now that he was old he still hurried, though he had become somewhat uncertain of his balance, and his left foot sometimes tended not to pick itself up as it used to do. If you had seen him at a distance— erect and lean, dressed in a dark gray suit, white shirt and tie, overcoat, and a felt hat smartly cocked—you might at first have thought him a much younger man than he was, though the cut of his clothes was somewhat out of date. But then, looking again, you would have seen that from time to time he swayed out of the line of his direction as though he might fall. Lately, Wheeler had begun to fall, sometimes hurting himself, though he had not varied from any of his purposes or consented to carry a cane. Mostly he just went ahead in his habitual eagerness and haste, leaving his feet to stay under him the best they could.

And so Wheeler hurried through the alleys of the yards, not defying gravity but just paying it no attention, and Danny walked at his side and half a step back, touching his elbow from time to time, not presuming to help him by "taking his arm" but alert nevertheless to steady him.

They found the calves. Wheeler stood long at their pens, seeing them now for the first time away from home, and settling his judgment of them. And Danny stood by, studying the calves himself and watching Wheeler.

Danny watched Wheeler with solicitude, interest, affection, amusement, and pride, seeing him as if not just with his own eyes but with the eyes of several of his elders to whom Wheeler had been a friend. The two of them — Wheeler swaying on the edge of the world as if he might at any moment disappear, and Danny, younger by thirty-two years, but gray-haired now and marked by work and weather — both were survivors and heirs of a membership going way back, of which more members were dead than living, and of which the living members were fewer than they had been in a hundred and fifty years. And so there could be nothing single-sighted in Danny's regard for Wheeler. If he was sometimes alarmed and always amused and touched by the small respect Wheeler paid to gravity and old age, he also felt for him an affection made manifold by its passage through the company of the dead.

When they had seen the calves sold, they went to the commissioner's office for the check. And then Wheeler, whose arm Danny had been so careful not to take hold of, took hold of Danny's arm and steered him into the cafeteria.

"It's dinnertime," he said. "Let's get something to eat."

His calves had sold well, he had estimated their weights almost exactly, and he had his check in his pocket. He was feeling good. He guided Danny into the serving line ahead of himself, making him his guest, so that he could prompt him to fill his tray. He had his wallet already in his hand.

"Now, Wheeler, I'm going to pay for mine," Danny said.

"Nawsir," Wheeler said. "You're not a-gonna do it." And then he said, as if he had said nothing before, "Help yourself, now, honey. Get plenty."

When they had sat down, Danny was obliged to remove his cap and place it on the floor by the table leg, revealing a head of hair that was as thick as fox fur and as mussed as a pile of straw, owing perhaps to his mother's mother's membership in the tribe of Proudfoots, no two hairs of whose heads had ever stuck in the same direction.

They liked their dinner and they took their ease over it, Wheeler talking, wandering in the maze of remindings and forgettings that his mind had become. Memories opened to him as aisles open among the trees when you are walking in the woods. He was drawn back toward an old feeling that had strung the generations together like beads on a string. The feeling could not be expressed, but had to be talked around. It had to do with the summation of the year, the fields giving up their bounty, the earth multiplying each thing after its kind. The feeling was as inward and powerful as lovesickness. By it, Wheeler recognized his father in himself; it put him at one with the desire in all things. That he knew this old hunger and delight to be passing out of the world made him the more eager to recall it, and all the happier in the company of the younger man with whom he fully shared it.

Danny Branch was one of Wheeler Catlett's last comforts, for Danny embodied much of the old integrity of country life that Wheeler had loved and stood for. In a time when farmers had been told and had believed that they could not prosper if they did not "expand," as if the world were endless, Danny and Lyda had never dreamed beyond the boundaries of their own place; so far as Wheeler knew, they had never coveted anything that was their neighbor's. In a time when farmers had believed that they had to take their needs to market or they could not prosper, Lyda and Danny ate what they grew or what came, free for the effort, from the river and woods. They drank water from their well and milk from their cow, and in winter sat warm beside a stove in which their own wood burned. Because Danny still worked mules, they grew much of their own fuel for farm work. They fertilized their fields mostly with manure from the animals. And so of course they prospered. And so in the last light of Wheeler's day and time he and Danny had one another's company, and that was prosperity too, in its way.

And so they ate together, and then Wheeler bummed one of Danny's cigarettes and they smoked. When they returned to the car, Wheeler was feeling so much himself that he was surprised to meet Danny at the door on the driver's side.

"I'll drive," Wheeler said, taking the keys from his pocket.

Danny said, "Oh, I don't mind to drive, Wheeler."

"I know you don't, honey," Wheeler said. He unlocked the door and got in beneath the wheel.

Danny went around and got in on the other side. Wheeler had already begun to talk again. He was, Danny said, "in a big way"—feeling fine and ready to venture forth into the world.

Wheeler's car was a large black sedan, one in a long series of such sober-colored vehicles, which he had used in the normal course of his work and pleasure, but also to travel in farm lanes and fields, to herd stock, and to haul various articles of freight, often his bird dogs, and now and then a sick calf or sheep. It's once-shining paint had been dulled and scratched by all the grass stems and weeds and tree branches that had lashed against it.

While they had been in the stockyards another car had parked too closely behind Wheeler's. Wheeler now eased back until his rear bumper touched the front bumper of that other car. He pushed the car backward until *its* rear bumper touched the front bumper of the car behind it. He then eased forward and made a similar adjustment in the position of the car in front. This enabled him to move comfortably out of the parking space and into the lane of traffic, which he did, skillfully enough, never having ceased to tell about buying a carload of Rambouillet-cross ewes in 1947, keeping what he needed of them and selling the rest. The ewes, he said, had not milked worth a damn.

Instead of taking the direct way to the interstate as Danny expected him to do, Wheeler made a series of abrupt turns that carried them deeper into the city.

"We'll just go home another way," he said finally. "We'll see different country."

By then, Danny did not know where they were, but he assumed that Wheeler did. They drove without talking for a while, Wheeler continuing to make from time to time a decisive turn into a different street, not always with due deference to the oncoming traffic. Noticing that Wheeler had not fastened his seatbelt, Danny fastened his own.

Wheeler, who often caught what others wished he would miss, said, "Honey, did you do that on account of my driving?"

"No," Danny said. "I about always do it." And ever afterwards, to keep from making a liar of himself, he about always did it.

After yet another while, Danny had to give up his assumption that Wheeler knew where they were. They were going down a muddy, chug-holey street through a new subdivision. Wheeler could not have known where they were, because where they were had been a different place only a short time ago.

"Well, sir," Wheeler said, "Andy hasn't got any sense of direction at all."

Wheeler was talking about his oldest son, who was two years younger than Danny Branch, but Wheeler was remembering him and speaking of him as if he were still in college and had grown no older.

"The poor thing," Wheeler said, "I took him with me to North Carolina. He didn't have a damned thing to do but sit over there and read the map, and he never knew where we were. He was *always* lost."

Wheeler said this without at all acknowledging that he was now lost himself. In fact, as Danny knew, Wheeler did not think he was lost. Wheeler assumed that being in motion was the same as being found. If he kept going, he would eventually see something he recognized.

Danny began to doubt that he would get home in time to bring up another load of wood. He wished a little that he had ungeared his team. Otherwise, he was content just to observe Wheeler's progress and wait for something that maybe *he* would recognize.

Wheeler said, gently, "Well," and Danny knew that Andy had again been forgiven for the failure of his sense of direction at the age of twenty-one, and Wheeler was thinking kindly of him.

Wheeler slowed down, turned into a just-graded driveway, and with some spinning of wheels drove across a miry patch of newly bulldozed building sites to another street, where he resumed his musing and drove along at the same ambling gait as before.

He was talking now about a bird-hunting trip to Tennessee that he had made with Elton Penn in 1955. Listening, Danny began to grin behind his hand, for the best story, so far, about Wheeler's driving came from that trip. They were coming home late at night, and Wheeler was driving fast. They were talking, absorbed in their conversation, when they came suddenly to a right-angle turn in the road that Wheeler saw a few seconds later than he should have. It happened that a farm gate was standing open right in the elbow of the turn. Wheeler drove through the gate, made a loop through a pasture, and drove back onto the road again. He never stopped talking.

That story told, among other things, what a good driver Wheeler had been. He did not always pay enough attention, but his reflexes were good.

Wheeler did not tell that part of the story. Maybe he had forgotten it, Danny thought. Or maybe he had not paid enough attention to remember it. It was Elton's story.

"Ay, Lord!" Wheeler said, and Danny knew that Wheeler had remembered again that Elton was dead and their hunting days a long time past.

There really was nothing wrong with Wheeler's sense of direction. From the time of his sudden change of course in the midst of the new subdivision, he had been going as straight home as the layout of the streets and roads permitted.

Presently they came to a main route that they both recognized, and Wheeler turned onto it. Throughout their circuit of wherever it was they had been — a passage that, for Danny, had involved several surprises and a modicum of worry — Wheeler had been completely unperturbed. His mood had been, as Danny would later describe it, "level." To him, the whole trip, the whole day, was an outing, with which he had been thoroughly pleased. Wheeler did not always take the world as it came. He had devoted his life to changing as much of it as he could — and to endless frustration and indignation at things he could not change. But there were days all his life when he found the world, though everywhere touched by sadness, to be boundlessly amusing and interesting. This was one of those days. As days went, it was a good one, and Danny knew it.

Now that they were leaving the city on a known road, evidently going back after all by the way they had come, Danny relaxed and settled himself for the trip. The sky had cleared, and now the sun was shining brightly. But Danny's complacency, as he later said, was "about five minutes premature." For when their road intersected with the interstate, Wheeler eased over into the left-hand lane and headed down onto the off-ramp amidst a suddenly risen cacophony of horns that would be with them for the next good while.

"Whoa!" Danny said. "Wait, Wheeler!"

But it was too late to wait. He might as well have been talking to the car engine. Wheeler had not caught on. He was experiencing his only moment of irritation that day. "What," he said, "are the sons of bitches blowing their horns about?"

He did not catch on, really, until he reached the bottom of the ramp and was forced leftward into the emergency lane by the onrushing traffic. The horn blowing continued as though all the herald angels were announcing chaos come again. The sounds varied from little admonitory toots of disinterested advice to sustained blasts and shrieks of outrage. Confusion and trouble passed over Wheeler's face. He put his foot on the brake.

And then he caught on. The very second in which Wheeler caught on was apparent to Danny, for in that second Wheeler started to grin. And then Danny felt the seatback press against him as Wheeler accelerated.

He did not speed up by much. He just resumed the amiable, ambling gait that he had maintained more or less ever since leaving the stockyards.

For a while Danny was thinking fast but not very purposefully. When he began to think purposefully, he concluded that the best thing for him to do was keep quiet. Now that they were on the interstate, one way to get off would be to stop and be towed away by the police. Or they could somehow turn around and go in the other direction. But Danny knew that Wheeler was not going to stop until he had to, and he would never turn around. Or, Danny thought, they could try to get through the traffic and across the median into their proper lanes. But the median would be wide and impassable most of the way, and the traffic was heavy. The only other possibility was to drive the emergency lane and get off on an on-ramp — and, for that, Danny thought, the farther out in the country the better. The best thing to do would be to go on to the Ellville interchange.

Having thought it through, he looked at Wheeler and knew that Wheeler had already come to the same conclusion. Wheeler was again in his level mood, evidently enjoying himself, driving along as if the wrong side of the interstate was simply one of the ways to go home. The passing horns continued to toot, hoot, blast, bleat, wail, and howl. From time to time Wheeler would become mindful of them, and he would nod and raise his hand politely to the drivers. "Thank you. Thank you. Excuse me. Thank you."

When Wheeler came to a car stopped in his way, he eased out to the left and went around on the grass. Or he waited for a break in the traffic and darted around on the right. Getting past the on-ramps required some hesitation and care, but that problem eased as they got farther from the city.

For maybe the next hour, Danny thought, he would have to live purely as a man of faith. He laid his hands in his lap then and just rode, paying close attention to Wheeler and to everything that was happening. If he survived, he thought, he would have to tell the story.

Danny realized that his mind had already entered into a profound concord with Wheeler's mind. They had both decided on the same course, not because Wheeler was thinking like Danny, but for the opposite reason. Watching Wheeler, Danny knew that he knew what it was like to *be* Wheeler, for that time and maybe for other times as well. He had felt himself in and had lived through Wheeler's moment of confusion as the ramp had led them into the opposing line of traffic, and he had felt the coming of clarity when Wheeler recognized their predicament and then accepted it and began to deal with it. He had felt the little stab of glee when Wheeler saw that it could be dealt with. He felt what it was like to be himself there with Wheeler in a bad situation, strangely elated, living by faith, going the wrong way home. If they got there, he thought, it would be the right way. He knew that he was living one of the clearest hours of his life.

And Wheeler was doing a splendid job of driving, keeping well off to the left, anticipating every problem, solving it with dispatch. His reflexes were working handsomely. He was just ambling along, still, keeping up the momentum to move fast if necessary, but maintaining too his level mood, grinning a little, watching everything. They were going to be all right, Danny thought. Maybe. If some misguided particle did not fly out of the torrent on the right and make the beginning of something entirely different. Dressed as he was, Danny thought, he would make a terrible-looking corpse.

Off beyond the highway they could see a farm that was becoming a housing development. The old farmhouse and a barn were still standing in the midst of several large new expensive houses without trees.

"Well, sir," Wheeler said, as if to propose a change of subject in a conversation that was becoming repetitive. "Years ago, that farm was owned by an old fellow by the name of Buttermore. He was a good farmer in his day, and a right good, decent man too. He was a client of mine. He never had much need for a lawyer, but I helped him in a few little matters over the years, wrote his will and so on. Or he would come in and we would talk."

An unusually vehement series of horn blowers went by, and Wheeler raised his hand and gave them a kindly wave. "Thank you. Thank you. Much obliged."

He drove on for a little while, thinking of Mr. Buttermore, and then he laughed. "When he got old, Mr. Buttermore became just pitifully forgetful. He would start a sentence and then forget what he was going to say, and what he had said so far. And then he would say, '—and so fo'th.' It got so that nearly every one of his sentences ended '—and so fo'th.'"

On their right, the stream of traffic hurtled by, and the brass of righteous invective continued—all the world bearing down and going by in the opposite direction. Fingers pointed. Fingers jabbed upwards in the sign that contradicts all contradiction. Horns wailed and bellowed in limitless indignation. On their left the fields and woods lay quietly, seeming to wait.

"I settled his estate," Wheeler said. "The old man had no children. But a fellow by the name of Rowd Dawson contested the will, claiming that he was Mr. Buttermore's natural son. His evidence was that his left eye was cocked at precisely the same angle as Mr. Buttermore's. Well, we wound up in court over it. And you can see where that cocked eye business put me with a jury of farmers who every last one believed in the inheritability of physical traits. And Rowd Dawson's lawyer had several witnesses who were experts on the angles of cocked eyes."

A state policeman went by, his head swiveled backwards like an owl's, and Danny made note of the fact by a rightward jerk of his thumb.

"I saw," Wheeler said.

"Well, sir," he said, "I learned just by chance, and nearly too late, that Rowd Dawson, as a young man, had been hit on the head with a beer bottle in a saloon fight. And I found witnesses who swore that that lick was what had cocked his eye."

They were coming down into their home river valley. They were coming to the Ellville interchange.

"Ellville," Danny said.

Wheeler nodded.

"So I won the case," he said, and he thought it over one more time before he added, "But, you know, I've had to wonder."

He entered the on-ramp and halfway up met a trailer truck coming down. Wheeler dodged off the pavement onto the grass. The truck went jarring by, honking furiously.

And that, suddenly, was all. They went on up the ramp, turned, crossed the overpass, and headed up the river toward Port William. Danny reached and patted Wheeler on both his shoulders, daring to encumber him now with half a hug.

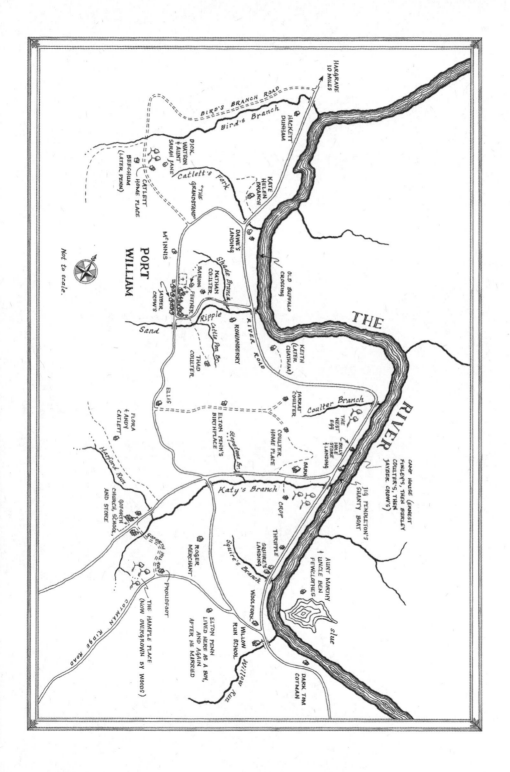

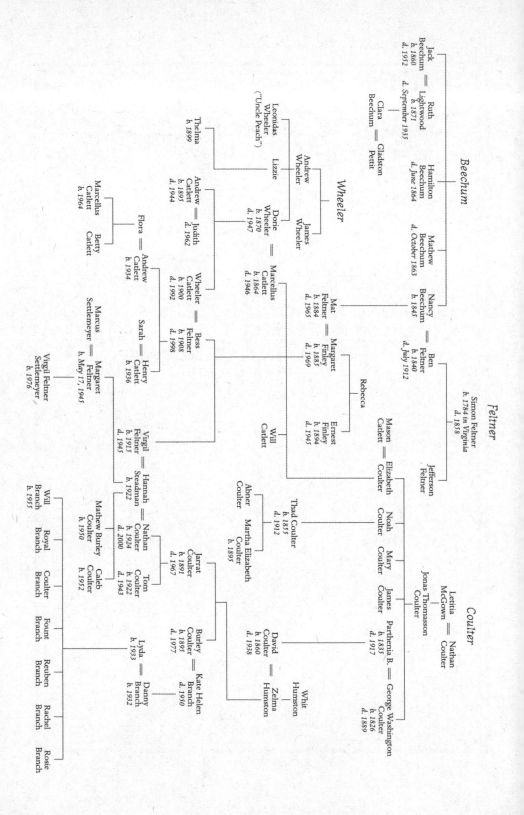